"Some tights, boots, a mask and
a cape — that's all I need in life!
Oh, yeah — and an archenemy!"

To Tim,

Enjoy!

ISBN 978-0-9768088-1-7

The Fearless Force, Night-Ghost, Skymaster, Aquarius, The Wizard and Titan are trademarks of Lee Rushton Howard

This story, though printed in 2007, was actually created in a finished form in 1986.

ABDIEL
Productions

THE FEARLESS FORCE

written and illustrated by
Rushton Howard

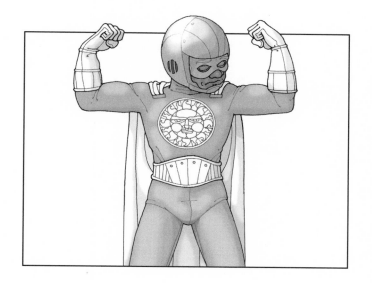

typesetting and layout
Selena Koosmann

business manager
Bunny Howard

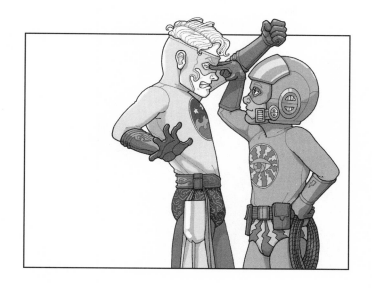

technical advisor
David E. Peterson

For Bunny.

Only with you can I . . .

> *bash through any barrier,*
> *speak wisdom beyond my years,*
> *explore the deepest depths,*
> *fly away from gravity itself,*
> *and break free from every snare.*

Only with you am I Fearless.

Introduction
In a Place Called Adelaide...

The story you hold in your hands is the Truth, as is every Fearless Force adventure to which it leads. Somewhere in the midst of my telling it, you might very well call me crazy, or an outright liar. I won't waste time trying to convince you. If you don't believe it — or *won't* believe it — then there's not much I can do about the limited workings of your brain. Such disbelievers can enjoy it as "fiction," if that's what makes them feel comfortable.

Perhaps you'll wonder if I was one of the superheroes involved. Or did I only *hear* these adventures secondhand from one of the heroes? This is a question I'd prefer to avoid answering. (As everyone knows, superheroes keep their true identities as closely guarded secrets.) Thus it is that names, faces and personalities have all been mixed, remodeled and traded around in an effort to maintain the safety of the daring crime-fighters whose tales I now relate. If any of their archenemies are still alive I wouldn't want them to discover a hero's secret identity and go seeking their long-awaited revenge. (As everyone knows, supervillains never really die, and they're always plotting their long-awaited revenge.)

Therefore, keep in mind that when I say such and such a character was a loudmouthed clown he might very well have been a quiet sort of child. Likewise, a character that I describe as bashful and polite could just as easily have been a cut-up. And perhaps the girl I've called "Maria" wasn't really as beautiful as I make her out to be (though, she'll *always* be so beautiful in my memory). Beauty is a tricky thing, as it means such different things to different people. On the other hand, she was *definitely* as friendly, bright and brave as I've written her to be; and these are qualities that are very clear in their definitions — unlike beauty.

I have even taken pains to hide the exact neighborhood where all these perilous capers took place. I have never lived in a town called "Adelaide"; nor did I attend a school called "Palisades Elementary."

And, though everything clearly takes place in the USA, I won't be revealing which particular state. Yes, I write that there are mountains on one side of the state and the sea on the other, and this may certainly sound like somewhere in Washington State. But the exact location of the real "Adelaide" will have to remain my secret.

As for the time? I'm not disclosing that either, but it's somewhere in the early 1970s. There were no computers in our homes in those days. There were only five channels on our television. Video games had not yet been invented. When my friends and I wanted to have fun... *we left the house!* We went out to the woods, meadows and creeks that surrounded our neighborhood. That's where most of a young superhero's battles against evil occur — in the patches of rough woods and vacant lots that hopefully still exist in commonplace suburban developments. (So if you're wondering why *you're* not a superhero, then ask yourself, "When am I going to fight crime if I'm wasting my day indoors, going 'blip, blip, blip' with a computer game, or flipping pointlessly through my 150 cable channels?")

Regardless of names, characters, towns and times, many things remain very precise in this account. For instance, you'll notice that all of my characters attend the same school even though one is in the sixth grade, while the rest are in the fifth grade. This is the way my elementary school was back then: kindergarten through sixth grade. I've recently discovered that all my old schools have switched, making grade school to be kindergarten-through-fifth grade; and what we used to call "junior high" (beginning at seventh grade) has become "middle school" (beginning at sixth).

I suppose I could have altered things in this story to reflect these current events, but I chose to leave the setting as I remember it — where sixth graders had that mixture of smugness and worry. Smugness, for they were kings of the elementary school, and worry, for next year junior high would put them back on the bottom again. Of course, the sixth-grade character that I've named "Doug" has neither smugness nor worry, as he's composed only of politeness and courage.

Speaking of the American public school system:

This tale tells of a battle to save civilization that happens within an elementary school, so you're going to be exposed to some outrageous acts that are taking place in a setting that's very familiar to you. The young heroes in my story are driven by circumstances to do battle against one of their teachers (as well as some other adults in positions of authority). *By no means* am I suggesting that you should go beat the living snarf out of your teacher! Don't be an idiot! If I get a letter from your parents (or your parents' lawyer) saying that my book has caused their otherwise loveable child to throw a bunch of pretend kung-fu at a teacher, then let me tell you this: I will spend all the money I have to put you behind bars! You're nothing but a maniac looking for an excuse. And I *will not* be your excuse! If you can't tell the difference between Right and Wrong, don't blame me; and don't blame The Fearless Force!

Which brings me to my next — and final — point: the most important thing that remains unchanged in this tale:

The heroes I knew were all good through and through. They were loyal, valiant, and respectful. Each one of them was the sort of squeaky-clean warrior for justice that I have a tough time finding these days. I pick up today's comic books and find crass, rude, and obnoxious characters instead of the righteous and honest protectors I recall from my childhood. When I was introduced to superheroing, the costumed champions that I knew wore bright colors and leapt into danger with a laugh. Sadly, comic books have been slowly losing their heroes and are replacing them with "bad dudes" in black leather trench coats, who wouldn't be caught dead in a bright yellow cape! They've lost the joy that is to be found in rescuing the innocent. Today's so-called "heroes" are as mean, immoral, and mentally messed-up as the villains they fight. But, then I suppose there are a lot of mean, immoral, and mentally messed-up children who root for the villains anyway! My books are *not* written for such children. I've set these events in type for anyone (not just children, but for *anyone*) with a noble light that shines inside them; anyone who sees a Grand Plan of Right and Good stretching out through all corners of all universes; anyone who longs to play a part in that plan.

And, of course, for anyone who thinks it would be a real kick to wear a bright yellow cape!

Part 1

The New Girl

Chapter 1

No Respect for the Costume!

Maria shut off the lawn sprinkler with a squeaky twist of the faucet handle. After the sprinkler's last gurgling sputter, the only noise was the faint drumming of soft moth-wings on the porch-light's glass.

Walking on squishing footsteps to the center of her front yard, she looked up into the darkening dusk of September. There was still that last, stubborn glow of bright blue on the edge of the world with the darkness of evening trying to push it down below the trees and houses. And with the dusk came a slight chill that said autumn was here. Now, it wouldn't *technically* be autumn for another three weeks. But children don't mark the seasons with proper scientific dates. They see fall as beginning when school does — and tomorrow was the Tuesday after Labor Day; the first day of the school year. This meant that, in a child's mind, it might as well be autumn.

Summer isn't about numbers on a calendar. It's about joy and freedom — a joy and freedom that ends, not when the rains come and the leaves turn gold, but when the first school bell rings and some old lady tells you to sit down, be quiet and open your math book to page one.

A sad little sigh escaped from Maria's lips, for tomorrow would be her first day in the fifth grade. What's more, there was the added misery that she would be starting in a *new* school. The Fuente family (for that was Maria's last name) had only just moved into this neighborhood a month ago. Shortly after moving in, she had begun ballet classes with a very strict teacher who settled for nothing less than hours of painstaking study and wholehearted dedication. The result of all this was that Maria hadn't been around her new neighborhood long enough to make a single friend.

She just knew that tomorrow she'd be the lonesome outcast in a class where everyone still remembered each other from the previous year. She'd wind up keeping to herself — maybe reading a book at recess, or some such pitiful thing — and pretending it didn't bother her to be so pitiful.

Things wouldn't be made any easier by the fact that it was the fifth grade. If she was going into kindergarten it would be a breeze. You don't have to work very hard to make friends when you're five years old. But in fifth-grade, everyone splits up into recognizable groups, gangs and armies. They start judging each other, making sure that a new girl is "cool enough" before declaring her to be a friend.

Now, you might think that Maria would be over-whelmingly popular when it's taken into account what a remarkably pretty creature she was. Most girls go through an awkward phase, where they think they're too ugly, too fat, too skinny, or too *something*. Then, they grow up and discover that they've become not so bad looking after all. (Most boys go through this too, but they'll never admit to it.) Maria, on the other hand, didn't seem like she would ever have those awkward years. She had been a beautiful baby, a beautiful toddler, and right now she was beautiful in grade school. She'd probably drive all the boys crazy in junior high and high school, then grow up to be a model or a movie-star.

With long, raven-black hair and big, brown eyes she was a sight that could stop a schoolboy's heart — not that any schoolboy would confess to such a sweet affliction. The problem with those schoolboys is that they would be sure to see any girl as "the enemy," for those later elementary school years are when the absurd "Boys versus Girls War" is at its worst. Your chances of finding a friend are instantly chopped in half when the boys detest you just for being female. But surely the girls would all like her, wouldn't they? Not necessarily. Consider the virus of jealousy. Many people fall for the notion that, just because someone is pretty, she must be stuck-up, shallow or just plain stupid — and jealous girls wouldn't trouble themselves to find out that, though Maria was pretty, she was none of those other things.

Her imagination was already playing-out the dreadful day that tomorrow would be. Although she wasn't at all the sort to fear the worst from an unknown situation, *no* reasonable person is going to assume that the first day in a new school is going to be fun! She breathed-in the twilight, only to form it into another woeful sigh. But she froze in mid-sigh as a flurry of shocking noises abruptly shattered the calm.

A single, jolting squeal of a police siren...

A shriek of tires skidding on the pavement...

The growl of a wild animal...

The dull thump of a car slamming into some large object...

All this was mingled with the laughter and shouting of children that flared up, then faded away.

It was impossible to tell where any of this mayhem was taking place. It was definitely close — but in which direction?

Then the hedges behind her seemed to explode. In

a furious burst of scattered leaves and twigs, someone or something leapt out of the shrubbery, crashing into the unsuspecting girl, and bowling her over.

After a clumsy tumble, she found herself sprawled on the freshly-watered grass. Her normally pretty tresses of raven-black curls were hanging sloppily across her face, and she had been blasted right out of her shoes. (Having only stepped outside to shut off the sprinkler, she hadn't bothered to tie her shoelaces.)

The intruder who had caused this calamity crawled out of the bushes where he had landed, and kicked off the sprinkler, which had become lodged on his right foot in the disaster.

Throwing her hair back away from her eyes, she discovered that the stranger who had collided with her was a very *strange* stranger!

He was a boy her age (somewhere around ten years old). And the "very strange" thing about him? He was a superhero!

Well, he was *dressed* as a superhero, anyway. That boy was decked-out in the sort of colorful costume one might see on a comic book crime-fighter. (Now, Maria wasn't a big reader of superhero comic books. She thought they were rather silly on the rare occasions that she saw them. Be that as it may, she could still recognize a superhero outfit.)

This young "crusader for justice" was dressed all in shades of purple — a mask and tight-fitting suit of medium grape color; his up-to-the-knee boots and up-to-the-elbow gloves were of a darker purple. He wore trunks of this same dark purple, covered with stars and clouds — a pattern to match his flowing cape, which was of that medium grape hue, decorated with white stars spread out above violet clouds, and topped-off with a hood, like that of a Catholic monk. At the center of this cape and upon his chest was the stern, white face of the man-in-the-moon.

At first, Maria was more startled than angry, being so taken aback by that bizarre getup. But her anger rose quickly and overtook her shock when she realized that her ungraceful somersault over the wet grass had landed her on her backside right in a marshy puddle.

A snarl of rage huffed from her lips as she climbed to her feet. The superhero held out his hand to assist her, but she batted that hand aside.

"Are you alright, citizen?" he asked, while untangling himself from the garden hose, which had looped itself around his left foot.

"Except for being soaked to the skin!" she snapped. And who can blame her for being so riled? When you're dry except for your hindquarters, well, that feeling has it's own particular unpleasantness! There's that clammy sensation of your blue-jeans and underpants hanging on you like your own personal swamp. *Anyone* would have been ticked-off at this point.

That lunatic pretending to be a costumed crime-fighter seemed fairly unconcerned with any sloshing discomfort in Maria's undergarments. Instead, he was caught up in a frenzy of excitement over something else entirely.

"You'd better get inside, Miss Fuente!" he said, trying to make his little boy's voice go as low as possible, to give his dire warning the dire tone it needed. Glancing around suspiciously in all directions, he added, "There's evil lurking about!"

He had an overly dramatic way of speaking that really irked Maria. It was little more than an imitation of a television superhero — talking slowly for a few words, to create some sense of doom, then suddenly speeding up to sound urgent. And that he called her "Miss Fuente" and "citizen" was just too silly to endure! To further aggravate matters, even after crashing into someone, he couldn't quit his make-believe crime-fighter game long enough to say he was sorry.

She growled back at him, "There's *stupidity* lurking about! Where are my shoes?"

"Your shoes?"

"My shoes, you idiot! I'm standing here in my socks!"

Needless to say, it's no fabulous feeling to stand around on a wet lawn in your stocking feet. This, along with her damp rear-end and the random soggy spots on her back, elbows and knees, added up to make one *seriously annoyed* Maria.

The boy-hero quickly scanned the area, gathering-up two shoes from completely different parts of the yard. "Are these them?"

"No!" she answered sarcastically as she snatched them out of his hands. "We *always* have shoes lying around in our yard! We grow them here! This is a shoe farm!"

"Huh?"

"Freak!"

Still looking over his shoulders for some approaching danger, he confessed, "I know I must appear rather peculiar to you, but—"

"Oh, grow up! What are you doing in that stupid getup, anyway?"

Muttering more to himself than to her, he wondered, "Why don't girls ever understand crime-fighting?"

Before she could construct another cross reply, the yard was lit by the bright-white beam of the spotlight on a police patrol car.

The purple superhero turned to run, but Maria caught him by the cape and tugged him to a stop — and not just to a stop, but right off his feet. Now *he* was the one being plopped down on his backside in the soggy grass.

The police officer opened his door and shouted, "Freeze, you two!"

The cloaked hero surrendered to his defeat, looking up to see Maria holding the end of his cape.

Unable to break free of Maria fast enough, the cloaked hero drooped in defeat.

Officer Rocco (for that was the policeman's name) stepped from the car and stomped across the wet lawn with a tight scowl on his face. In a scolding tone that told of a temper being held just below the boiling point, he asked, "Did you two pile all that grass in the street?"

"Grass?" Maria was understandably confused. "What grass?"

"The grass that I ran into!" The officer directed her attention to his patrol car. His proud vehicle of shining black and white was an utter disgrace. There was a thick coating of wet lawn-cuttings splattered from the headlights all the way over the windshield and most of the roof. He had indeed run into a pile of grass — an *enormous* pile of grass — and the collision had apparently been a hard and fast one.

That mess of damp green clumps and blobs steaming on the car's warm hood was such an astonishing sight that a little laugh snuck from Maria. She quickly buried that giggle and promised with full honesty, "I had nothing to do with that!"

Taking a strong stance with his hands on his gun-belt, the policeman spoke with every ounce of his authority: "Piling grass in the street is not just littering, it's creating an automotive hazard and a threat to public safety!"

Again, Maria firmly denied any assistance in the prank: "I *swear* I had absolutely nothing to do with it!"

But the officer was hearing none of it. He pulled out his writing pad and pen. "Give me your names, kids."

"I'm Maria Fuente, but I didn't—"

He jotted down her name as he asked the purple-cloaked boy, "And who are you?"

"I am... Night-Ghost." He hopped to his feet and took a dramatic bow, like a great stage actor. "Prowler of the twilight, child of the shadows, and escape-artist extraordinaire."

Officer Rocco looked up from his writing pad rather annoyed. However, at that moment when the lid should have exploded right off his temper, a slight grin appeared on his face — a quick little amused smirk that came and went in a flash. "I was wondering about your *real* name, but that's your 'secret identity,' isn't it?"

"Exactly!" Night-Ghost was quite relieved that the

officer understood.

With a disappointed sigh, Officer Rocco informed him, "As a champion of justice, you should know — and I'm guessing you're a super*hero* and not a super*villain*." (Night-Ghost nodded.) "Well, as a champion of justice, you should know that it's against the law to create an obstruction on a public street."

The young hero replied, "I didn't pile that grass in the street, officer."

"Then why did you run when you saw me coming?"

Night-Ghost looked him straight in the eye and answered, "The grass was *chasing* me. That was no ordinary pile of yard waste you ran into, Officer. It was the Compost Beast of Zetriak."

The policeman raised an eyebrow in surprise. "Pardon me?"

Maria rolled her eyes and groaned in disgust, "Oh, brother!"

"It was a being from an alternate universe," Night-Ghost explained in a very scientific tone of voice. "It was brought to life when Mr. Finley — the guy in the big, yellow house on Elm Street — left a bunch of grass on a magnetically unstable spot in his yard. The monster went on a rampage, and—"

The officer interrupted him, wondering, "How come I

didn't see any monster rampaging in this neighborhood?"

Night-Ghost shrugged. He hated to say it, but he did anyway: "The cops *always* miss the real action. I don't know why that is."

That comment didn't sit well with the officer, but, to his credit, he held his temper in check. "The 'rampage' around here was when two delinquents piled a bunch of grass in the street and made a run for it."

Maria simply *had* to respond to this! Pointing to the so-called "Night-Ghost," she declared, "I have *nothing* to do with this crazy person! I don't know him! I've never met him before! I only just moved into this neighborhood!"

Officer Rocco looked her up and down. "What's with the grass-stains and wet blotches all over your clothes? Looks to me like you could've been playin' around with that mountain of lawn-clippings that's now all over my car."

In a breathless frenzy she rapidly explained, "I was turning off the sprinkler, and this maniac came leaping out of the hedges like a... like a... maniac, knocking me over, and — well, *look at me!* He knocked me right out of my shoes!"

The officer threw a stern glance at Night-Ghost. "What sort of superhero goes around shoving innocent girls onto the ground?"

The would-be hero insisted, "A Compost Beast was

out to *kill* me!"

Maria threw her hands up in exasperation. "Boys are mentally deranged!"

"We *do* grow up eventually," said the policeman, feeling the need to apologize on behalf of every male human on Earth.

"Maybe *some* of you do!" Turning an unkind stare at Night-Ghost, Maria snarled, "The rest of you are hopelessly trapped in a never-ending Halloween!"

Night-Ghost shook his head sadly. "Girls! Always the 'Halloween comment!' They have *no* respect for the costume! I would have to save her from falling into a pit of bubbling acid before she'd admit that I'm not insane!"

"Even if you *did* save my life, that *wouldn't* mean you're not insane! You'd just be a crazy person with a whole lot of dumb luck!" And with that pointed remark, she stomped back towards her house (as much as a person *can* stomp in wet socks). She would have loved to have marched into her house and given the front door a good slam. *That* would have properly displayed her seething rage. But she couldn't go slogging indoors with those soaking socks. So she sat on the porch to peel them off and wring them out.

Still, Night-Ghost pleaded his case: "I'm telling you, the thing had glowing red eyes! It was eight feet tall!

And you didn't see it? Not even when you crashed your car into it?"

Officer Rocco led the would-be hero over to the grass-spattered squad-car, opened the back door, and said, "Get in, Ghost-Knight."

"It's Night-Ghost," replied the boy-hero as he surrendered to his fate and climbed into the backseat.

"Yeah, whatever," the officer muttered, half to himself. Then, getting in the driver's seat, he mumbled some police-code into his radio, scribbled something on his clipboard, and took the last swig of coffee from his thermos. Without turning around to look at the superhero in his backseat, he said, "Listen, Ghost-Knight..." (The policeman was getting the name wrong just to needle him.) "...girls don't go for all that comic-book stuff."

The strangely-dressed boy replied as if it were absolute fact, "I've teamed-up with a *few* girl superheroes on my adventures, but they're very hard to find."

"Let me clue you in on a few things." The officer was still looking down at his clipboard, scrawling out a report while he offered his advice. "I'm guessing you're about ten. Before you know it, you'll be looking to team up with a girl for something *other* than doing battle with red-eyed monsters. I'm not going to sit here and pretend that I know everything there is to know about women. But I do know that you are *not* going to be catching that Maria girl on the edge of a bubbling acid pit anytime soon. And if you want her to like you—"

"I don't want her to like me!" All the drama was gone from his voice, and he was squeaking his protests like any embarrassed ten-year-old. "Romance just interferes with crime-fighting!"

"Listen," the officer continued, "if you want her to like you, then dressing up like that and pushing her into a mud puddle is the *last* thing you want to do! So, lose the purple togs, and start... acting... like... a... normal... Huh?"

His lecture had sunk into a wandering mumble because he had spun around to find that the backseat was empty and the door was hanging open. Night-Ghost was nowhere to be seen.

At first, the officer thought it was downright disrespectful of that youngster to sneak out in the middle of a serious lecture. But then it hit him: That kid had been in a police squad-car. There are no door-handles in the back! There is no way to get out from the inside!

Looking at that unoccupied seat and open door, the policeman whispered, "Did he say... 'escape-artist'?" Then, regaining his senses, he assured himself, "I must've left the door unlatched. Yeah, that's it. I just didn't shut it all the way."

He got out of the car, and called over to Maria who was sitting on her front porch, "Did you see which way that crazy purple kid went?"

Maria was rather amazed that a ten-year-old boy — particularly a *nut* of a ten-year-old boy — could make such an easy getaway from an officer of the law. She paused for a confused second before answering: "Um... no."

Officer Rocco shrugged and whistled casually as if nothing had happened. Shutting the back door, he said the word "Coffee" to himself several times, then got back in the front seat and drove off in search of some.

...And perhaps a donut.

Chapter 2
Night-Ghost's Grand Mission

Even if you're an escape-artist extraordinaire called Night-Ghost, you can't escape the fact that your September will be ruined by the first day of school. You have to dress like a normal ten-year-old child, and trudge off to elementary school like everyone else.

You can't exactly say, "Sorry, Mom, but math and English are a waste of my time; I have to protect the planet from the forces of Evil!" Your mother hasn't the slightest inkling that you have a secret identity as a costumed crime-fighter, for you must keep your secret even from *her*. No mother is going to say, "OK, go ahead and fight evil; just try not to get any bullet-holes in your cape." (Mothers are too over-protective to let their precious "babies" fall into deathtraps like pools of fire.)

Now, your *dad* might understand. He might say, "Let the boy be a crime-fighter, Martha! It'll be good for him!

It'll build character! Why, I was a superhero when I was young!" And you might think, "Wow! Dad sure is cool about this!" But the next thing you know, your old man will be talking your ears off, telling you how to go about it all: "Son, let me tell you what to do when you're locked in a crushing-room with spikes on the walls." As if you don't know what to do when you're locked in a spike-walled crushing-room!

No, it's simply best to let your parents think you're completely normal, and go about your perils and adventures in secret. When September rolls around, you keep your mouth shut and attend school like you're expected to. Perhaps you stuff your costume in the bottom of your book-bag, in case evil rears its ugly head during lunch or recess. Injustice can strike anywhere — even an elementary school playground. (I've seen injustice there, and I'm sure you have too.)

Thus it was that Night-Ghost found himself sitting like an ordinary ten-year-old boy in an ordinary desk in an ordinary fifth-grade classroom. Had you been one of his classmates, you wouldn't have had the faintest notion that he had spent the previous night locked in a life-or-death struggle with the Compost Beast of Zetriak.

But had you known that a superhero was sitting next to you, you would have felt a little safer, for this particular fifth-grade class was one of the most perilous places on Earth! The teacher in charge was a monster far wickeder and more destructive than any Compost Beast.

Her name was Mrs. Flembaugh. Not a pretty name; not a pretty person.

She was only called "Mrs. Flembaugh" when she was actually *in* the room. When she was out of earshot, the students used her "real" name: "Sasquatch Lady" — a nickname invented years ago by students who had long since grown up and moved away. Even so, it had stuck to her down through the many years, and it was easy to see why.

She was a very old woman (not just when compared with her fifth grade pupils, but when compared with *anyone*), and her wrinkled features were locked in a permanent scowl. She was also very big (not just when compared with other old ladies, but with *anyone*), and she could throw a misbehaving student the length of a football field.

Gossip abounded that years and years ago she had sent a student to the hospital when she had picked up a desk and thrown it through a brick wall. It was never clear if the injured person was a student seated in the desk when it penetrated the wall, or if it was a person on the other side of the wall when the desk came flying through. (And, of course, some people said that the guy died.) There was no solid evidence to support any version of this tale. No one had ever proven that she had caused such serious property damage and personal injury. Yet, on this first day of the school year, as she stomped into the room and slammed the door behind her, her newest batch of students believed every wild myth they had heard.

She stared at her class wickedly, sending out a hateful energy from her eyes — an unseen lightning that leapt directly into the souls of her twenty-three horrified students. Each individual child got the eerie feeling "She's staring right at me and no one else!"

Writing out her name on the chalkboard, she then spun around, and gave a slight adjustment to the granny glasses perched on her nose. Her bright green sweater and pink paisley dress seemed far too sunny and cheery for the wrinkled scowl that was carved upon her face; and completely contrary to her hulking frame. At first glance, one might even assume, "That's not really an old lady, but a professional football player dressed-up in an old lady's costume and gray wig!"

After a pause to let an ungodly fear seep into her students, she spoke in a cold, unfeeling drone. "My name is Mrs. Flembaugh. As for my classroom rules: I have too many of them to list. When you break a rule, I'll tell you. For instance..." She pointed to a girl in the front row.

"What's your name, girl?"

"Rosalee," she answered timidly.

"Get rid of the chewing gum, Rosalee! Now!"

As poor, terrified Rosalee carefully got up from her desk to dispose of her gum, Mrs. Flembaugh told the class, "Now you all know: I don't allow chewing gum in my classroom. It's too late for Rosalee, who just made my Bad List, but the rest of you have learned a valuable lesson, haven't you?"

That cruel teacher held out one of her massive, wrinkled hands in a silent command. Rosalee surrendered the entire pack of bubblegum that she had in her desk.

Mrs. F.'s menacing eyes scanned the room like searchlights until they settled on another child. "What's *your* name?"

"...Uh...John." He was sinking low in his seat, desperately trying to shove a water-pistol deeper into his pocket where it wouldn't be seen. But with just a bone-chilling stare from his teacher, he surrendered his squirt-gun.

"John's on my Bad List," she told the class, "because... *I don't allow water-pistols!* And don't think that you can—" She interrupted herself when she spotted another sin. "You with the comic book!"

A boy with a comic book on his desk instantly froze in terror. He hadn't even been reading it at the moment.

Nevertheless, he offered it up in his outstretched hand and submitted his name for the Bad List: "Mike."

"None of this mindless rubbish!" the teacher grumbled, waving that comic book the way a preacher might wave a smutty work of the devil.

Then another forbidden act caught her eye. She walked right up to the desk of another boy, and loomed over him like the statue of a brutal god. She snarled, "You're doodling!"

That boy, who had been drawing a tiny picture of Sir Lancelot on the corner of a piece of paper, asked, "And there's no doodling, right?"

"This is *not* an art class, young man! What's your name?"

"Terry."

"Welcome to the Bad List, Terry!" She snatched the pencil right out of Terry's hand and scribbled furiously on his sketch. She scribbled until she had completely obliterated Sir Lancelot, then kept right on scribbling until she had snapped the tip of the pencil clean off. But that still wasn't nearly enough to express her ill temper. She tore that piece of paper away and wadded it up. Then she noticed another drawing underneath that first one. In fact, the sheet that she had ripped away was only the top page of a whole sketchbook full of artwork.

Sneering in disgust, she snatched the sketchbook away. Then she took her armload of confiscated items and locked them in her desk with a mean slam of the drawer and an overdone rattle of her keys.

She told those on her Bad List, "You'll get this rubbish back at the end of the day... *maybe!*"

Terry raised his hand. "Mrs. Flembaugh?"

"Yes?" She was clearly annoyed to see a child brave enough to speak-up. Her harsh display had been meant to frighten them all into utter silence.

"How do we get off the Bad List?"

She gave Terry a hardhearted stare-down. "You grow up, move to another state, grow old and die."

Perhaps that coldhearted old monster wouldn't have been so brazenly terrifying if she had known that one of the students in her classroom was secretly that masked defender of justice called Night-Ghost. He may have been dressed as a normal ten-year-old boy at the moment, but even without his purple mask, cloak, boots and tights, his superhero's brain was hard at work.

He stared at the bitter old woman with a cunning fire in his eyes, like some brilliant general plotting a battlefield strategy.

"Now," he thought silently to himself, "it's *very clear* why I've been sentenced to spend the fifth grade with Sasquatch Lady! Someone has to put a stop to her vandalism, theft and tyranny! Night-Ghost's Grand Mission has begun!"

Chapter 3
The Golden-Haired Stranger

While Night-Ghost was beginning his "Grand Mission" in Mrs. Flembaugh's torture chamber of a classroom...

In a different fifth-grade classroom at Palisades Elementary, Maria was undergoing that depressing nightmare known as "being the new student." She was lucky enough to have Mrs. Reynolds for a teacher — a kindly old lady who had never been given a nickname inspired by a legendary upright ape. Yet, even without a servant of Satan for a teacher, Maria was suffering a miserable first day in grade five.

She knew it was going to be miserable, so she had taken great pains to prepare. In a turtleneck of perfect white, along with a green plaid mini-dress (all the rage in those early 1970s), she had just the right balance of dressing not too flashy, for that would be "stuck-up," and not too drab, for that would make her a nerd. But, even with such preparation, she was an outcast from the start; not making a single friend. She hadn't even made an acquaintance. (That's a person who's not exactly your friend, but at least he or she knows your name.) But even when being totally ignored, the Marias of the world aren't known for sulking or pouting. She refused to grumble about her situation.

Looking on the bright side of her solitude, she thought, "No one's said a word to me, but at least they don't hate me." But then she heard otherwise.

Eavesdropping on a circle of girls, she heard one of them putting forth the ridiculous notion, "That new girl's pretty stuck up, don't you think?" And another agreed with this ignorant opinion, saying, "Yeah, she doesn't talk to *anybody.*"

"Well," Maria thought, "so much for keeping politely to myself!"

To disprove this "stuck-up new girl" notion, she decided that a more outgoing attitude was now in order. During the first recess of the day, she boldly approached a group of fellow fifth-graders and asked quite pleasantly if she could join their game. But, just as the whole pack of them were beginning their "Sure; why not?" sort of shrug, one less-than-pretty and more-than-jealous girl (who appeared to be the "leader" of the bunch) snarled, "Beat it, Barbie-doll."

Not one to take such cracks quietly, Maria snarled

right back, "Barbie's *blonde*, you toad!"

And the next thing Maria knew, she was running for her life.

She might have met with a pummelling from that toad of a girl, had not the playground supervisor been there to defuse the situation with a shrill blast of her whistle and a command of "Knock it off!"

Precisely as Maria had figured, she wound up sitting alone at recess, reading a book and pretending that nothing bothered her. Yes, every worry that had flitted through her mind the night before had come to pass precisely as she had predicted. The girls hated her when she talked; they hated her when she didn't.

And the boys? They also behaved exactly as she had assumed they would. Like brainless robots whose only programming was "Girls are dumb," they could only treat her like an inferior life-form, or ignore her completely.

Well, there was *one* boy who behaved differently towards her — a golden-haired boy who sat behind her in Mrs. Reynolds' class. His particular method of dealing with Maria was to stare at her as if she were a nine-headed monster, then drop his eyes to his textbooks if she looked back. On the playground it was the same: he would stare in some sort of astonishment, then take flight if she made a move in his direction.

Maria was sharp enough to know that his panicky behavior wasn't disgust. He obviously had a crush on her, which she found a little amusing and more than a little flattering. But, when all is said and done, he may as well have hated her guts or ignored her like everyone else, for he couldn't be her friend if he was too bashful to utter a word to her.

So, after that first recess, which was both dangerous and dull, she dragged herself through another dismal stretch of math and English lessons. And no matter what answers she knew, she never raised her hand to speak. If she was right, she only would've been seen as "the stuck-up new girl who's always showing off." If she had been wrong, she would've been called "the dimwitted Barbie-doll who doesn't know anything."

When the lunch bell rang, she picked up her lunchbox, and wandered off to a distant spot at the farthest end of a deserted courtyard to eat by herself. She could have chosen a grassy spot under the sunny sky. This would have brightened her up, but she didn't really want any brightening-up. The shadows between the pillars of the covered sidewalk were more to her liking. She sat on a cold cement step with no other company than ham and cheese on wheat bread, a thermos of orange juice, and an apple.

A single bite of her sandwich later, she had the odd

feeling that she was being watched. Looking up, she saw the shy, golden-haired boy staring at her from across the courtyard's wide patch of grass.

"Well," she thought to herself, "he's the only person who doesn't think I'm a disease! I should see if he can talk."

As nicely as can be, she sent that boy a long-distance greeting — a tiny little wave of her hand.

This, of course, threw that boy into a tremendous fit of confusion. He blinked in disbelief, his jaw fell open, and his face went white as a sheet. Maria's mysterious admirer couldn't have been more startled if she had ripped her own head off and flung it at him.

His fear of her was so adorable that she almost wanted to take him home and set him on a shelf with her collection of stuffed animals. That look of panic on his face was so amusing that Maria couldn't contain the itty-bitty laugh that snuck out of her. It was an *astonished* laugh, not a *mocking* laugh, for she had never seen such a terrible case of heartsick shyness.

Unfortunately, that itty-bitty laugh struck the boy as an itty-bitty *torture*. He blushed in absolute shame, and darted away as quickly as a sparrow.

Maria knew immediately that her wee little chuckle had caused immense damage. "Oh, no! He thinks I laughed at him! He thinks I'm a totally stuck-up creep!"

So she abandoned her lunch and raced after him, hoping she could explain the misunderstanding... and maybe find herself a friend.

Chapter 4

The Funny One, the Brainy One, the Quiet One, and a Sudden Theatrical Performance

Unaware that he was being followed, the golden-haired boy raced around the corner of the building, where he met up with three other boys. He was clearly a friend of these three, for he sat right down beside them, and opened his lunch sack.

When Maria saw that group of boys together, she skidded to a stop. Suddenly, it wasn't a good idea to confront her golden-haired admirer. She couldn't possibly embarrass him in front of his friends by asking him, "Why do you keep staring at me and running away?" Fifth-graders are extremely cruel when they find out that someone (even a friend) has a crush on a classmate.

And she wasn't too keen on walking up to a group of four boys and saying *anything*. So far, every boy had avoided her as you would avoid a mangy dog with a wet, hacking cough. Why should she put herself through the misery of being told to get lost again?

But she simply *had* to find out who that terrified, golden-haired boy was! She didn't consider herself to be a nosey person by nature, so she had no real desire to listen-in on some strangers' conversation. She promised herself that as soon as she heard what the golden-haired boy's name was, she'd go on her merry way. And as she stayed out of sight, lurking just around the corner of the building, she got the information she wanted immediately.

One of the boys said, "We'd ask, where you were, Dan, but we already know: you were staring at the one and only Maria Fuente and trying not to have a heart attack!"

And there it was: His name was Dan. Of course, if she was going to stick to the promise she had made to herself, she would've stopped her eavesdropping right then. However, the comment about Dan's danger of a heart attack from staring at "the one and only Maria Fuente" had sent a funny charge through her that kicked-up the speed of her pulse. Of course, she had already deduced that Dan had a crush on her; but it suddenly sounded like a breaking news bulletin to hear it spoken out loud by someone else. So not only was she going to keep listening in, she was going to shift into full spy-mode!

Feeling slightly bolder, she crept around the corner and hid in a shrubbery where she could spy on those boys without being seen.

She saw Dan looking discouraged as he prowled through his lunch sack. He groaned, "I had my lunch in my hand. For two seconds I was feeling all brave. You know: say 'Hi, can I eat lunch with you?' She was even alone. I'm such a loser!"

There it was again: that weird little jolt dancing through Maria's nervous system. Do boys *really* admit to this sort of stuff when no girls are around? Shouldn't his friends laugh at him? Shouldn't the conversation go something like this?...

"I wasn't looking at Maria!"

"Yes you were!"

"Shut up!"

"No, *you* shut up!"

"No, *you* shut up!"

"You shut up — times a million!"

"You shut up — infinity!"

But there was none of this simple-minded, "I'm cooler than you are" sort of talk. Either she didn't know anything at all about boys, or these four boys were completely different than anyone else their age.

The three sitting with Dan were Curtis, Peter and Terry — although she didn't get their names until well into the conversation. To start off with, she just thought of them as "The Funny One," "The Brainy One," and "The Quiet One." Curtis (The Funny One), was a tall, lanky boy with a broad, crazy grin. His bright-blonde hair was cut close at the sides with a tuft on top that swayed like a knot of yarn atop a fitful hand-puppet. He joked his way through the conversation, jumping from one cartoon voice to another — a fake British accent, a cowboy drawl, a pirate snarl. Maria could have listened to him talk all day long and still wonder what his *normal* voice sounded like.

The Brainy One — Peter — was shorter and of Asian ancestry, his close-cropped black hair spiked upwards. The thing that made him "brainy," was that he would answer with "I can comprehend that," or "that's logical to assume," when most people (especially a ten-year-old!) would simply say "Uh-huh." Even so, he never seemed to be self-impressed or pompous. He joked right along with Curtis, but used scientific brilliance as his form of comedy.

The last of the group was Terry — The Quiet One. He had light brown hair, which he left uncombed in the unruly way that a ten-year-old boy's hair should be. Dressed in a plain gray sweatshirt and blue jeans, he wasn't the sort of kid that anyone really notices. Maria decided to think of him as "The Quiet One," because he didn't clown around like his two buddies. However, he wasn't shy or withdrawn like Dan. He just seemed to prefer watching and listening to talking — rather like an alien from another planet sent here to observe us lowly humans without interfering in our business.

Terry had no lunch to eat, so he was just sitting there for the company. Whether he had forgotten his lunch or was too poor to have one, Maria couldn't guess, but his friends kept giving him whatever food they didn't want, as if he were the family dog taking the table scraps.

Those boys chattered about baseball (apparently, the Pittsburgh Pirates looked good this year) and comic books (apparently, the latest issue of Dr. Darkness had a guest appearance by Mystery Archer). It was nonsense that Maria found far from interesting. And just when she was thinking she should slink away, she heard her name spoken again...

Terry seemed to brighten-up with a flash of an idea: "So where is Maria eating lunch?"

Dan mumbled, "Back by the courtyard."

"And she's alone?" Terry started to stand up.

Dan pulled him back down to earth. "No! Do *not* go talk to her!"

"I was just going to tell her your name, and—"

"My name? The name of the guy who was staring at her like a freak?"

Peter asked, "Did her sensors indicate the presence of a guy staring at her?"

Dan confessed, "Aw, jeeze! It was terrible! She saw me!"

Terry, quite sensibly, suggested, "And that's when you're supposed to say, 'Hello.' "

"I'd sound like such a loser!"

"And turning around and running makes you look like a genius?"

"But 'Hello' is so lame!"

"Well, what do you *want* to say to her?"

"I want to say..." Dan lit up with a daydreamer's excitement. " 'Run for it, Miss Fuente! I'll handle this!' "

"You'll handle what?" asked all three boys at once.

"I'll save her from the chuckling blob of crud from Mars that's chasing her."

Peter wondered, "What if she never gets chased by a blob of chuckling Martian crud — or a globule of chortling snot from Venus, for that matter? What if — and call me crazy, for this is merely rapidly-formulated speculation — What if she has an ordinary, boring life? What do you want to say to her then? Have you concocted any sort of backup plan?"

Curtis interjected, "He already told you his backup plan: When she looks up, run! Run like heck!"

"I didn't run because she looked at me," Dan informed them quite sternly. But then he mumbled-out the rest of his response: "I ran because she... she smiled and waved."

Curtis snarled bitterly, "That creep! Smiling and waving!"

Peter added, "Why, it's an outrage! Call her parents!"

Curtis picked up the receiver on an invisible telephone, and as he pretended to dial it, he muttered crossly, "Those Fuentes are getting a piece of my mind! How dare they raise such a rotten little —" He suddenly shrieked, "Mr. and Mrs. Fuente, teach that barbaric little girl of yours some manners!"

Terry waited for Curtis to hang up on his make-believe phone-call, then asked Dan quite calmly, "You don't want her to smile at you?"

"I guess I do." Dan was lost. The worry that distorted his expression spoke of his fear that he just didn't understand anything anywhere in the world. "I don't know what my brain was doing!"

"Then I'll tell ya!" Curtis hopped to his feet and pulled Peter up with him. "OK, Pete, you'll be Dan, so all you gotta do is just stand and stare."

"Stare at what?"

"Stare at... Stare at Terry! Terry, you're Maria!"

"I'm Maria?" Terry was more puzzled than amused,

and he clearly didn't want to be cast in the role of Maria.

Curtis pretended to be enraged that he had to explain everything: "Just for the purposes of my little play, you're going to be Maria. You're not pretty enough, that's for danged sure! And you should really think about doing something with your hair. Maybe if we could find you a cute little miniskirt, you'd play the role better. You'd look good in something blue, I think."

"Just get on with it!" Terry grumbled, worried that Curtis was indeed weird enough to run off and find a miniskirt for him to wear. (For, in fact, Curtis was looking around to see if there was a girl anywhere near who was about Terry's height and who might loan her dress to them for a few minutes.)

Like some insane film director, Curtis described Peter's role to him: "You're Dan — a frightened young lad who is desperately in love with the stunning Maria Fuente." (Here he indicated Terry, and Terry dropped his face into his hands.) "So you just stare! You're unable to speak! Your thoughts are racing!"

Peter turned his face to Terry, locked his expression into an open-mouthed trance, and remained utterly motionless.

Dan was, of course, the object of the comedy to come, but he seemed at ease with it. He asked Curtis, "And what role are you going to play?"

Curtis grinned devilishly. "I am your innermost thoughts!" He ducked behind Peter and "the play" began.

While Peter stood perfectly still, staring at Terry with wide, worried eyes and gaping mouth, Curtis hid behind him and said, "There she is! Maria Fuente! She's... she's such a groovy, out-of-sight chick! Look at her! She always has the latest, far-out fashions on, but who cares? She'd still be beautiful if she wore an old trash-bag! An old trash-bag that's been *used* — *twice!* I should talk to her! But what do I say? 'Hello'? No! Too simple! I'll... Yes! I'll tell her, 'Miss Fuente, you would look beautiful in an old trash-bag that's been used twice! No, *three* times!"

Peter broke his trance to tell Curtis, "The word is 'thrice.' "

"No talking!" Curtis demanded. "You're in a trance! Just keep staring at her!" He pointed to Terry.

Terry took exception to this. "Don't call me a 'her.' "

"Act like professionals!" insisted the self-made director, and he went back to pretending he was Dan's mental voice. "No! She's noticed that I'm staring at her! I wonder what kind of ridiculous-looking blank stare I've got on my face! I wonder how long I've been staring at her — three hours? Four hours? No, she's still eating lunch, so it can't be more than twenty minutes. Man, I'm a great detective!"

Dan wasn't the least bit put-off by this "production."

He was actually enjoying it. It seemed to release all his frustrations and mock the confusion that he hated about himself. In truth, Dan seemed less annoyed to be ribbed in this way than Terry was to have to play the role of Maria.

And watching from her hiding place in the hedges, the *real* Maria was astounded. She had never seen anyone go to such elaborate lengths to be funny. Curtis didn't just spout off put-downs like any ol' class clown. He cast people in roles and produced miniature plays on the spur of the moment.

Curtis whispered to Terry, "OK, Maria, now you smile and wave!"

Terry waved, but didn't manage much in the way of a smile.

Curtis, playing the part of Dan's overworked brain, gasped, "Dang it! She smiled at me! My life is over! I'm crushed! …No, wait! A smile is good, right? What should I do? I should smile back, right? But do I look cool enough? Is my hair combed? Are my teeth brushed? Did I put on my coolest clothes this morn— Oh, no! Did I remember to put my pants on this morning? What if I forgot my pants? Oh, no! I'm too scared to look down and check! I don't feel a breeze, so I might be OK."

Much to his credit as an actor, Peter didn't even crack a smile. He kept right on playing his role of Dan

— holding his face in a perfectly vacant gawk while all this insanity went on behind him.

Curtis continued as Dan's inner voice: "It's not *my* fault that I don't walk up to Maria and talk to her! It's the fault of the Martian Crud-Blobs, who don't have the common courtesy to kidnap the girl I love, so I can shout, 'Run for it, Miss Fuente! I'll handle this!' Drat those blobs of— Oh! She's gonna smile at me again! I better scram! Run, feet! Get me out of here!"

After this bizarre routine, Curtis took a bow as if thousands were cheering him, when, in fact, Dan was his only audience in this deserted part of the school. (Well, yes, Maria was also there, hiding behind the hedges. She, too, would have clapped for that skillfully silly performance if it wouldn't have revealed her presence.) As Curtis bowed, he grandly thanked his other actors: "Let's have a big round of applause for Peter and his three-minute blank stare! And Terry for his fabulous portrayal of the lovely Maria Fuente!"

Dan applauded, having been mightily entertained, not caring a smidgen that he had been the target of this mockery. He leaned over to Terry and confessed, "Yep! That's pretty much exactly what my brain was saying!"

This prompted Terry to ask, "So, now that you know it's ridiculous, are you going to say 'Hello' to her?"

Taking a pause to try and imagine such an event, Dan finally answered, "Probably not."

"Then forget that one," Curtis advised him. "What you do is you bump into her. You make it look like an accident, and you oh-so-charmingly say, 'Pardon me, Miss Fuente. Sorry to collide with you, but I must confess it was grand to do so!' " (Of course, he put forth this suggestion in an overblown English accent, like some snooty millionaire.)

"I can't do a weird voice like that!" Dan argued (and rightly so). "And I'm such a klutz that if I bumped into her I'd probably knock her right into a wall and bash her teeth out. What do I oh-so-charmingly say then?"

Again, he fired-up that snooty English accent: " 'I must say, you have a lovely smile, Miss Fuente! Allow me to pick it up for you!' And then you pick up her teeth for her, the way a gentleman picks up a lady's hanky when she drops it."

Terry, who seemed to be Dan's voice of reason, asked, "Did you at least get a seat near her in class?"

"Yeah!" He finally had an accomplishment he could be proud of. "I'm in the one right behind her! As soon as I saw which desk she had taken — *voom!* — I rocketed straight to the next one in line! I'm tellin' ya, my feet didn't even touch the carpet!"

Maria thought that maybe she might step out of her

hiding place after all. This bunch of boys seemed very different from all the others she had run into. When they razzed a friend for having a crush on a girl, they did so pleasantly and with brilliance. To point at Dan and sing the snickering song, "Dan's got a girlfriend! Dan's got a girlfriend!" would have been utterly beneath them! A comic genius of Curtis's abilities would never have stooped to such an unoriginal put-down!

But, even if they sounded as nice as can be, it was unwise to step out of hiding and say, "Hi, can I eat lunch with you guys?" They were boys after all. She had stumbled upon them when they didn't know she was listening-in. Perhaps all it would take would be the appearance of an unwelcome girl to transform them from friendly, witty angels into sneering, insulting demons. She wasn't sure she wanted to hear Curtis's quick wit cutting her apart, or Peter calling her a slug by its scientific name. And Terry may have been "The Quiet One," but he *was* a boy. Even *he* might tell her to get lost.

The smart thing to do was to leave them alone. But just as she was about to walk away, she saw something tragic begin.

Fearless Force

Chapter 5

Attack of the Troglodyte

From across the schoolyard came Eddie Thigpen, the worst bully in America's public school system and the second evilest creature walking the Earth. (What with Mrs. Flembaugh being "the evilest creature walking the Earth," it hardly seems fair that Palisades Elementary School should also have to be home to the *second* evilest creature, but that's how it goes.)

Eddie put an ugly arrogance into his every step. He clenched and unclenched his pudgy little fists. He pawed at his unruly mop of red hair, pushing it out of his freckled face with an all-too-cool move, making sure that everyone could see his superior sneer. His faded denim jacket with its motorcycle advertisement on the back and tattered blue-jeans were a hoodlum's uniform that cried out, "Here comes trouble — trouble for no reason at all."

Seeing that chubby lout swagger across the playground, Dan groaned, "What's he even doing at this school? I thought he was going to be in junior high. He was in sixth grade *last* year."

"And the year before that," added Peter. "And the year before that."

"He's been at this school longer than most of the teachers," said Curtis. "He's got to be at least thirty by now!" This was, of course, an exaggeration. But if Eddie kept flunking, it would one day come to pass that he *would* be spending his thirtieth birthday in the sixth grade right there at Palisades Elementary.

Walking at either side of the gruesome Mr. Thigpen were two other grade school hoodlums. (Their names? Who cares if a bully's minions have names? It's not as if they're interesting people with personalities, or brains, or souls, or anything.)

Those two sidekicks of Eddie's were the proper age to be attending elementary school, so they were much younger than he was. Thus it was that they looked up to Eddie as their guide and role model. When Thigpen spat on the ground, they spat on the ground. When Thigpen sneered at something, they sneered at it. It's anybody's guess *why* they had chosen that meat-headed oaf as their master. Were they hoping that *they too* could take ten years or more to make it out of the sixth grade?

"He's headed right this way," said Terry, sounding annoyed, but still calm.

"What do you think his problem is today?" Curtis wondered. "We never even looked at him."

Peter remarked, "Who can guess what goes on in that sesame seed Eddie calls a brain?"

"Well, I'm not hangin' around here to find out!" Dan was hardly finished with that statement before he took to running. He fled to a different part of the schoolyard as fast as his feet could move him.

Witnessing all this from the shrubbery where she hid, Maria felt sad for Dan when she saw him take flight. However, she *did* think that he was the most sensible of the four boys. As she secretly watched those bullies close in, she wished that Peter, Curtis and Terry would get up and run as Dan had. She considered running herself — not because she thought that she might be spotted in her hiding place, but because she didn't want to watch the cruelty that was sure to unfold.

But she stayed put behind that hedge, and the cruelty unfolded...

In the wink of an eye, Peter and Curtis were lifted up and pinned against the building by the two junior bullies.

Meanwhile Eddie went straight for Terry, and hoisted

him right up off the ground. "You got some money for me, punk?" Flipping his victim upside-down, he shook him, waiting for loose change to come clinking out onto the sidewalk. And, as if Eddie were training his bullies-to-be, he told them, "This kid, Terry, is a gold mine! He *always* has a buck! His mom gives him lunch money, but he never buys lunch!"

To his credit, Terry didn't show an ounce of fear, even though he was being roughed around like a dog-toy. As calm as can be, he said, "I save it up to buy comic books on the weekends. You know, you guys could use a constructive hobby like that."

"*You're* my hobby!" Eddie laughed as he continued to shake him.

Eventually, a tiny scrap of green fell from Terry's back pocket: a folded-up dollar bill.

Peter, still held back against the wall by one of Eddie's henchmen, was the first to see that dollar bill drop onto the sidewalk. In order to distract the others as quickly as possible, he shouted, *"Thigpen, you're a troglodyte!"*

Eddie stopped his violent shaking of Terry, but still kept him suspended upside-down over the cement. After a befuddled pause, he turned an ugly sneer in Peter's direction. "I'm a *what?*"

"You're a troglodyte!" Peter informed him again. "A

bellicose mome! A truculent caitiff!"

Still concealed behind that shrubbery at the corner of the building, Maria nearly laughed out loud. She knew that a "troglodyte" was another word for "caveman," even though all of Peter's other put-downs had escaped her. She thought it showed amazing courage for a brainy kid to mouth-off at a troglodyte like that.

Still holding Terry by the legs, Eddie leaned in close to Peter and growled, "Just 'cause I don't know what you're sayin' doesn't mean I won't break your face anyway!"

"No," Curtis remarked, "the thing that's gonna keep you from breaking Peter's face is the fact that his big brother will break *your* face quicker, easier and into smaller pieces! And then he's gonna break the faces of your buddies here in alphabetical order! You guys want me to explain what alphabetical order is? You look confused. You know the tune, right?" And he launched loudly into song: "A, B, C, D, E, F, G—"

"Shut up, spaz!" Eddie wasn't as annoyed at the loud rendition of the alphabet song as he was by the mention of Peter's big brother. Everything said about that big brother must have been absolutely true, for Maria could see a cold fear take over Eddie's expression. His two bullies-in-training also looked queasy with terror.

One of those underlings looked up at Eddie, and

seeing the fear in his leader's eyes, asked, "Thigpen, you ain't scared of Doug, are you?" (Doug being the name of the big brother in question.)

Beefing up his pride, Eddie proclaimed, "No, I ain't scared of that loser!"

"You'd be afraid of him if you were intelligent," said Peter.

"Yeah? Well, I'm not!" replied Eddie.

It was all Peter could do to keep himself from laughing as he asked, "You're not what? Not afraid, or not intelligent?"

Striking a superior attitude, the bully sneered, "He ain't your real brother, anyway, 'cause he's black and you're Chinese."

Peter blew off this ignorant statement with a small correction: "Actually, I'm from Vietnam, not China."

"Who cares? What's the difference?"

"The difference? Simple: Vietnam covers one hundred, twenty-eight thousand and thirty-two square miles, and China is markedly larger at three million, seven hundred and four thousand, four hundred and forty square miles, but that's including Tibet, which—"

Again Eddie leaned in threateningly at Peter, saying, "I don't see your big brother here to do your fighting for you, so shut your mouth!"

It was right here that Terry decided to play a little

ruse. While still hanging upside-down in Eddie's clutches, he looked behind the bullies, waved his hand and casually said, "Hi, Doug!"

All three hooligans spun around with terror in their eyes. Their blood froze in their hearts at the thought of Peter's guardian angel sneaking up behind them. Of course, there was no Doug there. It was just a scheme of distraction — a none-too-clever plan, but enough to dupe those none-too-clever thugs.

During this distraction, Curtis made his move. He had gotten a small threatening shove from the bully that guarded him, so he performed an overdone crybaby whine... "You hurt me, you heartless brute!" ...and fell to the ground. Quick as a shark snapping at its dinner, Curtis grabbed up that loose dollar bill, and jumped back up to his feet.

The bully in front of him was just reaching out to catch him in a wrestling hold, when Curtis did something that few people would ever think of doing in a fight: he let loose with a shrill, startling noise two inches away from that bully's face. (It was the sort of sound that only the weirdest of kids can do. For it takes hours of diligent practice to learn how to master the ear-splitting wail of a turkey being electrocuted.) Having "said" this, Curtis burst into a run, and fled for his life, cackling like a madman.

The bully guarding him should have given chase, but

he just stood there, too shell-shocked from having that alien noise blasted directly at him.

Seeing his underling just standing confused, Eddie screamed, "Kick that spaz's butt!"

The junior bully snapped out of his trance, and ran after Curtis.

Maria wanted to stand up and cheer for Curtis's brilliant (if bizarre) escape, but she wisely kept hidden to see what would happen next.

Peter shoved his enemy aside and ran.

Terry wriggled out of Eddie's arms so easily that it was clear he could've done so at any time. He reached for his book-bag, which lay on the sidewalk, but before he could snatch it up and escape, Eddie had latched onto him again.

Shoving him up against the brick wall, Eddie poked a chubby finger into his captive's chest. "*You* don't have a big brother, so I guess it's OK to break your face!"

A feeling of dread filled Maria's bones as she watched Terry stand quietly in the shadow of the vicious Mr. Thigpen. She thought to herself, "I'll bet he wishes he *really was* one of those comic book superheroes he spends his lunch money on!"

Well, the Marias of the world don't just stand by and watch people get pounded-on by thugs. She figured that she could do something, even if it was nothing more than stepping out of hiding and yelling, "Knock it off, Eddie!" That would surely give Terry the split-second he needed to slip away.

But just as she took her first step towards the dangerous scene, she glanced down and saw something unbelievable.

Terry's book-bag was lying there at her feet. Its top was partially open, and she could see something purple inside. Her jaw fell open as she realized that it was the corner of a purple and violet, star-covered superhero's cape!

"Oh, no!" Maria was overcome with horror. *"Terry's that 'Night-Ghost' lunatic who crashed into my yard last night!* And he's actually carrying that ridiculous costume around in his book-bag! Is he out of his mind? What if someone sees it? They'll blab it all over the school, and he'll be laughed at all year! He'll be laughed at all the way through junior high! He'll be a joke until he graduates from high school!"

Maria knew that the very worst person who could possibly find that silly super-suit was the coldhearted punk who was looming over Terry at this very instant. She thought she had better grab that bag and get it out of there. Later, when this hubbub was over, she'd do Terry a second favor: she'd return the bag to him and say, "Don't *ever* bring this dumb purple costume to school again!"

As slowly and carefully as possible, she reached

out and caught a grip on that book-bag. Then, quick as lightning, she snatched it up and ran for all she was worth.

This caught Eddie's attention. Seeing that girl grab the bag and disappear, it instantly popped into his brain (or what Peter had referred to as "that sesame seed he calls a brain") that there must be something valuable in it. And if it was valuable, he wanted to steal it! "Hey! Get back here, girlie!"

The bully raced after Maria, and Terry sped off in the opposite direction, hoping to catch up with her by a different route.

Maria quickly outdistanced Eddie. It's a lost cause for a blubbery monstrosity of a boy to catch up with a girl whose twice-a-week ballet classes keep her nimble. She easily escaped him, ducked into the shadows behind a pillar, and looked into the bag. Sure enough, there it was — the hooded cloak, the purple mask, gloves and boots of that nut who called himself "Night-Ghost." The rest of the costume was missing, but she figured that, like most superheroes, he was wearing it under his regular clothes.

"He's off his rocker!" she whispered, as she zipped the bag shut.

Then, just as she stepped out of hiding, she found herself face to face with Eddie. They had a brief tug-of-war over the bag...

"Gimme that, girlie!"

"Get lost, you pig!"

...then he ripped it from her hands.

The bully unzipped the book-bag and snorted in triumph, "Let's see if there's anything in here I like!"

Horror shot through Maria's mind to see the thug's hand rummaging through that pack. This was *exactly* what she had dreaded! The rottenest of souls was about to pull out that purple superhero suit, and poor Terry would be ridiculed for the rest of his natural life!

Eddie had only just shoved his chubby hand inside the bag when Terry burst out of nowhere. Springing frog-like through the air, he whisked the bag right out of Eddie's hand, then darted around a corner and was gone.

Eddie hurried after him, leaving Maria alone and breathing a huge sigh of relief. All was calm again, as if the danger had never been. She returned to the shaded steps where she had left her lunchbox, sat down and thought, "Bullies! Why do some people get their jollies from shoving other people around?"

But this question turned out to be too huge for the moment. It led to thoughts that seemed to include everything on Earth: Why is there crime? Who chooses to be the one to ruin the lives of total strangers, and why do they do it? She quickly decided that this wasn't the time to analyze the whole world. This was the time to eat lunch. She took out her apple, but before a single bite, Eddie appeared in front of her again.

Between huffing for air, he barked, "Where's Terry?"

"I don't know," she answered with brave disrespect.

"He had to come this way! I chased him around that corner, and—"

She snapped, "Maybe he ducked into a phone booth to change into a superhero, so he can thwack you unconscious."

He strutted up to her in a threatening way. "Do you know who I am?"

She pretended to know nothing of him. "Um... Freddie something? I don't know."

"Eddie Thigpen!" he informed her with a self-impressed snort. "You're new, so I'm gonna give you a break. I won't pound your head in. I'll just take this apple instead."

With a triumphant grin of seldom-brushed teeth, he swiped that apple out of her hand and chomped into it just a few inches from her face. "You better have something else for me when I'm done with this!"

As that garbage-hearted caveman stepped forward to back her up against the wall, Maria felt a twinge of dread growing in the pit of her stomach. (She wasn't the sort to be easily frightened, but there's simple common sense that tells you it's not good to be backed up against a brick wall by a creature that delights in tormenting anyone and anything.) She glanced left and right, hoping to see some salvation headed her way — maybe that big brother named Doug that all the bullies feared. Even a crazy kid in a purple superhero suit would have been a welcome sight! But to her dismay, she saw no one. This shaded walkway where he had cornered her was suddenly as isolated as the South Pole.

Then a golden-haired figure came into view, peering cautiously around a pillar on the far side of the courtyard.

Yes, Dan had returned. He looked on in horror as the hooligan pressed Maria up against the side of the building and got right in her face to take big, slobbering bites from an apple.

"Here it is!" Dan thought. "I was wishing she'd be chased by a blob of crud from Mars! Eddie Thigpen stealing her lunch is pretty much the same thing! This is my one big chance to say, 'Run for it, Miss Fuente, I'll handle this,' just like I always wanted to!"

And with that well-planned-out sentence in mind, Dan strode boldly towards the scene of the crime.

Fearless Force

Chapter 6

The "Reverse-Bully"

Well, Dan's *first* step was a big, brave step — full of heroic determination to save Maria from the menace of Eddie Thigpen. But, as he got closer to the bully, each of his steps became a little less brave than the one before.

When he was finally standing right behind Eddie, he realized how unwise it is to march towards something without a plan of what to do once you've marched there.

Having never picked a fight in his life, Dan wasn't really sure how it was done. But he got a quick lesson in the "art" of fight-picking when Eddie's "playground bully radar" sensed the presence of a kid sneaking up behind him. He whirled around to bluster directly in Dan's face, "You got a problem, kid?"

Dan tried to babble something in response, but Eddie wasn't all that interested in an answer to his question.

Abrupt and jarring came the slam of the bully's foul hand into Dan's chest. Dan's next abrupt sensation was his hindquarters thumping onto the sidewalk. So there he sat for Maria to see — no damsel's champion, but a bug sprawled out and ready for an effortless squishing.

As if it wasn't bad enough that he'd be squished in front of Maria, the courtyard was quickly filled up with nearly everyone in the school (and what seemed to be seven hundred other kids from a couple other schools). In a bustle of excitement, a flood of kids had come rushing in from every direction.

First came Curtis, skidding around the corner, still waving that dollar bill in the air, laughing like a maniac and shouting, "I found a dollar! What a red-letter day!" Hot on his heels was the underling of Eddie's that had been pursuing him far and wide over the school grounds.

Next, Peter entered from the opposite end of the courtyard, chased-in by Eddie's other pet thug. Following in the wake of these two separate chases came the mobs and mobs of laughing grade-schoolers, eager to see some bullies pounding on younger kids. (Sad to say, mobs don't have any concept of right and wrong; they just want excitement.)

Yes, all the players in this miniature war were here — all except for Terry. After grabbing his book-bag, he seemed to have disappeared without a trace!

Everyone skidded to a stop at the sight of Dan cowering at Eddie's feet. Peter and Curtis getting chased wasn't nearly as interesting as Dan's situation. If Eddie was going to beat somebody up, then that was the main event! And Dan could feel every one of those unblinking eyes on him.

There was a cold gleam in Eddie's expression as he reached down, caught his victim by the shirt and hauled him up on his feet.

So much for Dan's dream of saving the day! There was a brief moment of terror as he saw his approaching doom in the shape of Eddie's beefy fist swinging directly towards his face.

And Dan *might* have gone home with a bloody nose...

...if not for a miracle out of the blue!

Out of nowhere, a hand appeared in front of Dan's face, catching Eddie's fist like a line-drive baseball, stopping it cold in mid-swing.

The hand that had zoomed in to save the day belonged to none other than Peter's big brother, Doug.

Although Maria had never seen him before, she knew immediately that it was Doug, for she had overheard that comment from Eddie, telling that Peter was "Chinese" (which he wasn't, really) and his big brother was black.

And this tall, strongly-constructed kid fit the picture she had drawn in her head: The stern "How dare you pick on a smaller kid" look on his face; the way he caught that flying fist and held onto it with a grip of iron. His whole person said "Big Brother."

And if all this hadn't told Maria that this was Doug, she could have guessed it by the look of terror in the eyes of Eddie and his henchmen. It was that same cold fear that had struck them when the very name of Doug had been mentioned — the same cold fear *times ten*, for now he was standing there in solid flesh and blood.

Doug was a "reverse-bully" — someone who had all the muscle of a bully, but used it to *break up* fights instead of *start* them; someone who saw smaller children as people in need of *protection*, not *torment*. Maria could tell all this in an instant. It was visible in his eyes.

Doug was the Anti-Eddie!

Every spectator was frozen in place as Doug stood there with Eddie's fist still clutched in his muscle-knotted hand. He plucked the stolen apple from Eddie's other paw, passed it to Dan, then dragged the bully across the courtyard and over to the side of the building.

Eddie offered such whimpering protests as "Hey, man, let me go!", "Come on, cut it out!" and "I never *touched* that new girl!" But Doug wasn't listening. He inserted the bully's head through one of the half-open windows of the school library. Pushing that window down so it was just a fraction of an inch away from the little monster's neck, Doug tightened the latch with a good, strong twist.

The upshot of this was that Eddie found his head inside the library, his body outside, and the window locked in place over his neck — not tight enough to strangle him. (Doug was very careful about this!) The window was closed just enough to hold him prisoner there while still allowing him to breathe. He squirmed and thrashed his limbs, screamed and cursed, beat and pounded the window-frame, all to no avail. That evil-minded kid was stuck.

Having dealt so swiftly and effectively with the ringleader, Doug turned his attentions to Eddie's two nameless underlings. It took nothing more than a steely stare from that "reverse-bully" to chase those cowards off like roaches fleeing a gust of bug-spray.

Then, without having spoken a word, Doug strolled casually away, his hands in his pockets as if this was just another boring morning. The only sign that he had been involved in a squabble was the disappointed shake of his head — a silence that seemed to say, "I can't *believe* some people get their kicks stealing apples from little girls!"

Half the crowd dispersed, somewhat let down that there hadn't been flying fists and bloodied noses. The other half hung around, thoroughly enjoying the sight of the universally-despised Eddie Thigpen trapped in the library window.

And there stood Dan with Maria's apple in his hand. He didn't know if he had been given the apple because he had been the closest person handy, or because Doug knew that Dan would want to be the one to return it. Whatever the reason, he was thrilled to be the one to present that stolen snack to the fabulous Maria Fuente. He gave it a quick polish on his shirt, and bestowed it upon her as if it were a fabulous, magical jewel being returned to a princess.

Much to his dismay, Princess Maria wasn't exactly thrilled to see that piece of fruit again. She tried to sound polite as she told him, "Um... Eddie bit that."

Dan looked at the apple and saw that a big, sloppy bite had been chomped out of its side. Then he noticed the pulpy smear of apple mush on the front of his shirt. (That'll happen, you know, if you try to polish an apple that's been bitten into.)

Maria said a grateful "Thanks anyway," but Dan had already vanished. She had only taken a quick look at Eddie trapped in the library window. When she turned back, Dan was gone — *utterly* gone — as if he had flown completely off the planet.

Meanwhile, the librarian was trying to loosen the

latch and free Eddie from his predicament, but Doug had twisted the lock with the strength of an angry elephant. Overcome with panic, the flustered librarian ran screaming for the janitor. And while Eddie waited for the janitor to come and set him free, the crowd in the courtyard pointed and snickered, thinking he looked like a wild-animal who had been trapped by a big-game-hunter.

Pushing through that giggling mob came Eddie's savior in green overalls: Charlie, the school's custodian, with his bright red toolbox in hand. He set to work with his screwdriver, pliers, vise-grips, and nearly every other device he carried, but couldn't get that latch to budge. Doug had tightened that latch with a positively superhuman amount of strength.

Maria wasn't interested in watching Charlie's attempt at rescuing Eddie. She was searching through the crowd for Dan, determined that she would find him and say, "Thank you for trying to stand up to Eddie." She hated the idea that a boy who was brave enough to march up to a bully twice his size was wandering around feeling like a failure.

Unable to find her would-be hero in the crowd, she left the courtyard. She ran around to the far side of the building, but Dan wasn't there either. Instead, she met up with...

...*Night-Ghost!*

Fearless Force

Chapter 7

An Insidious Plot Detected

Yes, Terry was decked-out in that crazy costume! The boots, the tights, the mask, the star-covered cloak with its monk's hood — the whole absurd getup!

After a moment of shock, Maria shoved him back into the bushes, hoping to hide him. "Are you crazy? What if someone sees you!"

"No one will see me!" he answered with his dramatic, super-heroic flair. "I am Night-Ghost; the prowler of the twilight, child of the shadows, and—"

"It's not twilight! It's broad daylight, you loony!" (It wasn't her intention to sound mean, but she was trying to snap him back to his senses, and to do that one must often speak harshly.) "And what do you mean no one will see you? *I* sure as heck see you!"

He seemed a little peeved by that remark (*and* a little embarrassed that she was right). "I haven't time for chitchat! I'm on a mission!"

"Eddie's already been taken care of," Maria told him. "Peter's big brother, Doug, trapped the creep in a library window."

"I'm on a *different* mission. I was *going to* leap in and stop Eddie, but once I saw Doug headed your way, I knew you'd be safe. So, now I have *other* injustice to stamp out!"

"Listen, I know why you're doing this." She put on a very intelligent air as she explained, "You feel kind of inferior to Doug because he can deal with Eddie so easily. Pretending you're a superhero makes you think you're brave."

He stared at her for a moment of amazement. "That's a brilliant analysis, Miss Fuente."

She shrugged. "Both my mom and my dad are psychologists. They talk about this stuff all the time."

"It's brilliant, but totally incorrect. Now, you'd better get back to your lunch. The case I'm on might be too hazardous for an ordinary human."

The way he spoke to her was positively absurd. That speeding-up and slowing-down speech pattern he had copied from a TV superhero. It was totally different from the quiet, ordinary Terry she had heard speaking before. Apparently, that purple mask had taken over his mind and put a completely new personality into his voice. And there was something about the long purple gloves as well: they seemed to have taken control of his hands, for his fingers clenched, then spread out, and danced strangely, as if wild schemes in his brain were putting clever fidgetings into them.

She groaned in frustration, then gave sanity another try: "Don't you think that you're a bit old to be running around in a costume, fighting make-believe dangers?"

"I can't waste time trying to convince you, Miss Fuente. If civilization is in peril, I have to act without delay." With that, he turned and ran away from her.

The rock-solid honesty in his voice was very disheartening to Maria. She was beginning to shift more to the belief that this poor kid wasn't merely pretending. "What if he really *is* out of his mind?" she thought sadly. "What if he's like those people they lock up in mental asylums for thinking they're Napoleon or George Washington?"

As he sped off on his "mission," he ran in perfect superhero form — crouched low, his hands curled into little fists, his cape flying out behind him.

And Maria followed (though she ran like an normal, *sane* person would run), for this mixed-up kid in the purple suit had become *her* "mission." She simply had to set him straight before he made a fool out of himself in front of the entire school.

Night-Ghost entered the building and sped through

the deserted hallway, heading directly for the door to Mrs. Flembaugh's classroom. Just outside the door, he flattened himself against the wall, like a secret agent who's about to go sneaking into a room.

Maria crept up beside him and whispered urgently, "I don't know what you have planned, but you can't go running around dressed like a—"

Night-Ghost turned and silenced her with the finger-to-the-lips signal. Slowly and carefully, he peered through the window in the door. He could see Mrs. F. sitting at her desk, busily correcting her students' papers.

"Mrs. Flembaugh's in there, isn't she?" asked Maria in a quieter whisper than before. "You don't want to mess with that woman! From what I hear, she's one wicked old lady, and she won't be amused by a kid playing superhero in her classroom during lunch!"

"I *have* to mess with her," Night-Ghost replied with steadfast conviction. "She's the insidious evil I'm up against!"

"But I heard she once got so mad that she threw a kid through a brick wall!"

"Don't worry, she'll never know that I was in her classroom! She's going to leave the room any second."

"Then you'd better get away from the door!"

"No! She'll go out the *other* door — the one that goes

outside." (Like all the classrooms at Palisades Elementary, this one had two doors opposite each other: one leading into the interior of the school, where Night-Ghost and Maria were at the moment, and one that opened up to the courtyards and playfields.)

As Night-Ghost watched through the window in the hallway door, things began to happen just as he had predicted. Mrs. Flembaugh grew very irritated by the commotion out in the courtyard. (Eddie was still stuck in the library window, screaming and cursing, Charlie was having no success freeing him or shutting him up, and the mob of onlookers was hooting in delight.) Finally fed up with the constant noise, Mrs. F. rose up from her chair and stomped out of the room to put a stop to the brouhaha — leaving, just as Night-Ghost had predicted, by the door to the outside.

Once Sasquatch Lady was out in the courtyard shouting, "What's all this racket about?", Night-Ghost made his move. He entered the empty classroom and ran right up to the teacher's desk.

Maria followed along, asking him, "What are you doing in here?"

"Sasquatch Lady has stolen something of great value," the boy in the cape explained. "It's in her desk."

Maria pushed him over to the window and said, "I'll

get it. You stand lookout at the window, in case she comes back." She gave the desk drawer a tug, finding it locked-up tight. "Well, whatever you're after, she's locked her desk, and you don't have a key."

"An escape-artist *never* needs a key!"

He pushed her gently aside, placed the heel of his hand over the keyhole, closed his eyes as if in some sort of meditation, then gave the drawer a little jiggle. It slid open as easy as anything.

Maria made no attempt to hide her astonishment. "How did you do that?"

Night-Ghost grinned. "Locks just... *obey* me."

He pulled out the sketchbook that Sasquatch Lady had stolen from him that morning (when he was Terry), and flipped through the pages to make sure it was still in good shape.

Looking over his shoulder, Maria remarked, "Those are amazing pictures!"

"They were drawn by a kid named Terry," Night-Ghost replied, unaware that Maria knew that *he* was Terry. "This sketchbook was unjustly taken from him right at the beginning of the day."

A smile grew on Maria's face as this make-believe superhero played his "secret identity game," as if Terry was someone else — someone for whom he was doing this good deed. She could very well have said, "Knock it off! *You're* Terry and I know it," but that would have served no other purpose than being mean. Instead, she asked, "So some stolen drawings — that's it? You said *civilization* was in peril."

As serious as a thing can be spoken, he told her, "The smallest of evils connect themselves to large evils, Miss Fuente. Where you find a tiny injustice, you'll soon find a huge one."

Having said this, Night-Ghost emptied that drawer of all the other items that Sasquatch Lady had seized from her students that morning — the pack of gum, the squirt-gun, the comic book, and many other objects that had enraged Mrs. F. in one way or another throughout the course of the morning. The purple-clad do-gooder distributed these things around the room, returning them to the desks of their rightful owners.

Suddenly, Maria understood that this kid wasn't so crazy after all. Sure, he didn't have to dress in such an outlandish disguise; and sure, he thought that what he was doing was an "act of justice" that "thwarted evil." But all the same, it was nice to see a kid whose heart was set on doing good — and doing so in secret. In particular, she watched the way he returned a package of bubble-gum to a desk marked "Rosalee." There was a gallant little grin on his face as he did so. Boy superheroes just love coming to the rescue of a pretty girl, even if it's just to return a pack of gum that an evil teacher has swiped.

"Well," Maria suggested, "let's see what *other* injustice lurks in Mrs. Flembaugh's desk!" At the very bottom of the drawer, she discovered a small metal lock-box. In a joking manner, she asked, "Hey, Mr. Escape-artist, you wanna work your magic on this?"

The cloaked crime-fighter leapt back to the front of the room. (There wasn't really any *need* for leaping, of course, but it made his cape flutter, and that's what capes are for.) He took the box from Maria, and performed the same lock-picking miracle he had done before. He placed the heel of his hand over the keyhole and the thing popped open.

Before Maria could say anything about his lock-picking being "just a trick of some sort," something more incredible met her eyes. That lock-box was filled with money! It was small portions of money — just one-dollar-bills and change — but there was a *pile* of it!

Maria gasped, "What's she doing with all that money in her—?"

Night-Ghost interrupted her when he found something else in that desk drawer: a collection of folded-up sheets of paper. "This might tell us something."

He unfolded those pages, to reveal that they were

scientific plans of some sort. They were sketches and designs for a mysterious-looking machine with wires, pipes, hoses and computer control panels all over it. These construction diagrams covered six pages front and back. The seventh page was a strange chemical formula — just a jumble of capital letters and small letters that would make sense to no one except a brilliant chemist.

"Looks pretty technical." Maria didn't think that they were *real* scientific plans — not for a *moment* did she think this. But playing along with his game, she said, "Of course, you know exactly what they mean, because you're a superhero."

"No," he replied in a very confounded way. "I'm not a scientist superhero; just an acrobat/escape-artist superhero."

"You know what I think? I think they're just some nonsense that that Terry-kid scribbled. I mean, he *is* an artist, so I'll bet he just—"

Night-Ghost had to cut her comment short. "We have to hide!" He re-locked that moneybox, returned it to the bottom drawer, and closed the desk. The scientific plans he folded-up and stuffed into his boot as he shoved Maria down close to the floor. "Keep low!"

The boy in the purple cape pulled her by the hand and headed for the door that would take them back out into the hallway from whence they had snuck in. But just as Night-Ghost opened that door a smidgen, he saw two kids out in the hall using the water fountain. So he abandoned his plan to escape into the hallway, and headed off in another direction, still pulling Maria behind him.

"We could have escaped back into the hall," she informed the purple-cloaked do-gooder, "if you weren't dressed in that silly suit!"

"Do you mind? We're in danger here!" (He was clearly needled by her remark. Superheroes *do not* like to have their costuming called into question!)

But she went on regardless of his level of annoyance: "It just seems to me that the crazy purple getup is making this adventure *more* difficult! If you want to be inconspicuous, why not just go around dressed like a normal—?"

Her confident questioning was cut short when she realized where he was dragging her next. The only other escape route was to duck into one of the two doors at the back of the classroom. You can guess what these doors were. One was marked "boys," and the other "girls." And before Maria had realized what was going on, Night-Ghost was pulling her straight into...

"The *boys'* bathroom? You can't drag me in there!"

Maria put her free hand on the doorframe and tried to hold stubbornly from being hauled into that alien territory.

But Night-Ghost gave an insistent yank that broke her grip and brought her clumsily inside.

The very next second, Mrs. Flembaugh returned from the courtyard. She was tugging Eddie Thigpen along by the ear, and Charlie the janitor followed close behind them.

"Shut the door, Moppy!" snapped the ghastly old teacher.

"Don't call me Moppy!" the janitor grunted. (He grunted it very quietly, for fear of riling Sasquatch Lady's temper.)

Turning her anger to Eddie, she commanded him, "Tell me how you got trapped in that library window!"

"Some kid named Doug did it! All I was doing was..."

And as Eddie explained the events that had occurred during those exciting first six minutes of lunchtime, Night-Ghost was listening from inside the boy's bathroom.

Maria *wasn't* listening. She didn't give a hoot what some creepy teacher, a playground bully and a janitor were discussing. At the moment, her mind was occupied with her own predicament. All in the space of a single heartbeat, she had gone from "confident Maria," who was teasing a pretend superhero about his absurd choice of attire, to "flustered Maria," who was trapped in a place where no sane girl should go. Afraid to touch anything, she scrunched her arms up at her sides — almost as if she feared that the sink, the paper towel dispenser, or some other fixture might leap up and touch her.

Thankfully, she realized that this bathroom was located between two classrooms, and there was another door leading out. She pulled that second door open just a wee crack to see if it was possible for her to get out without being spotted. But she never worked up the courage to peek outside. She just shut the door again, afraid that someone might be out there; someone who might catch a glimpse of her — even just a fraction of her face peering out. So she simply surrendered to the fact that she was trapped.

"Why am I in here?" she groaned.

"Because we're eavesdropping on Sasquatch Lady," Night-Ghost replied, as he kept his ear pressed up to the door.

"No, that's what *you're* doing! Why am *I* in here?"

"Shhh!"

But there was no shushing her: "Why didn't you pull us into the *girl's* bathroom? That would have been the chivalrous thing to do, you know, instead of putting *me* in this horrible situation! Or you could have told me that we were going to hide in the bathroom, and then I could have gone into the girls', you could have gone into the boys', and I'd be rid of you!"

This finally pulled his ear away from the door. *"You*

want to be rid of *me?* You're the one who followed me on this adventure!"

There was no point telling him that there was no adventure. He was utterly lost in his fantasy. She paced back and forth on a tiny spot of floor, muttering, "This is the worst day of my life! I'm going to get caught in the boy's bathroom with a nut dressed in a purple superhero suit!"

And during her distressed rant, Night-Ghost kept right on with his eavesdropping and whispered to her everything he was overhearing: "Eddie just admitted to Sasquatch Lady that he tried to steal some kid's lunch money! ...He admitted that he stole an apple from 'some new chickie' — I think that's you."

"Thanks for explaining that," Maria snapped quite impatiently. "But I don't care to listen to some thief's confession, or to hear some cranky old lady punishing him!"

"But she's *not* punishing him!" Night-Ghost was shocked. He listened some more, then reported, "They're talking about how they've split all the lunch money that Eddie has stolen over the years! ...That's what's in the box in her desk — stolen lunch money! ...Eddie and Sasquatch Lady have been running a stolen-lunch-money ring for years and years! He beats kids up and steals it; she pretends to punish him, and he gives her half of it!"

"Stop this ridiculous game!" Maria demanded in a

fearful whisper. "There's no such thing as a stolen-lunch-money ring! Get me out of here!"

Night-Ghost pointed to the door on the opposite side of the bathroom. "Go out that way. It goes into Mrs. Reynolds' class."

"I can't walk out there!" she argued. "That's *my* classroom! Someone is going to see me walking out of here, and they'll say, 'Hey, everybody! That new girl's a freak who uses the boy's bathroom!' "

"Everyone's at lunch. No one will see you."

"The way my day is going, I'm *sure* to be seen!" She tried to drag Night-Ghost away from the door where he was snooping. "I need you to go out first and make sure the coast is clear for me!"

"I can't!" He kept his ear up against that door, listening to the goings-on in Mrs. Flembaugh's room. "I've discovered a criminal plot!"

Desperate to get out of that place, Maria pulled the door open a half an inch and peeked out into her classroom. The room was completely empty... except for Mrs. Reynolds, who sat at her desk, going over some students' assignments.

Maria shut the door and whispered desperately, "My teacher's out there! She's sitting at her desk!"

"Then it looks like you're stuck in here with me,"

said Night-Ghost carelessly. "Now, please be quiet. I'm listening-in on the terrible scheme of a pack of nefarious lawbreakers!"

Maria dropped her head into her hands. "Why is this happening to me?"

"It's getting weirder!" Night-Ghost gasped. "...Sasquatch Lady's really cranked-off! She says that she gave Eddie orders *not* to steal anyone's lunch money today! ...She says that everyone at the school has to eat lunch... because she had Charlie put some sort of poison in the food!"

"Oh, this is insane!" Maria huffed as her temper began to boil. "I'm not going to play your stupid comic-book-hero game! Teachers *do not* split stolen lunch money with bullies! Nor do they kill their students by ordering janitors to put poison into children's sandwiches!"

Totally ignoring those protests that Maria was whispering in his left ear, the purple-cloaked crime-fighter kept his right ear planted against the bathroom door. His eyes widened in surprise as he relayed another bit of overheard information: "...Sasquatch Lady says that the stuff she put in everybody's food wasn't poison... it was *worse* than poison!"

Maria threatened him, "If you don't get me out of this bathroom, I'm going to scream!"

Night-Ghost's ear picked up yet *another* bit of startling

news: "...She just discovered that I took those scientific plans from her desk! We have to get out of here, right now!"

"Haven't I been telling you—?"

Night-Ghost ran over and clapped his purple-gloved hand over Maria's mouth. He whispered in her ear, "I have to put a stop to their food-poisoning scheme! Follow me, and I'll get you safely out!"

Chapter 8

The Genius Arrives

Leaping and climbing like a chimpanzee, Night-Ghost scrambled up the side of the narrow divider between the toilets, pushed open a ceiling tile, and disappeared into the shadows up above. Maria was frankly startled to see how acrobatic he was. It had only taken a single second for him to hoist himself up to the top of the divider, balance on its slender top, push that foam tile aside, and slink his way into the ceiling. Maybe *two* seconds, but no more.

She stood there, dumbfounded, while he looked back down from above and asked her, "Are you coming?"

Naturally, Maria was dressed for school, not for adventure. That morning, when she had put on her brand-new, green plaid mini-dress and slip-on loafers, it hadn't entered her mind that some nut in a superhero suit would be asking her to climb up the side of a bathroom stall and into the ceiling. *Of course* it hadn't entered her mind!

Regardless of this, she followed his lead, climbing up after him — up into the shadows above the bathroom ceiling.

As he closed the ceiling underneath them, he remarked, "You're quite agile."

"I study ballet. But where did *you* learn to climb like that?"

"Just my acrobatic super-powers," he answered with a smirk. "Come on; follow me."

So, quite contrary to her own good sense, Maria found herself with that kid in the crazy purple suit, clambering around in the dim crawlspace between the ceilings of the classrooms and the roof of the building. She and her strangely-dressed guide walked, crawled, and swung on the wooden beams, plastic pipes and dust-covered ventilation ducts that crisscrossed all around. If she had taken one step on the flimsy asbestos ceiling below them, she would have gone crashing down into a hallway or classroom. So she kept her wits about her, and made every move carefully — carefully but quickly; for she had to keep up with the so-called Night-Ghost, who was making his way through that cramped, dark and dusty area with reckless haste. Even so, he never slipped once.

Eventually, they came to a spot where Night-Ghost found a hatch above his head. It was locked, but that meant nothing to this escape-artist superhero who gave the handle a quick jiggle and twisted the latch open in the blink of an eye.

There came a bright burst of daylight as he threw back the hatch and climbed up onto the roof. Maria followed him up and, once out in the sunshine, she could see what a mess she had become.

"Honestly!" she grumbled as she brushed the smears of gray dust from that green plaid dress of hers. "I'm a complete wreck!" Crawling over all the pipes and beams within the school's ceiling had also made a mess of her turtleneck and knee-high socks, which had begun the day as pure white. She dusted herself off as best as she could. "Look at all this filth!"

But Night-Ghost couldn't understand why anyone would find fault with the magnificent thrill of creeping about in those always-unseen, totally off-limits places like the interior of a ceiling and a big, wide school rooftop. "Filth schmilth! Don't you just love it up here?" (A hint of a ten-year-old boy was sneaking its way into his superhero speech pattern.)

She took a quick look around, only to dismiss it as completely ho-hum. "It's a roof."

The rooftop of Palisades Elementary was a flat, level, black tarpaper surface from one side to the other with a raised edge all the way around — a little two-foot-high wall. So although they could hear the laughter of kids down on the ground, no one could see them up there. Still, Maria worried that they *might* be spotted, and before her crazy companion had closed the hatch again, she warned him, "We're going to get in trouble if we get caught up here."

But the boy in the purple super-suit completely ignored her concerns. He found a lost baseball lying by the trapdoor — a dirty, worn and faded ball that looked like it had been up there in the rain and rough weather for centuries. He picked it up and crawled over to the short wall at the roof's edge, crouching low and peeking over the top, looking for something very specific down on the ground. Once he found what he was looking for, he pitched that baseball down at the world below. Having caught someone's attention, he then gave a little wave.

Maria instantly pulled him back away from the roof's edge with the impatient demand of "Stop that! Do you want somebody to see you?"

"Just the guy I'm signaling," he replied. "I have to get another superhero on this case."

"Alright, stop it!" she demanded. "There *are* no other superheroes!"

"Fat lot you know! I'm the captain of a *whole team* of superheroes!"

"You're not even a superhero! We're climbing down

off this roof! And you, Mr. Night-Ghost, are going to get dressed in normal human clothes!"

"There's a tree over there..." He indicated some sturdy branches that overhung the roof. "You can climb down that way." Then he started to run off in the opposite direction. "I still have a mission!"

She caught him by the arm and dragged him to a stop. "Look, I have a cousin who pretends he's a superhero all the time. He does this silly thing..." (She struck a superheroish pose, and made a high-pitched science fiction buzzing/bleeping noise.) "...and he says that he can shrink down to the size of an insect."

"Well, he probably can," Night-Ghost replied casually. "Maybe I'll team up with him and fight crime someday."

He tried to run away again; again Maria pulled him to a stop.

She continued her tale: "My mom and dad explained to me why he does it."

Night-Ghost rolled his eyes in disgust. "Oh, here comes the wisdom of the psychologists again!"

"That's right!" she stated firmly. "We all have fantasies. It's because we find the real world is too difficult sometimes. But if you get too caught up in this superhero fantasy, well, one day you're going to break your neck climbing around on rooftops!"

Night-Ghost spoke quickly (but very nicely): "Yes, it is very dangerous to *play* at being a superhero... when you *aren't* one. That's why you don't have to worry about me. I actually *am* a superhero. So go find some kid who is only *pretending* to fight crime, and talk *him* down off a roof." He whirled about and sped away from her.

She followed after him, never letting up with her arguments: "Superhero comic books are really insulting to women, you know."

"Are they?" he asked with clear disdain for her opinion.

"They're always about some girl being held hostage by some criminals so some know-it-all boy can swoop in and save her and she can go all wobbly-kneed and say, 'Oh, you're so brave, Mr. Superhero!' Stories like that tell girls that they're helpless and weak, and that they can't do anything if a boy doesn't do it for them."

The tiniest little sneer appeared on Night-Ghost's face, and a snort of *"Humph!"* arose ever so slightly. A quick shake of his head seemed to say, "I have a million arguments for her, but I'm too busy!"

"Admit it," she demanded, "in your mind, a girl is just someone dumb who needs to be rescued."

He ignored her (or gave it his best try, anyway) and turned to go. But she wasn't done. She grabbed him by the arm again.

"So tell me: are there any girl superheroes on this team that you're the captain of?"

"Well... no."

"See? It's just a boys-only game to you! You would never think of letting a girl——"

"It's not my fault that there are no girl superheroes around."

"And why do you think that is?" She answered her own question quite instantly and quite insistently: "Because we have too much good sense to dress up like that and pretend that we have impossible powers that no one could ever have!"

"It's because you never read superhero comics, and that's where we get our powers." Having said all he needed to say, he turned and hurried away from her.

"That's it?" she chuckled. "Isn't it supposed to be that you got radioactive chemicals spilled on you, or some other dumb thing? Now you're telling me you get your powers just from reading comic books?"

He stopped, turned and replied sharply, "Y'know, I was actually thinking it was kind of groovy having you on this adventure. Next thing I know, you're having a conniption on me, telling me that it's insulting to women all over the world that there are no girls on my team, and then you make fun of being a superhero. You can't have it both ways! You can't say, 'Superheroes are stupid,' and then be all hurt when you're left out of the action!"

"I don't *want* to be a part of the action, because there is no action!"

"Fine!"

"Fine!"

"Good! 'Cause if you wound up in danger I *wouldn't* rescue you! Because, according to you, that would just be insulting to all women in the universe!" Again, he whirled around and rushed away.

Undaunted, she kept following, this time shouting out a threat: "I'm going to talk to the school nurse! You're mental!" And having shot out that parting insult, she spun around and headed for the tree that would take her down to the ground.

Suddenly, the sharp clank of metal against metal got her attention. Right next to her, a grappling hook of blue steel had been flung up by someone down below and latched itself onto the roof's edge. As she watched in amazement, a blue-gloved hand reached up next to that grappling hook, then another hand, and someone pulled himself up onto the rooftop — another superhero! (Well, another boy *dressed* as a superhero, that is.)

This one was outfitted in a suit of blue — light tights and dark boots and gloves. Over his mask he wore a shining steel helmet of blue chrome. On his belt hung a collection of equipment pouches and strange scientific hardware. The front of his shirt bore a large, unsettling design: a bizarre, staring eyeball.

"Not *another* one!" wailed Maria, driven nearly to her wits' end to think that there was a *second* boy at her school who enjoyed this lunacy of action-hero dress-up. "Who are *you* supposed to be?"

"The Wizard," he answered, but in a short way that seemed to say he wasn't interested in chatting with her. He took his grappling hook off the roof's edge, coiled up its long, blue rope and stashed it on his belt. Then, turning to Night-Ghost, he asked, "What's the calamity?"

His use of a far-too-impressive word like "calamity," told Maria that this blue-helmeted "super-scientist" was none other than Terry's friend Peter. (She could also see that beneath the blue mask was a Vietnamese face, and there weren't too many Vietnamese students at her school.) She was actually giving serious consideration to telling them right out that she knew their "secret identities," but then it occurred to her that if the two of them were going crazy it might push them deeper into craziness. And since she didn't want their minds to snap *completely*, she thought she had better refer to them by their superhero codenames. "That eyeball on your shirt gives me the creeps, Wizard."

The Wizard ignored her, and again asked his purple-cloaked partner, "What's up?" (Peter didn't appear to be as lost in the superhero game as Terry was, for he didn't use any super-serious TV hero voice. He just spoke like a normal ten-year-old boy... a normal ten-year-old boy who knew every word in the dictionary.)

Night-Ghost pulled the scientific diagrams out of his boot. "I found these plans in Sasquatch Lady's desk."

"Along with the proof of a stolen-lunch-money scam," said Maria with a disbelieving snicker.

Without a pause, everything seemed to make perfect sense to The Wizard: "So Sasquatch Lady and Eddie Thigpen have been in cahoots all these years to steal the lunch money from innocent kids?"

"That's only *part* of what we're up against," replied Night-Ghost in an all-too-serious tone.

Maria added some fake excitement: "Oh, Yes! Charlie the janitor is involved, too!"

The Wizard, on the other hand, was completely straight-faced. "The janitor too, huh? It's starting to sound like a pretty wide-ranging conspiracy."

"It appears," Night-Ghost continued, "that they've put something in everyone's food — something that Sasquatch Lady called *'worse than poison'!*"

The Wizard, who had been examining those intricate diagrams, flipped to the last page — the one with the chemical formula. "This must be the formula for whatever the worse-than-poison stuff is."

"Really? That's fascinating!" Maria had lost all patience with this make-believe game of theirs and she didn't care how sarcastic she sounded. "And what about the machine plans?"

Ignoring her sarcasm, The Wizard answered, "It appears to be a radio-wave transmitter of some sort — a very powerful one from the looks of it." He pointed out the wires and the electrical systems on the drawings (as if she was interested!). "You see, here's the primary wave capacitor, and here's the—"

Maria silenced the scientist with a cold stare.

Night-Ghost told his partner, "I don't think she's interested in the primary wave capacitor."

As The Wizard folded up the plans and stuffed them in one of his many belt-pouches, he made a faintly-muttered comment of annoyance: "Girls!"

"What about girls?" Maria wondered, a little irked.

"Girls never seem interested that the planet's in danger — *that's* what."

"If the planet was in danger," she argued, "we girls would leap right in and do what we could. But we just don't see the need to pretend it's in danger when it's not! And if I was going to make up some global threat, it would sure be better than a stolen-lunch-money ring!"

The Wizard gave up on her, turned to Night-Ghost and said, "If Charlie's got any of this worse-than-poison stuff leftover in a jug, I need to subject it to a chemical analysis. Whatever's in the food, I ate it just like everybody else! So I want to mix-up an antidote before it takes effect! That means I'll need your handy lock-picking power to get me into the janitor's room."

Maria was worried that they were getting in over their heads. "You guys can't go breaking into the janitor's room. You have to come to your senses!"

The Wizard gave her what (at the start) sounded like an official part in the plan: "Oh, and I'll need you for... let's see... nothing. Have a nice day!"

"That's OK," she sneered (though her sneer was far too pretty to have the meanness a sneer needs). "I can't come on any adventures, anyway. We girls don't have any super-powers, y'know, 'cause we don't read the right comic books."

The Wizard, shocked, turned to Night-Ghost. "You told her about that?"

But the boy in the purple cloak dismissed it as unimportant. "I didn't tell her anything specific." Then he reminded Maria, "And I told you: I thought it would be kind of groovy to have you on the adventure. *You're* the one who—"

Again The Wizard was startled. "You told her *what?*"

Night-Ghost now felt like *both* of them would start yelling at him, so he abandoned the whole conversation. "Come on! Let's get on with things."

The two superheroes made with all speed across the rooftop, Night-Ghost leading the way.

Maria chased after them, asking The Wizard, "You're a scientist; do you know what a delusion is?"

Without looking back at the girl running behind him, The Wizard spouted off a dictionary-styled definition as easily as you might describe a peanut butter and jelly sandwich: "Delusion; noun; a mistaken notion — specifically one that is held even at odds with obvious reality. Are you suggesting that we're living a delusion?"

"Well, are you just as lost in this comic-book-fantasy as your pal the so-called Night-Ghost is?"

Hoping to end the discussion, that super-scientist responded with a brief "Yep. I'm totally demented. Goodbye." And he waved her off like a pesky housefly.

Disregarding his rude reply, she stuck right there behind him.

Moments later, they reached a skylight that looked down into the custodian's room. Night-Ghost worked his unearthly talent on the lock — merely jostling the latch, and popping it open. The Wizard uncoiled the climbing-rope from his belt, attached its grappling hook to the frame of the skylight, and the heroes prepared to slide down it into the room.

Maria asked, "So now you're busting into the janitor's room? Isn't that called 'trespassing'?"

Night-Ghost's only response was "We're trying to save the world, Miss Fuente."

Not at all understanding the notion of crime-fighters who break-and-enter, she just let out a tiny, sarcastic "Who can argue with *that?*" Then she warned those boys one last time, "This game of yours is getting out of hand! You *can't* go down there!"

As he double-checked his grappling hook's grip on the edge of the skylight, The Wizard said, "Miss Fuente, your analysis of us has been very erudite, but you've had your say." He had thrown the word "erudite" into his sentence to make himself sound way too brilliant for her to talk to. (And in case you don't know, it's pronounced "AIR-you-dite.") And just to jab at her, he added, "Erudite, of course, means 'well spoken.' "

"I know what erudite means!" she snapped back.

"Yeah, 'cause I just told you." (He suddenly sounded more like a snotty little boy than a super-scientist.)

"I knew it *before* you told me!"

"No you didn't."

"Did so!"

"Did not!"

She rolled her eyes. "Some scientist you are! Einstein never argued like this!"

The Wizard quickly snapped back, "He did so!"

"No, he didn't!"

"Yes, he did!"

Maria got the sense that perhaps The Wizard was joking now, but she couldn't quite tell.

Night-Ghost stepped between them, and reminded them, "The world hangs in the balance. We haven't a moment to waste on this bickering."

Maria gave up on them and headed back towards the tree that overhung the roof — the one that would take her back down to solid earth. "I'm not going to snitch on you two, 'cause I wouldn't want to see you get in trouble while you're dressed like... well, like... freaks." (She had wanted to say something nicer, but "freaks" was honestly the best word to describe them.) "I'm getting out of here before I get caught with you. So get on with saving the world. It's boys' work, you know."

Night-Ghost, clearly disappointed, watched Maria walk away. "She thinks we're cuckoo."

"Get used to it." The Wizard slid down the rope into

the room below. "No one's supposed to know that our missions are for real."

Chapter 9
Custodian Combat

The inside of the custodian's room was gigantic, for it wasn't just a place for Charlie to keep his mops, buckets and brooms. It also served as the storage for the whole school. There were towers of cardboard boxes filled with books, paper, and all manner of supplies stacked up to the ceiling.

As Night-Ghost and The Wizard rummaged around, they found several boxes of blank paper and several more full of every imaginable color of paint. To an artist like Terry, blank paper and paint are a wondrous sight. Sounding more like Terry than Night-Ghost, he exclaimed, "Wow! Look at all this art stuff! I'd love to get locked in here for a month and just paint like crazy!"

"You're an escape-artist! You *can't* get locked in anywhere. It's simply *not* possib— Hello! What's this?" The Wizard held up a giant bottle, and carried it over to the janitor's workbench. The thing had a small portion of clear fluid in the bottom, but whatever the substance was it was a mystery, for the jar had no label. "Very suspicious, don't you think — this unmarked jug sitting in the corner?"

"If it's the last remaining bit of the poison that Charlie put in the food..."

The Wizard finished his partner's sentence: "...then it's just the evidence we need!" From a pouch on his belt he took out his portable chemistry kit, and eagerly launched himself into his studious chemist mode. "I'll take a sample of it, and run some tests on it after school. If it turns out to be the same as the chemical formula that you found in Sasquatch Lady's desk, then we can prove that she's—"

A key rattled in the door!

"Oh, boffo!" murmured Night-Ghost. (This is an old slang phrase for "Fabulous!" and he was groaning it sarcastically.)

The Wizard hadn't had a chance to collect a sample of that unidentified fluid. He had to abandon the idea, and pack away his portable chemistry set.

The two heroes began climbing up the rope to escape to the roof. The agile Night-Ghost zoomed up it in a heartbeat, but The Wizard had only just taken a hold on it when Charlie entered and screamed, *"What're you doing in here?"*

The angry custodian snagged The Wizard by the

belt, ripped him right off the rope, and hurled him across the room. The scientist crashed into a pile of boxes and slumped to the floor — more like a bag of dog food than a person.

Night-Ghost slid halfway down the rope, kicked his feet against the workbench, swung in a circle around the room, and slammed his boots into Charlie's face.

The custodian was slightly dazed, but he lashed out a hand and managed to get a tight hold on one of those purple-booted feet. With one mean tug, he pulled Night-Ghost from the rope and flung him the length of the storeroom.

But much to Charlie's surprise, that uncanny acrobat flipped in mid-air like a cat and landed squarely on his feet. The janitor charged forward and grabbed him in a stranglehold, but the master escape-artist effortlessly wriggled free.

"You're a slippery little eel!" The frustrated janitor reached up to the tool-rack above his workbench and got a massive crescent wrench as long as your arm. "But I'll take care of you soon enough!" Tightening his face into a wicked sneer, he took a swipe at his nimble foe.

Night-Ghost ducked, letting the wrench hit the wall behind him, where it knocked a chunk out of the bricks with a loud clank.

As for The Wizard, he hadn't been knocked out. He

had only been stunned for a second or two — that's all the time this fight between Night-Ghost and the janitor had taken so far. The hero-scientist jumped onto Charlie's back and wrapped himself around the man's shoulders. Super-scientist that he was, The Wizard understood everything about the human nervous system. He knew precisely where to jab a thumb into a person's neck — a little nerve-center that, when struck, sent a jolt of jittery pain through Charlie's whole body.

But like a grizzly bear, this mountain of a man was all the more dangerous when wounded. After a howl of agony, he reached behind, grabbed The Wizard, ripped him off his shoulders, and threw him into yet another pile of boxes. Again, the boy-genius drooped to the floor.

Charlie hoisted a heavy box of math books over his head and sent it flying at Night-Ghost, who dove aside and somersaulted out of the way, allowing that forty-pound box to fly past and burst against the wall. As the acrobat bounded up onto his feet, Charlie caught him by the shirt, pitching him at The Wizard, just as the young scientist was getting up again. The two superheroes collided and went down like bowling pins.

There they lay in a clumsy heap, trying to scramble to their feet and defend themselves as Charlie raised his giant crescent wrench to take a final, deadly swing. It was a perilous split-second where Night-Ghost and The Wizard needed a miracle.

And a miracle is just what they got, as help arrived in a flash of orange and yellow. From the open skylight above, a third superhero came leaping in, landing with all his weight on the janitor's shoulders, and shoving him face-first to the floor.

Charlie immediately rolled over and looked up to see who was behind such a sudden drop-in ambush. Much to his annoyance, it was another kid in a super-suit.

Standing boldly in boots of canary yellow and a snug-fitting costume of bright orange, the boy's chest bore a bright yellow sun-face — a symbol stern and humorless of expression. His wide belt had a plate of flexible, orange colored steel on its front. Upon his head was a helmet of the same orange chrome, looking like a perfectly polished steel tangerine, and underneath that helmet he wore a mask of orange to hide his identity. Flowing from his shoulders was a cape of bright yellow, and inside his gloves of that same brilliant hue, his hands tensed-up into tough little fists for the coming battle.

Charlie snickered smugly. "And who the heck are *you* supposed to be?"

"Titan."

"You don't look like a Titan," laughed the janitor,

rising from the floor. "Except for a goofy, orange suit, you look just like any other rotten, little grade-school snot!"

"Never underestimate a member of The Fearless Force!" Titan grabbed the enemy custodian by the coveralls and pulled him down nose-to-nose. "And *never* call our uniforms 'goofy!' "

Charlie wasn't the least bit frightened. With his face right there an inch away from Titan's, he snickered, "Come on, then! Let's see what you got, kid!"

Titan ignored this taunt. Releasing his grip on the janitor's coveralls, he responded with a calm (but knowing) smile. "I never throw the first punch... but I always throw the *last* one!"

His tone was so sincere that his spirit was fully explained in that remark. Staying true to the cause of justice, defending the defenseless, detesting hatred and cruelty — the entire heart of a good-guy was summed-up in his single sentence of warning. Titan was a good-to-the-bone "reverse-bully."

But Charlie only considered it ridiculous to meet an eleven-year-old who loved honesty and virtue. He laughed an enormous, jeering laugh at the do-gooder in the gleaming helmet. "Ooo! Big man!" He added to his insult by jumping back in a mocking, overdone fright. "I'm so scared! The kid in the orange suit is gonna hurt me!" Then the villain stopped, let a cruel grin control his expression, and curled up a fist. "Here comes that first punch you asked for!"

Titan stood peacefully still as that fist came speeding straight towards his face. In a matter of a hundredth of a second, when the janitor's massive knuckles were just about to make their impact, the orange-clad hero raised a hand with lightning swiftness and caught that fist, stopping it instantly.

With Charlie's hand caught firmly in the grasp of that tight, yellow glove, Titan spoke calmly and quietly. "Too bad you couldn't make anything of that first punch, 'cause it's the only one you get."

The confused, wide-eyed and terrified Charlie had nothing to say as Titan flung that fist aside and, once again, gripped his enemy by the coveralls, bunching-up the material in both his hands.

As the name Titan might suggest, that kid was a sixth-grade Samson. He lifted the six-foot six-inch, 280-pound custodian over his head and heaved him through the closed door. It tore from its hinges and split down the middle, scattering bits of wood in all directions. Charlie hit the floor on the other side, slid down the hallway, and lay there on his face, totally unconscious.

A sad shake of Titan's head seemed to ask the question,

"Where do all the evil people of the world come from?" For, even though he was a gold-helmeted superhero with the strength of a hundred men, or — who knows? — the strength of a *thousand*, behind his mask he was still just Doug: the kid who could never understand why some people get their kicks out of picking on people.

"It's a good thing you showed up when you did," said Night-Ghost as he shook Titan's hand in a very sincere superhero-ish way.

"Well, what the heck is going on?" asked Titan. "Someone want to tell me why I just beat the snarf out of the school custodian?"

A reply to Titan's question was shouted down from up above him: "Hey! 'Snarf' is *my* word!" The voice was that of Curtis (inventor of the word "snarf") as he looked down through the skylight. He climbed over and slid down the rope.

Like Doug (or, rather, Titan), Curtis was also dressed in a superhero disguise. His was all shades of green — bright green for his mask, shirt and boots; dark green for his gloves and tights, and darker still for his trunks. On his shirt was a symbol of green ocean waves with three stars above. The mask that hid his identity was open at the top to allow his tussled tuft of blonde hair to poke up into the air like it always did. And if the symbol of ocean waves on his chest didn't tell you that he was an aquatic hero, then it surely would've been apparent by the green swim-fins and clear plastic diving mask that hung from his belt.

Titan was frankly annoyed at that clownish kid's arrival. "What're you doing here?"

"What do you mean?" he asked right back. "The Fearless Force is never complete without the wondrous, weird and wild, water-breathing Aquarius!"

"There's no reason for the team fish-boy to be here," Titan told him with growing irritation. "Nobody's drowning."

"I don't know 'Nobody,' but if he's drowning I can save him!" Aquarius chuckled like a lunatic. Then, looking at the storeroom door broken all to pieces, he remarked, "Now I know why we have secret identities! Somebody's gotta pay for that door!"

"Hilarious," grumbled Titan.

Next, it was Dan who appeared on the scene, also decked-out in crime-fighting attire. As the fifth and final member of The Fearless Force, he was clad all in various shades of brown — from his boots, to his tights, to his gloves, to his shirt and the mask around his eyes. Over that mask, he wore a helmet of tough leather — the sort worn by ace pilots from World War One, with the rounded goggles set up on the top of it, just in case he should need them. The symbol on his chest was a somber, white cloud-face with orange rays of sunlight creeping through. Completing his costume was an immense, white cape, which, when spread out, had the shape and design of a dove's wings.

Dressed in this crime-fighting disguise, Dan, like his four friends, had a codename of his own: Skymaster. Likewise, he had a super-power of his own. As you might suppose from his codename, he could levitate, glide, and fly through the air with only his imagination to hold him up. So when he "dropped in" he didn't need to climb down the rope. He just drifted down slowly and gracefully through the open skylight, and landed gently in the midst of his four colorful partners.

(It was too bad Maria wasn't here to see this! It would've been utterly impossible for her mock their "make-believe superhero game" at such a sight. If she had seen Titan trounce the janitor, she might've thought he was pretty strong. If she had seen Night-Ghost flipping and dodging in his fight, she might've figured that perhaps he had studied karate or something. But there's no way a person can see a boy levitating slowly through the air and still scoff at the concept of real, live superheroes.)

"What's going on?" asked Skymaster. "I saw you guys climbing around on the roof, and I figured something's up."

"OK, Skymaster's here; that's everybody," said Night-

Ghost in a very get-down-to-business tone. (The purple-cloaked acrobat was the captain of The Fearless Force, so getting down to business was his job.) "Now we can fill you all in on the criminal plot that The Wizard and I have discovered. It seems—"

"Hey, heroes, we have a problem!" Skymaster's voice was overloaded with alarm. "Look out in the hall!"

All eyes turned toward the open doorway and a terrible sight met their gaze: A massive crowd marching slowly towards the storeroom, chanting, "Destroy the superheroes... Destroy the superheroes..." It appeared to be every person in the school — nearly three hundred people — shuffling in their direction on stiff, deliberate steps like a mob of mummies risen from their tombs.

This zombie army was made up of people who were ordinarily so nice and normal: the school nurse, the office secretary, the librarian, and zillions of students. Some of the adorable little kindergartners were waving crayons like knives. Peter's and Curtis's teacher, Mr. Lumley, who they thought was such a fabulous guy, was slashing a set of rubber-handled safety-scissors and chanting, like all the others...

"Destroy the superheroes... Destroy the superheroes..."

"Man! I once had a nightmare just like this!" Aquarius gasped. "Everybody in the school was out to kill me —

only, in the dream, I was in my underwear."

The Wizard pointed out his friend's superhero-suit and screamed, "You *are* in your underwear!"

Aquarius glanced down at his green tights and let out a comical, high-pitched shriek.

"Shut up!" demanded Titan. "Every time things get serious you two start up your comedy routine!"

"And you start lecturing them, Titan!" snapped Night-Ghost impatiently. "We don't have time for it! Let's figure out a plan!"

"We could shut the door," suggested Aquarius, his panic increasing. "That is, if Titan hadn't knocked it right off its hinges and busted it into sawdust with Charlie's head! We could shut it, we could lock it, we could sit in here and play cards, and have a big laugh over this! But no! Thank you, Titan, and thank you again!"

Titan began a threat: "Look, fish-head, if you don't shut your blowhole, I'm gonna... I'm gonna..." The strongman blinked several times, as if struck by a headache. "Anybody else hear a buzzing that's getting louder and louder?"

No sooner had he asked this than he was abruptly seized by some ungodly pain. He grabbed his head and crumpled to the floor.

At the same instant, Skymaster, The Wizard and Aquarius also dropped to the floor in a similar sort of pain

— overcome with tremendous headaches. They clenched their teeth, clutched the sides of their skulls, and rolled back and forth in agony.

Night-Ghost was the only one of the five left standing, and strangely enough, he was just fine. He urgently asked his teammates, "What's going on?"

"There's... a mean buzzing... in my head!" answered Titan through grinding teeth.

"Some sort of poison was snuck into everybody's lunch!" The Wizard told his strongman brother. "It must be taking effect now!"

"Is it deadly?" asked a panicking Skymaster.

"Wish I knew!" answered a moaning, twitching Wizard. But even in this pain, he explained, "Somehow it's turned everyone but us into zombies, and it's ripping our brains apart!"

"How can the same poison act different in different brains?" asked Aquarius, doubled-up in his misery.

The scientist's response was once again "Wish I knew!"

And those murderous zombies were now right outside the open doorway, still chanting, "Destroy the superheroes... Destroy the superheroes..."

Being the only member of The Fearless Force on his feet, Night-Ghost picked up a broom to defend himself and his team against the angry mob that shuffled towards them.

Fearless Force

Chapter 10
Mrs. Reynolds' Gruesome Advice

While Night-Ghost faces that mindless mob, it's time to find out what had happened to Maria. To do so involves stepping backward in time a few minutes to when she had parted ways with Night-Ghost and The Wizard on the rooftop of the school...

After abandoning those two ridiculous (and possibly insane) boys to play at their "pretend" superhero game, she climbed down that tree overhanging the roof. Once back on the ground where she belonged, she tried one last time to brush the dust and dirt of her "adventure" from her brand new dress. Surrendering to the fact that she'd be a wreck for the rest of the day, she returned to where she had left her lunchbox, picked it up, and wandered back to Mrs. Reynolds' classroom.

The kindly old teacher was sitting at her desk, sipping a cup of coffee and looking over some of her students' papers from earlier in the day. Seeing Maria come shambling sadly into the room during lunch, she asked, "Is everything alright?"

Maria's answer was carried on a defeated sigh: "Oh, I suppose."

"It's hard being in a new school, isn't it?"

Since that wasn't a question in dire need of an answer, Maria responded by wondering aloud, "Are all boys insane?"

Mrs. Reynolds replied (only *half*-jokingly), "Yes, Maria, all boys are unsound of mind. It's sad, but that's the way it has to be. Have the boys been picking on you?"

"No, not really. Well, yes, there was Eddie Thigpen; but I met some other boys. They were nice to start with. They let me play with them, but then I had to ruin it by making fun of their whole superhero thing. But come on! They were wearing masks and one of them had a cape and the other one had a weird... space helmet sort of thing. I really do think they were going off the deep-end about it. Why is it that instead of talking to each other like real people they have to get lost in some idiotic make-believe adventure and call each other by dumb codenames?"

"Oh, they're just having fun," Mrs. Reynolds assured her. "You know boys and their science fiction television shows and comic books and whatnot. However, if you think the boys were nice, then maybe there's something you're missing in all their fantasy. It's noble, isn't it? I mean, they want to be *heroes*, don't they? Good guys and crime-fighters?"

"I suppose they do," Maria confessed.

Her teacher wisely concluded, "It's not every day that you meet people who only want to do good. Even if they seem to confuse it in make-believe games, their wish is to be the good-guys. They're still people with good hearts."

Maria had to admit that her teacher was right. She thought back to how Terry (or, rather, *Night-Ghost*) had taken all the stolen items out of Mrs. Flembaugh's desk and returned them to their rightful owners. Even if he wasn't a real crime-fighter, he was at the very least a do-gooder. "So you think I should go find them and apologize for calling them crazy?"

Mrs. Reynolds didn't answer. For some unknown reason, she was frozen in position with her coffee cup raised halfway to her mouth.

This struck Maria as more than a little peculiar. "Mrs. Reynolds? ...Are you alright? I asked if I should apologize to those boys."

Mrs. Reynolds' response was *not* the sort of sober advice she normally gave out: "Destroy them!"

"Excuse me?" Maria was stunned in the extreme to hear such a violent suggestion coming from that kind old

lady's lips.

The teacher repeated herself, and repeated herself again: "Destroy them... Destroy the superheroes..." She rose from her desk and stalked robot-like to the door, her coffee mug still clenched in her hand. "Destroy them... They are in the janitor's room... Destroy them..."

Fear and disbelief were fighting for control of Maria's quickening heart. "How... how did you know they're in the janitor's room?"

Mrs. Reynolds' only reply was "Destroy the superheroes!"

As the zombie teacher left the room, Maria's pulse was pounding furiously. "OK, this isn't funny!"

She followed Mrs. Reynolds out into the hallway and found a throng of people walking with mechanically deliberate steps towards the janitor's room, chanting, "Destroy the superheroes..."

Maria shouted at the crowd, "This isn't the *least bit* funny!"

None of them answered. They just kept right on marching slowly on their way.

Caught up in the tightly-packed mass of shuffling bodies, she couldn't go anywhere but the same direction in which they were going. It was rather like being pulled downstream in the stubborn current of a river. She worked her way to the edge of the crowd and tried to make her escape into the nearest classroom. But, just as she was opening the door, a glassy-eyed teacher came out of that classroom and pushed her backwards into the marching mass.

Now more desperate than ever, she shoved through them, trying to flee into the library, where she hoped a window might get her to freedom. But that glassy-eyed teacher who had just joined the flock yanked her right back into the pack. He bent down, looked her directly in the face with his eerily bland expression, and reminded her of the common mission: "Destroy the superheroes!"

To have that blank-faced teacher speak so insistently (yet so lifelessly) only two inches from her nose was pretty disturbing! So Maria decided that it was best to play along. Extending her arms before her in typical sleepwalker fashion, she chanted in unison with the other voices, "Destroy the superheroes..."

Well, the Marias of the world aren't known for being slow-witted. If an entire school full of people could be transformed into mind-slaves who were programmed to kill some superheroes, then... there really must be superheroes! Suddenly, it was all too clear to her that those two boys who had been running around on the school rooftop were not *pretending* to be crime-fighters, and they were *by no means crazy!*

There was a brief moment where she muttered to herself, "Holy smoke! Night-Ghost and The Wizard are for real!" And this led to another improbable conclusion: "There really *was* a Compost Beast from another dimension running loose last night!"

But she couldn't take forever absorbing this astonishing new truth. She was surrounded by zombies! There were only two people she knew of who could explain all this madness.

She called out, "Night-Ghost! Wizard!" (She had almost called out for Terry and Peter, but she stopped herself, knowing that, since they actually *were* superheroes, then she had better not blow the cover on their secret identities.)

With neither the escape-artist nor his scientist-partner around, she had no choice but to follow along in that mob.

"I wonder why *I'm* not a zombie?" she thought. "I ate my lunch like everyone else, and I'm guessing that it's the poison in everybody's food that's affecting their minds. Maybe that apple that Eddie stole from me had my dose in it. Whatever the reason, I'd better just keep right on faking it!" So she continued with the common chant of "Destroy the superheroes!"

While she was still marching through the halls, acting

the part of just another mind-controlled human robot, she was near the back of this long chain of three-hundred-odd zombies. Far ahead of her, the front of the crowd was already at the door of the janitor's room, trying to push their way in as Night-Ghost stood his ground, armed only with that custodian's broom.

Fearless Force

Chapter 11

A Terrified Yelp Echoing Nicely in a Spacious Auditorium

Headache or no headache, The Wizard, Titan, Skymaster and Aquarius were in danger. They couldn't just roll on the floor, clench their teeth and groan. The Wizard was the first to get up. (Perhaps it was that his super-advanced brain could conquer a brain-poison more easily.) He looked up through the skylight and saw seven or eight murderous zombie students staring back down at him.

"We can't get out through the skylight!" he told his teammates. "They're up on the roof, too!"

"Well, we can't use this door!" Night-Ghost replied as the mob began to pack their way into the room like a human avalanche. The purple-cloaked hero struggled to hold them back, armed with nothing but that broom he had found.

The Wizard took a small canister off his belt — a blue-chrome object about the size of a soda-pop can. Pulling a trigger-wire, he flung it into the center of the crowd of approaching zombies. The little aluminum object hissed forth with a billowing cloud of pink smoke, and a circle of zombies in the center of the bunch collapsed into sleep. Still, there were over two-hundred of those blank-faced foes pushing their way towards the store room.

Night-Ghost was quickly losing the battle to hold them off with a broom. "Titan, are you *totally* out of it? This sort of thing really is *your* job, you know!"

Titan gathered himself up off the floor and shook his head a few times. The buzzing and pounding in his skull was there to stay, but the determined scowl he set on his face said that he was going to stubbornly ignore it. Taking the broom from Night-Ghost, he pushed the human tide backward with one arm and one mighty shove. Having thrown the mob back for a moment, he then lifted the janitor's massive workbench over his head and slammed it down to block the doorway.

With splendid seriousness he grumbled, "Now, let's get out of here!" (His seriousness was quite unlike Night-Ghost's. Where Night-Ghost seemed to be imitating a TV superhero as a way to have fun with his crime-fighting, Titan actually was that sort of superhero. When his eyes narrowed and his voice rumbled it made everyone stand back and think, "Oh, boy! There's gonna be some destruction!")

Pointing to the far wall, Titan curled up his small but super-powered fist. "I'll knock a hole in this wall and get us an escape route!"

"No good," The Wizard warned him. "That'll just take us to another hallway that's bound to be filled with more psychos!"

"Then it's up to the roof," said Night-Ghost as he scrambled quickly up the rope. "At least there aren't so many of 'em up there."

Since no one else could climb a rope as quickly as the purple-cloaked acrobat, Titan grabbed his teammates off the floor one by one, and tossed them up through the open skylight — even Skymaster. (He was having trouble flying, due to his rattling headache.) Finally, with one powerful leap, Titan jumped up after them, just as the mob pushed aside the workbench-barricade and broke into the room.

Up on the rooftop, The Fearless Force instantly discovered themselves face to face with a small crowd of twenty or so zombies who slowly advanced on them.

"Destroy the superheroes... Destroy the superheroes..."

More of those empty-eyed mind-slaves were climbing up from the janitor's room below, using The Wizard's blue rope that still hung by its hook to the skylight frame. So the hero-scientist had to put a stop to it — and quickly. On his equipment-belt was a small remote control: one touch of a switch and the grappling hook collapsed itself. All the zombies that were clambering up that rope were suddenly dropped to the floor, and all access to the roof through that skylight was instantly cut off. (The Wizard wasn't too worried about losing his rope and hook. He'd get it back later; or perhaps he'd have to abandon it and build a new remote-controlled grappling hook. These are the sacrifices you make when you're one of those "gadget heroes.")

The five crime-fighters turned to run, but suddenly found themselves facing a brick wall. It was the side of the gymnasium, which rose up a good twenty feet taller than the main part of the school. With the gym's huge wall blocking any escape, the heroes stopped and turned to face their enemies.

The mob slowly dragged towards them, and Titan stepped forward with a fighting smirk and two clenched fists.

The Wizard held his brother back and cautioned him, "If you throw anyone off this roof you might kill them! Remember, these aren't enemies like we usually fight. They're all innocent people under some sort of mind-control!"

"Hang on, Wiz," said Aquarius. "I see a few people in the crowd I want Titan to throw off the roof while we have this unbelievable opportunity!"

"I see one, too!" snarled Titan. And giving Aquarius a narrow stare, he added pointedly, "He's wearing a green superhero suit and carrying swim-fins!"

Night-Ghost ignored his team's comical squabble and asked The Wizard, "Do you have another knockout-gas grenade?"

"Too much wind. The gas will get blown away before it has an effect."

Night-Ghost's escape-artist brain quickly figured-out the team's next move: About fifteen feet above their heads was a row of windows that ran along the top of the gym wall. The purple-cloaked hero figured that those windows were his team's only possibility of avoiding the fight that was sure to erupt on the rooftop at any second. If they could all get up and through those windows, they could drop down into the gymnasium and find a few seconds of safety.

"Titan!" he called out in his most tense commander voice. "Throw me up to one of those windows above us!"

The orange-helmeted strongman obeyed, spinning around, grabbing his purple-clad partner under the armpits and flinging him effortlessly upwards. The agile Night-Ghost sailed skyward, in complete control the whole way, even striking a perfect "dramatic acrobat" pose as he flew up towards the window.

Catching a hold on the window-frame's edge with his fingertips, he planted his boots against the brick wall of the gym and clung there like a human fly. The latch that held the window shut was, of course, on the inside, but this was no problem for the boy who could command locks with a psychic force. He flattened-out his right palm on the windowpane, focused his mind, and the latch-handle on the other side of the glass began to turn, rotating as if moved by an invisible hand. When it was unlocked, Night-Ghost pulled the widow open — and this was no easy feat! Hanging onto a tiny half-inch-wide window-frame with four little fingertips while pulling a window open towards you is a clumsy event that can test the skills of even the most agile acrobat-superhero!

With the glass pane open, he hoisted himself up and sat on the windowsill, shouting back down, "Wizard! Throw me your rope, so we can climb down into the gym!"

"Can't!" The Wizard replied. "I sacrificed the rope!"

"You what?"

"I let it fall down into the janitor's room, so we wouldn't have any more zombies climbing up here!"

Night-Ghost suddenly got that somber look on his face that said, "Time to go to Plan B... So what *is* Plan B?" He looked down into the gym and realized that it was a place that already had ropes of its own. "Skymaster!

Can you fly? I need you to fly into the gym, get the end of one of the climbing ropes, and bring it back up here to the windowsill!"

Skymaster gave his purple-cloaked captain a confident thumbs-up. He shook his head to try and chase away the painful nuisance that pestered his brains. It didn't do any good. The headache was there to stay. So he got on with his mission. Concentrating as fully as he was able, he crouched down, then pushed his way up into the air. Flying (a bit unsteadily) he levitated up the side of the twenty-foot tall gymnasium wall; up to the open window where Night-Ghost sat. He paused for just a second on that windowsill — paused just long enough to give his head another shake and to hope that his flying power didn't fail him. If it did let him down, it would be a thirty-foot fall to the hard auditorium floor below. Then he shoved off from the windowsill and sailed out into the wide-open space of the empty gymnasium. *[Warning: **DO NOT** go launching yourself off of any windowsills unless you are a fully trained and fully qualified superhero who has been properly schooled in the complex secrets of human levitation!]* His flight-path was a little shaky at first, what with that pounding static in his skull, but he succeeded in floating through the air across the gym. Grabbing one of the long, sturdy climbing-ropes that hung from the ceiling, he flew the end of it back up to where Night-Ghost waited.

And on the rooftop below that open window, the throng of zombies closed in, grinning madly. Titan picked up The Wizard, threw him up to the window high above, then did the same with Aquarius (who — you guessed it — just *had* to squeal like a lunatic as he flew through the air). Night-Ghost, The Wizard, and Aquarius, perched up on the windowsill and, all three of them together, took a tight grip on the rope.

Aquarius leaned carefully inward to examine the thirty-foot drop to the gymnasium floor. "Did I mention that I don't like heights?"

"So close your eyes," Night-Ghost suggested before a quick, "Three, two, one, *go!*"

They launched themselves off the windowsill. (Well, Night-Ghost and The Wizard launched themselves, anyway. Aquarius just let himself be yanked out into space, emitting a terrified yelp that echoed nicely in the spacious auditorium.)

Swinging downward with incredible speed, they zoomed right past the floor, then shot up the far side of their arc, coming so close to the opposite wall of the gym, that Night-Ghost could touch his boots to it during the small weightless pause before they swung back downward again.

On this next trip past the floor, Night-Ghost released

his grip and somersaulted off, popping up on his feet, instantly balanced and surefooted. These sorts of stomach-flipping stunts were commonplace for him. But his two partners just kept a desperate, white-knuckle grip on that rope, letting it swing them back and forth for as long as it would take for it to stop.

As for Titan: well, he didn't need a rope. He vaulted through that open window way up by the ceiling, and just dropped — dropped the full thirty feet to the gymnasium floor, his yellow boots thumping solidly on their landing, as if a thirty-foot drop was nothing out of the ordinary. *[Warning: **DO NOT** jump off a thirty-foot drop unless you are a fully trained and fully qualified super-strong superhero whose bones have been enhanced to the toughness of steel!]*

When Aquarius and The Wizard finally felt that their rope-swing had calmed down enough, they slid to the floor, then took a moment or two to get their bearings. The Wizard took a few staggering steps on a crooked course, while Aquarius crawled around on all fours and finally collapsed on his hindquarters.

"I'm an *amphibious* super-guy!" he groaned as he fell back and lay out flat on the floor. "I shouldn't have to go swinging around on 'Lord of the Jungle' ropes! I think I'm gonna puke!"

"That's probably not a bad idea." Skymaster slapped the side of his head. "If the poison's in the food, we might want to chuck-up our lunches right away!"

"Whatever's in the food has worked its way to our brains," The Wizard explained. "It's already in our systems. Vomiting wouldn't help."

"Unless we puke in the right direction!" Aquarius suggested. "We could really teach those zombies a lesson if we messed-up their new back-to-school shoes!"

Titan didn't bother telling Aquarius to shut up this time. Instead, he asked The Wizard, "What kind of poison is it? Fish-head actually had a good question when he asked, 'How can the same poison turn everyone else into zombies, but just give us headaches?' "

"It's obviously some sort of mind-control drug," his scientist brother explained. "Maybe we're not zombies because our super-powers protect us better than ordinary people. Who knows? I won't have any *real* answers until I've had a chance to analyze the formula."

With all the drama a ten-year-old's voice can muster, Night-Ghost spoke two words: "The transmitter!"

The light of knowledge lit up in The Wizard's eyes. "The transmitter! Right!" He reached into his belt-pouch and whisked out the scientific diagrams that had been taken from Mrs. Flembaugh's desk. Examining the drawings with unbelievable speed, he flipped back and forth from page one to page three, from page five to page two. He studied the last page with the chemical formula, then flipped through the mechanical plans again. All the while, he muttered to himself, "Ingenious... ingenious in the extreme..."

"What is?" asked the other four.

At long last, he told his teammates, "High-frequency active auroral brainwave reorganization via specific targeted mineral toxicosis."

No one bothered to say "Try that in English." The confused looks on their faces clearly expressed this request.

He held up the chemical formula. "This poison gets into a victim's brain and does nothing. Nothing, that is, until Sasquatch Lady programs a command into this transmitter!" (And here he held up the mechanical diagrams.) "You see, the poison is soaked up by the victim's brain and it turns that brain into an antenna. The transmitter sends out a signal that latches onto any brain that's been poisoned, and the victim is forced to follow whatever order is transmitted. That explains why the whole school tried to kill us at once, *and* how we got those headaches at the same time."

"How so?" asked Night-Ghost.

"The command was obviously for everyone in the

school to 'Destroy the superheroes,' " The Wizard answered. "And since Titan, Aquarius, Skymaster and I can't follow an order to kill ourselves, our brains were rejecting the command — fighting against it — thus resulting in the occurrence of our cranial nuisances."

"I'm a *what?*" asked a confused Aquarius.

"A 'cranial nuisance' is a headache," the scientist explained. "You're a *general* nuisance. Anyway, if the command had been 'Everyone who isn't a superhero, destroy everyone that is,' then we never would have been hit with those headaches. We never would have known that our brains were contaminated with a noxious poison."

"I'm a *what?*" asked Aquarius exactly as before.

"A 'noxious poison' is a dangerous substance. You're an *obnoxious person.* Sounds the same, but different." (The Wizard seemed perfectly comfortable with his friend's interruptions. It was standard stuff for the two of them.) "Or, perhaps, if we had been given specific orders to fight each other — then *that's* a command we might have obeyed. Heck, Titan wouldn't need any mind-control order to strangle Aquarius! He wants to do that all the time!"

Titan and Aquarius nodded in agreement, for this was indeed the case.

The Wizard continued, "But a simple order of 'Kill the superheroes' would mean for us each to commit suicide, which is something we can never possibly do."

The rest of the heroes looked at each other and nodded in agreement. Their scientist partner seemed to have everything figured out from beginning to end.

"We have to find that transmitter," growled Titan, "so I can rip it apart!"

But right then the restless crowd of angry people burst in the doors of the gym — every door! In less than a second, The Fearless Force were totally surrounded. With their backs to one another, the five champions of justice gathered close together and tried to remember that they were supposed to be fearless.

Aquarius screamed, "Prepare to barf on my signal!"

"Or whatever battle tactic you think might work best," Night-Ghost added.

The zombies got within five feet, Night-Ghost yelled, *"Now!"* and the heroes charged headfirst into whomever faced them.

Fearless Force

Chapter 12

Maria, Morton, the Maniac, the "Moon-Man" and Much More Mayhem

Meanwhile, Maria had been going through the nightmare of being the only sane person in a crowd of murderous zombies. (It was almost as horrifying as being the only new girl in the fifth grade!)

Still pretending to be a zombie, she muttered, "Destroy the superheroes... Destroy the superheroes..." But, unlike that mob of mind-slaves, she had a fully-functioning brain inside her head — a brain that was busily assembling the puzzle-pieces of a remarkably bizarre first day of school:

"OK," she thought, "so there really *is* a drug of some sort in everyone's food, which means that Mrs. Flembaugh really *is* a supervillain. But even if Terry and Peter really *are* Night-Ghost and The Wizard, what good is that? They're just a guy who picks locks and a scientist. They can't do much against hundreds of zombies that want to kill them!" (She was, of course, unaware that those two heroes had three super-powered partners.) "Night-Ghost and The Wizard are going to need all the help they can get! I need to call the police. And — who knows? — maybe the army!"

As the mob of zombies marched into the entry hall of the school, they went wandering past the main office. Maria, knowing that there was a telephone in that office, finally made her move. She broke away from the pack, and hurried around a corner to hide. When the zombies had all gone shuffling away, she would duck into the office and put in her urgent call to the cops (and possibly the army). But as she peered around the corner to see if the coast was clear, she discovered that the office door was blocked. A bizarre scene was unfolding there:

Mrs. Flembaugh was out of her mind with anger, screaming at Mr. Morton, the school principal. She was holding him tightly by his wrist and pummeling him in the ribs with a meaty fist.

"Stop it!" the principal begged. "I'm sorry! I'm sorry!"

Maria was clever enough to deduce the truth behind half of what was going on: "Mrs. Flembaugh isn't a zombie, because Night-Ghost's right: she's the one who created all this madness!" However, there was still half the story that had her confused: "But Mr. Morton — he isn't a zombie either! And Sasquatch Lady seems to be pretty steamed at him for some reason! Did he find out about it, and is he threatening to call the police? Is *that* why she's punching him?"

Mrs. Flembaugh spotted Maria, and noticed immediately that the girl wasn't a mind-controlled robot like she was supposed to be.

Maria went back to her fake-zombie routine, and turned around to leave, but it was no use. The heartless teacher grabbed her by the arm, and gave it a wicked twist.

She pulled Maria up close and snarled through a devious, crooked smile, "You're not going anywhere, little girl! You've just made my Bad List! Do you know what that means?"

Maria tried to hold back her fright as she said, "*You've* caused this! You poisoned everyone's food!"

Mrs. Flembaugh's devious, crooked smile turned into a devious, crooked frown. "You know too much, missy!" She squeezed that claw-like hand into Maria's arm a little harder and let out a cold laugh.

Meanwhile, back in the chaos of the gymnasium...

The five members of The Fearless Force were still locked in mortal combat with the hundreds of students, staff and faculty of their school.

Titan was flipping people around as if they were nothing more than stuffed animals. The agile Night-Ghost ran through the midst of the crowd, avoiding every grasp like a greasy piece of wet spaghetti. Even The Wizard and Aquarius were doing well.

The Wizard, being a scientific genius, wasn't too bad in a fight. He was performing that battle-tactic he had used against Charlie earlier: punching and jabbing at his enemies' tiny nerve-centers. Behind a knee, behind an ear — wherever his studies in biology had told him that there was a natural weakness. He could make an arm or leg go numb, or knock the wind right out of somebody's lungs without having to hit very hard.

As for Aquarius... Well, being the water-breathing hero on the team, he obviously did a lot of swimming, which tends to make a person strong and limber, so he was quite useful in a struggle.

Skymaster was a different story, however. He wasn't what you might call a very skilled fighter. His power to fly was his only real crime-fighting asset. But, with that weird headache of his, he couldn't get into the air for more than a few seconds. He tried to fly, but his power failed him. He dropped right into the middle of the swarm and was grabbed by at least eight people. Some of the zombies began pulling on the young flier's arms and legs, while some others were fighting over who was going to get the treat of tearing his head from his shoulders.

Seeing Skymaster in the middle of a tug-of-war, Aquarius came to his rescue, diving into the fight and knocking people around until they dropped the helpless airman.

Skymaster gave him a quick "Thanks," and made another attempt to get up on the air. With a feeble push, he leapt off the floor, and slowly and weakly climbed about ten feet above the quarrel.

From this height, he spotted something quite startling: He saw through the window in the gymnasium door the scene that was unfolding in the hallway by the office — the struggle between Sasquatch Lady, Principal Morton and Maria Fuente. He saw as Sasquatch Lady latched her grip around Maria's arm and snarled right in the poor girl's face.

To witness that hideous old crone capturing the girl of his dreams, Skymaster knew that his moment had arrived! He could *finally* fly to her rescue! Sadly, while he was watching that whole scene in the hallway, he *wasn't* watching where he was flying. He flew face-first right into a basketball backboard with a thud, then dropped back into the skirmish.

This time, however, those clutching zombies weren't going to hold him for long. He was now a man with a mission, and *nothing* was going to stand in his way! In spite of his headache, he broke free from his clutching foes, and shot through the air to save the one and only Maria Fuente.

With his arms stretched out before him, the aviator-hero flew with ultra-urgent speed right into the door-handles, blasting the double doors wide open. He rocketed from the gymnasium, and straight to where Maria struggled to escape from Sasquatch Lady. In a heartbeat, he wrapped his arms around Maria with all his might and pulled her free of the monstrous old lady's grip.

As his flying powers weren't in tiptop form at that moment, he wasn't strong enough to carry her through the air. He and Maria clumsily crash-landed about thirty feet down the hall. It took another twenty feet for them to slide to a stop on the smoothly-polished floor.

Skymaster opened his eyes and discovered that he had landed right on top of Maria and was staring directly into her big, brown eyes. This was as close as he had ever been to her and it was *way too close!* He was so panicked to find himself nose to nose with her that, for a dangerous instant, he totally forgot about Sasquatch Lady.

But Maria still remembered that they were in danger. She looked over Skymaster's shoulder and saw Mrs. Flembaugh stomping down the hall towards them. Maria let out a startled scream right in Skymaster's ear that snapped him back to reality.

He jumped to his feet and whirled around to face-off with the malevolent teacher. However, Skymaster wasn't prepared for how quickly Sasquatch Lady could move. A wide, hulking old lady is not supposed to charge forward with such power. The young crime-fighter had barely risen to his feet when the villain was within reach; and when he whirled around, he whirled around right into her flying fist. That dastardly old woman's knuckles contacted with the side of the young hero's head and sent him tumbling across the floor.

The worst part was that he was about to yell that thing that he had been rehearsing in his heart: *"Run for it, Miss Fuente! I'll handle this!"* But, being totally unprepared for that punch in the skull, all he managed to say was "R—!"

As if all this wasn't bad enough, the gymnasium door burst open and Night-Ghost came rushing out.

Normally, it would have been great for the purple-cloaked escape-artist to come racing to the rescue. What made it not-so-great this time was that he yelled, *"Run for it, Miss Fuente! I'll handle this!"*

Skymaster was sprawled out on the floor thinking, "Now why did he have to say *that?*"

But it really didn't matter *who* had said it. Instantly up on her feet and sprinting, Maria had already gotten the idea that running for her life was the smartest thing to do. Unfortunately, she ran directly into Mr. Morton.

"Mr. Morton!" she said in a panic. "You've *got* to call

the police! Mrs. Flembaugh has done this! She's the one who turned everyone into zombies!"

To Maria's immeasurable horror, Mr. Morton gripped her by the arms, lit up a merciless smile, and repeated the very thing that Mrs. Flembaugh had said: "You know too much, missy!"

"Take her to your office, Morton!" commanded Mrs. Flembaugh. "We'll deal with her in a minute!"

Maria may have been fairly confused and scared when all this lunacy started, but she was quickly learning how to handle rapidly increasing danger. She booted the principal in the shin, drawing a sharp wail of pain from him.

Meanwhile, Night-Ghost was engaged in a fierce brawl with Mrs. Flembaugh. The star-cloaked acrobat may have been as nimble as a monkey and able to duck and dodge with superhuman skill, but he was up against a woman whose all-too-suitable nickname was "Sasquatch Lady." She was three times his size, and extremely brutal. Each punch she threw was sped through the air by the diabolical hatred that burned in her nerves. And when those punches managed to connect (for even Night-Ghost couldn't dodge them all), they hit like bony little meteors and bashed the hero straight to the floor. In the space of two short seconds, he would collapse, seem defeated, gather himself up, hop to his feet, and the battle would continue.

His mastery of acrobatics was almost like a strange form of kung-fu that was all his own invention. He would leap, spin, jut out a foot or fist, and deliver a solid thump to Mrs. Flembaugh — a solid thump that would have instantly ended a fight against any *normal* person. But a "Sasquatch Lady" can easily take such a hit and keep right on going.

Their fight was so swift and ferocious that, for a brief moment, Maria and Mr. Morton stopped struggling with each other and watched. They were both struck dumb to see the hideous old teacher and the nimble superhero fighting for their lives.

Night-Ghost managed to land a few hits and kicks that sent Mrs. Flembaugh reeling backwards. He hadn't yet knocked her down, but he was starting to have an effect! Perhaps a hundred more punches and he would see her fall. Sadly, he wouldn't get the opportunity to do so. A little problem arose. Actually, it was *four* little problems — four of those zombie-students came bustling out of the gym and tackled the acrobat-hero.

This freed Mrs. Flembaugh from her bout with Night-Ghost, just as Skymaster was climbing to his feet.

Now, Skymaster knew he'd never be able to tangle with the crazed old teacher as fiercely as his purple-cloaked partner had. His best hope was to use the one super-power that set him apart from other humans: he needed to get up on the air. Once he was flying, he could strike at her from above.

Sadly, the moment he launched himself off the ground she grabbed a hold of his ankle and yanked him right out of the air. Then she performed a wrestling throw on him (one called a "helicopter-toss"), and slammed him into the floor with incredible strength, leaving him dazed and feeble.

She dragged him back over to the gym, opened the door, and flung him in as if she were feeding a sardine to a pool of sharks.

Yet, Night-Ghost wasn't finished. An escape-artist is a tough person to pin down for long. He squirmed free of all four of those zombies and sprang at Sasquatch Lady like a purple-caped panther. He landed on her with such force that he bowled her over onto the floor.

While she wrestled with Night-Ghost, the wicked old teacher shrieked, "Get rid of that girl, Morton!"

"I'm trying!" Morton whined as he struggled to contain Maria. "But she's more dangerous than she looks!"

Sasquatch Lady was fighting with a super-skilled, super-agile superhero. She did *not* want to hear that Morton was helpless against an ordinary ten-year-old girl! She was about to growl out an even angrier command at him, but, at long last, Morton managed to haul Maria into his office and lock the door behind him.

Once more, those zombies came to Mrs. Flembaugh's aid and pulled Night-Ghost away from his fight with the devilish teacher. They dragged him back into the gymnasium, and Sasquatch Lady slammed the door on them.

Now the front entry hall of Palisades Elementary School was calm and empty. Only Mrs. Flembaugh remained, resting against the gymnasium door and catching her breath. She could hear the muffled roar of an insane riot seeping through the door behind her, and it made a spiteful grin grow upon her wrinkled face.

Slowly turning around to peer through the window in the door, she watched as the five heroes fought for survival. She laughed a savage laugh and muttered, "Destroy them, my slaves! *Destroy them all!*"

Fearless Force

Chapter 13

The Unsurpassed Master of the Faster-Track Tasks Whacked Back and Unmasked

Mr. Morton was a rather tall, awkward creature; a fragile, narrow frame leading up to a generally uninviting face set with heavy, black-rimmed spectacles. The greasy quantity of black hair atop his head was combed down against his skull with a slick, cheap grooming product, though there was forever a little rooster tail popping up at the back. His smile always seemed like a poorly rehearsed imitation, for it was rarely an expression of joy; usually it was just a clumsy attempt to hide the many sicknesses of his dimly-lit soul. He always wore a bland, black business suit that must have been tailored to his skinny shape, for they don't commonly sell them in such thin sizes. With a white, button-down shirt and slender black necktie, he always hoped that he looked like a dangerous government agent, though no one had ever mistaken him for one.

With the captive Maria in his clutches, he dragged her

through the school's main office and into that hideous place that is the office within the office: the principal's office — the place that conjures up dread in the imagination of any grade school student. However, the young Miss Fuente's sense of dread was heightened by the fact that she wasn't being taken to that place for having used a naughty word on the playground, but for having discovered too much about the villainous practices of her faculty.

Once inside the principal's office, Mr. Morton shoved Maria into a chair and quickly locked the door with the frantic jingle of a key. As Maria jumped up, sped for that only exit, and fought uselessly with the doorknob, Morton dropped the key-ring into his jacket pocket and stood triumphantly over her.

"You're not getting out, little girl." A grin coiled across his face. "Sit."

Standing her ground, she spun around and boldly asked, "Alright, Mr. Morton, what's going on here?"

"You must be insane to think I'd tell you anything!"

"You *have* to," Maria informed him. "This is a public school! I have a right to know why the building is loaded with zombies and lunatics! If you don't tell me, I can get a lawyer and sue you!"

He thought for a moment, and his grin collapsed into a worried expression. "Is that true? I *have* to tell you?

...You can sue me?" He suddenly realized that she was bluffing him, and he scolded her for it: "Knock off the fibs, little girl! There's nothing more dishonest than lying!"

"How 'bout turning people into zombies?" she asked. "That seems pretty dishonest to me!"

"Don't talk back to your elders!" He was trying to sound important and intimidating, but the whole time he kept rubbing his shin. It was still in agony from that kick Maria had given him out in the hall.

"So am I under arrest?" she asked. "If I am, I get to make one telephone call, you know. That's what I learned in social studies — one phone call when you're arrested. So hand over the phone!"

"Hey! I don't take orders from you, kiddo! I'm the principal! This is my school! And I don't do anything I don't want to do... unless Sasquatch Lady tells me it's important."

"I don't believe what I just heard!" Maria put on an act of shock and disgust. "Did you just call her 'Sasquatch Lady'? I'm tellin'!"

"Please don't! *Please!*" Morton's eyes grew wide with fear, and his hands were shaking like jackhammers. "I'm begging you! Don't tell her I said that! I didn't mean to!"

Maria just looked away from him and pretended she didn't hear.

There was a sudden, sharp knock at the door. Mr. Morton knew it was Mrs. Flembaugh, and he was scared to death to let her in the office.

He whispered to Maria, "Don't say anything! Have a heart! The last time she heard me say that name she went totally berserk, and she—"

"Open this door, Morton!" screamed the angry voice outside the office. (Yes, it *was* Mrs. Flembaugh.)

After dropping his keys twice, trying the wrong one three times, and the right one upside down, he finally opened the door.

Mrs. F. stormed in.

Morton asked her, "What did you do with the purple moon-man?" (He had no idea what Night-Ghost's name was.)

"He's back in the gym getting ripped apart by the zombies," replied the victorious Mrs. Flembaugh.

"Why are all the students and teachers zombies?" asked Maria. "What's going on in this place?"

Mrs. F. stared down on Maria with a demonic scowl. "Don't worry about it, missy! In a few minutes you won't even remember seeing them. We're taking you to the basement to erase your brain. We'll wipe out everything you've seen today."

Maria laughed a nervous laugh and backed away from

the villainous teacher. "I'd really appreciate it if you didn't do that. You see, I read a chapter of my English book, and I'm supposed to answer the questions on it after lunch."

"No brains are getting erased today!" said a voice from another part of the room.

They all spun around as Night-Ghost leapt through an open window. Everyone was completely startled. No one had even heard him open that window. What's more, they all thought he was in the gym being torn to bits by murderous zombies.

He looked at Maria with a heroic smile, telling her, "I promise, you'll remember everything you've seen here!" Then he fixed a steely-eyed stare on the villains and told them, "I'll make sure you two remember it as well... for a long, long time!"

Sasquatch Lady didn't utter a word. She wasn't concerned with exactly *how* her proud little foe had managed to escape the gym. All that concerned her was making absolutely certain that he was crushed — and instantly! Picking up Morton's chair, she sent it sailing at Night-Ghost. His super-acrobatic skill allowed him to dodge the flying furniture, letting it shatter on the wall behind him, then he darted boldly forward at his foe.

The fiendish Mrs. F. caught the young hero in an iron grip, her wrinkled (yet unnaturally tough) fingers clamping mercilessly around his throat.

Well, Maria wasn't about to stand idly by and let a superhero be murdered for her sake! (She was feeling bad enough that she was someone who needed rescuing in the first place.) With a charge of courage worthy of any comic book crime-fighter, she sprang onto Mrs. Flembaugh's shoulders and latched a chokehold around the elderly villain.

Mrs. F. wasn't all that troubled by the girl trying to strangle her. (Sadly, Maria's act was better described as "brave" than "effective." Being new to life-or-death struggles, the young Miss Fuente wasn't putting *nearly* enough gumption into that chokehold.) The murderous teacher was pretty much able to ignore the girl on her back and focus her hate on squeezing Night-Ghost's windpipe shut. And it was taking an unbelievable amount of mental focus, for she could feel him slowly but surely wriggling out of her grasp. Furthermore, he was lashing out with his feet, booting her in the shins and knees.

Thus it was that the villain came up with a dastardly plan to rid herself of both Night-Ghost and Maria in one fell swoop. With her hand that wasn't throttling the escape-artist she reached out towards Mr. Morton's desk-lamp. Gripping the hot, glowing light bulb in her palm, she closed her hand around it and clenched tight, shattering that bulb in her fist with a loud pop and a jangle of broken glass that flew out from between her fingers.

Her hand was now clamped around the hot innards of the light bulb. The electricity that usually sizzles through those bare coils untouched was now sizzling up her hand and straight through her entire body. The 120 volts that had been feeding the light were now speeding through her frame, transforming her into a human power-conductor. Of course, your average person would be quickly killed by such an act *[and don't you try it!]*, but Sasquatch Lady merely laughed as the dangerous voltage shot through her nerves. (She even laughed-off the jagged shards of glass from the bulb that were digging into her palm.)

The force of that electrical surge threw Maria from the old lady's shoulders and dropped her to the floor. Not really sure what had happened, Maria sat on the carpet with her eyes unblinking and wide-open, her electrically-shocked hair standing out sideways in excited surprise. She was a comical sight, quite at odds with the deathly seriousness of the battle.

As for Night-Ghost, he was held in Sasquatch Lady's horrible grasp while the current of energy shot through the old woman's body, down her arm to the hand that clutched the hero's throat, and jolted through his body. At last, he succeeded in prying himself from her clutches — just moments before the electricity did him any serious damage. Understandably stunned by this experience, he crouched on the floor, catching his breath and collecting his senses.

Unfortunately, he didn't collect those senses of his fast enough. Mrs. Flembaugh, still clutching that shattered lamp in her hand (and thus still charged through and through with a dangerous electrical current), shot out her other hand, bashing her fist brutally into Night-Ghost's side.

One hit, then another and another — each one smashing Night-Ghost in the ribs as a flurry of yellow-white sparks flew from the vile old woman's knuckles. The helpless hero, pummeled by that electrically-charged fist, could only crumple to the carpet as each clobber sent a shock through his nerves.

When she felt that she had finally rendered him feeble enough, Sasquatch Lady made her move! She grabbed Night-Ghost's mask, gave it a twist and a tug, and pulled it right off his head.

Upon seeing Terry's face, she howled, "One of my own students? It's an outrage!"

Of course, Maria, who was witness to this disastrous event, already knew Night-Ghost's secret identity. And where only a few minutes ago she had been thinking that he was a lunatic lost in a fantasy, now her heart was breaking for him as his precious secret was so rudely exposed before his enemies, Sasquatch Lady and Mr. Morton.

Terry turned a serious face to Maria — perhaps as if to say, "Please keep my secret." Then, turning to Mrs. F., he gasped out feebly but bravely, "I suppose you're going to erase my mind along with Miss Fuente's."

"Oh, you don't get off *that* easily, young man!" Morton cackled treacherously. "I'm going to see to it that you go out like a real superhero!"

"Real superheroes don't 'go out!' " Terry answered sternly. "They escape in the nick of time!"

Morton gave him back a cold stare. "Not from *this* principal's office, they don't!"

On the principal's desk was a wood block with the name "Milton Morton" engraved on a brass plate. (Yes, "Milton" was Mr. Morton's unfortunate first name.) Atop this nameplate block were two ballpoint pens standing up. It was the sort of normal desk-set you'd see in any principal's office. But when that criminal principal pulled back the pen that stuck up on the left side, it turned out to be far from normal. There was a sharp click as that pen activated a hidden switch. With a low electronic hum, the bulletin board on the far wall rotated, and on the backside of it were four shackles. Mrs. Flembaugh slammed Terry to the wall while the chuckling principal latched the shackles to the boy's wrists and ankles.

As Terry hung there on the wall like some sort of human artwork, Morton pulled back the right-side pen on his desk-set. This activated another hidden switch, and the portrait of Abraham Lincoln on the wall opposite Terry slid to one side. Behind that picture of our sixteenth president was something that looked like a bazooka... aimed right at the captive fifth-grader.

"That is an electro-burst death-ray cannon," Morton explained as the weapon began to pulsate with a droning buzz and an orange glow. "I bought it just in time for the new school year — part of my usual back-to-school shopping. It shoots a powerful bolt of energy that can stop an elephant dead in its tracks and leave *nothing but* the tracks! Its trigger is wired directly into those shackles on your arms and legs! If you try to escape... *Zap! Poof!* You're finished!"

"And what if I just hang around all day?" asked Terry.

Morton lit up his lizard-like smile. "What kind of superhero is going to hang around all day with a death-ray pointed at him while two supervillains are dragging a pretty little girl into a basement to erase her brain?"

Terry narrowed his eyes and tightened his jaw. He hated the fact that the principal was right. There was no option for a hero but to escape!

"I wish I could see your attempt to break free," Morton

laughed, "but it's a very powerful weapon and this is a very small office. We might *all* get fried!"

Mrs. Flembaugh turned a threatening grin at Maria. "Poor little girl! Having to hear such ghastly things! You might have nightmares! We'd better take you to the basement and make sure that you forget all of it!"

If Maria had any fear, it didn't show. "Well, Sasquatch Lady, before you wipe out my brain, I think you should know something: While you were out, Mr. Morton called you Sasquatch Lady."

Mr. Morton started to scold her: "You little snitch! I told you that if—" Then he suddenly corrected himself: "I mean... You little liar! I meant to say 'liar,' not 'snitch'!"

Mrs. F. snapped, "Oh, shut up, Morton!"

He whined desperately, "I *swear* I didn't say it!"

She threatened him casually: "I'll deal with you later!"

To which he whined all the worse, "Please! She's lying, I tell you!"

The door slammed behind them, and their bickering voices faded off as they dragged Maria down the hall. Terry was left alone with that electro-burst death-ray cannon humming quietly as it waited for him to make a move.

He knew he could be out of those shackles faster than anyone on Earth. (He may not have had his mask on at this moment, but he was still the untrappable Night-Ghost!) So he immediately set to work.

His power to make locks "obey" was a psychic power. He focused his thoughts into what might be called "an invisible sixth finger" that penetrated the handcuff's mechanism and operated its inner workings. This caused the electro-burst death-ray cannon to let out a sputter — not a fatal burst, but only a warning.

He instantly stopped what he was doing. If he went any further with unlocking one of those handcuffs he'd be atomized. (Which is a fabulous word meaning "blasted apart into separate atoms.")

"Perhaps this calls for a more old-fashioned escape-artist's talent! I'll slip my hand out of the shackle *without* unlatching the thing."

Moving as slowly and gently as a surgeon, he squeezed his thumb and fingers together to make his hand thin enough to slide out of its cuff. He hadn't gone more than a quarter of an inch when there was a slight click and the cannon let out another sputter and a spark. If he tried anything more, the deadly weapon would let loose at full power and roast him to ashes.

He shoved his hand back into the shackle and took a deep breath.

"I can worm my way out of these restraints in a second. The only snag is that it'll take a *half* of that second for the cannon to fry me to a purple-clad crisp!"

Still, he was fully confident that he'd come up with *something* before Maria's brain was erased in the next two minutes or so.

"They think they've got me! Ha!"

Fearless Force

Chapter 14

The Purple Perpetrator of Pernicious Peril Prevention

The humming and glowing pulsations of the electro-burst death-ray cannon seemed to say, "Come on! Try and escape, so I can blast you into a bunch of charred cinders!"

Night-Ghost's escape-artist brain instantly whipped-up a plan of action:

Fact: This spot on the wall where he was shackled was actually the flip-side of Mr. Morton's bulletin board.

Strategy: If the captive hero could get the wall to spin around again, then it would be the notices tacked to the bulletin board that would be facing the electrical cannon instead of him.

Escape: The board would act as a shield to take the brunt of the blast, while Night-Ghost would be safely on the other side, working his way out of his shackles.

Problem: How could he get that wall to twirl around again?

He had seen how Mr. Morton had activated the motor to spin the bulletin board: The pen sticking up on the left side of the desk-set was the secret switch. Night-Ghost needed something to throw at that pen to trigger it once more.

He got hold of his cape with his teeth, and tugged it out from behind his back. Wagging his head from side to side, he swung that cape back and forth until he could grab a corner of it in his right hand.

"I better get this right the first time," he muttered as he bunched up the cloak in his hand. "It's not three throws for a quarter."

With a flick of his wrist, he threw the balled-up cape at the pen on the desk that would activate the rotating bulletin board. He scored a direct hit. (A great escape-artist's skill is always good under pressure.) The left-side pen was knocked over and the switch clicked on. The wall began to spin slowly, and Night-Ghost found himself rotating around until he was hanging in a dark space inside the wall, instead of in the principal's office. This, of course, put the bulletin board between his back and the death-ray.

Once he was shielded, he twisted his left arm free of its handcuff. There followed the sharp snapping noise of the cuff's trap-switch being activated and the deadly device was triggered. He heard the crackling of electricity back in the office, and felt the heat behind him as the death-ray cannon started to destroy the principal's bulletin board and all the messages pinned to it.

"I hope Mr. Morton didn't have anything important on there," he laughed.

Precisely according to his plan, the bulletin board behind his back shielded him from any danger. However, as he started to work his other hand free, a horrible thing became apparent: When he had thrown his cape at that pen-switch on the desk, he had knocked the switch into the "on" position for good. The wall kept right on spinning, and he was rotating around with it to face the death-ray head-on!

And that cannon was still firing away at full blast! It hadn't just gone "Zap!", and destroyed the notices on the bulletin board. No; its beam of hot, fatal energy was *continuing* to roar as Night-Ghost spun towards it.

Even a cool-headed expert escape-artist can know a moment's frustration. When this young hero realized that he was being turned towards a roaring bolt of lightning his heart sank.

"Oh, boffo!" (Again, this was groaned sarcastically.)

He fought with the restraint on his right arm as the spinning wall to which he was bound steadily rotated him back into the principal's office; back into the path of destruction. Smoke and bits of burning wood filled the air as he tried to wriggle loose from his right-hand shackle.

The lightning bolt roaring from the mouth of the cannon was cutting a straight line right for the man-in-the-moon on his chest when he pulled his right hand free and ducked. When the rotating wall was totally broken and burnt to pieces, it collapsed and dropped the escape-artist to the floor.

As he crouched on the carpet catching his breath, he watched the cannon reduce the spinning bulletin board to a crumbling mass of smoky, black ruins. There was a whine, a grind and a mechanized howl as the weapon overheated and shut itself off.

Laying on the floor, surrounded by charred pieces of that bulletin board, he undid what was left of the shackles from his ankles. He gathered up his mask and cape from off the desk, and made himself back into a proper-looking superhero. Then, vaulting the desk, he speedily unlocked the door with his strange power to command locks. Darting from the principal's office, he raced through the main office, and headed with all speed for the basement.

Passing the gym, he looked through the window in the door and saw his four teammates fighting for their lives against the swarm of zombies.

"It wouldn't do any good to help out in that madhouse.

I have to stop this insanity at the source!"

Just down the hall from the storeroom (which was still missing its door, because Titan had bashed it apart with Charlie) there was another door marked "Boiler Room." (That's a room where one finds a water-heater.) The latch was locked, but again this meant little to Night-Ghost. He worked his magic on the door handle, then opened it slowly and carefully.

The super-agile hero entered the Boiler Room as silently as if he were in a movie with the sound turned off. The door opened up on a stairway leading down into the school's gray cement basement. But Night-Ghost didn't use those stairs. Instead, he climbed up on the railing, then leapt straight up to the big, rectangular light-fixtures that hung from the ceiling. Grasping the narrow chains that held the basement's lights suspended in midair, he climbed, monkey-like, from one to the next — but not by swinging. Had he *swung* from light-fixture to light-fixture, he would have caused those lights to swing, and this would have called attention to him. Instead, he was moving up there next to the ceiling with perfect muscular control, in a smooth, steady way that didn't disturb the lights at all.

From this high viewpoint he could observe the entire basement from one end to the other. In the far corner stood the school's water-heater — an immense tank of drab green connected to the walls through a conglomeration of plumbing. And beside that boiler was a machine twice its size — a device covered with blinking lights, metal pipes and plastic hoses that snaked around on all sides. Yes, it was the very machine that had been sketched-out in the mysterious plans that he had taken from Sasquatch Lady's desk; the device that The Wizard had figured to be a transmitter.

And next to that machine was the scene of peril:

Mrs. Flembaugh clasped tightly onto Maria while Morton attached two wires to the girl's forehead and plugged them into the machine. Maria struggled with all her might against Mrs. Flembaugh's clutches. She tried to kick Mr. Morton as he stuck those wires on her head. She tried to stamp on Sasquatch Lady's foot, but the villainous teacher held onto her with an insistent grip.

Mrs. F. assured Maria with a sickly sweet laugh, "This won't hurt a bit."

Maria replied defiantly, "That's not your usual style, Sasquatch Lady."

And this got a scream of a response from Mrs. F.: "You *want* to hurt, brat? I'll hurt you!"

Knowing it was time to act, Night-Ghost grabbed the power cable that fed electricity to the light-fixture upon which he was standing (which fed power to all the other light-fixtures). When he yanked the power-cable, the room was instantly plunged into total darkness.

But, as you can guess, total darkness means nothing to someone with a name like "Night-Ghost." His eyes could penetrate darkness better than a cat's. Dropping from the light-fixture, he ran to the fuse-box on the wall, and began flipping switches at random until one of them shut off the strange machine that was hooked to Maria's head.

Mrs. Flembaugh, not knowing that Night-Ghost was in the room, presumed that there had been a power overload. Her voice thundered out in the dark: "Morton! You blew the fuses, you dolt!"

Since Night-Ghost had no trouble finding his way in that pitch-black cellar, he charged straight across the room and threw a good, solid punch at his teacher's mouth. *[Warning: **DO NOT** punch your teacher in the mouth, unless you have actually caught her in the act of erasing the brain of a classmate with a mind-control machine!]*

Not having seen that hit coming, Mrs. F. was knocked completely off her feet, and her false teeth were sent flying. She released her grip on the imperiled Miss Fuente, who instantly made a break for it.

Maria plucked the wires from her forehead and ran for her life through the darkness. She was headed in what she *thought* was the direction of the stairs. But after two steps she ran blindly into a mop and bucket, then fell right into Night-Ghost's arms.

"Don't worry, Miss Fuente," he whispered. "I have you. Take my hand and follow me."

As he led Maria up the stairs and out the door, they could hear the top-volume commands of the crazed, old woman: "Morton! Fix the lights! Get that girl! Find my dentures!"

Chapter 15
Maria's Very Unpopular Brain

Out in the light of the hallway, Maria stared at Night-Ghost in total disbelief. "You actually escaped from the principal's office?"

"That's what an escape-artist does, Miss Fuente." Night-Ghost pulled her to a stop in a side hallway.

Remembering what he had said up on the roof, she jokingly told him, "I thought you said you weren't going to rescue me!"

Remembering what she had said the night before, he jokingly replied, "Oh, I'm just a crazy person with a whole lot of dumb luck!"

Always one to admit when she was wrong, she instantly began overflowing with apologies and explanations. "I am *so* sorry I called you crazy! But, come on! A kid tells you he's a superhero — well, what's a person supposed to think?"

"Don't worry," he laughed. "I'm fairly used to being called crazy."

Their conversation was interrupted by the sound of the gymnasium doors bursting open. Maria and Night-Ghost spun around and saw the mob of zombies shuffling their way.

"Here we go again!" Maria groaned as she and Night-Ghost braced themselves for the onslaught.

But to their surprise, the crowd wandered right past them. It was as if Night-Ghost and Maria were utterly invisible. The murderous zombies had lost all interest in killing, and they were sleepily shuffling away.

"They didn't even notice us!" Maria breathed a sigh of relief.

Night-Ghost struck up that fast-and-slow TV superhero way of speaking: "Now that the machine is shut down, Sasquatch Lady's commands are wearing off."

With the threat of murderous zombies now dissolved, Maria caught her breath. More to herself than to Night-Ghost, she said, "It's a bit much to take in. My principal tried to erase my brain! A teacher at my school is creating zombies! And superheroes... *are for real?*"

"As real as real gets," said the escape-artist with a wise smile. Then he pulled the monk's hood of his cloak up around his head — the better to appear mystical as he added, "There are more things in heaven and earth, Miss Fuente, than appear on the evening news."

While she was still processing this weird, new reality through her brain, Night-Ghost took her head gently in his hands and gazed into her eyes.

Her first thought was that he was going to kiss her, which didn't seem like a half-bad idea. After all, isn't the hero *supposed* to kiss the girl that he rescues? Sure, she had thought that this was a silly habit of comic books and adventure movies. But, after all the day's goings-on, it suddenly seemed like the next natural event in the process.

However, when the hero's eyes began to glow with an unearthly purple light, she asked suspiciously, "What are you doing?"

"I'm sorry," he answered, "but I have to hypnotize you."

" 'Hypnotize me'?"

"Yes, you saw me without my mask; you know my secret identity. I'm afraid that's just not acceptable. I'm going to make you forget my real face."

She broke free of his grasp, and backed away. "Hold on, buster! All this freaky stuff is going way too fast! First that crazy old lady wanted to erase my memory — now *you?* Why is everyone after my brain today?"

"I have to hurry!" He urgently tried to take her face

in his hands again.

Again she backed away. "What did you tell me when you came jumping into Mr. Morton's office? 'No brains are getting erased today!' and 'You'll remember everything you've seen here!' Is that just heroic bunk that you say when you leap into a room, or did you mean it?"

"That was before you saw me unmasked! Look, I really have to hypno—"

The purple-cloaked hero was interrupted by the sound of Sasquatch Lady and Mr. Morton stomping up the stairway from the basement. Night-Ghost pulled Maria around another corner, ducking farther out of sight as the two villains rushed by. Mrs. Flembaugh was slapping Morton on the back of the head and barking out orders: "Get back to your office! Get this place looking like a normal school again!"

Maria listened to those villains hurry past, then spun around to find herself looking right into Night-Ghost's glowing purple eyes. She wanted to turn away, but the harder she tried, the more impossible it seemed. That purple glow intensified until the hero's irises were burning like twin violet sunbursts with tiny white and pink sparks dancing in spirals.

In the space of a few gasps, her free will dissolved under his spell. He waved his hand in front of her face, her eyelids fell shut, and she stood there before him in a trance.

With his voice in a steady drone, he took away a single piece of her memory: "You never saw Sasquatch Lady remove my mask..."

In a sleepy mumble she answered back, "I never saw her remove your mask..."

Then he placed a false image in her mind: "You'll remember everything as it happened, except that when I was shackled to the wall in the principal's office I still had my mask on."

She answered back, "...You still had your mask on..."

"You can wake up now."

And, just like that, her eyes opened and she swooned, as if about to faint. Night-Ghost caught her around the waist, and kept her from falling over.

As she regained her senses, she realized that she was being held in his embrace. At the same instant, he realized that, yes, he had stopped her from falling, but he was *still* holding onto her. There followed a tiny little pause where they both thought, "Hey! This is kind of pleasant!" Then both their brains abruptly decided, "Ten-year-olds are supposed to think this is stupid and embarrassing!" So they broke away from each other and tried to pretend that they hadn't enjoyed that embrace one bit — no, not one bit! (Sure!) Their pulses were pounding twice as quickly now as they had during the most dangerous parts of their adventure.

She asked, "What just happened? You hypnotized me, didn't you?"

Night-Ghost replied, "I had to. In our little adventure together, you saw my real face."

Maria said, "Well, you know best," but she was *really* thinking, "The joke's on you, Terry! I still know who you are! I *already knew* you were Night-Ghost before I saw your real face! I saw the purple costume in your book-bag!" She wisely kept this information to herself, and let the hero think that he had succeeded in protecting his secret identity.

The clang of the bell signaled the end of lunch. Night-Ghost advised Maria, "Get back to class and pretend that nothing weird happened."

"Shouldn't I get out of this school?" she wondered. "Sasquatch Lady and Principal Morton will be looking for me! They'll search every classroom until they find me!"

"If you skip school," he explained, "your teacher will wonder where you went. That will raise suspicions."

"But I'll just get called to the principal's office," she said, "and get chained in front of his death-ray like you were! I don't know how to escape from a death-ray! I'm just an ordinary person!"

A friendly gleam appeared in the boy-hero's eyes as he told her, "You, Miss Fuente, are no ordinary person!" Returning to his serious ways, he told her, "Head back to class and act like nothing happened. If the principal comes looking for you, try to duck out of sight. Now, I'd better see how the rest of The Fearless Force are doing."

He ran back towards the gymnasium and Maria followed. As he threw open the door, she was right behind him, looking over his shoulder at the four battered and beaten heroes smeared on the floor.

"They don't look too good," she gasped. As Titan rose to his feet, shaking his head, she asked Night-Ghost, "Who's the guy in the orange and yellow suit?"

"Titan," Night-Ghost replied, rather impatiently. "He's the strongman of our team."

"Is he more powerful than a locomotive?" (Now that she had discovered real superheroes, she wanted to know how they measured up against the play-acted ones on TV.)

"It depends on how fast the locomotive's going." Night-Ghost could see that Maria's curiosity was growing in leaps and bounds, so he decided to get all the introductions out of the way in one fell swoop. Pointing out his partners one by one, he said, "You already know The Wizard. The one in green is Aquarius — he's our water-breather. And that..." (He indicated the boy in the flier's helmet.) "...is Skymaster."

"And he can really *fly?* That was for real?"

"Yes!" answered Night-Ghost, his impatience mounting. "Now, *please* get back to class!"

The Marias of the world are very perceptive. She knew right away that, since the brilliant Wizard was the brainy Peter, then the super-strong Titan *had* to be his big brother, the "reverse-bully" named Doug. Aquarius she recognized as Curtis by the way his green mask was cropped off at the top, and his plume of blonde hair stuck up in the air. Besides, she knew when she met The Wizard on the rooftop that if he was Peter, then it wouldn't be long before Curtis appeared as yet another costumed crime-buster.

But as for Skymaster? She had no idea who he could be. She didn't connect him to Dan because the ever-too-bashful Dan didn't seem to be the type to go racing through the air like a human missile, plunging headlong into peril. After all, she had seen Terry, Peter and Curtis all face up to Eddie Thigpen and his cronies at lunchtime. But Dan had been knocked right on his hindquarters.

When she had seen Skymaster in the midst of battle, she never would have guessed that the brain under that leather helmet was packed full of worries and self-doubts.

All she saw at that time was a superhero rushing to the rescue as boldly as any of his teammates would have.

She kept her mouth shut about all of this. If she had been fool enough to say, "Hey, that's Peter, Doug and Curtis," then a cranked-off Night-Ghost would only hypnotize her again. Taking his advice that she should return to class and act natural, she went on her way. But after three running steps, she stopped in her tracks. Her brain began arguing with her heart, and it went something like this...

Her heart: "After a girl is rescued by a superhero isn't she supposed to kiss him?"

Her brain: "No! It's embarrassing enough that you let a boy rescue you in the first place! If you kiss him, he'll think that women are weaklings who can't save themselves!"

Her heart: "If kissing the hero is so horrible, then why does it seem like such a splendid idea?"

Her brain: "OK, you can thank him — but with a *handshake* and that's all!"

The quickly spreading grin on Maria's face said that she would ignore her brain's stuffy complaints and give-in to her heart! She spun around, ran back to Night-Ghost and said, "I forgot to thank you. "

He was about to say, "You're welcome," but before he

could utter a word, she gave him a quick little kiss. Quick though it may have been, it was still on the lips. (She had to. His superhero's mask covered most of his face — even his cheeks. It was either kiss his lips or a purple, rubber mask.)

As his face flushed red, he thought, "Thank heaven for superhero masks that cover nearly your entire face! They make it so a girl has to kiss you on the lips, and then they hide the fact that you're blushing like an idiot!"

After that mind-melting thank-you, Maria hurried off, leaving Night-Ghost as blank-faced as one of the zombies he had recently been fighting.

As for Skymaster, he was just sitting up, groaning miserably as he discovered several awful bruises on his body — bruises going deep into the muscles and probably going all the way to the bone. He shook his head and started to stand very slowly and carefully. His headache was gone, but his vision was still somewhat blurry. Unfortunately, as his blurred vision came back into focus, the first thing he saw was Maria's "Thank you" kiss to Night-Ghost.

This was simply *not* a good day to be Skymaster. He gave up trying to stand, and toppled back to the gymnasium floor.

"Hey, Boss!" Aquarius grinned and jabbed Night-Ghost in the ribs. "How come the zombies are all smoochie-face with you, but the four of us get the snarf beat out of us?"

"She wasn't a zombie," he answered humorlessly.

"She must not have eaten anything with the poison in it," The Wizard guessed.

"Eddie stole her apple at lunch," said Titan. "That probably had her dose of poison in it."

In his dead-serious voice, Night-Ghost told his team, "I saw the transmitter. It's down in the basement. Sasquatch Lady and Mr. Morton had Maria's head wired up to it. They were going to use it to erase her memory of what she had seen. I'm guessing they had to plug her brain into it because she never ate any of the poison."

"Exactly," The Wizard replied. "If she had no poison in her system, they would have to attach the mind-control machine directly to her head."

Aquarius jokingly chimed in, "You expect me to believe that there's a mind-control machine in the school basement? On the other hand, I still believe the rumors that Mr. Morton has a diesel-powered spanking machine in his office."

"Actually, it's an electro-burst death-ray cannon," replied Night-Ghost in all seriousness. "It's hidden behind the portrait of Abe Lincoln."

"No lie?" Aquarius was clearly impressed. "Come to think of it, it's illegal for principals to spank students these days. But I don't think there's any law against a mind-control machine or a death-ray."

The Wizard headed for the door. "I've got to get my hands on that mind-control machine and dismantle it!"

" 'Dismantle it'?" Titan clenched up his yellow-gloved fists and followed after his brother. "Let me *smash* it to pieces!"

Aquarius stopped them both by asking, "Isn't the important move right now to return to our classes and act like nothing happened? We have to protect our secret identities."

"A bit of a snag for some of us," said Night-Ghost. Then, without sugarcoating the disastrous news, he informed them, "Sasquatch Lady got my mask off me."

The jaws of his four teammates dropped in horrified unison.

After a shocked pause, The Wizard asked, "Do you think you can use your power of hypnosis on her?"

"Perhaps I can hypnotize her," Night-Ghost replied, "if I can get close enough to give her a good stare in the eyes. But, if I can't..."

"If you can't..." Aquarius finished his thought for him: "Your life is ruined, man! I mean *totally* ruined! Bam! It's over! You're 'Dead-Meat City!' "

Night-Ghost gave him a cold stare that silently said, "Thanks for pointing that out!"

Aquarius patted him on the hand like a loving grandmother. "If you can't put the whammy on her, well, it's only fair. The four of us have her mind control juice in our brains, y'know."

As they left the gym, Skymaster walked past Night-Ghost and shot him a nasty look.

"Skymaster, it's not my fault," said the escape-artist, knowing his friend was upset about Maria's kiss.

Skymaster stopped, and turned towards him with a look of depression and disbelief. "It's always the same, boss. On our adventures you get kissed by girls from outer space, girls from other dimensions, girls from the past, girls from the future... And you don't even appreciate it, man! You always do that I'm-too-busy-fighting-evil-to-fall-in-love routine!"

"Listen, Skymaster, I—"

"There's only *one* girl that I've ever..." Skymaster sighed in defeat. "Aw, the heck with it! You might as well get the girl on *this* mission too!" As he turned and walked off, he added, "And you just had to say, 'Run for it, Miss Fuente, I'll handle this'! Of all the things to say!"

"Come on, listen. It just sort of fell out of my mouth! I wasn't—"

The heartbroken flier wouldn't hear a word of explanation as he shambled away in silence.

Fearless Force

Chapter 16

Suspicious Stares & Nagging Doubts

Nowhere at Palisades Elementary School was there a sign that a lunchtime struggle had ensued between a mob of zombies and a team of superheroes. Students studied, teachers taught, and everything appeared quite ordinary.

In one hallway the janitor whistled casually as he swept up some sawdust and bits of broken wood; while in the main office, the secretary was calling a hardware store to get a new door for the custodian's room. (Apparently, no one could remember how the old one had been blasted to pieces.)

While Charlie swept up that evidence of his brawl with Titan, Sasquatch Lady and Mr. Morton had some cleaning up of their own to do if they were going to keep a lid on their schemes. One thing that was a plus for those villains was the fact that no one could recall being mind-slaves. Every person seemed to have phony memories of what he or she had done for the second half of the lunch break. (Brains tend to do that, you know. They patch together fake recollections when there's a blank spot in the memory.)

The other plus on the villains' side was that they had unmasked Night-Ghost. Once Mrs. Flembaugh got back to class, she would (with immeasurable glee) unleash her vengeance upon Terry.

But knowing the secret identity of only *one* of the five was too tantalizing for words. Determined to learn the true identities of the other four heroes, Mrs. F. swore that she'd get the information out of Terry if she had to fling him through a brick wall to do it.

As for Principal Morton, he stood outside his office, staring suspiciously at each student that passed by, wondering, "Is *that* one of the superheroes? Is *that* one?" And the students stared back nervously, wondering why their principal should be glaring at them in such a paranoid, narrow-eyed fashion.

Never one for being smooth or clever, Mr. Morton went so far as to stop kids at random — grabbing them by the arm and ordering them, "Spill your guts! Are you one of 'em?"

Of course, the students just looked at him funny, and one little kindergarten girl broke down and cried.

Finally, the none-too-brilliant principal received an overdue slap on the skull from Mrs. Flembaugh.

"None of them were five-year-old girls!" she snapped.

"How do we know for sure?" was his defense. "They were disguised!"

Gripping him by the necktie, she hauled him into his office, where she barked out a plan: "*I'll* take care of the superheroes. *You* go to Mrs. Reynolds' class and get that black-haired girl. Her name is Maria Fuente."

Still he went on arguing, "How can one little girl be any threat to our—"

"Morton!" she snarled. "I'm having you hunt her down just to keep you busy! You're dangerous to the operation when you're on the loose without an assignment!"

With a mumbled, "Yes, Mrs. Flembaugh," the principal hung his head in disgrace and shambled away.

And what of Maria?

She had returned to her class, remembering *all too well* that something out of the ordinary had occurred, but there was nobody she could talk to about it. Yes, there were five others who remembered the truth — Terry, Peter, Doug, Curtis, and whoever Skymaster was in real life. (She still had no clue that the hero in the flier's helmet was the tremendously bashful boy who sat directly behind her!) Of course, those five were experienced superheroes.

It must have been fairly common for them to put their normal clothes back on, and go about their day as if nothing outlandish had happened. In fact, they probably loved sitting there at their desks, pretending to be ordinary kids, and knowing things that the people around them would never believe.

Maria, on the other hand, was *not* an experienced superhero. So to have been right in the middle of a skirmish between killer mind-slaves and costumed do-gooders was pushing the limits of her understanding. Regardless of the fact that she had lived through it, everything was now back to normal. She was beginning to doubt if any of her wild adventure had happened.

She took a good, long look around the room to see if anyone else looked as bewildered as she did...

...But no; nothing appeared out of place, except for the outlandish memories in her own head.

Of course, casting a suspicious gaze around the room tends to make everyone else think, "That new girl is even *weirder* than I thought!" And it didn't help matters much when she asked another girl, "What did you do at lunch?", just to see what the girl's answer might be.

That other girl snipped back a snotty response: "I ate food, you ditz! What'd'ya think?"

"Well, *she's* back to normal," Maria muttered to herself.

Next in her investigation, she decided to ask the shy, golden-haired boy who sat behind her — the one named Dan. The moment she turned around to look at him he froze in panic. When she asked, "What did you do at lunch?", he raised his book in front of his face to hide behind it.

"And *he's* sure back to normal," she muttered as she faced forward in her chair. Then she thought, "I'm so stupid! He got shoved to the ground by Eddie, just before all the madness broke out. *That's* what he did at lunch. I must've sounded like a jerk reminding him about it!" Turning back around again, she gently lowered Dan's book and tried to apologize: "Sorry. I forgot Eddie was pushing you around. I didn't mean to— I mean, I was just wondering if you did anything interesting *after* Eddie pushed you— Oh, forget it. I was just trying to make pointless conversation."

Dan (as usual in Maria's presence) was utterly incapable of speech. There was *no way* he could tell her, "Oh, after Eddie shoved me around, I changed into my superhero suit and snatched you out of Sasquatch Lady's clutches." Revealing his identity was strictly forbidden by the Superheroes' Code of Honor. And being unable to conjure up any "pointless conversation" to take its place, he accepted Maria's apology with a shrug, then hid behind his book again.

All the while, his brain groaned silently in his skull,

"She thinks I'm a wimp! I wish those zombies *had* torn my head off!"

Mrs. Reynolds' voice broke through this after-lunch chatter: "Take out your English books. Let's review nouns and verbs, which I'm sure you learned last year. On page twelve you'll find..."

Blah, blah, blah. This ordinary school day was underway once more. And it was all Maria could do to pretend to pay attention while she thought...

"Superheroes aren't real! Somebody played a joke on me! No! *Everybody* played a joke on me! The whole school must've gotten together and said, 'Let's fake-out the new girl!' But I'm nobody's chump! I'm wise to 'em!"

She did another slow, suspicious glance around the room, until she was peering back over her shoulder at Dan. Again, when his eyes met hers, he raised his textbook as a protective shield.

Seeing Dan avoid her gaze, Maria thought, "There's my proof! That boy has a crush on me, so he feels bad about the fact that the whole school is ganging up to play a prank on me! *That's* why he can never look at me!"

"Maria...? Maria Fuente...?" (It was Mrs. Reynolds' voice snapping her back to reality.) "Face the chalkboard, please."

"Yes, ma'am." Maria spun back around as instructed.

Mrs. Reynolds continued, "The verb in this sentence,

as you can see, is..."

Blah, blah, blah. The moment Mrs. Reynolds' chalk was squeaking and clacking on the blackboard, Maria's pondering picked up right where it had left off:

"Wait a minute! A *whole school* doesn't gang up to play a trick on one single, solitary new girl. To make that Skymaster-kid look like he was flying they'd need some pretty expensive Hollywood special effects. No school is going to go through all that trouble just to say, 'Ha, ha! The new girl fell for it!' That's as ridiculous as the whole thing being true!

"The only explanation left is that I've lost my marbles! While everyone else was eating lunch, I was running around like a lunatic *thinking* I was in a crowd of zombies; *thinking* I saw superheroes leaping and flying about. I must've looked insane, running through the school, screaming and fighting with nothing!"

Again, she scanned the room — this time with worry and dread in her eyes. "They all think I'm out of my mind! That's why everyone hates me! ...Well, Dan doesn't hate me." Of course, when she glanced back at Dan, he hid behind his book again. This caused her to assume, "He doesn't hate me, but he's afraid of me because I'm insane! He's thinking, 'She sure is pretty, but she's crazy!' He must *really* have a crush on me, if he can still like me when

I'm a nut!"

"Maria...? Maria...?" (Yes, it was Mrs. Reynolds' voice calling out from the real world a second time.)

Quickly facing forward again, Maria promised her teacher, "I'm paying attention — honest!" Then, glancing down, she noticed something strange. While her mind had been wandering, her pen had been doing the same. There were scribbles all over the front of her notebook — and interesting scribbles they were! A stern man-in-the-moon face surrounded by clouds and stars! A giant heart decorated with intricate swirls, curls and curves. And at the heart of that heart was the name...

...written in that way young girls have of writing the name of a boy they like. (You know, *that* sort of like!) It looked as if she had spent a day and a half just drawing the "T", giving it all the careful detail a medieval monk gives to a capital letter in a hand-copied Bible.

Seeing that she had doodled Terry's name inside a heart, she very quickly assured herself, "I am *not* in love with that kid! He's *not* Night-Ghost. He *didn't* escape from any death-ray in the principal's office. It was all a delusion of mine!" Even so, she went right on drawing that heart around his name, thinking, "But what if it was true? That sure would be something!"

Although she had convinced herself that none of the outrageous lunchtime events had actually happened, she could still see Night-Ghost in her mind. His fists and feet darting around with superhuman skill; his cape flying and fluttering behind him; his stern eyes peering out from under that shadowy hood — it seemed as real as any memory in her head.

With such images in mind, her expression was brightened by an amused smile — a self-mocking smile as she thought, "All my talk about how comic book adventures are insulting to women, but you know, maybe superheroes aren't so stupid! Someone who does good deeds with a mask on, and never accepts a reward — that's a nice idea. Of course, they don't have to dress so weird!"

She was dragged out of this tangled briar-patch of daydreaming when Mrs. Reynolds yanked the notebook out from under her pen, saying, "Let's just see what has your interest, young lady!"

Now, Mrs. Reynolds was by no means a harsh taskmaster. On the other hand, she wasn't about to let a student sit there and doodle — not after telling that student twice to pay attention. Thus it was that the (usually) kind old woman held Maria's notebook up for the class to see.

"Well, there's the man-in-the-moon," said the teacher

with comical amazement. "That's very pretty! And what's this here? A heart with the name Terry in it? And who is Terry, I wonder?"

Maria threw together a hurried lie: "A boy... from... my old school."

This embarrassing event brought howls of laughter from everyone except Dan. He was wide-eyed in shock, for he knew just what those scribbles on her notebook meant.

His brain wailed in silent misery, "Night-Ghost's man-in-the-moon symbol and Terry's name... in a heart! She knows his secret identity... and she's in love with him!" He dropped his head onto his desktop with a bang.

And right when Maria was feeling the humiliation of her classmates' jeers, something even worse caught her eye: Outside the window she could see Mr. Morton heading towards her classroom. He was marching across the courtyard, and he looked like he had a mission in mind.

"He's after me!" she thought. "It's because I went nuts at lunch and thought there were zombies loose in the school!"

Knowing that it just wouldn't do for the daughter of two psychologists to be sent home from school because she had lost her mind, Maria figured that the best course of action would be to hide under her desk. (Not a very dignified move, but it just might do the trick.)

As she sank slowly out of sight, everyone assumed

that it was because she was being ridiculed so fiercely for having drawn a heart and a boy's name on her notebook. And just as she had ducked down all the way, the door popped open and the principal stuck his head into the classroom. He scanned the room for Maria, but couldn't see her as she was completely hidden under her desk.

Speaking loudly over the ruckus of laughter, Mr. Morton asked Mrs. Reynolds, "Are you missing a student? A girl... I don't remember her name."

"No," the teacher replied. "They're all present and accounted for."

Satisfied with her answer, the principal closed the door and left.

"Alright, Maria," said Mrs. Reynolds. "Sit up."

She cautiously crept up from below her desk, looking suspiciously around to make doubly sure that Mr. Morton was nowhere near.

Mrs. Reynolds returned the scribbled-upon notebook. "I apologize for making such a spectacle out of you, Maria, but I hope you've learned your lesson."

"I certainly have, ma'am," she replied in all sincerity. "I'll get to work now."

Miserable as their lives were, Maria and Dan were both thinking the same thing: "My life could be worse... I could be Terry!"

Fearless Force

Chapter 17

The Achilles Factor

Yes, after his lunchtime adventure, Night-Ghost had changed back into everyday, ordinary Terry. And though returning to Mrs. Flembaugh's class was certain doom for him, superheroes *do not* flee from what must be done.

Once her students were seated and the bell had rung, a cold smile spread across Mrs. F.'s face. "Terry, I want to see you at my desk right now."

The whole class went silent. Each student thought, "It sure looks like Terry's gonna get it for something! I'm glad I'm not *him!*"

Bold and unflinching, Terry walked up the center aisle of the classroom, approaching his archenemy's desk and his certain doom.

Mrs. F. would have delighted in exposing Terry's secret identity to the whole room, but that would've meant exposing her *own* evil deeds at the same time. What's more, she didn't want the class cheering Terry, for they'd be sure to practically worship him if they knew he was a real, live superhero. That's why she kept her voice low throughout the following conversation, and none of the class could catch a word of it, no matter how far they all leaned forward.

Her cruel voice rumbled out a command: "Tell me who your four cronies are."

With a smart-alecky smirk (one that would have seemed more natural on Curtis's face), he said, "Their names are... Skymaster, The Wizard, Titan and Aquarius."

"I want their *real* names!" (She was trying to keep her volume down, but as her anger was flaring up, this was becoming impossible.)

"That would be a secret," he replied in a calm tone (which was much more Night-Ghost-ish). "*Four* secrets, to be precise."

Sasquatch Lady could tell that she was up against someone as stubborn as herself. Surrendering to this fact, she told him, "I know who *you* are, anyway."

"So I suppose it's back to the death-ray in the principal's office?" whispered Terry.

"Absolutely not!" She reclined confidently in her chair. "I'm not going to dispose of you — not now; not ever. I'm going to see to it that you're in the fifth grade for the rest of your life! You don't worry me anymore. With your secret identity exposed, you're finished!" Her satanic glee increased as she asked him, "Do you know what an 'Achilles heel' is?"

Terry had read almost as many Greek myths as he had superhero comics. He proudly replied, "Achilles was an indestructible soldier in ancient Greece — indestructible everywhere but a tiny spot on his heel where he had ordinary mortal skin. That's where he was hit by an arrow, and he was finally killed."

Not bothering to be impressed by her student's knowledge, Mrs. Flembaugh continued her threat: "Every superhero is like Achilles. No matter how powerful they are, they *all* have a weakness. And I know what *yours* is!"

Terry's heart froze! As far as he knew, Night-Ghost *had* no weakness! Sure, he wasn't bulletproof or anything like that. He was as human as anybody else — liable to drown if held underwater; to splat on the ground if dropped from a plane. But was there some *very particular* thing that was specific to dooming Night-Ghost? If there was, he had never heard of it. He had never in his crime-fighting career run across any alien meteor, toxic potion, or occult spell that could sap away his super-acrobatic skills, his mysterious lock-picking ability, or his hypnotic talents.

Bursting with curiosity, he carefully asked his teacher, "So what *is* my weakness?"

It didn't seem possible, but Sasquatch Lady's grin grew wider. "Remember, I caught you this morning scribbling your little drawings? I think *that's* what your super-weakness is! *You can't focus on schoolwork!* You're a hopeless scribbler — an incurable daydreamer! You'll have no time to thwart my schemes if I give you a mountain of homework every night... *forever!"*

His heart sank into a cold hole in his stomach. She was utterly correct! A mountain of homework *would indeed* be his undoing! This devilish old woman had not just unmasked him; she had seen straight through him, figuring out his innermost fears. Unable to conjure up a single bold word, he stood there clearly conquered.

Delighted to see him so robbed of hope, she gave the order, "Back to your seat, mister. It's time to crack the books!"

But Terry didn't move. He stood his ground and aimed his eyes directly into his enemy's. Those paranormal eyes of his began to glow with their intense purple light.

In a very mysterious tone of voice he said, "Mrs. Flembaugh... you will forget my secret identity... you will forget that you unmasked me..." (With his back to the class, none of the other kids could see the unearthly glow in his eyes.)

Sadly, the old woman was too immensely evil to be so easily entranced. Before that boy-hero's power could take a hold on her thoughts, she swatted his knuckles with a ruler, telling him, "I'll have no hypnosis in my classroom, young man!"

To see Terry get that swat across the hand, the rest of the class flinched in sympathetic pain. None of them could have guessed what had just gone on. They thought perhaps that Terry had mouthed off at her. Never would they have suspected the *true* strangeness of what was being said just a few feet in front of them.

Still, Terry held fast to his bravery. "You're dealing with a member of The Fearless Force. I won't be defeated by some simple homework!"

"Oh, you'll be dealing with more than homework when you get home today! You're going to have to deal with something *no other superhero has ever faced!*" The old lady's wicked grin spread out from ear to ear. "I called your mother and told her what you were up to at lunch!"

Terry's jaw dropped, and he was left speechless. *That* was dirty pool! *That* was totally against the Rules of War between superheroes and supervillains! You do *not* go calling your archenemy's mother!

The villainous old monster was absolutely correct:

This was something no other superhero had ever faced! But Terry would have to wait until after school to find out how it would conclude.

Satisfied with her underhanded victory, Mrs. F. repeated her dread command: "Back to your seat, mister."

Part 2

After School
(Several Different Kinds Of Terror & Adventure)

Chapter 18

Closer to Heaven

After Mr. Morton had failed to spot Maria in her classroom, she had been safe for the rest of the school day. Eager to stay that way, when the last bell sounded, Maria made her way carefully off the school grounds. She snuck behind shrubberies, ducked behind corners and pillars, escaped across the play-field, and at last made it safely to the cover of the woods.

Taking a path that twisted its way in and out of the shadowy pines and alders, hurrying over the bumps and dips of the uneven terrain, she finally burst out into the open sunshine again. On this far side of the woods, she stood at the edge of a wide, rugged meadow. It was a lovely stretch of freedom rolling ahead of her in ups and downs — every imaginable color of grass, from waist-high pale yellow to stubby crab-grass clumps of deep emerald.

With that barrier of shadowy forest between her and

the school, the feelings of danger finally let go the grip they'd had on her. There didn't seem to be any enemies disturbing the September breezes in this meadow, so she stopped, took a breath, let it out, and set off again with a calmer stride. Strolling through the grassy field, she had hardly walked twenty steps when she got the peculiar feeling that she wasn't alone. Spinning quickly around, she was surprised to find Skymaster standing in the sunlit meadow.

Maria thought she had settled on *not* believing in superheroes, so to see him standing there in the tall, pale yellow grass... well, she wasn't sure *what* to think.

As for Skymaster, he didn't have a word to say because this was Maria Fuente he was looking at, and his voice *rarely* worked within a mile of her.

Finally, after that nervous pause, it was Maria who managed to speak first. She tried a polite (if uneasy) "Good afternoon?"

He answered in that serious tone most superheroes use, "Good afternoon, Miss Fuente."

And a fanfare of brass trumpets burst to life in his heart, for *he had finally spoken to the one and only Maria Fuente!* Although he appeared calm on the *outside*, on the *inside* his soul was exploding with those brass trumpets... and confetti... and cascading balloons... and millions of voices screaming in joy.

He may have been thrilled that he could speak to her in an oh-so-serious superhero voice, but Maria actually found him rather cold, like some royal character that is bored when speaking with the common folk. Night-Ghost always sounded mysterious when he used a superheroish tone (adding to it a little sparkle of the eye that play-fully suggested, "I-know-something-you-don't-know"). Skymaster's attempt at sounding serious just came out terribly bland.

"You're Skymaster... right?" she asked in the same polite but nervous way.

"Skymaster," he answered in the same serious (but actually bland) tone.

Deciding that she had best get to the bottom of things, she marched right up to him and jabbed a finger into his chest. He was indeed a solid object — no ghost or hallucination. Skymaster wanted to squeal in delight, "She touched me!", but he managed to keep up his cool posture, and pretended to be annoyed by her.

She demanded to know, "Is this some prank that's being played on me because I'm the new girl?"

He shook his head "No," without saying it.

"Don't talk much, do you, Skymaster?"

He shook his head "No," without saying it.

She crossed her arms, and gave him a shrewd look up and down. "Anyone ever tell you that your mommy dresses you funny?"

He seemed needled by her humor. "This is a crime-fighting uniform. My mother did *not* make it."

"I didn't think so. It looks too good — like a real, honest-to-gosh super-suit. The leather gloves; the perfectly-fit boots and mask... Where'd you get it?"

"That's another secret."

"Is it a *magic* super-suit? Is that where you get the power... to..." She stopped herself. "You wouldn't tell me anyway, would you?"

He shook his head in another silent "No."

"Well, if you guys *don't* get your powers from your suits, I don't know why you wear the silly things."

"It's a tradition," he explained, "and really quite sensible. It's like being a circus acrobat or a ballet dancer. Normal-person clothes would just get in the way. You can't be fighting a fifty-foot-tall monster, and say, 'Oh, hang on while I tie my shoelace.' "

At the mention of ballet dancers, Maria *finally* understood. "I take ballet, and you're right. I'd fall on my face if I had to do it in 'normal-person clothes.' Still, I don't get the whole super-suit design. I mean, why the underpants on the outside of the tights?"

Now he was *really* agitated! "I don't know. Why do you ballet dancers wear those weird, fluffy skirts that stick straight out?"

She pretended to be as agitated as he was. "You makin' fun of my pink tutu?"

He stiffly answered, "We'll just call a truce."

She jokingly asked, "So, do *you* dance?"

"I fly."

Well, Maria was quickly getting the impression that this particular hero was a snob or something. He wasn't a hallucination, but he might very well be a robot. Still, she was so curious about him that she was determined that she'd crack through his icy exterior. "So, Skymaster, can you *really* fly, or is it a trick?"

Again no word for an answer. Instead, he picked his feet up off the ground. Hovering about two feet over the grass, he drifted in a quick circle around her, then landed again. She let out an astonished laugh, hardly believing her own eyes.

This was where her smart-alecky attitude vanished. Up until this point, she had still been thinking it might all be some gag. But when he glided a loop around her she was utterly breathless.

Stepping closer, she examined his feet. "Are there rockets in your boots?"

He raised up one foot to show her the very normal sole of his brown boot.

She darted around behind him and lifted up his cape to see if he was hiding some sort of jetpack beneath it. Rather embarrassed to have a girl snooping around under his cape, he pulled it back down and leapt away from her.

"Sorry," she laughed. "I was seeing if you had a rocket engine under there."

"No. All I have under there is my... my *rear end*, if you don't mind." Though he was turning red in the face, he also found this very humorous. Still, he wouldn't permit himself to laugh. That might shatter his serious superhero air, and he didn't want to do that! Ah, but if only he *had*. For Maria, seeing him turn red but not give the slightest chuckle, well, she figured that she had offended him.

"Sorry," she said again. "So how *do* you fly?"

"I just... fly, that's all."

"Well, where did you learn to fly?"

"Don't you know that superheroes have to keep the source of their powers a secret?"

"I don't read much about superheroes." With a near-to-exploding curiosity, she asked, "What's it *like* to fly?"

Try as he might, that boy with the power to fly didn't have the power to describe it. After a failed search for the words that would explain the glories of levitation, he gave a halfhearted response of "It's... interesting, I suppose."

This didn't come out *at all* as he had intended. It didn't seem that he was at a loss for the perfect words. No, it sounded more like he just didn't want to be bothered with "dumb" questions.

Becoming quite put-off by his emotionless ways, she crossed her arms and gave him a wise look. "So why are you here? I mean, if everything's a secret with you, we don't have anything to talk about, do we?"

"It's my mission to see that you get home safe." He had *hoped* to respond in a very dashing manner — perhaps to bow to her like a gentleman-knight — just like the "dramatic stage actor bow" that Night-Ghost usually did when introducing himself. Sadly, he was too nervous about standing there, holding a conversation with the all-too-wonderful Miss Fuente. Again, he just sounded like a lifeless robot.

"Your mission?" she asked in a lighthearted fashion. "Was this a direct order from Night-Ghost, or was it *your* idea?"

Though it was completely untrue, he replied, "Oh, it was Night-Ghost — a direct order. He's the boss-man, you know."

Assuming from his attitude that she was annoying him, she replied somewhat coldly, "That's OK; I can get by without a babysitter. I don't need to be walked home, thank you." And she turned to leave.

The heartbroken hero suddenly realized that he had failed miserably in his attempts to sound "cool." As she walked away, he called out, "Um... actually... I wasn't going to *walk* you home!"

Maria stopped in her tracks and her stomach came alive with butterflies. She spun around, and with no attempt to conceal her excitement, asked, "Are you going to *fly* me home?"

He nodded a silent "Yes."

Her jaw dropped and her brown eyes brightened at the notion of a trip through the heavens. Dan could hardly contain the joy he felt behind his Skymaster mask. To have put such enchanted surprise on that most wonderful of faces was the high point of his ten years. A grin appeared on his android-like expression, which Maria noticed instantly.

"You finally smiled!" she remarked. "Are you laughing at me because I'm just an ordinary human who thinks flying is amazing, while it's just an everyday, boring thing to you?"

"Oh, flying *is* everyday to me, but it's *not* boring!" He took a step towards her and said, "I was just smiling because I'm about to show you the world like you've never seen it!"

"So how do we do this?" she wondered, taking a step towards him.

The hero spoke with a shy mumble. "Umm... I'm... I'm... going to have to... Um... If I'm going to fly with you, I'll need to put my... arms around... you."

Maria thought it was funny to see his somber ways decay into nervous ramblings like that. His seriousness had failed at last, and she was amused to find that he was terrified at the thought of this embrace. Still, she couldn't feel all that superior, for she also blushed a timid crimson as she clumsily replied, "Oh, yes... right. That... makes sense."

She clasped him tightly around the shoulders, but he only took a slight hold on her waist. She thought it was funny to meet a bashful superhero, but she didn't want him to be so bashful that he'd drop her from a mile in the air.

"You'll have to hold me tighter than that," she suggested quietly.

"Yeah, right."

And he pulled her even closer, hugging her right up against him.

As their noses touched and their gazes were locked together, Maria felt like she was posed for a kiss in an old black-and-white movie. How long they stood in the meadow like that, staring into each other's eyes, no one can say, but finally the hero spoke:

"Ready?"

She blinked herself out of a trance. "Huh? 'Ready'? Oh! To *fly!* Yes!"

"Hold on tight," they reminded each other at the same instant.

Slowly and without a sound, all four of their feet raised up out of the grass at once. She let out a startled gasp and took a new grip around him. Shutting her eyes tight, she buried her face in his shoulder as he put on a sudden burst of speed and propelled them high into the endless September blue.

Chapter 19

Walking On Air

"Open your eyes," Skymaster whispered. "You don't want to miss any of this."

Maria carefully opened one terrified eye and saw blue — nothing but blue — the blue of a bright afternoon. Turning her pale face away from his shoulder, she glanced downward. There were her feet and then nothing else for a mile or two — or possibly a *thousand*, for all she knew. The town of Adelaide was a miniature collection of toy cars, trains and houses far below. Dots of people scurried back and forth like insects.

Though she may have been scared to begin with, the Marias of the world are very bold people. It was no time at all before she felt perfectly comfortable in midair.

Up there the winds blow stronger and colder. Though it may have been late summer, it felt like a crisp winter chill blowing through her long, black tresses, telling her that this was no dream.

"How can you stand to keep this a secret?" she wondered.

"I just do. I have to."

"If I could fly, I wouldn't bother keeping it a secret for two seconds!" She spread her arms out wide to feel the wind against her hands. "I'd fly everywhere just for the fun of it! I don't think I'd go around bashing people — even if they *were* criminals. I'm not like you. I can't go charging headfirst into a fight."

Skymaster laughed big and loud. Poorly done though his super-serious act had been, Maria really *did* think of him as someone who goes charging headfirst into a fight. "The thing is, no matter who you are — even if you hate fights — if you promise to stand up for virtue, you're going to have to make a fist *someday.*"

She recalled, "I suppose I *did* kick the principal in the shin today."

Skymaster laughed again. "All for the cause of virtue!"

His laughter was a relief to her. It meant that he *wasn't* annoyed with her as she had first imagined. Then a new thought struck her: What if it wasn't *annoyance* or *boredom* that made him so serious? What if it was *sadness* instead? She didn't know a lot about superheroes, but she did know that some of them fight crime for very unhappy reasons, like having to avenge the death of a loved one who had been unjustly killed. She was right on the edge of asking about this, but if it was the case, it wouldn't be right to pry into such terribly gloomy and personal matters.

Instead, she asked him, "Don't pilots ever see you up here? What do they think when you fly past the windows of their planes?"

"Oh, I stay away from planes — unless I'm on a crime-fighting case where I have to get right up next to them. A propeller would chop me up if I wasn't careful, and a jet engine would do even worse if it sucked me in! So I'm not about to get very close to them just for the fun of it."

"Still, a pilot or two must have caught a glimpse of you."

"They probably think I'm just a huge bird or something. You see, there's this weird thing that most people's brains do: when their eyes see something they don't believe in — like a flying superhero — their brain remembers it wrong. Without even realizing that it's happening, their brain automatically makes up a phony story about what it must have been. The Wizard explains it a lot better than I do. It's really sad that people can't believe in flying superheroes even when they see superheroes flying."

She agreed. "Imagining why something *can't* happen is a horrible waste of imagination."

"That's brilliant!" In fact, it was such a brilliant

comment that if Dan didn't already have a crush on her he would have *developed* one at this moment.

But then she confessed, "Before you call me brilliant, I should admit that after all the craziness at lunch, I told myself that none of it happened; that I had hallucinated. Just now, when you met me in the field, I was sure it was all a joke."

Skymaster didn't think less of her. As long as she was there in his sky with him, he didn't give a hoot what she believed. And her honesty to confess just made her all the more beautiful.

With the view of the sea on one side and the mountains off to the other, she suddenly realized, "I never told you where I live! You've taken me *miles* away from my house!"

"I thought you might like the whole grand tour of the heavens."

In case you've never looked up, September skies are not like any other skies. It's the time of year when summer is crawling away and autumn is creeping in. Bright white clouds of summer were reaching far off to the southeast. From the northwest, the great, gray clouds of autumn came marching forward.

When the clouds were under them and the planet Earth was blocked from view, Maria felt like she had been transported to a countryside of gray and white mountains and valleys that were in the process of shifting, drifting and changing. She forgot for the moment that if Skymaster let go of her those "mountains" wouldn't support her for an instant and she'd drop to her doom.

As he rotated around to swoop off on a new heading, she mumbled (mostly to herself), "It feels sort of like dancing."

"I wouldn't know. I can't dance!" he laughed, for the idea was completely out of the question.

"If you can learn to fly, you can *certainly* learn to dance! I'll show you. Stop right here."

He brought their flight to a halt, and they hovered in place several thousand feet up in the sky. While he stood upright on the thin air, she stood on the tops of his feet, then posed his arms in the proper arrangement for a waltz — his right arm extended and his left around her waist. Putting one hand in his and the other around his shoulder, she said, "Here we go... One, two, three, and, one, two, three, and..."

She guided his feet to the rhythm, and they began waltzing across the wild blue yonder. It wasn't long before this waltz brought a romantic glow to her bright, powerful eyes of brown.

He wished he had the courage to kiss her. Nothing

big — just a pleasant, tiny little touch of his lips to hers. As this wish hammered away in his soul, he was convinced that his brain would explode at any instant. It seemed that only his leather airman's helmet was keeping the plates of his skull from blasting apart and flying off to the four corners of the Earth.

Overcome by the romance of it all, he tried something new: Only holding her by one hand, he twirled her out as ballroom dancers are supposed to do. Unfortunately, he wasn't thinking too clearly, and he wound up twirling her right out into empty space.

Maria slipped away and dropped through the hazy gray clouds.

Skymaster hesitated for a split-second of *"What have I done?"*, then chased downward through the mist after her.

Maria found herself in a few harrowing seconds of freefall through the clouds (which was pretty scary because she couldn't see anything). Then she fell out the bottom of the clouds and had a few more seconds of freefall in the open (which was pretty scary because she could see the Earth rushing up at her).

After these few seconds of spine-shaking fear, an embarrassed Skymaster had his arms around her again. They circled and spun together until he had slowed her descent; then once more they were flying safely.

"Well," she laughed in relief, "*that* was a scare and a half!"

"I *told* you I couldn't dance!" (He mumbled this so low she almost didn't catch it.)

Since they were already quite close to the ground now, she pointed out where she lived. Of course, he already knew where she lived; but, playing the secret identity game, he couldn't let her know this. He sailed over the woods and made a direct line right for the rough patch of wilderness behind her house.

Once he had set her safely on solid ground again, he took three running steps and rocketed back up into the sky.

"Well," she remarked aloud, "I had him laughing for a moment there. Maybe he isn't a robot after all."

She waved a good-bye that he never looked back to see, for he was too busy scolding himself. "Man, I'm a klutz! For a minute I was cooler than Night-Ghost, then I had to go and wreck the whole thing!"

Chapter 20
Trap of Distractions

The first thing Terry saw when he walked into his home was his mother's disappointed frown.

"OK, mister," she said. "What were you up to at school?"

He faked innocence (and faked it poorly). "Uh... Nothing."

"Your teacher called here, saying that you were a superhero!" (Terry's mother never was any good at getting angry. All the same, she did have a way of speaking her disappointment in a very jarring manner that was almost as bad.) "She said that you were creating all sorts of havoc at school. Come on; out with it! What's the story behind *that?*"

He sighed a huge, defeated breath, and drooped his head. After a moment of staring at his feet, he looked up and spilled the whole truth: "Yes, I'm a superhero — an acrobat and escape-artist, if you must know. I'm the leader of a whole team of superheroes. And Mrs. Flembaugh is a supervillain who has a plot to rule the school — and possibly the whole planet — with a mind-control machine. She turned everybody into zombies during lunch in an attempt to slaughter me and my team."

His mother was no longer disappointed. Actually, she seemed slightly amused. And yet, she didn't want her son to know that she found his story entertaining. "Well, as long as she's the villain and she started all the chaos, then I guess you're in no trouble."

Terry could see that his mother didn't believe a word he had told her, but he didn't mind as long as he was off the hook. "Can I go, then? I have to thwart her nefarious scheme."

His mother caught him by the shirt as he tried to hurry away. "Not so fast, escape-artist-guy! You have another job to do first. Mrs. Flembaugh said that she gave you a math assignment to do as punishment — everything on pages seven and eight of your arithmetic book."

He froze in his tracks. A math assignment! In forcing him to do two pages of his math book, Sasquatch Lady was getting the leader of The Fearless Force out of the way so she could follow through with her plans for control of every mind on Earth!

"She'll take over the planet while I'm still on the first page!" he argued.

"Well, can't a superhero just buzz through his homework at lightning speed?" she wondered innocently.

"That's not my power! I told you: I'm an escape-artist and acrobat! Math is my one weakness! And she knows it because she's my archenemy!"

"Listen..." (Mom was finally going to lay down the law here.) "I don't know what went on at school. When your father gets home *he* can get the truth out of you." She gently pushed him up the stairs towards his bedroom. "But, as for right now, you've been given an assignment to do, so get cracking."

"Can't you see what's going on here?" he pleaded as he was shoved into his room. "The world's most dangerous supervillain is turning you into an unwitting dupe! You're being made into my prison guard, and my own room is being made into my trap!"

"You're an escape-artist. So, let's see you escape." And with that dare, she closed the door to his "prison."

"What now?" he asked himself. "Perhaps the window...?"

The door opened again, and his mother poked her head in the room. "Don't you dare go out the window, mister! You're not leaving this house until I see a math assignment completed and in my hand."

With that stern warning, she closed his door again.

"Guess I don't have any choice," he groaned as he opened his math book and flung himself onto his bed.

Flipping to the proper pages, he saw the long columns of math problems lying in wait for him...

1.) $36 \div 6 = ?$

2.) $45 \div 3 = ?$

3.) $51 \div 17 = ?$

...and scads more just like those. (Page eight looked far worse!)

"Division!" he snarled. "Sasquatch Lady is truly the most deeply evil villain I've ever been up against!"

Taking a sheet of paper out of his notebook, he wrote his name at the top, then copied down that first division problem.

"Thirty-six divided by six.... Hmmm.... Well, six and six is twelve... and... twelve and six is eighteen... and..."

Hardly realizing what he was doing, his pencil began drawing a picture on the top of the paper. Halfway through a sketch of an armored English knight, he screamed, "No!", wadded up the paper, and threw it away. Getting out a second sheet of paper, he wrote his name at the top, and began again.

"Thirty-six divided by six... Hmmm..."

He thought and thought about it, but got nowhere; for he only thought that he thought and thought about it.

His eyes wandered right out of the math text, and found their way to the colorful pages of a comic book. When he finally realized that he was neglecting his homework, he threw the comic book aside and howled, "No! Sasquatch Lady's insidious plan is working! It's working *all too perfectly!* She's cleverly deduced that the best prison cell for me would be my own room! It's loaded with too many distractions!"

He hopped to his feet and paced around his "cage."

"I need a plan — some sort of brilliant strategy! If a missile was coming at me I could duck! How do I duck a math assignment? If these walls were moving in on me and they had spikes on them I'd be able to think of a way out! But, no, this time I'm trapped by my own wandering imagination! I've just doodled all over the paper! I haven't answered a single math problem!

"Math!" he snarled. "It's such a ghastly thing that it has 'problems.' In history, I have 'questions' to answer. Math has 'problems.' That's *proof* of how lousy it is! Science has 'experiments.' Art has 'projects.' " This sparked an idea. "Art project! By heaven, that's the answer! I'm an artist! I can draw knights and dragons that look like knights and dragons! Why don't I just draw a math assignment that looks like a math assignment?"

So, with all possible speed, he scrawled out a

collection of math equations and their "answers." Not one of them was the *correct* answer, but that didn't matter. All he had to do was make it *look* correct. As long as there were numbers after the equal signs, it would appear that he had done a whole assignment. His mother wouldn't be *grading* it; she only wanted to *see* it. (That's what she had said — "I want to *see* a math assignment." She didn't say he had to do it *correctly*.)

As for Mrs. Flembaugh, well, he would never be handing the paper in to her. Once he escaped his bedroom, he'd rush right out as Night-Ghost and have her in jail by morning of the next day. She would never be grading anyone's papers again!

At last, he had covered the whole sheet of paper, front and back, with realistic (yet phony) arithmetic. Quite proud, he chuckled to himself, "It looks very convincing! This might actually be a better skill than being good at math!"

Rushing out of his room and down the stairs, he yelled, "I'm going out to stop Sasquatch Lady's plans for global control!"

"Wait a minute, kid!" his mother yelled in reply. "Let's see that math assignment!"

"Oh, yeah, right. The math." He gave her a rapid glimpse of the phony assignment, then took it away. "There it is. Well,

I gotta hurry!"

"Hold it!" She gave him a doubtful stare. "Hand it over."

He reluctantly surrendered his forgery.

She gave it an examination, and quickly discovered his ploy. "Fifty-one divided by seventeen is *not* forty-four!"

"So I'm terrible at math!"

"You didn't even try! You just scribbled a bunch of garbage, hoping I'd never look at it!"

"I'm not kidding!" he protested. "I'm a superhero, and I have to go save everyone on the planet — *including you!*"

"Let me ask you something: As a superhero, would you stop some crooks who were printing counterfeit money?"

"Of course. Why, just three days ago, my team and I—"

"And would you stop some crooks who were pretending to be police officers?"

"Certainly! In fact, last week there were some phony cops who—"

"Well, I'm a mom. It's sort of like being a superhero. I'm sworn to stop crooks who make counterfeit math assignments and pretend to be good students."

"Crook? I'm no crook! What I do, I do to help save the world!"

She sighed sadly. "Sit down, Amazing Boy, or whatever your name is."

Terry sat (without revealing his actual super identity).

"Why," she asked him, "would a superhero try to fake-out his own mother? I thought you all fought for right and justice. It looks like *you're* Sasquatch Lady's unwitting dupe, not *me*. She's made you into a rotten little faker who tries to cheat his way out of homework. I think you're right when you say that she's the evilest person on Earth. That's why I'm not allowing you to do battle with her."

"What?" He couldn't believe his ears. His heart sank into the depths of despair, and he felt like the worst failure alive. What kind of superhero is stopped from fighting crime because his mom won't let him?

"You're obviously no match for her," his mother told him bluntly.

"What do you mean? I rescued a girl from her clutches today, and I escaped from a death-ray in the principal's office!"

His mother grinned a teasing grin. "A *girl*, huh?"

"I am *not* in love with her, Mom! Sheesh! Romance just interferes with crime-fighting! Don't you know that?"

"I just don't think you're such a fabulous superhero, if you can be tricked into faking your homework. If you can be tricked into wrongdoing so easily, who knows what *else* she'll fool you into doing? Why she might even get you to join her side and become a supervillain! I say, let some more experienced superhero stop her. Now, go to your room, and wait for your father to come home."

Terry slumped out of the chair, and slowly dragged himself up the stairs to his room.

Alone in his "prison," he thought, "She's right. I blew it! I let Sasquatch Lady turn me into a... into a... criminal!" A new idea struck him, and aloud he said, "I've been going about this all wrong! I've been acting like a ten-year-old kid trying to escape his homework, instead of a superhero trying to escape a trap! This is a job for Night-Ghost!"

Chapter 21

The Captive Outer Space Princess

In a few short seconds Terry was clad in his full Night-Ghost outfit — mask, boots and all. Next, he scooted his bed in front of the door, so he could set to work without fear of his mother popping in and catching him in that wild costume.

Now that he was the ever-untrappable Night-Ghost, he set to work. And, like the over-dramatic superhero that he was, he muttered his plan out loud:

"What am I up against? Two pages of division. How is that worse than sliding walls covered with spikes? It's not!

"I have to remember that it's *not* an ordinary homework assignment! It's a trap! People are counting on me to get out of this!

"What if I was on an adventure, and this math was put before me? What if... let's say some aliens have taken some innocent girl captive, and I snuck aboard their flying saucer to save her? Then what if they said, 'Do these two pages of division problems in ten minutes, and we'll let her go free'? What would I do? Would I say, 'I can't do division that fast; you aliens can go ahead and keep the girl'?

"No! I'd do the danged division, because it's a part of the adventure!

"Well, I'm turning the tables on Sasquatch Lady! Instead of letting my imagination *trap* me, I'm going to let it *rescue* me!"

Turning to the mirror over his dresser, he stared into his own eyes and brought to life his super-hypnosis power. The unearthly purple fires came to light in his pupils and spread their glow to every part of his eyes. He gazed into the soft glow and the violet sparks that danced in his irises until he felt a warm hum move across his skull and down his spine. Once locked into a trance, he gave himself a command:

"You will believe that some aliens have a beautiful princess held captive... and the only way you can save her is to do pages seven and eight of your math book!"

At that instant, his imagination kicked into high gear.

Terry's ordinary, rectangular bedroom shifted shape to become the round-walled, silver chamber of an alien spacecraft. Gone were the toys, comic books, socks and sweatshirts that normally littered the floor. The blue-green

The cloaked hero surrendered to his defeat.

*Maria found the halls of her school packed
with crazed zombies.*

Maria locked a stranglehold on Mrs. Flembaugh.

"Don't talk much, do you, Skymaster?"

The fantasy sequence got rather out of hand.

*High above the town, Skymaster spotted
something very suspicious.*

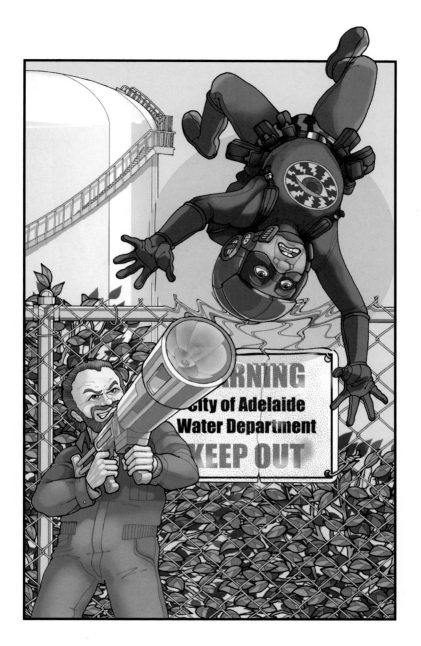

The Wizard was thrown by Charlie's
gravity-wave-disrupter.

Mr. Morton attempted to slice-up Aquarius.

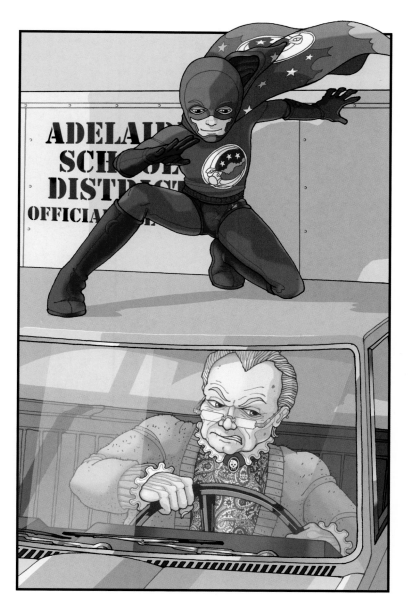

Mrs. Flembaugh was unaware of the stowaway
on her roof.

*Maria's embarrassing question drove the hero
quite near to insanity.*

Aquarius was the only one who could save them!

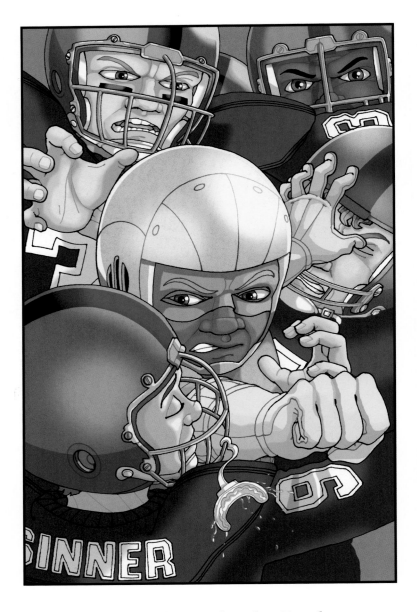

In physical hostilities such as this, Titan became
The Fearless Force's most important asset.

Maria tugged her principal by the necktie, pulling his face down as she brought her knee up.

Maria was helpless against the mind-controlled heroes.

The Wizard hurried to dismantle the transmitter.

He wrapped one of his iron-muscled arms around her
waist and told her, "Hold on!"

shag carpet was replaced with a steel-grid floor, through which puffs of steam came hissing forth. Gone were the wooden furnishings — the dresser, the bed, the desk. There were only complicated intergalactic computer screens that were curved to fit in the circular flying saucer chamber. Gone was the sound of his mother's vacuum cleaner downstairs. All he could hear now were the mechanisms of the spaceship's light-speed engines rumbling below his feet.

And, captivated by his own hypnotic power, this new room was all completely real to him... as were the occupants!

Encircling him on all sides were cruel-looking creatures in gray, leathery jumpsuits: green-skinned extraterrestrials with enormous melons for heads and wide, black eyeballs. Pointing their pencil-thin fingers at him, they asked, "Why have you entered our vessel, Night-Ghost? It is forbidden for you to be here! It can only mean your death!"

Held to the wall by a silver chain was a girl — an Earthling girl. She looked a bit like Maria Fuente. No... She looked *exactly* like Maria Fuente! Yes, there was the lovely Maria Fuente shackled to the framework of that ship with a chain of alien steel on her wrist. Dressed (as most outer space slave-girls are) in a tiny, futuristic costume of glossy silver, she was a heart-stopping vision.

(Why, you ask, do aliens dress their captive Earth-girls in skimpy, shiny outfits? Because, at the moment, we're inside a boy's imagination, that's why.) What's more, her face was painted with little interplanetary designs of pink and blue, and her long, black hair was decorated with glittering garlands of silver stars. Those aliens may have been evil, but they *did* know how to get a slave-girl gussied-up!

One look at that space princess, and Night-Ghost was wide-eyed with surprise. He mumbled to himself, "I just said 'a beautiful princess'; I never said it was supposed to be *her!*"

"You have to get out of here!" that imaginary Maria warned the hero who had rushed to her salvation. "These aliens have frightening mental powers!"

The alien captain hissed at Night-Ghost through needle-sharp teeth, "The girl is to be taken back to our planet as a gift for our Imperial Majesty. She is to be a princess on our world... for a day." He pointed a laser pistol at Maria. "...Then she will be disposed of!"

Night-Ghost snarled boldly, "You're not taking her anywhere!"

The spaceship captain narrowed his bulging black eyes and aimed his laser-gun at Night-Ghost.

But another member of that otherworldly crew pushed

his captain's weapon aside, saying, "Wait! If the Earthling superhero loves the princess, then he can—"

Night-Ghost immediately shrieked, "I don't love her! I'm just here to rescue her!"

"We can read your thoughts, Earthling. You do love her!"

Maria was completely surprised. "He does?"

"They're lying!" Night-Ghost insisted. "They're just trying to get us all flustered!"

The alien shrugged. (He couldn't figure-out *why* it would get the superhero flustered if someone mentioned that he loved a girl.) "If the Earthling wishes to rescue the princess, then let him take the death-challenge!"

Maria cried out in alarm, "Don't do it! They can read your mind! They know all your weaknesses! They'll give you something impossible!"

The expert escape-artist ignored her cautions, and boldly accepted his enemies' dare: "Go right ahead with your death-challenge!"

Laughing with terrible glee, the aliens tossed a book at Night-Ghost's feet — a mathematics text. They dared him, "Do pages seven and eight. You have ten of your Earth-minutes to accomplish this task. If you succeed, the princess is yours. If you fail, you die."

They placed a pencil and a sheet of notebook paper in front of the young hero, then gave him one final warning:

"Don't think you can trick us by scribbling out a bunch of fake answers! It's the real thing, or we'll vaporize you!"

"What have you gotten yourself into," Maria moaned as her spirits sank.

Night-Ghost walked over to her, lifted up her head, and gazed into her beautiful, brown eyes. "Don't fret, Miss Fuente. I can do this. It's only two pages."

"But it's division!" she sighed hopelessly as the aliens dragged him away from her. "You're *lousy* at division!"

He replied with a confident smirk, "Then I'd better get started. The clock is already running."

And indeed it was...

09:50... 09:49... 09:48...

He wrote out the first problem, and muttered to himself, "Thirty-six divided by six... Hmmm..."

From where she was still chained to the wall, Maria shouted, "It's just like multiplication, only in reverse!"

"No help from the captive!" snarled an alien, putting a razor-sharp sword to her throat. "One more word from you, Earthling female, and you shall die!"

"So, six times six is thirty-six," Night-Ghost muttered. "That means thirty-six divided by six is... *six!*"

He moved right onto the next problem, then the one after that, then the one after that. He answered each one at a lightning pace, writing faster than he had ever written in his life. When he had reached the bottom of page seven and was moving on to page eight, he heard Maria's voice...

"Four minutes left!"

...and the alien guard's voice...

"Remain silent, female, or perish!"

The purple-cloaked hero pressed on, answering everything on the eighth page with even greater swiftness than before. And yet, these equations were far more difficult. They were moving into triple-digit numbers, such as...

$$144 \div 12 = ?$$

He couldn't let this strike fear into him, however. He had to keep going! There was a life hanging in the balance — the life of a beautiful girl in a skimpy space princess costume! Few things in the universe are more important than that!

When he finally shouted, *"Done!"* and slammed the book shut, the countdown to disaster was...

00 : 02

"Now..." He cast a determined expression on the aliens. "Unchain the girl!"

"Never!" shrieked the starship captain, diving at Night-Ghost with his long, narrow sword.

The nimble hero dodged to the side, twirled around, and knocked the weapon from the villain's hand with a solid thump of his boot. Grabbing up the sword, Night-Ghost took a huge swing, and brought the thin-but-unbreakable blade crashing down on the chain that held Maria. With her chain snapped, she instantly ripped a laser-pistol from the hand of one of the aliens, and began firing bursts of crimson energy in all directions. When the first alien fell limply to the floor, she snatched-up his pistol and continued her self-defense with a weapon in each hand.

Night-Ghost and Maria were an unstoppable team. The aliens were dropping like flies under his sword-thrusts and her well-aimed laser-blasts.

When all the aliens had perished or fled the scene and the two heroes were alone, he threw a proud grin her way, telling her, "I was right, Miss Fuente; you're no ordinary person."

She looked into his eyes, then turned shyly away. "It looks like I'm your princess. You won me fair and square."

His proud grin transformed into a delighted grin. "I suppose that's true." He coughed nervously and quickly added, "But no person can own another person, you know. That's what I fight for: freedom for everyone."

She cast aside every ounce of her shyness, flung her arms around him, and launched into kissing him as if she had waited her whole life to do so.

He suddenly felt terrible about this whole wild fantasy

he was having. What was he doing kissing the girl his best friend had a crush on? Even in a daydream, he shouldn't do such a thing! Yes, he felt so horrible about it that he *almost* stopped kissing her!

At this baffling moment, he heard his mother's voice outside his bedroom door: "What's going on in there?"

And that shout from the world of reality ended the kiss and broke his hypnotic trance. The daydream vanished. Gone were the round, steel walls of the spaceship interior; gone were the green-skinned alien villains; gone... (sigh!) gone was the image of the stunning Miss Fuente in her science fiction princess attire.

Night-Ghost was standing there in the very ordinary bedroom of a ten-year-old boy. Dirty socks and sweatshirts on the floor; comic books strewn everywhere — things were as they should have been.

However, he was still dressed in his super-secret superhero suit. So when his mother tried to open the door, he leapt to hide behind it.

She was only able to open the door an inch, what with the bed blocking it.

"Why is your door jammed shut?" she asked rather suspiciously.

"Um... 'Cause I'm doing my homework!"

"It sure doesn't *sound* like you're doing any homework

in there!"

True, it *didn't* sound like anyone was studying. Night-Ghost had been hopping on his bed and leaping about the room, making all sorts of zapping noises as his game of hypnotic-make-believe had reached its peak of laser-warfare.

"Why do you have to block your door to do home-work?" she asked.

With outrageous impatience (which came out at a very comical level), he shouted, "I'm a superhero! Everything I do is in secret! How many times do I have to tell you?"

"Well, less noise in there," she commanded, and then walked away.

He took a moment to catch his breath. Then, glancing down, he saw laying at his feet the math assignment that he had finished. Every answer to every problem on pages seven and eight! Accomplished in ten minutes... and with two seconds to spare!

Staring at his own handiwork in amazement, he muttered to himself, "You mean I can actually do my math homework in nine minutes and fifty-eight seconds?"

His whole life he had been one of those people who took forever to do his homework — if he ever bothered to do it at all! When faced with a single page of math, he would always moan, groan and grumble. He would waste all of a sunny afternoon whining, "Can't I just go out and play? I don't need to know any of this math! I'll never use it anywhere in life!"

All at once, he had learned a valuable lesson: His whining had been foolish. No teacher had *ever* given him *any* bit of homework he couldn't have done in a flash if he had just sat down and done it. All those other kids — the ones who always had their assignments finished and ready the next morning — they weren't "smarter" than anyone else. They probably just put-off the whining instead of putting-off the homework. (And, when you think about it, homework may be no fun; but is whining any more fun than homework?)

This was one of the best lessons Terry had learned since gaining his Night-Ghost powers. He had discovered that there are things we all complain about doing, but we would do quite eagerly if the situation was different.

Think of something you hate to do, something you're afraid to do, or something you think you're simply unable to do. Now, consider this: would you be able to accomplish it if some evil aliens double-dared you? Would it become an easier task if the reward was a kiss from Maria Fuente — or whoever your own personal "Maria Fuente" is? (This, of course, is only a theory of mine. You're free to call me a fool if you like.)

Throwing off his cape, mask, gloves and boots,

he stuffed them away in their book-bag. He put his commonplace clothes back on, threw that bag over his shoulder, scooted his bed away from the door, and sped from his room. Waving that homework assignment in the air, he ran downstairs, and slapped it into his mother's hand.

"Here it is!" he announced proudly. Dropping his math book on the table, he opened it to pages seven and eight. "Go ahead, check it out! They're all there!"

After a speechless pause to check a few of the answers, his mother gasped, "It *is* all here! How did you do it so fast?"

"I turned the tables on Sasquatch Lady!" (Even though he was Terry at the moment, he could still use his always-serious Night-Ghost voice.) "She was hoping to use my imagination against me! Instead, I used it as a superhero should — for the fight against injustice! It's amazing what a guy can accomplish when there's some evil aliens, a death-challenge, and a space princess in a silver bikini." Then, more like an excited ten-year-old than a superhero, he babbled out the rest: "Can I go now? I have to continue my crime-fighting!"

"Sure," she replied, still surprised at his victory. "Go right ahead."

"I'll be at Dan's," he told her, then rocketed out the front door.

After he was gone, a worried look appeared on his mother's face. " 'A silver bikini'? That can't be good!"

Fearless Force

Chapter 22

A Soothing Air and a
Wicked Plan

When Dan arrived home there was no one there to meet him — only a note on the kitchen table:

I'll be back at 5:00.

Don't forget to practice your music.

Love,

Mom

He was actually glad to find his house deserted. He didn't want his mom to ask, "Why so glum?", for how could he tell her the truth?: "Oh, I finally spoke to Maria Fuente today, and then I took her 10,000 feet into the sky... but then I dropped her!" When your superhero identity is a secret, so are all your superhero failures. (A message for parents: When you ask your son or daughter "What's wrong?" and he or she responds with a glum "Nothin'," it might mean that he or she has had some terrible superhero setback. Don't pry. They can't reveal any of the truth to you. It's not safe for you to know a superhero's secret identity — even if that superhero is your own kid!)

The stupidity of Dan's near-fatal blunder with Maria had put his mind into a flaming tailspin. And whenever his mind was this turbulent, there was only one thing to put him on a steady course again: his music. There never was a need for his mother to write those reminders for him to practice, because he actually *enjoyed* it.

Dan was a skillful flute-player — quite astonishingly skillful. He had even played with a big, snooty orchestra last summer at some big, snooty event. This meant dressing up in a tuxedo and performing with men and women five and six times his age. It was a lot of fuss, but that didn't ruffle Dan's feathers. If he was playing his flute, not even a tuxedo could annoy him. His music made all other earthly cares fall away.

One reason he enjoyed his daily practice of sharps, flats, rests and rhythms is that, unlike every other child who has to learn a musical instrument, he didn't have to stay cooped-up in his bedroom. No, his rehearsals usually took place a couple of miles up in a wide expanse of unbroken sky.

So less than five minutes after Dan had walked in the front door, Skymaster launched out an upstairs window, a silver flute clutched firmly in hand. High up where the cool winds snapped at his dove-wing cape, he inhaled deep on that thinner atmosphere, then exhaled it through his flute as an elegant rhapsody.

Soon a flock of starlings had gathered behind him, imitating every twist and turn of his flight-path. They seemed charmed by this flying piper's tune. Even as he looped in wide, graceful arcs and twirled in tight barrel-rolls, he never let up on that melody. On the contrary, his tune became all the more frenzied to match his aerial stunts.

Dizzy from all this spinning and flute-playing, he stopped his music and hovered in place to catch his breath. As the birds looped around him, he yelled at them, "So, there we were, dancing, laughing, everything's groovy... Then I have to go, 'Oops! Dropped you, Miss Fuente! Sorry about almost *killing* you!' She's probably calling the cops right now to report a butterfingers superhero who just committed attempted murder!"

But his audience didn't give a hoot about girl problems. They just wanted more music. With the "concert" over, the birds lost interest in him and sped away.

Left alone in his sky, the musician-hero sighed sadly and looked down. About five-hundred feet beneath him was his school... and some very suspicious goings-on!

The parking lot was empty... except for one truck. It

was one of those cargo trucks that belonged to the school district — the sort with the cab up front painted a bland shade of green and the big, boxy rear section a plain aluminum color — but it wasn't making any sort of official pick-up or delivery. Sasquatch Lady and her henchman, Charlie the janitor, were loading a huge metal canister into the truck's cargo compartment. Skymaster didn't need three guesses to know what was in that canister.

"I'll bet that thing is full of her mind-control serum! She's got big plans brewing! I gotta tell The Fearless Force!"

Spinning around and tilting his course downward, he aimed himself at the wide, wild woods that lay spread out behind his neighborhood. As he rushed into this untamed mass of emerald wilderness, he wove his way through an obstacle course of towering pines, maples and alders until he arrived at The Fearless Force's tree-house headquarters.

And this was a tree-house unlike any you have ever seen.

Normally, when a tree-house is thrown together by a pack of kids it's a crooked shack composed of random boards — most of them rotten and warped; some of them being old "For Rent" signs — sloppily hammered together with bent nails. But this place was constructed with professional quality lumber, and every wall was made precisely straight. Yes, it may have been a tree-house put up by grade-schoolers, but it was also the base of operations for a team of real-life superheroes. (Can you picture a genius of The Wizard's quality, or a hero of Night-Ghost's serious nature calling a ramshackle hut their HQ? No way. Neither can I. A solidly built structure would be the *only* proper command center for such an expert team.)

Skymaster's boots thumped down for a rooftop landing, and he climbed down a ladder to a side door. Night-Ghost was alone inside, seated at the round table that took up almost the whole interior of the place. The Fearless Force's captain was busily scribbling something in a spiral-bound notebook.

All in a frenzy, Skymaster told him, "Sasquatch Lady's got some huge scheme in the works! I just saw her and Charlie loading a big barrel of their mind-control poison into a truck! Where are the other guys?"

"Probably on their way," answered Night-Ghost, closing his notebook and putting it away on a bookshelf. "I just came here to write about the lunchtime zombie-war in my journal."

Skymaster set his flute safely on a shelf, then suddenly let himself boil over with rage. "Make sure you write-in the part where you told Maria your secret identity!"

Night-Ghost was taken utterly off-guard by this accusation. "I never told her! She was in the principal's office when Sasquatch Lady unmasked me! But it doesn't matter, because I hypnotized her right after I rescued her from the basement. She'll never remember it."

"She still knows!"

Night-Ghost was taken off-guard all over again. "No way!"

"She's got your man-in-the-moon symbol drawn all over her notebook! Underneath it there's a big, fat heart with 'Terry' written in it! There's all these flowers and... and... it's just sickening!"

"I'll fix it," the escape-artist assured him. "I don't know why my hypnosis didn't work, but I'll fix it. Just don't tell the other guys that she knows. Deal?"

Skymaster gave him a sideways stare. "You kiss her.... She knows your secret identity.... Sounds pretty fishy."

Night-Ghost was naturally put-off by this distrust from his best friend. "I didn't kiss her! *She* kissed *me!* A tiny kiss!"

"On the lips?"

"I have too much mask on my face! There's really not much else she could have done, you know."

"She could've shook your hand," he grumbled.

"I'm tellin' ya, it was quick, it was small, it was nothing."

A sigh of agony drooped Skymaster's whole frame. "She'll never kiss me. Now, *that's* what 'nothing' means!"

They hushed their argument as The Wizard, Titan and Aquarius came scrambling up into the tree-house by the rope ladder hanging underneath. Night-Ghost and Skymaster had been so caught-up in their Maria-talk that they hadn't even heard their teammates approaching.

The Wizard threw open the trapdoor in the floor, and climbed up into the place, saying eagerly, "OK, Night-Ghost, it's time for you to get me into the school so I can deactivate that mind-control transmitter."

But the purple acrobat replied, "That'll have to wait."

Skymaster retold the urgent news: "Right now Sasquatch Lady and Charlie are taking a whole, humongous barrel of their poison somewhere! They were loading it into a truck, and—"

"And you're gonna follow that truck!" The Wizard took a small, hand-held radio off a shelf and plopped it into Skymaster's hand. (Remember: there was no such thing as a cell-phone back then.) "Take this walkie-talkie. Call me when you find out where they're going! Although, I think I already know what she's up to."

"The water-tower?" Night-Ghost suggested.

"Precisely," The Wizard replied. "She's going to dump that stuff into the water-tower on the hill, and take control of every mind in this neighborhood!"

"Can I sit this adventure out?" Aquarius asked. "I should've told you guys a long time ago: I'm afraid of water."

Of course, it was a feeble attempt at a joke — the team's amphibious superhero suddenly confessing that he had a fear of water. It was a gag that didn't get one laugh, but just annoyed stares from the other four. After a long silence, Titan asked the absurd amphibian, "Tell us again, why did we let you join The Fearless Force?"

Aquarius pretended to be ashamed, turning his eyes down toward his feet. "I paid each of you guys five bucks."

Always eager to get back to the serious subject of superheroing, Night-Ghost ordered Skymaster, "Scout ahead!"

"I'm on it!" With a quick salute, the boy in the dove-wing cape launched himself out the window and sped off into the wild blue yonder.

The Wizard took a blue backpack off of a hook on the wall, and quickly loaded it with scientific gadgets he might need in the forthcoming action.

As the four teammates climbed down through the trap door in the floor, Aquarius asked, "When you guys finally *do* fire me, will I get my twenty bucks back?"

"We'll never fire you," Titan assured him. "One day

we'll just look the other way and whistle while some mad scientist's robot stomps on you."

"Or," The Wizard chimed-in, "we'll tell Titan that you've turned into a supervillain, and let *him* stomp on you."

"You'd actually let Titan beat the living snarf out of me!"

The Wizard informed him, "Superheroes don't *'beat the living snarf'* out of supervillains; we *'defeat'* them."

"Same thing!"

"But a nicer word!"

Night-Ghost looked up to Heaven and mumbled, "One guy lost on a girl and the other three are the Marx Brothers! Why couldn't I get a *real* superhero team?"

Chapter 23

Headfirst Into a Fight

Skymaster soared over the treetops, and put the woods behind him. Zooming quickly to the other side of the neighborhood, he approached the huge water tower on the hill above the quiet little community. It was an enormous, silver aluminum tank nearly a hundred feet high, placed among the oldest and largest homes of the neighborhood — those houses that are so big and so antique that they can't help but look haunted. And the surrounding trees, having grown undisturbed for so many long decades, towered high and put those huge houses into continuous shade, only adding to the mysterious effect. But Skymaster wasn't on the prowl for haunting spirits (that's a different adventure altogether), he had business at the water tower.

Standing high above the trees and surrounding homes, the massive aluminum cylinder of a tower looked as if some wandering giant had set down his giant's soda-pop can on the edge of town and forgotten it there.

As the airborne hero closed in on the tower, he saw that the villains were way ahead of him. Their green and silver cargo truck was parked in a gravel alleyway between the tower and the neighboring houses, and Sasquatch Lady and Charlie had already begun their dreadful business. They were hauling their sinister, black drum of mind-control toxin up the long, skinny staircase that circled the side of the structure. Charlie had a welder's torch and fuel tank strapped to his back, so that he could cut his way into the water tower once he and his boss-lady reached the top.

Skymaster came to a stop in mid-air, pulled the walkie-talkie off his belt and hit the talk-switch. "Wizard! I'm at the water tower! They're here! Sasquatch Lady and Charlie are here! They're dragging their barrel of poison up the stairs on the side of the tower!"

The Wizard's voice crackled back through the little speaker: "We're on our way! In the meantime, *you're* going to have to stop them!"

Skymaster didn't bother to hide the panic in his voice as he replied, "Stop them? Me? I'm just 'the scout-ahead-guy'! *Titan* is 'the beat-people-up guy'!"

"Do what you can," was The Wizard's only advice.

Skymaster clipped the radio onto his belt and groaned, "How did I ever get this job?"

Although he wasn't "the beat-people-up guy," he *was* a superhero. So with Maria's words about "launching himself headfirst into a fight" echoing through his brain, he thrust his fists out forward, picked up speed and aimed himself at the criminals on the stairway. He swooped down and rammed into Charlie, knocking him into Sasquatch Lady. Thrown off balance, the teacher, the janitor and the heavy steel canister tumbled and bounced over one another, falling down the narrow staircase. The rattling and clattering of the barrel on the metal stairs was almost as loud as the villains' cries of pain. Though the barrel dropped off that circular stairway and crashed on the ground, the two criminals managed to catch themselves after a few somersaults.

Mrs. F. pointed to the top of the tower and yelled at Charlie, "Get up there, Moppy! Cut the hatch open! I'll get the canister! Now! Move!"

While muttering, "Don't call me Moppy!", the janitor grudgingly headed up to the top of the stairs, while Mrs. F. headed back down. Displaying the sort of inhuman strength that had earned her the name "Sasquatch Lady," the wicked old woman picked up that enormous barrel; and, lugging it on her back, she started marching up the stairs again.

Skymaster landed on a nearby rooftop, leaned back

against the chimney and hummed a tune. He was waiting for Mrs. F. to carry her canister up to the top of the stairway again; then he would launch himself at her and deliver another nasty shove to send her back down to the bottom.

When Charlie had fired-up his cutting torch and Sasquatch Lady had made it to the top of the tower, Skymaster figured it was time to knock his enemies down again. He took to the air and circled the tower a few times to build up speed. Unfortunately, as he came around on his final pass, Sasquatch Lady snatched the torch from Charlie, and waved its hot, blue flame at the flying fifth-grader.

Skymaster yelped in surprise and flailed off course, totally out of control. His foot hit the peak of a rooftop, causing him to flip end over end. Then there followed a tumble down the far side of that steep roof, a painful thump against one of the gables, and he finally dropped off the edge to fall two stories into a shrubbery in the front yard. There was a quick series of snaps and cracks, which were the twigs and branches that broke his fall, but the crash-landing hero was certain it was the sound of his arms, legs and ribs shattering.

And while Skymaster was lying tangled in the shrubbery, looking like an abandoned puppet that had been flung from the window of a passing car, the villains continued their vile handiwork.

Charlie finished cutting through the hatch in the top of the tower, and Mrs. Flembaugh popped open the valve on the sinister barrel. The villains hoisted it high and laughed wildly as they began to pour the serum into the water. Every "glug, glug, glug" of that dangerous toxin sloshing into the town's water supply could be counted as another family that would soon be under Sasquatch Lady's control.

Skymaster knew the situation was grave. However, his midair spin and clumsy tumble over the rooftop had shaken him up more than he had first thought. He tried to remove himself from the shrubbery, but with every motion he discovered that the bruises he had received in the lunchtime war were now bruises-within-bruises.

Then, out of the corner of his eye, he caught a glimpse of something orange and yellow flashing by. It was Titan, running towards the water tower — running faster than a champion racehorse, churning up whirlwinds of dust behind him as he sprinted through the gravel alleyway on his super-muscular legs.

"I'm sure Titan can handle this," Skymaster told himself as he lay there in the bushes. "I'm gonna take a break, and wait for my head to stop throbbing and my muscles to stop spinning... or should that be the other way around?"

Titan skidded to a stop — yes, actually *skidded* — like a speeding car; his heels digging two fifty-foot-long channels in the gravel as he slid to a halt. Rushing to where Skymaster was sprawled in the bushes, he quickly asked, "You OK?"

Skymaster just as quickly replied, "Around the back of the house — at the tower — they're pouring their mind-gunk in the water!"

Titan was off like a shot, leaving his partner where he lay.

And with "the beat-people-up guy" now on the case, Skymaster breathed a sigh of relief. He made his awkward exit from the shrubbery, tussling and thrashing about, as if the greenery were a living thing that refused to release him. He was still stumbling and tripping even after he was fully free of the thing.

Then, as he got his balance and got his cape straightened, he realized that there was an old gray-haired man watching him. This elderly gent looked understandably puzzled to see a kid in a white cape, brown tights and airman's helmet crawling out of his hedges. Having witnessed Skymaster's unsteady steps, the man wondered, "Aren't you a bit young to be drunk?"

" 'Drunk'?" Skymaster took this as a terrible insult. "Superheroes don't get drunk!"

"So you're a superhero?"

"Duh! The mask, the cape, the boots! What did you think?"

"Thought maybe Halloween was here a little early."

Skymaster grumbled to himself, "Do people *really* think that's clever — the Halloween remark?" Then aloud, he proclaimed, "For your information, I'm helping to save the world today — and that includes you, pops! So a little gratitude would be appreciated!"

"Just save the world without messing up my yard, and *that* will be appreciated."

Skymaster waved the old timer off, as if to say, "I don't have time for this," then flung himself up into the air.

Unfortunately, his flying power was malfunctioning, what with the nasty fall he had taken. No sooner had he thrown himself heavenward than he plopped right back down, belly-flopping onto the lawn with a comical thud.

The gray-haired man shook his head and chuckled as he went into his house and shut the door.

The hero on his front lawn shouted at the closed door, "If my flying power hadn't been messed-up by my battle with those supervillains, you would've seen something pretty cool!"

Fearless Force

Chapter 24

The Sinister Canister

A mean snarl had grown on Titan's face. Having seen Skymaster lying painfully in a shrubbery, he had that "reverse-bully" wrath building up inside him. It always brought the strongman's anger bubbling to the surface to see a smaller kid being picked-on — even if the kid was a superhero. With his eyes narrowed in rage, The Fearless Force's muscleman ran straight to the base of the water tower, grabbed the metal stairway and began shaking its framework with all his super-strength.

Up on the top platform, Charlie and Mrs. F. were nearly vibrated right off their feet as the staircase rattled violently. They watched in horror as the nuts and bolts holding their platform to the side of the tower started jiggling loose. Mrs. F. knew that she and Charlie would be shaken right off that platform any moment.

"Throw the canister in!" the teacher shrieked.

They dropped the entire drum of poison through the hole, and heard the echoing splash from inside the great well of water.

Charlie howled, "Now let's get off this stairway before we *fall* off!"

Titan continued to shake the stairs as the villains clambered down, tripping on the last few steps, and sprawling on the pavement at the feet of the grinning hero.

At this point, Night-Ghost, The Wizard, and Aquarius finally caught up with their super-strong partner.

Desperately trying to catch his breath after having chased the fleet-footed Titan across the country-side, Night-Ghost said, "Your mad scheme is at an end, Sasquatch Lady!"

"*You're* the one at an end, Terry, my boy!" she chortled as she rose to her feet. "That barrel is already deep in the town's water supply, fulfilling my 'mad scheme'!"

"We have our aquatic teammate here to get in there and take care of it," said The Wizard as Aquarius took a bow. (OK, Aquarius *didn't* take a bow. He curtsied like a ballerina, weirdo that he was.)

Skymaster joined his friends at this point, still looking a bit shaken.

"You OK?" asked Titan.

"Just had a crash-landing," he replied.

Titan cast a threatening eye upon Mrs. Flembaugh and Charlie, telling them, "I don't like creeps picking on my pals!" Then he tore a long piece off of the metal staircase with a loud squeak and snap of twisting, breaking steel.

Afraid of getting smacked with that chunk of metal, Charlie flinched backward and asked, "What're you gonna do with that?"

"Oh, I just needed something to tie you up with," Titan grinned. Then he gave that steel bar an effortless twist, showing how he could tie it in knots as easily as a normal person might twist a length of rope.

But before he could bind those criminals, a red-hot beam of light cut through the air and zapped the strongman in the hand, forcing him to drop the steel bar. The Fearless Force spun around to see a black sedan parked at the end of the alley. Mr. Morton was seated at the steering wheel, waving a laser-pistol out the driver's side window.

"You kids are in big trouble," Charlie grinned. "The principal's here!"

The laser-pistol-packing principal swaggered out of his car, trying to look as smooth and dangerous as he could. He kept his heat-ray trained on The Fearless Force while he slicked back his hair, straightened his tie, and pulled up his socks.

Aquarius leaned over to The Wizard and muttered,

"Old lizard-lips was looking pretty cool there, until the yanking-up-the-socks part."

The scientist didn't answer back with any comical quip. His eyes were locked on Morton while his hand was carefully removing a pellet from his weapons-belt. An instant later, the young scientist tossed the pellet at the ground, and a huge cloud of blue smoke exploded between the heroes and their principal.

Morton fired several laser-beam shots blindly into the billows of gas, but The Fearless Force had scattered in all directions.

Mrs. Flembaugh's voice hollered out of that blue cloud: "Don't shoot into the smoke, you fool! Charlie and I are in here too!" She stomped out of the smoke and right up to Principal Morton, scolding him harshly: "I have the gnawing fear that I'm going to conquer the world, only to die the next day because of *your* stupidity!"

He cowered in fear from her, and tried to get on her good side by telling her, "At least I remembered to bring my heat-ray this time!"

Still she scowled and gave him the threat that angry grade-school teachers always give: "I hope you brought enough for *everyone!*"

Morton opened the trunk of his car to reveal a miniature arsenal of outlandish weaponry. He handed a strange-looking, fat-barreled rifle to Mrs. F., telling her, "This is a gravity-wave-disrupter. It'll send those heroes flipping in every direction!" Handing an even bigger cannon to Charlie, he said, "This is a thermo-charge-thrower. It launches grenades that pop in fiery little explosions."

Sasquatch Lady instantly switched weapons with Charlie, taking that thermo-charge-thrower for herself, and caressing it as if it were a beloved pet. "I want *this* one! It sounds... *brutal!*"

Now armed with deadly force, the villains went on a superhero-hunt.

And, though none of the residents of that quiet hilltop cul-de-sac knew anything out of the ordinary was occurring in the gravel alleys between their homes, a full-fledged battle to save civilization erupted.

Seeing that fat, silver rifle in Charlie's hands, Night-Ghost immediately shouted, "Wizard! What's that thing Moppy has?"

"Not sure." The scientist looked it over. "It could be a..."

But "not sure" was all Night-Ghost needed to hear. If The Wizard didn't know what the thing was, then there was only one way to find out: to charge at "Moppy" and get him to fire it. So the purple-cloaked hero bolted forward, making unpredictable leaps and handsprings to the left and right as he did so.

But all of Night-Ghost's acrobatics were futile, for Charlie's weapon didn't need to hit the hero *exactly*; he merely needed to aim in the general area. And so he did. Pointing his gravity-wave-disrupter at the rapidly-approaching acrobat, he squeezed the trigger, and a circular, orange blast sprang from the barrel of the weapon: a wave of energy that distorted the world in a wide "zone of madness" all around Night-Ghost. The caped crime-fighter was lifted right up off his feet, and, along with a fair amount of gravel and weeds, he was spun wildly in midair, then thrown clumsily into the chain-link fence that encircled the area.

The Wizard was also knocked off his feet, as he had been just on the outside edge of that pulsating, orange "zone of madness." Flung sideways, he shouted out the solution to Night-Ghost's question: "It's a gravity-wave-disrupter. Do you need a definition, or did Moppy just explain it to you?"

Night-Ghost hopped up on his feet, straightened his cape, and grumbled, "It's been thoroughly explained, thank you."

Now that Charlie knew what his weapon was capable of, he took only enough of a pause to grin an evil grin, then he launched into an all-out attack on The Fearless Force. He fired off one quick shot after another, sending Titan, The Wizard, Aquarius, and again Night-Ghost flipping and crash-landing, and throwing them roughly into one another.

Skymaster figured that, since he was the only one of his team who could "ignore gravity," he would be immune to the effects of a gravity-wave-disrupter. But he discovered, to his unpleasant surprise, that there was no way his flying power could work in a "zone of madness" where gravity was being thrown into chaos. Just like his earthbound friends, he was yanked this way and that by disordered gravity, twirled in confusion and flung against the ground.

"Check it out!" the janitor shouted in fiendish glee. "It even works on the flyin' guy!"

And, of course, the gravity-wave-disrupter wasn't the only danger to dodge! While the heroes were being tossed around like rag-dolls, they still had to be on their guard as Mr. Morton's heat-ray sliced the air with burning beams, and Mrs. F. was launching projectiles from her thermo-charge-thrower. These were shiny, round objects the size of ping-pong balls — grenades that burst into deadly fireballs. A single one would blast a superhero to bits if it ever got too close.

Thus the conflict was in full swing, and the heroes weren't getting in a single punch. They were too busy ducking laser beams, dodging grenades, and being flung around by disrupted gravity.

During this insanity, The Wizard pointed to the top of the water tower and shouted to Aquarius, "Get up there!"

The amphibian's reply was a disbelieving shriek of *"Say what?"*

"Get inside the water tower and close off the valve on that drum of toxin they dropped in there!"

Aquarius looked up the narrow staircase that led up the side of the tower. *"I ain't goin' up that stairway!* The way Titan shook it, it's all ripped loose and nearly falling over! And that's, like, a thousand feet up!"

The Wizard took a quick glance at the top of the water tower. "It's ninety-two feet, seven inches."

"That's way too high for *this* guy!" Aquarius insisted. "The reason I'm a frogman-kind-of-superhero is because water is always, you know, really low. You never have to *climb up* to get to water. It's always at sea-level."

"You're the amphibious member of the team! You go where the water is! Today, the water is in a tower, so you're goin' up into a tower."

"If it's up, then it's *Skymaster's* job!"

The Wizard shouted back, "Skymaster can get up there, but then what's he going to do? He can't swim!" He then rolled his eyes in frustration. "A flier who can't swim and an amphibian who's afraid of heights! What kind of super-team is this?"

Throwing his protests aside, the green-clad water-breather headed for the rickety staircase. "OK, Wiz, I'm on it. But you're only the *second* in command. The moment I get back, I'm reporting you to Night-Ghost! Bein' way too bossy is *his* job!"

So, with thermo-charges popping and heat-rays sizzling all around him, Aquarius hurried up the wobbly staircase on the side of the water tower. Or, rather, it *had* been on the side of the tower until Titan had shaken it loose. Now with its framework unbolted from the tower, it was a dangerously swaying set of stairs that made for a precarious journey up to the top.

Clutching tensely to the railing, Aquarius muttered to himself, "Don't look down, don't look down... I looked down! OK, *that's* a long drop... so *don't* drop, idiot! ... Halfway up... nearly there... don't look d— Oops! I looked down!"

Then, quite abruptly, his panicky climb to the top of the tower went from merely unnerving to downright horrifying. At the halfway point in his climb (which, according to The Wizard's estimation, would have been roughly forty-six feet above the ground) Charlie noticed that Aquarius was headed up the rickety stairway. The criminal janitor aimed his gravity-wave-disrupter at the amphibious hero and pulled the trigger.

Caught in the nature-confounding effect of that weapon, Aquarius was nearly yanked right off that unstable staircase. If not for the fact that he already had a tightly-terrified grip on the railing, he might have been thrown out into the air and dropped to his doom. But he held firmly to that railing, even as gravity went haywire around him and his feet were lifted up over his head.

Of course, he shrieked the loudest and highest note his voice could produce (or *any* voice, really).

At this moment, Aquarius may not seem like much of a hero — first, that he was so frightened to climb that shaky stairway and, second, that he would wail like an infant when the danger got out of hand. But, to his credit (and we can suppose this is what made him "hero material"), he continued his journey to the top of the tower — even though he was still caught in that gravity-interrupting beam of energy. Upside-down with his feet flailing in the air, he clutched tightly to the railing and climbed hand-over-hand, still heading upward…

…and still howling like a baby the whole time. No words; just high-pitched howling.

Finally, the gravity-disruption stopped. (Charlie had four other heroes down there on the ground to worry about.

He couldn't focus on Aquarius forever.) And with the laws of nature returning to normal, Aquarius' feet dropped back down. This was a harrowing moment: the sudden shift in his weight, his body swinging back downward. He had to wrap his arms around the railing to keep from plummeting to his death. Then, at last, he got himself back onto the stairs, caught his breath and took a moment to calm the shaking of his limbs. Continuing upwards, he arrived at the top platform — right where the open hatchway was, which would lead him down into the watery interior of the tower.

Well, actually, the open hatchway wasn't *right* there. It *would* have been if the stairway hadn't been shaken loose and unbolted from the side of the tower. There was, in fact, a space of about four feet between the platform and the side of the tower. Four feet may not seem like much space to cross, but when one is looking down ninety-two feet to the ground, and when one is afraid of heights, a gap of four feet can feel like the Grand Canyon!

Standing on that tiny metal platform (which swayed side to side with his every little move), Aquarius anxiously examined the four-foot chasm he needed to cross, and mumbled quietly to himself, "Don't say, 'Don't look down,' because it always makes you look d— Oops! I looked down!"

Sitting down, for there was no way he could keep his

balance on that swaying platform, he squeezed his flippers on. (They were made to fit right over his tight-fitting superhero boots.) He slid his clear diving mask down over his eyes and stood up slowly and carefully. Then he pulled-in a great big breath and hoped there was a healthy dose of courage mixed in with that oxygen. He hesitated twice (because he was Aquarius), but at last lunged forward (because he was a superhero).

Flying out over the four-foot span of nothingness, he caught a hold on the edge of the open access hatch. His hope was that he could pull himself up and into that hatchway, but when he looked down and saw his flippered feet and then nothing else for ninety-two feet, it sent a panic through him that turned his arm muscles to Jell-O. The best he could manage was to hang there from the open hatch and kick his flippers uselessly against the side of the smooth aluminum tower.

"No, God!" he cried out loudly to the sky. "Please don't let me pee my pants! Not when I'm about to get into the town's water supply!"

Thankfully, he kept control of his bladder (as the best superheroes do). And while he struggled to hoist himself up and into the hatchway, he glanced down again to see Charlie on the ground below him, aiming that gravity-wave-disrupter up at him.

"No, Moppy! I'll never call you Moppy again! Just don't shoot me with that thing!'"

Needless to say, Moppy ignored the desperate appeal of his helpless victim and pulled the trigger.

The gravity-baffling surge of energy instantly surrounded Aquarius, twirling him upside-down. It was all he could do to keep one hand locked tightly on the edge of the hatchway. There was a spit-second of heart-stopping fright as he found himself looking straight down and thought he was being thrown off to his death. But then he found that by having his legs pitched upwards like that it was actually flinging him forward into the open access hatch. To his colossal relief, he was hurled right through the hole and into the water tower.

With the splash of the cool, water all around him, his panic instantly dwindled away. He was finally in his proper element!

Once fully submerged, he activated his miraculous super-power. In a blast of bubbles, he exhaled every bit of air out of his lungs, then inhaled a huge gulp of the water that surrounded him. *[Warning: **DO NOT** inhale water unless you are a fully trained and fully qualified amphibious superhero whose lungs have been modified by some mystical process into fish-like gills!]*

"OK, then!   Where's that drum of mind-control

juice?" He asked this of himself out loud. Now that he was breathing water, he could just as easily talk underwater, and he always loved the weird, garbled and echoing tone of his voice whenever he spoke in that element. (Of course, he didn't have to worry that he was breathing water that was contaminated with mind-control serum, for he already had that evil toxin inside him, as he had eaten it in his lunch at school.)

To be on the inside of that massive water tower was a truly fascinating experience. Imagine a building — a huge, windowless building — flooded nearly all the way to the ceiling with crystal clear water. Of course, it wasn't meant as a place for people to be swimming, so there were no lights at all; for why would anyone light the inside of a water tower? The only light to see by was the single shaft of daylight streaming in through the open hatch far above him; and, even though it was reflecting off the silver aluminum walls, it still wasn't enough to brighten that enormous place. The aquatic adventurer found it rather difficult to see all the way to the bottom of the tank. So he dove deeper into the dimly-lit water, searching for the canister of serum, which must have sunk straight to the floor.

And outside, where the battle was still raging...

Mrs. F. had spent all of her thermo-charges in no time while trying to pick off the all-too-nimble Night-Ghost. The super-acrobat was quite an uncooperative target, refusing to stand still for a moment. When her ammunition was spent, she tossed the thermo-charge-thrower into a nearby trashcan and snatched Morton's heat-ray from him.

"Hey! That's *my* laser-gun!" he whined.

"I have a different job for you," the crazed old woman replied. "Inside the truck you'll find some scuba equipment, a knife and a spear-gun. Get in that water tower, and make sure that the fish-boy never comes out of there alive!"

Morton chuckled, taking delight in this new assignment, and hurried off to get suited up.

Meanwhile, the battle raged on...

Charlie would send the other four members of The Fearless Force flipping through the air with his gravity-wave-disrupter and Sasquatch Lady would try to pick them off with her heat-ray. Thus, the heroes were too busy to stop Mr. Morton as he emerged from the back of the truck in full scuba gear and made his way up the tower stairway.

The villainous principal had a tough time climbing those stairs to the top of the tower. If you'll recall, Aquarius had put his flippers on when he reached the upper platform. Morton wasn't that bright. He had equipped himself completely in his wet-suit and diving gear — *flippers included.* This made him a ridiculous sight as he stumbled his way up the stairs.

Inside that tower, Aquarius had swum to the bottom where he found the drum of serum. He twisted the valve shut, so it wouldn't leak any more of the mind-control poison into the town's water.

He instantly congratulated himself. "Ta-da! The world is safe once again, thanks to the wondrous, weird and wild, water-breathing Aquarius... and his special guests, The Fearless Force!" And imagining that he could hear all of humanity applauding for him and screaming his name, he added, "Thank you, thank you! It was my pleasure, really!"

Just when he thought everything was going fine, he noticed a shadow had crossed the beam of daylight that shone through the open hatch up above.

There was a splash behind him that thundered loud and echoed through the water. He whirled around to see his principal in a frogman suit swimming towards him, a loaded spear-gun in his hand.

Chapter 25

Fishin' Season

Mr. Morton wasted no time pulling the trigger on his spear-gun.

Aquarius screamed and quickly darted to one side as the spear whooshed past his hip, just an inch from skewering his kidney. It was no ordinary spear, but a rocket-powered one with a spinning knife-blade on its tip. And it had one more surprise: just as it zoomed past Aquarius, it exploded.

The villain took aim and fired again.

The green-clad hero dodged this spear, but it was even more dangerously close than the first one. He hadn't been ready for a second spear to come flying at him so rapidly after the first. A normal spear-gun only fires one shot, then needs to be reloaded. But this version in the hands of Mr. Morton was as high-tech as the other weaponry that he and his nefarious cronies had been using. Not only did it shoot rocket-powered, saw-blade-tipped, exploding spears, but it shot them in rapid succession.

As that second buzz-tipped spear zoomed right between Aquarius' legs and exploded behind him, he shrieked, "Yikes! That ain't no normal spear-gun!"

Principal Morton was taking aim again when he suddenly realized the strangeness of what he had just heard. He nearly spat the air-hose out of his mouth as he thought, "A kid who can talk underwater! This is getting weirder and weirder!"

Aquarius noticed the shock in his attacker's eyes and knew exactly what was on the man's mind. "Don't worry! I'm not really talking underwater! What you're hearing is an optical illusion, only with your ears. Is there a name for that?"

Morton fired another rocket-propelled projectile.

"Hey!" Aquarius dodged this miniature torpedo as deftly as the others. "So I don't know what it's called! That's no reason to shoot at me, bub!"

The aquatic crime-fighter darted left, right, up and down, while a flurry of spears zoomed and exploded all around him. In that chaos of fire-and-bubble streams and thundering blasts, he was doing a lot more than just avoiding spears. He was counting, "One alligator, two alligator, three alligator," in an effort to figure something out: How much time was there between the launch of a projectile and its explosion.

When he finally had the timing worked out, he performed a most daring maneuver: He watched a spear come hissing forth from the weapon...

"One alligator..."

...then he ducked to the side, reached out and caught it...

"...two alligator..."

...spun that little torpedo around, and sent it racing right back into the gun-barrel.

"...three alligator!"

Mr. Morton dropped the spear-gun just as it was blown to bits by its own returning projectile.

But that vicious principal wasn't about to call the game lost! He pulled a long, gleaming diver's knife from the sheath on his leg and lunged forward. The villain tried his best to stab, jab or grab his prey, but Aquarius was as agile as a squid; as quick and nimble underwater as Night-Ghost was on dry land.

That aquatic hero figured that if he kept his opponent swimming in circles long enough, the principal would use up all the air in his tanks faster than normal. Morton knew he was never going to get his hands on this slippery amphibian, so he decided to get the barrel of serum opened up and get out.

He took another swing with his knife and let Aquarius duck out of the way. Then the principal swam straight for the canister and banged on the valve, trying to open it.

"No way, pal!" Aquarius latched onto his enemy's air tank, and tried to pull him away from the drum of mind-control serum.

Morton swung his knife around at the bothersome water-breather on his back, but the hero dodged the blade and clung on like an octopus.

"You want me off your back? Fine!" He loosened Morton's weight-belt, pulled it down around the man's ankles, tightened it up, and then swatted the knife from his hand. "It's all over, Mr. M.," he laughed as he dragged his principal back up to the surface.

Once Aquarius' head was above the surface, he blew a steady stream of water out his mouth and started breathing air again. He found that there was a ladder on the inside wall of the water tower leading up to the access hatch through which he had entered. Climbing up, he stuck his head out into the world of daylight and shouted, "OK, I saved the world! Now get me out of here!"

Glancing down to the ground far below, he saw that the battle between his fellow heroes and their enemies was reaching its conclusion...

Mrs. Flembaugh had finally decided on a retreat,

caring little that she was abandoning Morton and Charlie. Leaping behind the steering wheel of her truck, she reached out the window and fired several zaps of her laser-pistol to keep the heroes at bay while she started the engine, spun her wheels in the gravel, and raced off.

Night-Ghost hurried after her, jumping onto the back bumper of the escaping truck and hanging on as it bounced down the alleyway.

Now it was just Charlie who was left to face The Wizard, Titan, and Skymaster, and it wasn't long before Skymaster swooped down and kicked the gravity-wave-disrupter out of the janitor's hands.

With Charlie unarmed, Titan pounced upon his enemy and, with only a fraction of his super-strength, delivered an uppercut to the villain's chin that knocked him unconscious. The orange-clad dynamo picked up the slumbering custodian, dropped him in the nearest trash-bin, and slammed the lid down on him. Then he picked up the gravity-wave-disrupter, crumpled its barrel shut with an easy squeeze of his hands, and dropped the now-useless weapon to the ground.

All was calm.

In this moment's pause, Titan, The Wizard and Skymaster caught their breath; then they heard Aquarius screaming, "Somebody get me outta this tin can!"

So Titan and The Wizard hurried up the water tower's loose staircase. Unlike Aquarius, these two boys were laughing all the way up, clearly amused by the "funhouse" aspect of the side-to-side swaying. Skymaster, of course, took the quicker way up — as only a flying superhero can. They helped Mr. Morton out of the tower, and onto the dangerously unstable platform, which was quite an awkward event, what with him wearing his scuba gear and all. The Wizard restrained his principal with a set of steel-blue handcuffs from his equipment-belt.

As Titan and The Wizard led Mr. Morton back down to the ground, Skymaster lifted Aquarius out of the tower and carried him quickly down to solid earth. Aquarius dug his fingers into Skymaster's shoulders and kept his eyes squeezed shut during this brief act of levitation. He hated these times when his flying teammate would have to transport him from place to place. As he had told The Wizard a few minutes ago: The reason he was a frogman-kind-of-superhero is because water is always really low.

It looked like things were generally under control. Aquarius was on his knees, kissing the ground; Morton was safely in superhero custody; and Charlie was unconscious and stuffed in a trash-bin.

...Actually, that last item on the list wasn't quite accurate. Titan had made a tragic error. He had stuffed Charlie into the same trash-bin where Mrs. Flembaugh had deposited her thermo-charge-thrower. While the heroes were getting Morton and Aquarius back down from the water tower Charlie came to his senses. He found himself upside-down in a rubbish container... with a thermo-charge-thrower right under his head. And, contrary to what Mrs. F. thought, the weapon was *not* useless! It may have been empty of ammunition, but there was a back-up cartridge of an additional two-dozen projectile-charges attached to the top of it. (Whether Charlie knew more than Sasquatch Lady did about thermo-charge-throwers or whether he discovered this by chance is unknown.) He clicked that new ammo-cartridge in place, popped up from his trash-bin, and leveled his weapon at the heroes.

"Don't move, tough-guys!" the criminal janitor grinned. "Me and Morton are getting out of here! Un-cuff him!"

The Wizard just stared at Charlie with an overdone expression of disgust.

"You in the blue helmet!" Charlie waved his thermo-charge-thrower menacingly at the boy-scientist. "I'm talkin' to you, Astro-Boy! Un-cuff him!"

"Alright, I'll do it," the scientist grunted sullenly. "But it's *'Morton and I* are getting out of here,' not 'me and Morton'."

"Shut up and unlock him, wise-guy!"

The Wizard followed the orders of the armed and dangerous custodian, releasing Mr. Morton's hands. Morton scooped up the broken gravity-wave-disrupter (hoping that he could send it in for repairs later), and the two villains fled, disappearing down the street in the principal's car.

Titan hurried in pursuit on his superhuman legs. But, as he was approaching forty miles an hour, Charlie leaned out the passenger-side window with his cannon, firing a projectile that erupted on the pavement just inches away from those speedy, yellow boots. Titan was knocked right off his feet by that fiery little explosion and went for a violent crash-and-roll on the rough roadside while the villains made their getaway.

"Skymaster!" shouted The Wizard (who was officially in command when Night-Ghost wasn't around). "Follow them!"

"I'm on it!" He hopped up into the air. "But I don't think I can keep up at the speed they're driving!"

"Do what you can," replied The Wizard. "But stay up high! They have that grenade-launcher!"

"Looks like we blew it," mumbled Titan as he shambled back to where his partners waited.

"Not so!" answered Aquarius. "I closed that canister tight! Those clowns may have gotten away, but they didn't get away with anything. Night-Ghost's on the back of

Sasquatch Lady's truck, and Skymaster's hot on the heels of Morton's car."

In the middle of saying this, Aquarius activated another of his super-powers: He shook himself in a rapid frenzy, like a dog does after a bath, which flipped all the water off of him and out of his hair. Quicker than it takes to count out three seconds, he was completely dry (or so close to completely dry that "completely dry" isn't much of an exaggeration). This was indeed a necessary power to have if one was to be an amphibious superhero!

The Wizard uncoiled the rope on his equipment-belt. "Come on. We'd better get that barrel out of the city's water. Aquarius, you'll dive back in there and tie this rope around it, and Titan can haul it up through the hatch."

"I ain't goin' up that stairway again!" Aquarius protested. "I'm the man of the hour, not the clean-up crew! And besides, I just dried off!"

A wordless stare from Titan told the amphibian that if he didn't *climb* to the top of the tower, he'd be picked up and *thrown* to the top of the tower. Aquarius quickly ascended the steps, and the "clean-up crew" was in action.

Meanwhile, out on the highway...

That green cargo truck was rumbling along, with the ghastly old woman at the wheel totally unaware that she had a purple-cloaked stowaway crouched on her back bumper. There weren't too many cars on that stretch of road, as this was the part of the highway that circled out through the back country; out past the campgrounds and state parks. So there weren't many motorists to notice that a truck labeled as...

ADELAIDE SCHOOL DISTRICT
FOR OFFICIAL USE ONLY

...had a kid in a purple superhero costume hanging onto its rear.

In fact, of all the cars that the truck passed, Night-Ghost only noticed one driver who spotted him: a woman whose face instantly dropped into a look of shock. The acrobat-hero gave her a snappy salute, and then she was gone — fading off into the distance as Mrs. Flembaugh zoomed forward at double the speed limit. All the other drivers out on the highway that afternoon, were just lost in their boring, everyday thoughts — too busy focusing on the important, grown-up things in their lives to notice an acrobat crime-fighter going about the business of saving civilization.

After riding on that back bumper for a few miles, Night-Ghost climbed up the back of the boxy cargo container, using whatever handholds he could find: the handle of the sliding cargo door, the edge of the container. Any tiny thing he could wrap his tough little acrobat's fingers around was enough for him to hoist himself upwards, until he was crawling across the roof of the cargo box.

When he reached the front, he hopped down onto the roof of the cab. Right below him, in the driver's seat was Mrs. F., still unaware of her uninvited passenger. She clutched the steering wheel in her withered hands, swerving the truck from one lane to the other, snarling at the other cars to get out of her way (and in the most offensive language!). Night-Ghost, untroubled by the left and right lurching of the vehicle, stood steady on the cab's rooftop, and readied himself for his next move: to swing down through the passenger-side window.

Sadly, this maneuver was not to happen.

A small explosion popped in the air next to the hero's head.

With his best "What the devil was *that?*" look on his purple-masked face, he glanced back over his shoulder and saw that there was a car speeding along just behind the truck and driving just as irresponsibly. At the wheel was Mr. Morton — still in his scuba gear, of course. Charlie was in the backseat, with both his left and right windows open, so he could lean out either one of those windows with his thermo-charge-thrower — the weapon that was currently aimed right at Night-Ghost.

As that car veered to the right and started pulling up

next to Sasquatch Lady's truck, the villainous old woman looked over and saw her two henchmen there, speeding along beside her.

Morton rolled his window down and hollered, *"The purple moon-man's on your roof!"*

Before Mrs. F. could react to this news, Night-Ghost was snapping into action. He dropped off the roof and down onto the left-hand side of the truck cab — and not a moment too soon, as Charlie fired-off another miniature bomb in his direction.

As Night-Ghost hung there on Sasquatch Lady's side-view mirror, he looked up to see her worst expression of shriveled rage scowling down upon him. She rolled her window down, and snarled, *"You?* I'll teach you what happens when you hitch rides with the wrong people!"

Sticking her heat-ray-pistol out the window, she fired a blast of searing-hot energy, which he skillfully dodged, while at the same instant bashing the weapon out of her hand. That deadly item went bouncing off into the distance; just another lost article lying on a highway somewhere.

As Mrs. F. jabbed her arm out to get a hold of Night-Ghost, he swung on the side-view mirror and flung himself up onto the hood of the truck. As he stood up to run up to the roof again, she jostled her steering wheel, which swung the truck violently side-to-side. This time, the cloaked acrobat wasn't as surefooted as he had been before. This time, he was in mid-run when she jerked the truck back and forth.

He was falling off, heading straight for the hard concrete of the highway, but he managed to slap his left hand onto the top edge of the truck's cargo compartment. This was only a temporary salvation, for the moment he grabbed onto the slick, metal corner of the truck's roof, he felt his fingers beginning to slide off.

Glancing downward, he saw his feet dangling over the blurred pavement that raced below. He tried to get his right hand up to the roof's edge, but the more he tried to reach up with his right hand the more he lost his grip with his left. He gritted his teeth and growled at the top of his lungs — straining every muscle in his body to keep his painful, three-fingertip hold. All the while, Mrs. F. was swerving the truck back and forth to try and shake him loose.

The squealing of tires ripped through the air, and the hero glanced to the rear of the truck. To his horror, he saw the black sedan with Morton and Charlie racing around behind Sasquatch Lady's truck and motoring up quickly on the side where he was hanging.

"Oh, boffo!" (Yes, it seems Night-Ghost *only* used this phrase sarcastically.)

The principal's sedan was now right across from him,

and Charlie aimed his thermo-charge-thrower directly at the white crescent moon on the hero's chest.

Night-Ghost's hand slid down to a two-fingertip grip...

Charlie slowly squeezed the trigger...

The acrobat's two little fingers finally gave up and slipped off the edge of the roof.

Chapter 26

The Ravine

As Night-Ghost fell from the truck, he slammed his heels into the side of the truck's enormous cargo box. The huge, steel-panel wall vibrated like a gong and launched him out towards Morton's car.

Seeing as how Charlie was leaning out the window of that car, Night-Ghost wrapped himself around the man's shoulders, and clung desperately to him while hanging over the highway. But, even though he was clasped onto the janitor for dear life, the acrobatic hero was still clever enough to knock the thermo-charge-thrower out of Charlie's hands, and send it clattering off into the distance behind them.

Idiot that he was, Charlie wasn't wearing a seatbelt, so when that nimble hero latched onto him the janitor was hauled halfway out the window. The two of them hung out over the road as Charlie pleaded frantically, *"Get him offa me! He's pullin' me outta the car!"*

Morton and Mrs. Flembaugh got the same diabolical idea at the same instant: If they scraped the sides of their vehicles together, they would squish Night-Ghost between them — as if he were a blob of jelly in a steel sandwich. (Of course this meant that Charlie would be squished between the car and the truck right along with Night-Ghost, but neither Mr. Morton nor Mrs. F. seemed to care about Charlie's fate.) So, the principal jerked his steering wheel to the right, the teacher jerked hers to the left, and the car and truck moved quickly towards each other.

Just before the thudding impact of the collision, Night-Ghost grabbed onto the truck's side-view mirror and swung himself back up onto the hood. He hopped onto the roof of the cab, then up onto the top of the huge cargo bin. Charlie narrowly missed a squishing as he crawled back inside the car and screamed at Morton, "Are you tryin' to kill me?"

With the acrobat on her roof again, Mrs. Flembaugh hit the accelerator and a blast of black smoke swirled behind them. The engine roared and the truck's speed doubled. The wind blew past Night-Ghost so fast that he could barely breathe. He lay down flat and tried to hang on, although there was nothing to hang onto. The roof of that cargo compartment was just a big, flat, smooth surface.

"Has she no concept of a speed limit?" he groaned.

The truck kept picking up speed and Morton's car vanished in the distance far behind. The escape-artist clinging to the top began to slide slowly across that smooth roof — sliding closer and closer to the rear of it, no matter how much he struggled to crawl forward. As the truck bounced and jarred him, he felt his feet fall off the back end of the cargo compartment, and he knew that the rest of him would follow any second.

Then the driver's door flew open, and Sasquatch Lady let out a shrieking laugh as she jumped from the cab. Glancing over his shoulder, Night-Ghost saw his teacher hit the ground, rolling in the gravel on the roadside. Then she stood up, completely unhurt, and shook her fist at him.

A leap like that from a speeding truck would've killed any normal person. A shiver went up Night-Ghost's spine as he thought, "She *can't* be human!"

With no one at the steering wheel, the truck was left to veer off at random, ignoring the highway's twists, turns, and painted caution-lines. It rocked and lurched as it broke through a guardrail, careened over a steep drop-off, and nose-dived into a valley. It pitched forward, catapulting Night-Ghost off the roof and out into the air. As he sailed through space, he saw a tree-filled ravine spread out hundreds of feet below him.

He spun like a rag-doll into the whirling green blur

and reached out desperately, hoping to catch a hold on a branch or *anything* to break his fall.

But something caught *him* instead.

"Gotcha, boss!" said Skymaster, flying down from above and wrapping his arms around Night-Ghost.

Though the flying hero had saved his escape-artist partner from a fatal fall, they were going too fast, and Night-Ghost was too heavy a burden for Skymaster to keep control of their flight. They spiralled wildly through the sky, smacked into the treetops, then went bumping and scraping through the snapping pine branches. Finally, they crashed into the hillside and rolled to a stop in the dirt.

The truck had hit the bottom of the ravine before them in a deafening confusion of crashing, groaning, and shattering sounds. It now lay silently on its side in a cloud of dust and leaves.

Night-Ghost stood up and straightened his starry cape. "Nice save. Thanks."

"No prob." Skymaster put his own cape in order and brushed away the pine needles that covered him. "What's next?"

"We find some clues in that wreck." Night-Ghost ran to the ruined truck, crawled in through the driver's side window, and began searching the cab.

Skymaster wondered to himself, "Doesn't he take a

breather after a near-miss like that?"

Night-Ghost emerged from the wreck with a morning newspaper, which must have been a clue of some sort, because he did that Sherlock Holmes thing of saying, "Hello! What's this?"

"You didn't have to go over a cliff on top of a truck to get a newspaper. You can get one of those anywhere."

"One with a big, red circle around an article like this one?" Night-Ghost showed him a page of the paper and, sure enough, there was an article circled with red ink.

Skymaster read the article with growing interest...

Mayor Lane to appear at local elementary school

He mumbled the rest to himself and stopped partway through. "This is *our* school! The mayor of Adelaide is going to be at our school tonight!"

Night-Ghost's voice took on a grave tone. "If Sasquatch Lady slips her serum to Mayor Lane and gets control of his mind, she'll have control of the city. Next it'll be senators, congressmen, military leaders... the president..."

Skymaster went on, "Then it'll be the Queen of England! The Pope! The Emperor of China! She'll be in control of the whole world!" (If The Wizard had been there he could have informed them that China doesn't have an emperor anymore, but neither one of these two knew any better.) "This is starting to look seriously ugly!"

Night-Ghost's eyes narrowed to a look of grim concern. "We're putting an end to this dastardly scheme *tonight!* While Mayor Lane is giving his speech, we'll be down there in the boiler room making sure that Sasquatch Lady's machine never transmits another mind-controlling command! Go find the rest of The Fearless Force. Tell them they need to assemble at HQ again at seven-thirty."

Skymaster took a step and was about to fly away when Night-Ghost stopped him, adding, "But first... how 'bout a lift home?"

His flying partner gladly complied: "All aboard for Fearless Airlines!"

A piggyback ride is a fairly normal thing among childhood playmates. So things certainly looked ordinary as Night-Ghost jumped on his friend's back, and Skymaster hooked his arms around his passenger's legs. But a moment later, the boy in the pilot's helmet gave a shove of his mysterious levitating energy, carrying himself and his captain high into the air.

Night-Ghost — like just about any ten-year-old — burst out with a holler of delight to feel the wind on his face and see the trees shrink rapidly below him. The pair had travelled in this manner quite frequently on their many crime-fighting capers, and Night-Ghost never failed to remind him, "You have the coolest power *ever!*"

Though it's always nice to do a friend a favor, Skymaster couldn't help thinking how much nicer it had been that afternoon to share his sky with you-know-who!

Fearless Force

Part 3

From Afternoon into Evening

(A Security Breach and Some Hidden Truths Revealed)

Chapter 27

All-Too-Human

Although Maria had missed out on that ruckus at the water tower, she was about to get herself back into the adventure in a big way. In order to tell her story it's necessary first to step backward in time a little ways — back to just a short while after Skymaster had left her in the wilderness behind her house.

Every Tuesday and Thursday meant ballet class for Maria. She was normally an excellent student, but today her mind was on wilder adventures than practicing her pliés and arabesques. (If you'd care to know what those are, just go ask the nearest ballerina.) Her dance instructor, Mrs. Salter, was quick to point out every misstep: "Focus, Miss Fuente! Do it again! Pay attention, Maria! Do it again! Where is your brain, girl? Do it again!"

Regardless of this harsh instruction, Maria had always felt like a fairy princess at her dance lessons. Dressed in her pale pink ballet tights, and a ribbon of a similar shade gathering back her enormous mounds of black hair into a ponytail, she always enjoyed this art of floating gracefully — even though it was difficult labor to learn all those proper pliés and arabesques. (You still need to go ask a ballerina what those are, don't you?) However, there was no "fairy princess" feeling today. It was just fifty minutes of an old lady yelling and a clock ticking far too sluggishly.

Somewhere out there in the world five boys were battling evil and having the time of their lives — dressed like lunatics, to be sure, but still having the time of their lives.

When those fifty slow minutes finally crawled into the past, she doffed her pink fairy princess attire and threw on the perfect costume for a wide-open summer afternoon: careless, comfy sweatpants, sneakers that looked like they'd been around the globe several times, and a well-worn rock-band t-shirt from a concert she hadn't been to. And standing on the sidewalk outside the dance studio, she waited for her father to show up. All the while, she was terribly confused. Should she sigh a weary sigh for having uselessly frittered away most of the afternoon? Should she pace and fidget, knowing that there might be more adventures on her horizon?

Maria's parents — both busy psychologists — had carefully arranged their schedules so that Dr. Fuente (Mrs.)

could be home to take Maria to ballet practice and Dr. Fuente (Mr.) could pick her up afterwards. And when her father's station wagon pulled up outside the dance studio, Maria couldn't jump into it fast enough.

Before Mr. Fuente could ask, "How was ballet?" or "How was the first day of school?", Maria asked him, "Where would I find a superhero?"

A strange question, he thought, coming from his daughter, who had never shown any interest in such things, but he answered it all the same: "In the pages of a comic book."

"No, I mean a *real* superhero."

"There's no such thing."

"Well, if there *were*, where would I find one?"

There was a tiny sigh of exasperation from her father. This question seemed to be beneath his dignity. "Oh, I don't know." He gave a fussy tug on his wide necktie, as if to draw attention to that "serious person's article of clothing" (although the very wide neckties of the 1970s drew attention without any help!).

"I just figured that, since you're a boy, you might—"

"I'm a man, dear, not a boy — a man with a Ph.D." (That's an official title given to someone who has studied quite deeply any sciences of great consequence.) "I don't read comic books anymore."

"But you did at one time, right?"

"Yes; long ago. I certainly don't recall much about them." This topic of nonsense put a crinkled map of frustration on his forehead. "When did you acquire a taste for comic book superheroes?"

"Some boys I met at school are really into them — and I mean *really* into them!"

" 'Some *boys'*?" he asked in a teasing way. Now that he realized the significance of the subject, he was sorry he had been such a spoilsport about it. Much more eager to be of help now, he searched the volumes of his memory for anything he could recall about superheroes. "Well, the way you'd normally find a costumed crusader for justice is to get into danger — you know, fall off a building or something."

Overjoyed that her father was finally proving useful in this area, she urgently prodded him for better information: "What if he's already saved me? How do I find him again?"

"In that case, you'll have to be pretty sneaky," he advised with a wink. "Their secret identities are *extremely* vital! They usually have a hidden lair somewhere — at the North Pole, or on a satellite in orbit, or in an underground cavern. It takes some cunning detective work to find a superhero's HQ."

The wheels in her mind began turning at full speed.

Yes! There *had* to be a secret base that The Fearless Force shared, and she was determined that *somehow* she was going to find it! (She just hoped it wasn't at the North Pole or in orbit!)

The moment her father's car had pulled into the driveway at home, she leapt out, saying, "I'll be back in time for dinner," and raced off to begin her search for The Fearless Force's secret HQ.

But where was she supposed to begin looking? She knew the real names of four of the five heroes — but only their first names. And she had no idea where any of them lived.

When this depressing realization came to her, she stopped in her tracks. One second ago she had been exploding with energy, rushing enthusiastically into another adventure. Now she was standing motionless on the sidewalk, drooping like a wilted houseplant, looking bewildered and defeated.

Shielding her eyes from the sun, she looked up. That blue sky was so far away, so untouchable. She *couldn't possibly* have been floating through it a couple of hours ago. She didn't belong in it. Nobody did but the birds.

She sighed. "Maybe it *was* all in my imagina—"

An itty-bitty, boy-shaped speck suddenly launched out of the woods like a silent missile. (It was, of course,

Skymaster, and this was right at the point when he was racing off on his scouting mission to the water tower.)

Maria's heart jumped. And, just like that, she once more believed in the impossible!

That airborne crime-fighter was flying so straight and true — like an arrow shot from the bow of a warrior-god — he *had* to be charging into some sort of mind-boggling danger!

Following that flying hero, Maria was soon tangled in the thick forest where dusty pathways ended in waist-high underbrush. Backtracking and choosing different turns where the trails split, she still wound up in dead-ends overgrown with briars. Climbing up on a fallen tree, she scanned the green confusion that surrounded her.

Off in the distance, she could see a flurry of colorful forms racing through the forest — purple, blue, and bright green, with a swift blur of yellow and orange at the lead. These flashes of color were the rest of The Fearless Force hurrying off to join Skymaster. Knowing every path of this wilderness, those four adventurers zigzagged swiftly through the greenery and disappeared over a ridge. And all Maria could do was watch them sprint out of sight.

She had never in her life felt so ordinary...

...so held down by gravity...

...so human.

Chapter 28

Intruder in the Dark

Maria kept searching those woods through the remainder of that sunny afternoon. Even though The Fearless Force were long gone, and most surely in the midst of their newest crime-fighting case, she wanted to find the path that had taken them over the ridge and out of sight (just so she'd feel like she had accomplished *something*). After a long expedition, she succeeded in finding the dusty path that wended its way through the ferns and undergrowth.

"There's the path. But, whoop-de-doo and big stinkin' deal! I can't possibly catch up to The Fearless Force!"

After this groan of disappointment, she decided to shamble homeward. She lost her way and found her way several more times, until she left the forest behind and was back on her own street.

Kicking off the vines that were looped around her legs, and carefully extracting the sticker vines that had latched onto her t-shirt and sweatpants, she slowly wandered down her avenue. Dropping one last length of briar-vine on her front porch, she dragged herself into the house, slouching, depressed and all in a shambles from her wasted time of ripping through the wilds. When her mother questioned her about her untidy appearance, she answered with a feeble sigh, "I was sort of playing a sort of hide-and-seek sort of game... sort of. And I sort of wasn't very good at it."

Mrs. Fuente gave her daughter a loving caress on her wilderness-smudged face. "You can tell us all about it at dinner. Now go wash-up, and change out of those filthy clothes."

While soaping away the fraction of forest that she had brought home on her hands and face, she stared sternly into the bathroom mirror and told her reflection, "The Fearless Force's headquarters is out there in the woods somewhere, and you're going to find it! And you'll be with them on their next mission, whether they know it or not — whether they *like* it or not!"

These notions fueled her enthusiasm, and when, as commanded, she changed out of her filthy clothes, she dressed in something that would be just as adventure-ready. She pulled-on some tattered blue-jeans, and a pink butterfly-design shirt that was cute when she got it last year, but was now worn enough that she didn't care if it got too close to a laser beam or an explosion. She might have put on her same ragged and dirty sneakers that had trudged all over the woods, but chose instead some sneakers that were nearly as beat-up as her others. (They didn't look like they had been around the world, but they did look like they had crossed North America two or three times.) As she tied them on, she reminded herself, "I wouldn't *want* to be a superhero! Imagine! Having to go into every adventure in the same clothes day after day!"

Then she hurried to the dinner table, where she was determined to eat whatever was put in front of her as quickly as possible. When there were battles against evil to attend, who would be foolish enough to argue about eating broccoli?

So she sat down at the kitchen table and chomped down her dinner in a wild frenzy. Much to her parents' surprise, she didn't try to strike a bargain whereby she could leave her broccoli uneaten. Instead, she just bravely shoveled it in and asked them, "How does a person fly?"

Her all-too-sensible father responded with an all-too-sensible solution: "They go to the airport and buy an airline ticket."

This logic in no way satisfied her. "How do they fly *without* an airplane?"

"No one can do that." Mr. Fuente was very firm on this point.

"What if I've *seen* someone fly?"

Her mother chimed in, "They tricked you, dear."

"Yes," her father explained, "they used ropes or wires or a jetpack."

Her mother added, "If people could fly we would have heard about it by now."

Maria still rejected their logic. "Maybe a person could fly but keep it a secret."

"Nope." Mr. Fuente was quite definite. "Someone would look up and see this flying person, and there you go — the secret would be out." Then he linked his fingers, leaned his elbows on the table, and drew upon his studies as a psychologist to tell her, "There are people who *think* they can fly, but it's really just mental illness. Once we discover the *reason* that they got such a wrongheaded idea, we can cure them of it."

Mrs. Fuente wondered, "If a person could fly, why would they need to keep it a secret?"

To which Maria sheepishly replied, "So... you wouldn't cure them of it?"

There was a short silence while the two grown-up doctors of psychology thought this over. Then Mr. Fuente mumbled, "Nonsense," and that was the end of the discussion.

Mere minutes later, Maria had scraped up the last of her dinner, gotten her "Be home by nine o'clock" warning, and was gone. With the closing of the front door behind her, she was out of the place where superheroes were "mental illness," and free in the world where they were "as real as real gets."

The horizon was dimming with the faintest traces of dusk as evening was beginning its creeping advance. Maria stood out on the sidewalk where earlier that day she had spotted Skymaster sailing in an arc over the trees. She drew an imaginary line across the sky that marked his journey.

If he had lifted off from Fearless Force HQ (which she was banking on), then the start of her imaginary line would be the location of that very HQ.

Keeping this point in sight, she ran straight for it. Climbing over a neighbor's back fence she went thrashing through the wilderness again.

Once in the depths of the woods, she trudged forward, trusting that she was onto something big with this hunch of hers. She looked upward into the trees (in case the heroes had a tree-house headquarters); and down at her feet (for they could just as easily have an underground fort with a doorway hidden in the dirt).

The day was dimming and the shadows between the trees were rapidly thickening into a clotted, impenetrable darkness. Soon it would become near-to-impossible to spot any sort of secret hideaway.

Then, at long last...!

High overhead, she could only just barely see a rectangular shape mingled in the silhouettes of branches and leaves. That had to be it — the tree-house held high in the branches of three sturdy alders. Without a moment's hesitation, she grabbed the nearest branch and hoisted herself upward. Then it was up through a trap door and into the place she went.

She could hardly make out anything through the gathering gloom, but she could see well enough to be vastly impressed. Seeing that perfectly-built headquarters, and comparing it to the rickety shacks that most kids build in trees, she could only think, "Of course it's expertly constructed! I would expect nothing less from these guys!" There were openings — windows without windowpanes — on three of the four sides, and a door that led to an outside platform, where a ladder extended up to the rooftop.

Most of the room inside was taken up by a round table with five wooden chairs around it. And this was the only thing that looked out of place, for those chairs didn't match one another — each one being in a different shape and style; each painted a different color. So, even though the headquarters itself was perfectly built, at least the *furniture* looked like children had put it together!

Wall compartments and shelves all around were filled with various items — among them a flashlight, which Maria was delighted to find. It was a huge, heavy camper's flashlight that lit up the whole place when she clicked it on. Now she could see this superhero base in all its glory. There were maps covering every wall, which gave an air of authority to the place, even though it still was a tree-house. At the same instant it was both a place where super-powered guardians gathered to discuss the protection of civilization, and a place where ten- and eleven-year-old boys gathered to trade comic books.

Now with the light on, she discovered that those five mismatched chairs weren't a sloppy, childish touch at all. Each was carefully painted to match a particular hero — orange for Titan, blue for The Wizard, and green for Aquarius. The other two were very detailed — Skymaster's had a white cloud pattern all over it, and Night-Ghost's was purple with white stars to match his cloak.

The compartments on the walls were labeled for the items stowed in them:

Maps & Charts.
More Maps & Charts.

Walkie-talkies, Telescopes & binoculars.

Night-Ghost's books. (These were things such as *True Ghost Stories,* and an *Encyclopedia of Witches, Demons and Spirits.*)

The Wizard's books. (These were all thick volumes meant for college professors — *Atomic Physics, Essays on Nuclear Radiation*, and the like.)

The Wizard's Gadgetry. (This was a shelf the length of an entire wall, crowded with radio components, wires and boxes of transistors. Some of these items looked like inventions that the team's scientist was working on; others appeared finished, though Maria couldn't even guess at what they might be.)

Aquarius' Junk. (This shelf contained a radio/tape-player, some Beatles cassettes, and a pack of playing cards. Apparently, he didn't have any extra needs as a superhero. The diving mask and swim-fins he carried with him were enough.)

Titan's Stuff. (This held a few comic books, a dog-eared science fiction novel, and a jar of beef jerky. These relatively useless items told of a hero who needed nothing other than the energy in his fists and his do-gooder's heart.)

Lastly, she found the most interesting shelf of all:

Skymaster's Flute.

This struck her as very amazing. (And on a day like this one, a thing had to be *particularly* noteworthy to be amazing.) Most kids only know the simplistic pop music on the radio. But because of her background in ballet, Maria had a better understanding of music than your average ten-year-old kid. She was very familiar with the likes of Mozart and Stravinsky. The fact that Skymaster could play such a complex and beautiful instrument as the flute made him all the more mysterious to her. No, that "sad hero" *wasn't* a robot. He had a soul as complex and beautiful as that flute, even if he was too serious to smile.

Then, underneath that flute, she noticed something on Night-Ghost's shelf: Wedged between *Unsolved Disappearances* and *Mysterious & Unexplained Sightings,* she discovered a spiral-bound notebook. Carefully sliding it out a little ways, she saw written on its cover...

Night-Ghost's Journal

She had actually hunted down this tree-house in hopes of meeting The Fearless Force, and coaxing them into letting her go on an adventure. She hadn't planned to be nosey, but this was too good to pass up!

First looking over each shoulder to make extra-sure that she wasn't being observed, she pulled her shirt-sleeve around her hand (so she wouldn't leave any fingerprints), and removed the journal from its place. Laying it on the table and sitting in Skymaster's chair (she liked that one the best), she opened the notebook to a random page, and found herself in the middle of a wild adventure...

...The bomb was about to go off, but I had nowhere to dispose of it. I was really starting to sweat, and I remember yelling, "Some days you just can't get rid of a bomb!" The pounding at the door was getting louder and I'm pretty sure I only had about twenty seconds left...

Maria figured, "It's a diary! Then it should tell somewhere in here *how* they all got their powers, and who Skymaster really is!" (It was so exciting that she suddenly didn't feel nosey at all. No, she felt more like "Maria Fuente: Girl Detective!") She flipped back to the inside front cover of the journal and found scribbled there...

The Fearless Force timeline.

AUGUST 2: I become Night-Ghost.

AUGUST 8: Skymaster learns to fly, He and I team up.

AUGUST 17: Titan and The Wizard get their powers, and they AGREE TO team up with Skymaster and me.

AUGUST 21: Aquarius gets his powers, But we don't know him Yet.

AUGUST 27: Aquarius moves into the neighborhood. He gives us each $5, so we let him join. Plus, he invented the name "Fearless Force."

Well, it was fairly interesting to discover that Night-Ghost had been a solo superhero for a week or so before teaming up with Skymaster, and *then* the others joined in. And it was also interesting that Night-Ghost had been a superhero the longest, and that was for only a single month. Furthermore, it was funny to discover that Aquarius had to *buy* his way onto the team!

All that aside, it wasn't very enlightening in regards to the actual source of the boys' super-powers, or the secret identity of Skymaster. So she quickly began at page one, where the story portion of the journal began...

It's rather embarrassing to admit it, but before becoming Night-Ghost I was actually afraid of the dark. This was back in August that I—

That's as far as she had gotten when a voice whispered in her ear...

"Boo!"

Fearless Force

Chapter 29

Hypnotic Eyes of Purple,
Hypnotic Eyes of Brown

That simple joke of a "Boo!" nearly scared Maria right out of her skin. Springing up in a panic, she toppled backwards over her chair, and crash-landed in the corner of the room. As her heart pounded like a locomotive engine, she looked up to see Night-Ghost staring down on her.

With his cloak gathered around him and draping down almost to the floor, he peered out from under his shadowy hood in the fashion of some ancient holy mystic. (If ancient holy mystics ever wore purple, that is.) He scolded the intruder: "This isn't a library, you know."

"Um... well... I... um..." Maria was quite understandably at a loss for an excuse. "I'm not normally a nosey person — I swear!"

He smirked slightly. "But here you are, going through my private journal." Closing the notebook, he returned it to its place on the shelf.

"It was kind of an investigation. I've decided to call myself Maria Fuente: Girl Detective."

A grin appeared on his face, but he ordered it to be gone. "You still know my secret identity, don't you?"

She nodded. "Your name's Terry."

"How did you overcome the hypnotic spell I put on you?"

"I didn't. You just told me to forget that I saw you without your mask. But I already knew you were Terry, because, at lunch, I saw the purple cape in your book-bag. That's why I took it and ran. I didn't want Eddie Thigpen to see it."

"Well, I *do* appreciate that. But I still have to hypnotize you again."

"Why can't I know who you are? I could help you on your adventures... maybe?" She had begun this very boldly, asking the first question with a strong-minded upward tilt of the head. But two words into the second question she had started to feel foolish. By the time she arrived at the ending "maybe," it was a timid whisper.

He actually considered her requests before responding grimly, "No. Sorry. That's just not possible. I know what we do looks like fun and games to you, but... Well, take today for example. There were lasers and explosives everywhere. I nearly got squished on the highway, then I was on top of a truck when it went over a cliff. It's serious business."

Maria was instantly all agog. *This* was just the sort of adventure she had hoped to find! Scrambling up off the floor, she set Skymaster's chair aright, sat down and urgently pleaded, "So tell me! What happened?"

The hero pulled back his hood and took his seat across the table from her. "Look, you know too much as it is."

"Just your secret identity. But why can't I know what you've been up to?" He was still reluctant to talk about his day's dangers, so she struck a bargain: "You tell me where you guys were rushing off to, and then I promise I'll sit nice and quiet and let you hypnotize me."

He didn't believe for an instant that she'd happily submit to hypnosis. But she had really turned on the charm in those big, brown eyes of hers. He may have been too serious about fighting crime to waste time with romancing girls, but he was still a boy. He couldn't bring himself to refuse her request. "We were headed for the water tower up on the hill..."

And with that opening, Night-Ghost launched into a retelling of the afternoon's adventure. All the while, Maria sat with hungry ears taking-in every syllable. She was spellbound by each flying punch and thermo-charge; entranced by each close call and peril-upon-peril. Yet, even while listening eagerly, she was churning in misery that she had missed it all.

As for Night-Ghost, it wasn't long before he wasn't just retelling the day's events but *acting them out.* Though he had begun his tale as blandly as a voice reading a radio news report, by the middle of it he was waving his arms wildly, striking every action pose, and adding in every sound effect from screeching tires to the zip-zap of heat-ray-beams. Having always written these capers in his journal, it was a new and exciting experience to have a live audience.

Upon the conclusion of this tale, which any "reasonable" mind would consider totally ridiculous, Maria sank in her chair with a sigh. "I missed *everything!*"

"You're *supposed* to miss everything, Miss Fuente." He was using that super-serious superhero voice again, for the time had come to hypnotize her. Turning his purple, star-covered chair around, he sat backwards on it, leaning on the back, and locking his gaze straight into hers. "Now, look into my eyes."

She did as he instructed. But just as his eyes began to glow with their supernatural, violet light, she closed her eyes (and, just for good measure, covered them with her hands). "Wait! I changed my mind!"

He groaned in frustration.

With her hands still clamped over her closed eyes, she asked, "What's wrong with me knowing your secret identities?"

"Because there's nothing so important to a superhero as— ...Hang on. Did you say, 'secret *identities'*— as in *more than one?*"

As guilty as can be, she peeked out between her fingers with one eye and fumbled for a response. "Um... I... um... meant that *if* I knew..." She surrendered to her mistake and spat out the whole truth: "OK, OK! I know that The Wizard is really Peter, Titan is his big brother Doug, and Aquarius is that weird friend of yours, Curtis!"

Night-Ghost jumped from his chair and paced angrily on the meager bit of open floor that was available in that tiny tree-house.

Since the annoyed superhero was saying nothing, Maria broke the awkward silence by half-jokingly asking, "So what's *Skymaster's* real name?"

Night-Ghost finally spoke: "No one's ever guessed our secrets like this! And we've been fighting crime since—"

She playfully interrupted: "Since a month ago. Well, all of you weren't together until the end of August, when Aquarius joined the—"

"Stop that!" He clenched his fists and snarled to think that someone had picked his team apart so easily. Then, with a fresh determination, he planted himself in his chair again. "This is ending right here and now!"

"The whole secret-identity-thing is just silly!" Again, she hid her eyes from the hypnosis he was about to activate. "If superheroes are so keen on helping people, why not let everybody know who you are and where you live? That way, if someone's in trouble and they need a super-strong guy or a guy who breathes water, or whatever, they can just walk right up and knock on your door."

He was irritated that he had to explain it, but he did so anyway: "If our enemies know where to find us, they'll blow up our homes and our families. I have a mom and a dad to protect, you know."

"Oh." Maria was pretty embarrassed to have asked such a dunder-headed question.

"And that's why *you* can't know our real names or faces," he explained. "If someone found out that you knew, it would make you a target."

Again his eyes glowed; again she covered hers.

"You promise you won't wipe out any *other* memories of mine?"

"I'm just going to make it so you don't remember my secret identity — *or* Peter's, *or* Doug's, *or* Curtis's."

"Good," she replied (still covering her face). "Because I flew with Skymaster today, and I don't ever, ever, *ever as long as I live* want to forget that!"

Reaching out and taking her hands away from her face, he asked, "When did you go flying with Skymaster?"

"He flew me home from school," she answered innocently. "Remember? It was *your* order for him — to make sure I got home safe."

Of course, Night-Ghost *hadn't* given Skymaster any such order. But the purple-cloaked hero was clever enough to figure out the truth: Skymaster had made up that fib of a "mission," just as an excuse to take the girl of his dreams for a trip through the heavens. Night-Ghost wasn't the least bit vexed that his flying partner had perpetrated such a ruse. He would have shouted, "Way to go, Skymaster!", if it wouldn't have given anything away. Instead, he just held down his grin and mumbled, "Oh, yes, the order to fly you safely home. I forgot about that. Busy day, you know."

"OK." She sat up straight in her chair, and looked right at him. "If I get to remember my flight with Skymaster and all the other weird things that happened today, then you can go ahead." She finished-up with a cunning smile, adding a little warning: "But I'm going to find out your names all over again — *Skymaster's included* — because I'm Maria Fuente: Girl Detective, and I'm going to be right there with you on your next adventure!"

Like a bucket of cold water on a campfire, he snuffed out her enthusiasm with a gloomy comment: "Miss Fuente, don't take this as an insult, but I'm going to make extra-sure that we don't cross paths with you again."

And the sparks of purple in his eyes glowed brighter and brighter still.

In her panic to hold onto her memories for a few more minutes, she proposed a quick deal: "Let me ask three questions! Just three questions, then I *swear* I'll go straight into a trance!" She faked a comical sleepwalking spell with her arms outstretched and a drone of "I will obey you, master."

"*One* question," was all he would agree to.

"*Two* questions!" was her next bid.

He settled for this. "OK, two. But nothing I am sworn never to reveal!"

"Great. Two questions. Um..." She had whipped-up this deal quite impulsively. She hadn't gone so far as to think of any questions. She figured, "You probably won't tell me Skymaster's secret identity."

"Nope," he affirmed.

"Dang," she grumbled. "I wanted to know that — just for two minutes. Knowing all five names — it's like collecting a whole set of something."

"Come on. Question number one. Make it good."

She thought and thought, until she had finally wrung a question out of her brain: "When you have me in a trance, are you..." (Her smile spread out wide as she tortured him by making him wait for the second half of the question!) "...are you going to kiss me?"

He sprang from his chair and stomped around the tree-house. "I'm a serious superhero! I *don't* use my powers for such— *Grrr!* I don't need to hypnotize girls to get them to do that! For your information, I've kissed girls from the past, girls from the future, girls from outer space, girls from other dimensions—"

"And probably the Compost Beast of Zetriak," she smirked, just to needle him.

"No! But I've kissed *you!*" he reminded her quite pointedly. "That is, you kissed *me!* That's right, *I* didn't kiss *you! You* kissed *me!* So what makes you think that I'd need my hypnotic powers to get you to do it again?"

She laughed to see him in this flustered condition. Just a minute ago he was a grand, mysterious figure. Now he was huffing and puffing like a humiliated ten-year-old boy whose proud sense of "cool" had been swiped away.

Realizing that his loud protests were only feeding her laughter, he fought to calm himself down (though he wasn't very successful). "If you would read comic books, you'd know that we superheroes are too busy saving the world... and sometimes the galaxy! We can't waste our time on silly things like having a crush on somebody! *Most* of us are like that, anyway — and *I'm* one of them! A girlfriend? Urgh! Some tights, boots, a mask and a cape — that's all I need in life! Oh, yeah — and an archenemy!" After this rant, he took a breath and calmed himself down. "You know, if you like this sort of gossip, there's a kid who sits behind you in class—"

"Yeah, Dan," she said lightly. "I know he's a friend of yours; and he's nice and everything. But he's so bashful that I'm surprised he can leave his house every morning. He won't say a word to me."

Night-Ghost was a bit disappointed to hear that she didn't much care for his friend. So he suggested, "What about Skymaster? I'll bet *he* liked flying you home."

Maria dismissed the flying hero too. "Skymaster is kind of weird. Once I got him to laugh, he was an OK guy, but the rest of the time, he was a real 'Mr. Robot.' Since you know both of them, maybe I should tell you: Skymaster could do with some of that cute 'puppy-dog' shyness that Dan has way too much of; and Dan really needs to be a little gutsy like Skymaster."

It was all Night-Ghost could do to keep himself from laughing out loud. With a smirk threatening to take control of his entire face, he mumbled, "Right; I'll be sure to tell them... *both* of them. Now, what's question number two?"

She thought for a moment as her teasing grin grew wider and wider. Apparently, she had cooked-up a second question, and Night-Ghost wasn't going to like it any better than the first: "How are you any different than Sasquatch Lady?"

"What?" He was thoroughly disgusted. "She's a villain who wants to rule the world! I'm a hero who's going to save it! She and I are *nothing* alike!"

"Well, she wanted to erase my memory of something I wasn't supposed to see; and here you are just about to do the same thing! I'm telling you, if Sasquatch Lady showed up right now to rescue me from you, I'd go with her!"

Night-Ghost was utterly confounded by her logic. His jaw fell open and he stared off into space.

Proud of her wisdom, Maria sat back in her chair, her arms folded victoriously. "Everybody wants to vacuum-out my memory today! Nobody wants me to have the tiniest bit of truth."

Night-Ghost had never been so defeated as he was at this moment. How was it possible that this girl (who never read any superhero comics) could teach him (the captain of The Fearless Force) what it meant to be a defender of justice?

But that's exactly what had just happened!

He was tremendously ashamed, and feeling like an exposed fraud. He turned his eyes down at the floor. He looked off to the side. He looked everywhere but at Maria.

She reached out and turned his face towards hers. When their eyes met, she told him softly, "I'm sorry I said you were the same as Sasquatch Lady. That was mean. I was just kidding. Go ahead and do what you have to do. Hypnotize me."

But he couldn't possibly bring himself to do it. Staring into her big, brown eyes, he discovered that *she too* was a hypnotist of sorts. He seemed completely powerless, as if it was *Maria* controlling the will of *Night-Ghost*, and not the other way around.

This utterly brilliant girl had chosen the only two questions in the whole universe that could have cut right through him and sting his very soul. That pair of questions had thumped him like a "one-two punch" on his pride. With that first question about kissing her, it seemed that she had looked right into his most private thoughts to see the fantasy that he had enjoyed that afternoon, where he won the "outer space princess." And while he was still staggering from that invasion of his heart, the second question of her "one-two punch" had shattered everything he believed about himself.

He told her, "You're like Sasquatch Lady, too, you know."

"I am?"

"She discovered my weakness today — math homework. I thought that it was my *only* weakness, but I guess I have *all sorts* of weaknesses."

"Like what?"

"Like thinking I'm always right." He spoke these words very quietly, and in a *truly* serious tone that made a complete joke out of that super-serious voice he used the rest of the time.

"But you *are* right. I shouldn't know your secret identity."

"I've been thinking that, just because I'm the good-guy, I can do whatever I want to do and it will automatically be right. I thought I could fake my homework; I thought I could erase your mem—"

He was interrupted by a commotion from down below — the voices of the other superheroes coming through the woods. They weren't discussing any important matters of crime-fighting; they were merely chattering on like ten-year-old boys. (Aquarius was telling some terrible joke about four nuns arriving in heaven after getting run over by a bus.)

Night-Ghost jumped up in a frenzy, whispering, "The

guys are here! I gotta hide you until they're gone!"

With the three heroes climbing up from below, Night-Ghost hoped to hide Maria on the roof. But just as he was about to shove her out the side door that led to the ladder, there came the thump of two boots over their heads. It was Skymaster making a landing on the roof.

With the rooftop now out of the question, Night-Ghost told her, "Hide in the corner!"

She did so, and quickly! Then he set his chair in front of her, sat down and spread-out his cape to shield her. With his journal in his lap, he pretended that he was reading over his writings as Skymaster entered through the side door, and The Wizard, Aquarius and Titan popped up through the trap door in the floor.

Crouched in the corner behind Night-Ghost, Maria heard him telling his team, "Let's get going! We haven't a moment to lose!"

Then she heard The Wizard reply, "Hang on. I'm gonna need some extra gadgets." And she waited breathlessly while that scientist collected his inventions from the shelves and stuffed them into his backpack. She didn't think they'd ever get going, as Aquarius kept asking, "What's that one for, Wiz?" Or he'd tell The Wizard, "Take this one! I love the way it shoots sparks everywhere!"

She wanted to scream, "Aquarius! Will you please

shut up and go save the world!" But, of course, she was smart enough to keep her cool.

The team of crime-fighters *finally* hustled out of the place and Maria breathed a sigh of relief. Night-Ghost, being the last to leave, turned to her and said, "Sorry I can't hypnotize you right now, Miss Fuente. I have to get my team into the school so we can destroy that mind-control transmitter!"

He leapt out the window, dropping branch-to-branch in ape-man fashion to the ground. Maria peeked ever-so-cautiously over the windowsill. She saw those four colorful shapes vanishing into the tangled twilight woods, and the outline of Skymaster above their heads sailing away under the summer evening's first lonesome star.

She asked herself, "Did he tell me where they were going because he was *inviting* me on the mission?"

Fearless Force

Part 4

Evening Darkens Down to Night

(A Missile, a Bomb and the Most Dangerous Pack of Zombies Yet)

Chapter 30

Going Underground

Skymaster glided swiftly over the woods towards Palisades Elementary. But he wasn't flying at top speed, for he had no desire to get there ahead of his teammates, as he had done at the water tower that afternoon. This time he wanted to make sure "the beat-people-up guy," Titan, was right there at his side when the action started. So he only flew as fast as Titan could run.

As before, the strongman was thundering through the woods like a freight train, clearing a path for his partners. He had done this many times on previous adventures — blazed a trail by ripping madly forward at racehorse speed — and the evidence of his past efforts were crisscrossed throughout this patch of suburban wilderness. The kids of the surrounding neighborhoods rode their bikes on these trails, *never guessing* that they had been carved out of the woodlands by a super-strong crime-fighter.

Polite strongman that he was, Titan stopped several times, so his three earthbound teammates wouldn't fall too far behind. Skymaster would hover and circle overhead and wait also. When the others were just catching up, the orange-clad Hercules would set off again and plow straight through the branches and briars.

Where the woods ended and the school parking lot began, Titan skidded to a stop — as before, by grinding the heels of his yellow boots into the soil and sliding about thirty feet in the rattling rocks and dirt. While waiting for his partners to catch up with him, he removed the collection of blackberry vines that had wound around his arms and legs.

In a moment, Night-Ghost was right there at his side, followed by the others. The heroic five hid there at the edge of the woods, keeping in the shadows of the trees, spying on their school's parking lot. It was a beehive of activity. Hundreds of grown-ups had come from far and wide to hear Mayor Lane give a speech.

Seeing that swarm of people, Titan said, "We can't exactly go marching in the front door. We'll have to creep in through the back of the school."

"That won't do us any good either," replied Night-Ghost. "The door to the boiler room is just across the hall from the gym where this crowd will be. No matter *which* way we go to get into the school, we'll be spotted the moment we try to get into the basement. We need to sneak down there unseen."

"Why should we *sneak?*" snorted Aquarius snobbishly. "I *wanna* be seen! I look great in my green duds! Besides, we're superheroes. Nobody's gonna ask questions if we just waltz in there and beat the snarf outta the principal and the old lady."

This string of silliness brought a humorless glare from Night-Ghost.

"I was only joking, Nightie," the water-breather muttered. "Can't you chuckle a *little?*"

The purple-cloaked hero narrowed his humorless glare. "I've told you before: never call me 'Nightie.' "

The absurd amphibian seemed a bit frightened by that cold response. "I know. It slipped my peanut-sized mind. I remember now."

The Wizard asked Night-Ghost, "You know a different way into the basement?"

Night-Ghost crouched low, crept out of the shadows of the trees, and into the parking lot. He stopped and directed his teammates' attention downward to a storm drain at his feet. His plan was clear: they were to crawl through the drain system under the pavement and into the school's basement.

"Oh, right!" Skymaster laughed a nervous laugh and let loose with heavy sarcasm: "After flying through a clear blue sky all day, I always like squeezing into a pitch-black hole in the ground!"

Titan removed the heavy iron grate, breaking it free of the years of moss and rust that held it tightly in place. The heroes peered into the square, vertical shaft that led straight down — deep, deep down — into complete darkness.

Skymaster declared, "You're crazy if you think I'm going down there!"

The Wizard asked innocently, "You're scared of tiny, cramped, dark places?"

Skymaster replied to this with a heavily sarcastic "Duh!"

Aquarius casually remarked, "I thought you were afraid of water."

"I'm afraid of water *and* cramped, dark places!"

"Weird," the amphibian mumbled. "I'm just a-scared o' heights."

"I can have as many phobias as I want!" Skymaster insisted. "It's not a 'pick one' sort of deal! And I ain't goin' down in that hole!"

"We're sticking together." Night-Ghost stated this in his matter-of-fact manner. "Down we go."

So Skymaster surrendered with a grim sigh and

joined the expedition. One by one the heroes climbed down the square hole. One by one they were enveloped by its uninviting shadows.

As the captain of the squad, Night-Ghost led the way, his superhuman eyes seeing perfectly in the lightless dim. Next went The Wizard, who clicked his flashlight on so he and the others could see. After him went Aquarius, then Skymaster (after a sad sigh of defeat), and finally Titan, who put the iron grate back into its place above him.

With their backs against one wall and their feet against the opposite one, they scooted downward into the gloom.

The tunnel grew darker with each inch they went down, and The Wizard's flashlight provided little help in that crowded drain-shaft. As they lowered themselves down into the darkness, Skymaster could be heard grumbling to himself, "I can't believe I let these guys talk me into this kinda stuff!"

When Night-Ghost reached the bottom of the vertical drain shaft, he discovered a square chamber — a junction-point between four sideways shafts leading off in different directions. He chose the tunnel that pointed in the direction of the school and crawled forward.

Skymaster felt like screaming, or throwing up — anything but going deeper into those drainpipes. But a mission against evil is a mission against evil, so, like his partners, he crawled into the next tunnel without a complaint.

That second tunnel was even smaller than the first one, and the heroes had to squirm along on their stomachs like worms. It would have been totally dark if not for The Wizard's flashlight. Sadly for Skymaster, that light was way ahead of him, so he was pretty much in total blackness as he crawled along.

Thankfully, the third tunnel was almost big enough to stand up in, and the heroes climbed into it with immense relief. The Wizard's light reflected off a slender trickle of water that flowed at their feet, casting reflections on the walls.

"Good thing the tunnels are getting larger," said The Wizard calmly. "We were almost out of air in that tiny one."

" 'Out of air'?" screamed Skymaster.

"Well," The Wizard explained, "five people can't survive very long in a pipe as small as that one we just came through." He held up a small compressed-air canister. "That's why I was releasing oxygen from this tank the whole time we were in there. It kept us from suffocating."

None of this soothed Skymaster's panic. "Why didn't you *tell* us we were about to suffocate?"

The Wizard shrugged, and returned the empty oxygen tank to his backpack of gadgetry. "I had the whole thing under control. So why discuss it?"

Skymaster couldn't believe that his scientist-partner was so casual about this. "Because I don't like crawling in dark, cramped underground pipes, that's why!"

"We're out of the cramped pipes now," Night-Ghost remarked. "We're into the big ones, so there's nothing to worry about."

" 'Big'? You think this pipe is big? We're all hunched-over in here!"

"Just hang in there," Night-Ghost told his frightened partner in a tone that was half soothing and half official. "We'll keep moving forward and be out of this in no time."

"Yeah," The Wizard joked, "we'll soon be out of this and into something else that'll scare the snarf out of ya."

"So it's cramped spaces and water?" Aquarius asked. "Anything else on that list?"

"I'm afraid of *everything*, OK?" Skymaster was too panicked to feel any shame admitting this. "Water, cramped sewer pipes, spiders, snakes, worms, lizards, bats, laser-guns, bombs, the sight of blood, and crazy fifth-grade teachers! Can we just get out of here?"

"You forgot Maria Fuente," chuckled Aquarius. "You're *completely* terrified of her."

If Skymaster could have fired lasers from his eyes, Aquarius would've been burned to a cinder at this point.

The amphibious comedian ignored that scorching stare and went right on with his mocking: "I'm serious, fly-boy! This is supposed to be The *Fearless* Force. We might have to change the name on account of you."

Before Skymaster could respond, an unbelievably loud slamming sound echoed all around them. All five hearts jumped, stopped, stuttered, then started again at double speed.

Huge cement doors had closed-off every tunnel except for the one ahead of them, which was blocked by a heavy steel gate. They were now trapped right where they stood.

Aquarius whined, "OK, I'm pretty danged scared! I guess I don't wanna be in something called 'The Fearless Force,' either!"

Titan pushed his way between his teammates with a "Let me take care of this" sort of posture. He compacted his right hand into a little yellow fist, drew back his arm and launched it forward with paranormal velocity. His knuckles pounded painlessly into the cement, bashing a little fist-sized indentation into that barrier — an indentation with several cracks radiating out from it. He pulled his fist out of the hole it had made and saw that he hadn't managed to break through to the far side.

"Couple more," he promised, as he pulled his arm

back for a second hit. "Couple more an' I'll have it!"

"Don't bother." Night-Ghost stopped him and pointed to the steel bars at the other end of the tunnel. "*That's* the way we're headed. Pull those bars apart, instead."

Titan nodded and headed for the gate. (Bending steel bars is every bit as fun to a super-strongman as is bashing through solid cement.) He wrapped his hands around the bars, planning to bend them apart. Believe it or not, his superhuman strength wasn't going to be enough this time. After a lot of sweating and straining, he only managed to put a slight bend in one bar.

The Wizard produced a soda-pop-can-sized canister from his weapons-belt. "Stand back. I'll blast 'em apart with a bomb."

But Titan wouldn't hear of it. "We are *not* setting off a bomb in an underground tunnel! That bomb is huge! It could cause a cave-in! Just give me a minute! *I'll* get us out."

Before the young strongman could take a second try at bending those bars, a wall of water thundered down the tunnel and knocked him backward. The rushing water pushed the heroes back against the three stone doors that had just shut them in and held them there with its crushing force.

Now it was obvious why there were three stone barricades and one set of bars making-up this trap: the bars were to allow this flashflood to pour in and fill the sealed chamber.

"Did I mention that I'm afraid of water?" asked Skymaster in a horrified frenzy.

"Wizard!" shouted Night-Ghost. "Any oxygen left in that tank?"

The Wizard hardly had time to say, "Nope," as the place quickly filled with water. His flashlight floated to the top and lit their panic-stricken faces as they gasped their last breaths.

Night-Ghost called out to the one hero who couldn't possibly drown: "Aquarius! Get the—"

Whatever his plan of escape was, he couldn't finish speaking as the tunnel flooded completely and the last pocket of air was gone.

Now all was silent as the water-breathing Aquarius swam madly about, looking for some way to save his suffocating teammates.

Chapter 31

Drowned Rats

The Wizard fumbled for his flashlight, but the water currents were tossing it all over and everything was a confusing blur. When he finally did get a grip on it, Aquarius instantly snatched it away from him.

"Don't worry, Wiz!" said the amphibious hero. "I know what to look for!"

He began a rapid search for the bomb that The Wizard had planned to use on the steel gate. It had been knocked from the scientist's hand by the flood, and it had to be somewhere near. He shot the beam of light all around, but it was difficult to see through the trash and pollution that had washed into the pipes. (This was also pretty foul water for him to have to breathe.)

He finally found the explosive device, but Skymaster kicked it right out of his hand. (Skymaster didn't mean to, of course. But, as he had said, he was terrified of water, and he was thrashing around in a blind panic.) Aquarius reached out again for a shadowy shape that he thought was the bomb, but instead found his hand wrapped around something mushy and furry. A closer look revealed it to be a dead rat.

After a quick, high-pitched (and very "girlie") sort of shriek, he flung it away, wiped his hand on his pant-leg and mumbled, "I could've gone all day without *that!* Now where's the bomb?"

He scanned his flashlight beam all around, and at last it shone on the little blue cylinder he was searching for. To his horror, it was now on the other side of the bars — on the other side of the bars and *out of his reach.* He tried to squeeze his body between the bars as he grunted, growled, howled, and made noises that can only be made underwater — and by a person who *breathes* water.

He stretched his arm out as far as it could go, but that bomb was still several feet out of reach. His muscles began to strain and tear as he tried to worm his way farther and farther through the bars.

He wasn't getting much closer to that bomb, but then an idea popped into his brain. He waved his hand in a circle until he had created a current that pulled the bomb towards him and drew it right into his grasp.

"N'yuk, n'yuk, n'yuk! I'm so smart it hurts!" Yet,

right when he had that bomb in his hand; right when he was feeling so altogether smart, he realized that he had gotten himself stuck between the bars. "Oh! This is *unbelievable!*"

He struggled, shouted, and finally pushed himself free of the gate, then swam back towards one of the cement doors that blocked the far end — the one that had Titan's fist-sized indentation in it.

Aquarius called out a warning — "Grab the bars, everybody!" — then set the bomb's ten-second timer and stuffed it into the little indentation in the heavy door of stone.

The other heroes paddled frantically to the steel bars and clasped on tightly. Skymaster couldn't find his way there, as he was out of his mind with fear. So Titan tucked him under his arm and got him to where he needed to be.

Scant seconds later, there was an immense explosion at the far end as the bomb blasted that cement door to pieces. Then came a powerful rush as the water rapidly poured out of the tunnel. They all tightened their hold on the bars as the violent current tried to pull them toward the hole that had just been blown open in the cement barrier.

Skymaster had been suffocating for far too long. He lost his grip on the steel bars and was swept down the pipe. Aquarius instantly let go of the bars, caught the airman by the shirt with one hand and snagged Titan's ankle with the other.

After a few rapid seconds that seemed like a few long minutes, most of the water had drained out and air returned to the tunnels. The gasping and coughing of the heroes echoed down the stone corridors as the water calmed to a trickle once more.

"You done great, pal!" said The Wizard. He slapped Aquarius on the back as the amphibian spit out a stream of filthy drain-water.

"Anybody got a breath mint?" asked Aquarius, wiping the gray-brown water from his teeth. As he had done earlier that day, he did a quick "dog-shake," and was almost completely dry in three seconds.

The heroes hopped to their feet. Well, *four* of them, that is. Skymaster remained on the floor, shaking all over, the filthy water still dribbling off of his face. His pale face and unblinking eyes told the full story of the panic that had been running chaotically through his skull for the last minute.

Titan glanced down at him and muttered carefully, "Uh-oh. He's got that 'I don't want to be a superhero anymore' look on his face."

"Yep," The Wizard replied. "He usually goes all shaky and blank like that when we nearly die by drowning."

Aquarius joked, "That's because when you're all drowning it's time for Aquarius to save the day! He ain't afraid of water. He just don't got any faith in *me!*"

Night-Ghost looked down on Skymaster with encouragement on his unworried face, and extended a hand to help his shaken friend to his feet. Skymaster took that hand, stood up, and tried to collect his rattled wits.

Though there may have been a joking atmosphere in the air, no one was making fun of Skymaster or the terror he had experienced. Rather, they were just trying to lighten-up the seriousness of the situation. For everyone knew that the flying hero had suffered a horrendous shock. His limbs were still quivering (and that they would be for awhile), but none of his friends would ever ridicule him for that. They each gave him a pat on the back or a bit of advice on how to carry on:

"Take a few deep breaths, pal."

"Shake it off."

"We survived."

Skymaster did indeed try to shake it off, then grumbled to Night-Ghost, "You actually *enjoy* death-traps!"

The escape-artist's half-grin was a clear sign of agreement.

"Let's get going," said Titan, wrapping his powerful hands around the bars and putting all his strength into them.

This time he was angrier than when he had previously tried to bend them. (Being nearly murdered has a way of getting *anyone* ticked-off!) After a grizzly bear snarl from the strongman, there came a creak and a snap of metal. He broke two of those bars and bent them out of place, so he and his team could pass through.

"Man, those're tough bars!" the muscleman mumbled to himself, very much relieved that he had finally snapped and bent them. If he had taken any longer at it, he might have been in for a bit of embarrassment.

The five journeyed forward, and soon rounded a corner where light streamed down through a grate above them. They had arrived underneath the school's cellar — right below either the boiler room or one of the other rooms next to it. Titan bent his head down and jumped straight up, knocking the metal grate into the air with his shoulders. It flew through the cellar and hit the floor with an enormous clang.

The five heroes climbed up and into the school's basement. There they found Mrs. Flembaugh, her gigantic mind-control transmitter...

...and an entire peewee football team in full gear.

As The Fearless Force invaded her lair, Mrs. F. picked up a microphone that was plugged into the transmitter. She grinned savagely as she spoke into it: "Falcons!"

The football team snapped to attention.

She growled out a command to them: "These five costumed clowns are The Fearless Force! They are your worst enemies!"

The zombie athletes snarled and sneered as they moved forward together with one big, threatening step.

"Those are Fenton's Flower Shop's Falcons!" said The Wizard, recognizing their colors of red and black. "They're the toughest peewee team in town!"

To which Aquarius replied, "I guess you *gotta* be tough when you're playing for a flower shop, huh? Hey, Wiz, toss a can o' knockout-gas at 'em!"

"Room's too small." The scientist's speedy three-word answer meant that a windowless basement is no place to set-off a knockout-gas grenade. Yes, it would have sent the football players to sleep... along with The Fearless Force.

Sasquatch Lady raised her control-microphone to her mouth again and let loose with a bone-rattling cry: "Falcons! Annihilate the superheroes!"

The mind-controlled team followed their orders, leaping forward in one huge red and black wave. Even Titan was bowled over as the heroes were buried under the crush of attackers, and the fists began to fly.

"Unnecessary roughness!" shouted Aquarius in a perfect sportscaster's voice. "Fifteen yard penalty!"

Fearless Force

Chapter 32

Punching Fiends &
Foisting Punch

And while those five champions of justice were down in the basement fighting for their lives, an ally of theirs was also entangled in the war against evil. This sixth hero was, of course, Maria Fuente, and her evening's adventure was only just beginning.

After leaving the tree-house HQ, she had let the heroes get a head start, then followed the path that Titan had carved out of the forest. She had arrived at the edge of the crowded parking lot a few short minutes behind The Fearless Force. Watching from the shadows as they vanished into the storm-drain, she waited until Titan had put the iron grate back in place above him, then made her move.

She wasn't about to follow them underground — not out of a fear of crawling around down there, but because she knew that most of the superheroes would take an instant dislike to having her tag along. (Well, she *did* have some qualms about crawling through drainpipes, but we'll call it "good sense" and not "fear.") She figured that she would let The Fearless Force lead their attack from down below while she would sneak into the school by a different route.

So she went around the side of the building. Although the front entrance of the place may have been buzzing with people and activity, the backside of the school was just the opposite: dim and deserted. The classroom hallways were either half-lit or left completely dark.

Looking for some way to get inside, Maria prowled cautiously through the dark courtyards, feeling more than a little creeped-out by the darkness and silence of the playground. (A closed-up and dark elementary school is many times gloomier than any other building, because it's normally a place full of such life and noise. There's something dreadful about a grade school in a darkening dusk — particularly when you happen to know that it's the scene of an evil plot to control the minds of the human race!) Finding all the back doors and side doors locked, Maria stood for a moment with a "dang it!" expression on her face. But, now that she was feeling like Maria Fuente: Girl Detective, she wasn't about to call it quits! She crept close to the side of the building, trudging through the shrubberies that were outside the classrooms, until she found a window that had been left unlatched.

Pulling that window open, she climbed up and in. Once inside that dark, deserted classroom, she quietly shut the window behind her and hurried out into the halls of the school. Tiptoeing through those half-lit, shadow-filled corridors, she headed for the boiler room (which, of course, would be perilously close to the front entryway).

She kept her eyes darting left and right, for if she was spotted she'd be dragged straight to the principal's office to face the death-ray that had nearly zapped Night-Ghost into lifeless ashes.

As she stalked carefully towards the boiler room door, and came closer to the brightly-lit entry hall, she began to hear the stir and burble of conversation. Peeking around the corner ahead, she saw the throngs of adults making their way to the gymnasium for the evening's big event.

Among the crowd was Mr. Morton, welcoming everyone to his school with a vigorous handshake and a sleazy, reptilian grin. On the farther end of this entry hall, was the corridor that led to the boiler room. *That's* where the adventure was to be found.

Still moving as stealthily as a spy behind enemy lines, Maria snuck past Mr. Morton and his guests by crawling under the school's trophy case, then ducking for cover behind some tall potted plants. Once in the shadowy side hallway, she made with all haste for the door marked "Boiler Room."

With this door locked tight, she asked herself, "How does Night-Ghost do that lock-unlocking thing?" Hoping she might discover a superhero's magic trick by accident, she gave the doorknob a little jiggle — just the way she had seen the purple-cloaked escape artist do it. Nope. The door was still locked. Super-powers simply do not come that easily.

Before she could come up with a "Plan B," Charlie the janitor appeared on the scene, pushing his mop along. (Having spent his afternoon trying to poison the town's water supply and massacre a team of superheroes, he had to work these late hours tending to his *actual* job of mopping the floors of Palisades Elementary.) Seeing Maria ("that black-haired girl" that Morton and Sasquatch Lady had been searching for) trying to break into the boiler room, he dropped his mop and charged at her.

The mad-eyed custodian was already at top speed when Maria spotted him out of the corner of her eye. As he reached out his massive arms and dove at her, she spun away and bolted for her life, avoiding his grasp by mere inches.

At first, she figured, "That's it! My adventure is over!

I'd better just get the heck out of here!" Then a bolder thought occurred to her: "He wouldn't dare kill me in the middle of a crowd!"

So she ran straight for the gymnasium and pushed her way into the center of the sea of people. Hot on her heels, Charlie hurried into the crowded room, and began searching frantically for her. Ducking for cover behind a pack of grown-ups, Maria tried to stay out of Charlie's line of sight as he hunted for her in the crowd. Then she noticed that Sasquatch Lady and Mr. Morton were *also* in this crowd, so she was forced to keep out of their view as well.

Maria had to stay continually alert as to where each of those three villains was if she wanted to remain unnoticed. This involved switching from one hiding place to another every few seconds. Huddling up behind a loud woman in a big green coat; crouching behind a bald man in a brown suit; shifting position to behind a fat man in an argyle sweater — nowhere was safe for more than an instant. Charlie was closing in on her, even though he didn't know he was.

In this cat-and-mouse game, Maria found herself hiding behind and between adults who hadn't a clue that she was in danger for her life — if they even noticed her at all. They were caught-up in their very grown-up discussions of politics. They argued about the city budget; the roads and fire departments. And Maria thought, "Maybe all these topics are important. But nothing's *nearly* as important as the fact that there's a mind-control machine in the basement! Or the fact that the janitor is out to kill me!"

All the while, Mr. Morton was over by the refreshments, shoving a glass of punch into every empty hand.

"Have some punch!" he'd giggle. "It's great stuff! Have more!"

Maria's eyes narrowed to a determined squint, and she muttered to herself, "There's gotta be mind-control juice in that stuff!" (For that little instant she had become as overly-dramatic as Night-Ghost!)

Weaving her way through the crowd, she made it right up next to the refreshment table, but stayed carefully hidden behind a small group of adults. As she watched unseen, Mrs. Flembaugh came stomping up to Morton and pulled him aside.

"Stop acting like an idiot!" the devilish teacher growled. "I'm going to the basement to make sure the machine is ready! I expect you to act intelligent while I'm gone."

"I will!" he promised quite indignantly, as if he had never been anything else but intelligent. Naturally, the moment she left the room, he lit up his repulsive smile and resumed his practice of thrusting a glass of punch at anyone who walked by.

(Of course, when Mrs. Flembaugh left the gym and

headed down to the basement, that's when she encountered The Fearless Force climbing up through the floor-drain and ordered her zombie football players to attack them. So, that brawl was going on down there while the following events occurred in the gym...)

As the villainous principal handed out his glasses of perfidious punch and giggled his secret giggle, Maria stepped boldly out of hiding. (With Mrs. Flembaugh out of the room, she wasn't nearly so scared about coming out in the open.) She asked quite brashly, "Why don't *you* have some punch, Mr. Morton?"

He looked down at her with horrified surprise. There she was: that same troublesome black-haired girl.

She wore a sly grin as she prodded him again, saying, "Go ahead; let's see you drink it!"

Morton fumbled for an answer as he felt more and more people turning to look at him with growing suspicion in their eyes. All nearby conversation had ceased. There was no more chatter about politics. Everyone was more interested in why a school principal and a ten-year-old girl would argue about who's drinking punch and who isn't.

"I... I had some earlier," the principal told everyone. Then he bent down and whispered in Maria's ear. "You women are all demons! You're going to grow up to be just like Sasquatch Lady!"

"Drink it," Maria demanded with a stern stare. "It's great stuff. You said so yourself."

"I think I will!" Morton smiled his sewer-rat smile and lifted his glass. "Mmm! Smells good! ...Boy, am I ever thirsty!" Then (very much on purpose) he tipped his glass, sloshing the punch everywhere. "Oh, I've spilled! What a clumsy goose I am! And look at that — a wet spot on the floor! That's terribly unsafe! Someone might slip and break their neck! We'd better go find the janitor, little girl! He's good at cleaning up messes!"

This was where Charlie stepped forward, asking villainously, "Did someone call for the janitor?"

"Yes!" Morton cackled with devilish glee, and rubbed his hands together in the fashion of a classic maniac, then quickly tried to put a lid on this clearly evil behavior. "There's been a terrible spill here! Let's go look for your mop — *all three of us!*"

The curiosity of every onlooker was turned up a notch. Yes, there certainly was something very weird about the way this principal and this girl were behaving, but no one could figure out what it was.

Mr. Morton grabbed Maria by the arm, and rushed her quickly out of the gymnasium, and Charlie followed close behind. As he was leaving, Morton hollered out to the entire room, "Ladies and gentlemen, you know him, you love him, you might even have voted for him — our very own beloved Mayor, Theodore J. Lane!"

This introduction wasn't supposed to come for at least another half-hour, but Mr. Morton needed something to distract everyone's attention away from the fact that he was dragging the little black-haired girl out of the room.

Maria shouted desperately, "The punch has mind-con—"

Morton clapped his hand over her mouth.

The criminal principal riled up the crowd's applause by yelling, "Let's hear it for Mayor Lane! Speech! Speech!" Then he hustled Maria out the door.

Mayor Lane, taken off guard by this early introduction, was pushed up to the little riser at the front of the room and fumbled with the pages of notes for his speech. "Um... uh... Good evening, citizens of Adelaide... Um..."

All eyes turned toward the mayor at the microphone; all ears were attentive to these serious matters. And as quickly as that, the crowd forgot that something bizarre had been going on.

Once out in the hall with the door closed, Morton laughed right in Maria's ear, "It's curtains for you, little girl!"

As abruptly as a thing can be done, Maria tugged her principal by the necktie, pulling his face down as she brought her knee up, smashing that knee right into his nose. The principal's eyeglasses rattled across the floor as he collapsed in a withered heap, and Maria made a hasty escape. *[Warning:* **DO NOT** *knee your principal in the face, unless he is a maniacal supervillain who's trying to rule the world through mind-control!]*

Charlie raced after the fleeing girl, but her ballerina's feet were too swift for him. She headed straight for the principal's office where she darted inside and locked the door behind her.

Charlie pounded on the door, yelling, "That was stupid, kid! You're *cornered* in there!" Then he ran back to where Mr. Morton lay groaning on the floor, and dug around in his coat pockets for the office keys.

Inside that office, Maria grabbed the portrait of Abe Lincoln and yanked it off the wall. And there it was: the electro-burst death-ray cannon that had almost massacred Night-Ghost during lunch.

Twisting the bolts that held the cannon in place, she unfastened it from its brace and looked it over to see if she could figure out how it worked. On one side she found a switch that could change its power-level from "Total Annihilation" down to "Mild Discomfort" and several in-between settings. Seeing as how she was up against some very dangerous criminals (whom she didn't much care for), she didn't want to be as tame as "Mild Discomfort." So, instead, she settled for the slightly harsher "Brutal Stun." She discovered the trigger on the underside, then hoisted the device up on her shoulder like a bazooka.

Outside, Charlie was just finding the proper key to unlock the office.

When the janitor threw the door open, he was confident that he'd find a terrified little girl cowering in the corner behind a filing cabinet. Much to his jaw-dropping, heart-stopping shock, he found himself staring straight down the barrel of an electro-burst death-ray cannon.

And while the janitor stood frozen in horror, the girl with her finger on the trigger growled, "Eat lightning, Moppy!" with all the gruffness of a U.S. Marine.

Charlie made a panicked retreat, but couldn't outrun a bolt of energy. A "brutal stun" blasted him in the tailbone and he ran yelping down the hall.

Mr. Morton was just coming to his senses when he looked up to see Charlie getting stunned (and brutally so!). The principal leapt to his feet and ran for his life, as Maria dealt him a zap of lightning between his shoulder blades.

As those two villains scurried off down different corridors, Maria stood triumphant in the empty front hall. The door of the gymnasium opened up and a woman stuck her head out. Seeing Maria with that massive silver ray-gun on her shoulder, the woman automatically assumed it was only a toy. So it was with no amazement on her face that she told Maria, "It's OK for you to play out here, but keep the noise down. The mayor's making a very important speech."

Well, it would've been pointless to reply, "No, you're mistaken. This is a *real* electro-burst death-ray cannon, and I'm saving you all from a mind-control plot." Maria could only nod and say, "Sure. OK."

The woman went back into the gym, and the girl with the electrical-cannon hurried off towards the boiler room.

At first, she was thinking, "Won't those Fearless Force guys be surprised when I come bursting in with this thing!" Then she thought, "Maybe they haven't even gotten to the basement yet! If that's the case, they're gonna get the surprise of the century when they show up to find that I've already blown the mind-control transmitter to bits!"

But as she was running with these thoughts dancing around in her brain, the power cord on her electrical-cannon reached its end. (Yes, the thing was still plugged into a wall socket back in the principal's office.) That wire stretched out tight and yanked her right off her feet. With absolutely *none* of her ballerina's grace, she crash-landed on her backside.

Always one to be honest with herself, she said aloud, "OK, I don't feel so cool all of a sudden."

Cool or not, she gathered herself up again, ran back to the office, unplugged the power-cord, and hurried to the boiler room door. Plugging the cannon's cord into an electrical socket in the hallway, she took aim at the doorknob and fired a blast of energy that knocked the latch loose. Pulling the door open, she heard the uproar of the battle raging down there in the basement.

It was instantly clear that she wasn't going to get there before The Fearless Force — they were already in the thick of a clattering tumult. But, first on the scene or not, this was her night for adventure!

Poised with her weapon held high in a perfect secret-agent pose, she took a deep breath to ready herself for danger, then leapt forward into battle.

Chapter 33

The Missile & the Syringe

Maria could hardly believe the chaos that greeted her eyes when she came down the stairs into the screaming mayhem of the boiler room. This was a smaller brawl than the lunchtime madness had been, but it was far more savage. During the ordeal at lunchtime, it was just teachers and students thrashing on The Fearless Force. The zombies in *this* war were — as The Wizard had said — the toughest football team in their league. Once Fenton's Floral Shop's Falcons, they were now Flembaugh's Fiendish Falcons. The diabolical teacher's mind-control had transformed the young athletes into enraged killers and the heroes were taking a terrible pummeling.

It was in physical hostilities just such as this that Titan became The Fearless Force's most important asset. Yet, strong as he was, he was only one person, and this tussle was going on in every corner of the room. He didn't bother protecting himself against the knuckles that flew at his own face, nor the fingers that clutched at his throat. His only concern was for his teammates. Even as he was being wrestled down, he would reach out between the bodies of his opponents and pull the zombies off his friends. Protecting his little brother was his top priority, after which came the need to rescue Skymaster — and, yes, even Aquarius! He didn't worry too much about Night-Ghost, because he couldn't even keep track of where the agile acrobat was half the time.

With that orange-clad muscleman's assistance, Skymaster broke free and took to the air. He grabbed a broom from the corner, tripped up a few of the zombies with it, and jabbed a couple others as he swooped high and low.

Although that flying hero fought valiantly, he was quickly distracted when he noticed Maria on the stairway. He shouted to her, "Run for it, Miss Fuente! We'll handle—"

The Falcons plucked him from the air and flung him right back into the skirmish.

Upon seeing his flying teammate taken down, Aquarius yelled, "Interception!" (Of course, that lunatic amphibian would be shouting out his radio sportscaster's play-by-play for the duration of this entire fight.)

Maria began unleashing a series of blasts from the

barrel of her borrowed electrical cannon. Standing high on the stairway as she was, she had command of the whole basement, knocking back the crazed footballers with one stun-burst after another. She set Skymaster free by zapping his attackers, and told him, "This girl does *not* 'run for it!' " (And she told him this not in any snotty, self-impressed way, but with a bright smile that set Skymaster's heart aflutter.)

Maria then turned her electrical weapon on Sasquatch Lady, who was watching the battle with demonic delight. That ghastly teacher managed to duck out of the way and hide behind her enormous transmitter, moving faster than any old lady should reasonably be expected to move.

Titan grew angrier as more and more punches landed on his face; and with his increasing anger came increasing strength. The Falcons began piling on him in greater numbers — doubling and tripling their team effort until the strongman was forced to leave his teammates to their own powers and defend himself. But the good, golden heart that thundered away in his chest wouldn't let him inflict any serious injury upon his enemies. Thankfully, those footballers were equipped with all their safety gear, so the super-strong hero could slam his fists into them without the fear of breaking anyone's bones.

Maria's onslaught of lightning bolts was just what

The Fearless Force needed to scatter that army of enslaved athletes.

The Wizard shouted up from the battle, "Maria! Clear me a path to the machine, so I can shut it down!"

Happy to be of service, she began zapping all the football players who were in The Wizard's way. He made a mad dash for the mind-control machine, but one of the athletes who had been zapped got right back up and tackled him from behind. As the scientist was dragged back into the fight, he screamed, "Maria! Destroy the machine!"

She took a shot at the mind-control device, but it had no effect. Her weapon was only set for "brutal stun," which couldn't damage the giant, steel mechanism.

The Wizard shouted, "Turn up the juice!"

Maria checked the lever on the side of the cannon, and decided to set it for "complete destruction." But while she was standing there halfway down the staircase, re-setting her weapon, one of the football players was flung across the room and collided with her. As she was bowled over, the cannon was bashed out of her grasp and knocked across the room. Its power cord was stretched to the limit, and yanked out of its electrical socket.

Maria ran down into the midst of the conflict and retrieved the cannon, but until she could plug it in again, it was a thoroughly useless item. As she looked all around for an electrical outlet, she found a ring of football players closing in on her from all directions.

She made an embarrassed little request: "Can you boys hold on until I get this thing plugged in?" And as the zombies stepped ever closer, she mumbled, "I didn't think so."

But before those zombies could strike at the disarmed Maria, Mrs. Flembaugh stepped out of hiding and shrieked, "Falcons! Stop!"

The Falcons instantly quit their attack and stood like statues.

Aquarius grinned victoriously. "Had enough, eh?" (And it was absurd of him to grin so victoriously, for at this moment he was being held upside down by two of his foes.)

"No, you buffoon!" replied Mrs. F. "That was merely demonstration number one! Now it's time for demonstration number two!" She laughed a rumbling laugh and spoke quietly into her microphone. "Titan... Aquarius... Skymaster... Wizard..."

As she spoke their names, each of those four heroes went into a glassy-eyed trance.

"They may still have your serum in their brains," said Night-Ghost defiantly. "But *I* don't!"

"Titan!" she commanded. "Hold Night-Ghost and

don't let him go!"

The strongman obeyed, clasping his mighty arms around his team's leader.

Maria tried to make a break for the exit, but Sasquatch Lady spoke another command into her control-microphone: "Aquarius! Get the girl!"

The amphibian did as ordered, darting after Maria and catching her in a tight bear-hug. The strange thing about Aquarius was that, even though he was under mind-control, he gave a mischievous "N'yuk, n'yuk" sort of giggle and screamed, "I get the girl!" Still chuckling his stooge-like chuckle, he dragged her back to the center of the room to stand her next to the captive Night-Ghost.

Maria struggled, but to no avail. Aquarius' swimmer's muscles were just a wee bit too strong for her.

As for Night-Ghost, breaking free of Titan was just about the toughest thing he had ever attempted! Every time he wriggled an arm free, the zombie strongman would grab a leg.

Seeing this constant struggle between the two of them, Sasquatch Lady gave another order into her control-microphone: "Wizard! Tie Night-Ghost with every knot you know!"

While Titan held Night-Ghost, The Wizard uncoiled the climbing rope from off his belt, looped it around the captive acrobat from his shoulders to his ankles, tying it snug with more knots than are known to the entire British Navy. He used the bowline knot, reef knot, double sheet bend, sheepshank, timber hitch, slippery hitch, rolling hitch, plus several that his computer-like mind made up on the spot — finishing up with a weird variation on the fisherman's bend. Then he threw his grappling hook up over a pipe in the ceiling, hoisted Night-Ghost off the floor (upside-down) and secured him in place with a monkey's fist knot on another nearby pipe.

That done, the zombie scientist dusted off his palms with industrious pride.

Night-Ghost instantly set to work worming his way free. His mental power that could trip the inner mechanisms of door-latches worked just as well loosening up knots. Even so, it would take time!

Maria had faith that the purple-clad escape-artist could conquer those ropes, so she tried to stall for the time she knew he needed. She asked Sasquatch Lady, "How much stolen lunch money did it take to buy that mind-control machine of yours?"

"None of your beeswax, girl!" she answered tartly.

Maria countered with, "You may get your poison into every skull on Earth, but you can't control every single human being with one transmitter in the basement of an elementary school."

"Oh, you better believe I'm prepared to rule the planet!" Sasquatch Lady flicked a switch.

At the activation of that switch, one whole wall slid back and part of the floor moved away, revealing a pit below — a circular cement well that went down fifty feet or more. Inside the pit stood a giant, towering missile of gleaming white.

The insane old teacher related her plan with pride: "That missile carries a satellite that I've connected to my command center here. Once I've launched it into orbit, it will transmit commands to every point on the planet! And when I've gotten the poison into everyone's brain, I'll be able to make *anyone anywhere* do my bidding!"

The insidious schoolteacher punched a red, flashing button on her control panel. The rocket began to rumble, as smoke billowed-up from the pit and into the room.

"The launch sequence has begun!" she bellowed triumphantly. "Now to make sure you two get in step with the rest of the people on Earth!" She held up a syringe full of clear fluid. (A "syringe" is, of course, the hypodermic needle that a doctor uses to inject a dose of medicine into a patient.) Then came another command into her control-microphone: "Skymaster, I want you to inject a dose of this serum into Night-Ghost and the girl!"

The hero in the flier's helmet took the hypodermic needle from Mrs. Flembaugh, and walked directly up to Night-Ghost. The captain of The Fearless Force was helpless as Skymaster stuck the needle into his flesh.

"Don't do it, Skymaster!" Night-Ghost begged.

Skymaster was deaf to his friend's plea. He slowly drew his thumb in, squeezing the serum out of the syringe, and pumping it smoothly into his captain's bloodstream.

Sasquatch Lady could barely contain her mocking laughter as she held up a second syringe full of venom. "Now... give the girl a dose."

Skymaster tossed the empty hypodermic aside, took the fresh one from Mrs. Flembaugh, and walked towards Maria. The zombie-airman pulled up Maria's sleeve, and she winced in pain as he jabbed the needle into her arm.

Fearless Force

Chapter 34

I Got Your Mind Set On Me

With that needle jabbed into her flesh, Maria moaned a dreadful and quiet, "*Please* don't do it, Skymaster!"

And at the pitiful sound in her voice, he stopped. He was still holding that needle in her arm, but not injecting the serum; not making any move at all.

Mrs. Flembaugh snarled into her control-microphone, "Inject her, Skymaster!"

Skymaster got ready to do so, putting his thumb on the syringe's plunger.

But again, Maria begged, "No!", and again, Skymaster became immobile.

There was something about this girl's voice that was cutting through the poison in the flier's foggy brain.

Maria was awestruck by the effect her voice was having on this zombie hero. She had just heard Night-Ghost begging him to stop and it hadn't worked. Why would his own captain's words have no meaning to him, but she could make him freeze with a simple "No"? She thought she should see just how far Skymaster would obey her — and quickly! She told him, "Take the needle out of my arm!"

Skymaster followed her command to the letter.

Boiling with rage, Sasquatch Lady hollered, "What's wrong with you? Inject the girl, Skymaster! Inject the girl!"

Skymaster started to obey that villainous directive, but again Maria shouted out, "Don't do it!", and again he stopped in his tracks. Back and forth it went. The zombie airman was a human Ping-Pong ball between these conflicting orders. He'd back off from Maria, then advance on her, then back off again, depending on who was giving him instructions.

After a few of these back-and-forth orders, a startling truth became clear to Maria... a miraculous truth... and it was as clear to her as an endless summer sky:

The boy in the flier's helmet was Dan!

He *had* to be. The only thing that could possibly overpower Sasquatch Lady's mind-control system would be the intense crush he had on Maria. (Love conquers all, as they say!)

At last, Maria gave the command that turned the tide of battle for good: She leaned in close to Skymaster and whispered, "If you inject Sasquatch Lady and don't obey anything she says from now on... I'll give you a kiss!"

That was it for Skymaster! His new mind-control mission was to follow the order to inject Sasquatch Lady and to ignore any other directions. He took to the air and swooped around the villainous old teacher like a hunting hawk.

"Skymaster! Back off!" wailed Mrs. F. as she dodged left and right to avoid getting stabbed by that syringe. "Obey me!" In her panic, she backed up, fell over a chair, and sprawled across the basement floor.

Skymaster jabbed the needle right into her backside, and released the toxin into her bloodstream. Then, throwing that empty syringe aside, he shouted out a simple "Ha!" and turned to Maria with his arms outstretched. Yes, the zombie hero was ready to take that kiss he had been promised! Even though he was in a trance, he had a look of excitement on his face — a strange sort of blank-faced zombie excitement.

"Later!" was Maria's quick response. (She wasn't about to kiss that creepy-looking zombie!)

Skymaster drooped in disappointment — a strange sort of blank-faced zombie disappointment.

As Mrs. F. climbed up off the floor, she tried to regain her dignity by claiming, "It doesn't matter if I have the serum in me! No one's going to speak any orders into this mind-control transmitter but me! So, I don't care if—"

She froze in horror when she noticed that Night-Ghost was gone. The rope that had been holding him prisoner was hanging limp and empty. The escape-artist was now loose in the room somewhere!

But he had her mind-control serum in him now. He would obey her voice. So she called into her microphone, "Night-Ghost! You are my slave! Come out of hiding!"

Much to Sasquatch Lady's confusion, the escaped hero didn't appear. So she barked out more commands: "Titan! Wizard! Find Night-Ghost!"

The evil teacher's confusion increased as Titan and The Wizard just stood there. They ignored her orders and stared straight ahead with uninterested looks on their zombie faces. Thinking there must be something amiss with her transmitter, she turned around to find that the control-microphone had become unplugged. What's more, it was *Night-Ghost* who had unplugged it!

The purple-cloaked hero was standing there, twirling the cord's plug in his hand, and grinning triumphantly. With a tug of the cord, he made the microphone leap from her grasp and fly right into his hand. He plugged it back into the mind-control machine and his smirk grew into a wide smile as he whispered into the microphone,

"Sasquatch Lady...?"

The teacher went blank-faced. The serum and the machine were working perfectly to take over her thoughts. She was now a mind-control slave of that heroic escape-artist.

"Well, what do you know!" Maria laughed in surprise. "She answers to the name Sasquatch Lady!"

Night-Ghost rattled off his commands: "Sasquatch Lady, you will forget my secret identity... You will forget about the homework you gave me today."

"I will forget your secret identity," she droned. "I will forget your homework."

Another thought occurred to Night-Ghost: "Wait! I actually *did* that homework! *Don't* forget about it, Sasquatch Lady! I actually want to hand it in."

"I will *not* forget about the homework," she droned in the same dull manner.

Then he gave his teacher some commands to keep Maria safe: "Sasquatch Lady, forget that this girl saw me without my mask. And never pester her again! She knows *nothing* about The Fearless Force."

Mrs. Flembaugh droned, "I will leave her alone. She knows nothing about The Fearless Force."

"That's great," said Maria, "but could you tell Aquarius to let me go?"

"Oh, right!" Night-Ghost gave the command to his team: "Hey, Fearless Force! Wake up!"

The Wizard, Titan, Aquarius, and Skymaster shook their heads and blinked their eyes.

Aquarius popped out of his trance to find his arms locked around Maria. With an impish grin, he asked her, "Hey, toots, what have we been up to?"

Night-Ghost shouted out, "Wizard! You have work to do! Stop that missile from launching!"

"Missile?" asked The Wizard — along with the other three members of The Fearless Force. (Having only just snapped out of their trance, they hadn't a clue what had gone on for the past few minutes.) They looked over to the side of the room where the floor had moved away. For the first time they saw the deep pit with the missile standing in it — and that missile was smoking and shaking, getting ready to lift off.

But the monster known as Sasquatch Lady was too evil to be controlled for long. She broke out of her trance, bounded across the room, snatched the microphone from Night-Ghost, and barked out a dire command to her mind-slave football team: *"Falcons! Obliterate The Fearless Force! Grind them into dust!"*

Night-Ghost tried to wrestle the control-microphone from her, to give the football players a new command, but she threw it to the floor and crushed it under her shoe, saying, "Now you'll *never* stop them, you purple vermin!"

The five guardians of truth were instantly swallowed by the charging crowd of screaming-mad athletes. Maria found herself being ignored by the peewee army. This was due to that last command of Sasquatch Lady's to "Obliterate The Fearless Force." So the Falcons focused all their violent attentions on the five costumed crime-fighters, and paid no mind to Miss Fuente. As far as they were concerned, she was utterly invisible.

She tried her best to pull the zombies off of The Wizard, knowing that the scientist would be needed to stop the launch of the missile. But the football players trying to massacre The Wizard swatted her aside as if she were nothing more than a pesky mosquito.

She tried to get her hands on the electro-burst death-ray cannon, but that weapon was being kicked all over the floor in the scuffle, and it was finally kicked over to the edge of the fifty-foot-deep pit wherein the missile stood. It balanced on the pit's edge for a moment, while Maria dove towards it, arms outstretched. It teetered over and dropped into the pit just as Maria's fingers got near, and she was a fraction-of-an-inch and a fraction-of-a-second too late to get a hold on it as it fell out of reach. Its power-cord whipped chaotically hither and thither and followed the falling cannon, but Maria couldn't get a grasp on that cord either. The weapon was lost.

As she heard it hit with a distant clank at the bottom of the missile's pit, she felt her hopes hitting the bottom of her soul with the same sort of clank.

Meanwhile, Mrs. Flembaugh was up to something. The devilish teacher was at the controls of the mind-control machine where she was frantically punching in a secret code. This bit of business done, Mrs. Flembaugh raced up the stairs, ran from the room, and slammed the door behind her.

Having witnessed Sasquatch Lady's actions, Maria rushed to the mind-control machine and looked at the video monitor. She shouted out over the battle, "Wizard! We have trouble!"

The scientist's blue-helmeted head popped up from under a pile of zombies. He asked, "What *sort* of tr—?", then vanished under the pile again.

Maria told him, "This view-screen says, *'Transmitter self destruct'!*"

"Titan!" cried The Wizard. "Get this mob off of me! I have work to do!"

Titan gave a big, growling shove and freed himself from his own pile of attackers, then hurried over to tear the mountain of zombies off of his little brother. Picking

The Wizard up off the floor, he threw him (gently!) in the direction of the mind-control machine.

Knowing he had only a few moments before he was attacked again, The Wizard punched the machine's keyboard and didn't like what he saw. "Just what I was afraid of." He hurried over to the missile's launch-pit, leaping and dodging several flying tackles on the way.

"What's going on?" asked Night-Ghost from under a crush of zombies.

The young scientist replied, "The transmitter's going to pop! It's gonna pop with enough force to wipe all of Adelaide clean off the map... in ten minutes!"

"We'll try to keep the maniacs off you," said Titan. "You just worry about defusing that bomb!"

"First things first!" The Wizard replied, standing at the edge of the missile's launch-pit. "This rocket's lifting-off *now!* I still have ten whole minutes to worry about the bomb!"

Grabbing onto his rope (which still dangled from the ceiling where Night-Ghost had been trussed-up) he swung out over the pit, landing on the nose of the missile. Producing a crescent-wrench from his weapons-belt he started to disassemble the smoking, rumbling monstrosity. He removed a few large sheet-metal panels and started working on the confusion of wires and tubes inside.

All this time Maria had been thinking that The Wizard didn't really have much of a super-power — he was just smart. How could *that* be considered a super-power? It was nowhere near as astonishing as flying or breathing water.

But now she saw him clanking away with his wrenches and screwdrivers, working with paranormal swiftness. He dug through the guts of that missile like a magical elf from Santa's toyshop. What Maria was discovering was the limitless mental might of that boy-genius. A single two-second glance at any mechanical device was enough for him to know *exactly* the function of every wire, hose, gear, and piston.

In a matter of seconds, he had unbolted a quarter of the nose-cone and flung away that curved aluminum panel. This exposed the inner compartment at the top of the rocket, wherein sat the satellite — the transmitter satellite that was expected to cruise in orbit around the Earth, broadcasting Sasquatch Lady's orders to a zombie planet. This device was a shiny, silver, odd-shaped box about the size of a small car, with its dish-antennas and solar-power panels folded-up to compact it for flight.

Crawling around and underneath this cumbersome gadget, The Wizard tried to get at the mechanisms that would shut-off the missile's launch sequence.

As Maria watched the hero-scientist clank away at his job, she thought, "I'll bet I can actually help!" (She was no good at beating-up crazed football players, but turning bolts and screws might be a possibility.)

Of course, it was going to be a tough job convincing The Wizard that she could assist him. The other four members of that superhero team didn't seem annoyed to have her on the adventure. But she could sense that The Wizard was somewhat irritated to have a girl — a normal, human, un-super girl — hanging around. Even so, she was going to lend him a hand.

Jumping onto The Wizard's rope, she swung across the pit, and landed next to him on the missile.

"Look," she began, "I know I'm a girl, but—"

"How perceptive!" He spoke hastily, without looking at her. "I was just thinking, 'I hope she knows she's female; I'm way too busy to explain something like that to her.' "

She was going to call him rude or snotty or something, but he beat her to it. Finally turning to look at her, he said sincerely (but still quickly), "Sorry. You can call me a jerk later. Right now I need your help."

"You got it!"

He thrust a socket-wrench into her hand. "Climb down the side of the rocket, remove the third access panel on the fuselage

She was pretty sure that the "fuselage" was the body of the rocket (and she was right), so she didn't waste time asking about that. She just nodded her head quickly and asked, "Then what?"

He continued, "Find the secondary control cable for the ignition sequencer, then—"

"In English!"

He knew she was right. Nothing was going to get done if he tried to dazzle her with engineer-talk. "OK, later on you have to call me a jerk *twice!* Find a green pipe running vertically next to a red pipe."

Another hurried nod of the head and she snapped into action, sliding down the rope, deeper into the pit, down the side of the gigantic rocket. She undid the bolts that held the third access panel in place. A moment later, she had crawled inside the guts of the missile and called out, "I found the green pipe!"

From up above on the cone of the rocket, The Wizard shouted down, "Follow it to a shut-off valve. It should be connected to a whole series of black hoses…"

And thus began the rapidly-thrown-together technical team of The Fearless Force's scientist and Miss Fuente. While the brawl continued in the basement, they worked diligently on dismantling that soon-to-launch missile.

Sadly, they weren't to remain free from that brawl for

very long.

Five Falcons leapt onto the nose of the missile and tried to tear The Wizard limb from limb.

Titan hurried to his brother's rescue. He sprang into the air and landed in the thick of the fight, which was a pretty clumsy fight, what with there being very little room in the open nose-cone of that rocket. He pried the villains' clutching hands from his little brother's throat, held them back and asked, "How long do we have?"

"Well... Not long," answered the scientist as he clattered and pounded his wrench in the smoking machinery. "It would speed things up if this satellite wasn't in my way!"

Titan gripped the massive satellite and tore it out of place. While still fending off the maniacs who were clawing at him, he dropped the satellite to the bottom of the pit. "There ya go! It's outta your way. *Now* how long do we have?"

"Well, we have about seven minutes and fifteen seconds till the self-destruct on the mind-control machine goes off."

"I mean the *rocket!*" shouted Titan over the ever-growing rumble of its engines. "How long till this thing launches?"

The Wizard looked his brother straight in the face and told him, "About twelve seconds."

Titan's heart nearly stopped. *"What?"*

"I'm trying to disconnect the engines! Don't worry! I have one of them shut down already!"

The rocket began to shake like mad.

The ceiling above them opened up, clearing the way for the missile to head skyward.

"Get off this thing, *now!*" (Titan sounded more like a protective big brother than a superhero.)

"No! I'm almost finished!" (The Wizard sounded more like a defiant younger brother than a scientist.)

The pit burst alive with orange fire as the missile began its liftoff and crept skyward. Titan picked up his brother and threw him to safety — out of the missile's launch-pit and into the basement. The strongman was about to jump to safety himself, but five zombies held him fast within the open nose-cone of that rumbling missile. The rocket lifted off, rose up through the open roof, and climbed into the night on a growling pillar of flame and smoke.

The Wizard called out, "Titan! Maria's inside the missile! Get her out!"

Sadly, the strongman heard nothing. His little brother's warning was drowned out by the rumble of the launch.

During the lift-off, Titan was still held down inside the nose of the thing by those five zombie footballers. And unknown to him, Maria was still somewhere inside its guts. When she realized that the thing was launching, it was far too late to jump out. All she could do was hang on.

Everyone in the boiler room ducked behind the mind-control machine to shield themselves from the blast. Then, once the missile had shot high into the air, they all resumed the fight.

As the missile climbed into the night, The Wizard shook his head sadly. "Hope I do a better job on the time-bomb!"

Chapter 35

Maria's Brilliant Save

Thankfully, the rocket never made it into orbit. Because The Wizard had disconnected one of its engines, the thing was running on half power. Of course, it wasn't carrying the heavy satellite it had been intended to carry, but it did have the added weight of Titan and the five zombie football players in and around its nose compartment.

It was a bad combination: that burden of struggling enemies on the top and the lopsided thrust coming from only one engine. It meant that the missile was completely out of balance. After shooting up out of the school on a crooked course, it rose a few miles over the city, then whirled and spun without direction.

Of course, Titan was still in his right mind, so he was having trouble adjusting to the fact that the missile on which he was standing was looping madly like a carnival ride. Had any of his four younger teammates been up there with him, he would have made sure that he had his "strongman face" on. But as he was in this predicament on his own, he didn't worry about the queasy expression that rolled in his eyes.

He tried to remind himself that superheroes never barf — especially when they're high above the city they're supposed to protect!

Seeing as how The Wizard had been tinkering with the missile before it took off, there were plenty of wires, cables, and hoses dangling from its sides. Titan and his enemies held tightly to these loose wires and whatnot while their brawl continued.

The punches flew with ferocious intensity. Titan and his foes would hold tightly to a wire or engine hose with one hand, take a swing with the other, slide off the missile and dangle in space for a moment, then pull themselves back up and do it all over again.

In the midst of this mile-high conflict, Maria climbed out of the missile's innards, and let out a gasp of distress to see the lights of Adelaide so far below.

Titan glanced back over his shoulder, shocked to the core to see her there. *"What are you doing here?"*

"I was helping The Wizard stop this thing!" she answered, hanging onto the rocket's frame with her most intense grip. "I guess we didn't do so well."

Titan's momentary distraction of noticing Maria was something the Falcons immediately took advantage of. They tore loose the cord that the strongman had wrapped around his wrist, and flung him the length of the rocket. He bounced down its smooth, metal surface, unable to find a handhold anywhere, and sailed out into the open air.

To her increasing anguish, Maria now found herself alone on that runaway missile with five brainless mind-slaves. But the Marias of the world don't despair — even in such horrendous circumstances. In a speedy burst of inspired brilliance, she came up with a plan to save Titan before he met with a splattering doom on the earth below. She knew he was tough, but she didn't think he could survive a drop from this height (and she was correct).

She climbed out of that cubbyhole in the side of the missile, and put her plan in motion. "Phase one" of her plan was to get those football players to attack her. Knowing they would only attack a member of The Fearless Force, she yelled out a big announcement: "Guess what? I just joined The Fearless Force!"

This little fib made their faces twist up in hate, and they lunged at her.

Now, "phase two" of her plan was to get them to chase her all around that rocket. Holding tight to the many hoses and cords that flapped in the wind, she led her enemies on a chase from one side of the rocket to the other, and from the back to the front. In so doing, she was shifting the weight that the missile was carrying, and this succeeded in steering the thing through the sky!

She steered it straight downward, toward the orange and yellow speck below her, which was the free-falling Titan.

Seeing that missile headed towards him, the plummeting hero knew right away what Maria was up to. A delighted smile spread across his face as he said, *"That's* why Skymaster's in love with her! She's a genius!"

A second later, the missile sped close to him, and he stretched out a hand. Two of his mighty fingers caught the very tip of a tail-fin, and that was enough to save his life. Once his weight was on that tail-fin, the rocket tilted upward, and raced high into the atmosphere again.

Climbing up that fin, he made it to the main body of the rocket. Ramming his fingertips into the thing's aluminum skin, he started to crawl toward the front. Those powerful fingers bent, twisted, and ripped holes in the side of the missile as the Herculean hero made his way to the top. The squeak of that warping metal could be heard even over the rushing wind and the dull rumble of the engine.

Up at the nose of the missile, the football players gave up on chasing Maria and watched Titan creep inch-by-inch toward them. Little hints of surprise and fear actually flashed in their zombie eyes.

The rocket turned a few hair-raising spirals, spinning everyone upside-down again and again. It bucked up and down, climbing skyward one second and plummeting downward the next. Still, Titan was able to hold on just by punching his fingertips into the metal.

Maria felt very relived to have that muscleman back onboard the missile with her. "I can't believe my idea worked!"

Titan replied with a simple "Miss Fuente, you're brilliant!" And the smile that delivered this compliment was as dashing as any movie musketeer's. For the briefest moment, Maria forgot that she was a few dangerous miles off the ground.

Titan's smile dissolved into a narrow-eyed scowl as he turned toward the zombies. "So you guys wanna play 'King of the Rocket,' do you?"

Chapter 34

The Getaway

And down in the gymnasium, none of the crowd of grown-ups had the slightest idea that a missile had just launched from the school's basement. The roar of the blast-off had disturbed the mayor's speech, but Mr. Morton came running into the gym and quickly announced, "The rumbling sound you just heard was the water heater exploding! Don't worry! It was just the boiler bursting! The janitor already has it under control! Have some punch, and forget all about it!" He advised Mayor Lane, "Go right ahead with your speech, Teddy," then rushed out of the room again.

The second he was out of the gymnasium, a cruel hand gripped him by the ear and a voice boomed out, "Morton! We have to get out of here!"

"Sasqua— I mean, Mrs. Flembaugh!" (He knew who it was without even looking.) "What was that explosion?

Did you launch the rocket? I didn't think we were launching that until Saturday! There's a couple hundred people in the gym! I had to tell them that the boiler burst! Why did you—?"

"Clam up!" She dragged him out the front door and into the parking lot. "I set the self-destruct on the transmitter! We have less than eight minutes to get out of Adelaide!"

"But, why?" he howled. "If you blow up the transmitter, we'll have to build another one! And if the school is destroyed I'll be out of a job!"

"I told you to stop whining!" She gave him a quick slap to knock him back to his senses. "The missile's launched, and soon the satellite will be in orbit! Once the transmitter explodes, those stinking superheroes will be no more! Getting another machine built isn't so difficult! We'll rule the world by the end of next week!"

"I disagree, Sasquatch Lady!" said a familiar voice.

She looked over her shoulder, and there — not really to her surprise — stood Night-Ghost.

He stepped out of the shadows and crossed the parking lot with a determined expression. "Your demented plot is finally at an end!"

Unimpressed by his victorious manner, she snarled out a cold threat: "Once I rule the world, I'll find out who you are again! I'll make your life an eternal fifth-grade nightmare! How'd you like to clean every blackboard eraser in North America?"

"What do you mean you'll 'find out who he is again'?" asked Morton. "Don't you know who he is? You took his mask off him today!"

Frustrated beyond belief, she growled, "The little creeps injected me with my own serum and used the transmitter to make me forget! But *you* saw him, Morton! Who is he? Tell me!"

Morton thought for a moment. "Hmmm... I remember you said his name a couple of times... What was it? Keith? Greg? Carl?"

"You're useless!" shrieked Mrs. Flembaugh. "Get in the car!"

She opened the passenger door of her car, throwing Morton inside.

Night-Ghost sprang to the car's roof and struck a battle-ready pose. He fired-up that TV hero's serious speech pattern to full-blown intensity: "You're going nowhere, Sasquatch Lady!"

Quick as a cobra, she snatched his ankle and hurled him across the parking lot. He hit the side of a car with a thump and slid to the ground. Suddenly, all those stories about her picking up a desk and throwing it through a wall seemed perfectly believable.

She jumped into her car, locked all the doors, and fired up the engine. But just as she was skidding out of the parking lot, Night-Ghost leapt at her car and snagged a hand on the passenger-side door-handle.

"He's on my door!" Morton wailed. "Shake him off!"

Spinning the steering wheel this way and that, she tried to jar the hero loose from the car while he used his escape-artist power to undo the door-lock. Before Morton could scream again, Night-Ghost had flung his door open and grabbed the man by the coat.

"You're coming with me, sir!" said the boy-hero as he pulled his principal from the speeding vehicle.

Both acrobat and principal landed hard, and tumbled on the side of the road. Morton didn't think about whether he had broken any bones. He just wanted to get away from that weird kid in the purple cape. He was on his feet in an instant, running after Mrs. Flembaugh's car, and screaming, "Come back, Sasquatch Lady! Don't leave me here with him!"

His pitiful cries were useless. The car vanished in the distance.

He whirled around and snapped at Night-Ghost, "I know who you are! It's over for you, Phil... Mike? Is your name... Tony? OK, I may not remember your name, but I remember what your face looks like behind that mask!"

"That's right, you do," the hero answered. "But you're going to forget." Then he smiled, and the eerie purple light glowed in his eyes. He waved a hand before Morton's face and the principal was locked into a trance.

"You will forget my name... You will forget my face..."

Chapter 37

Defusing and Descending

With Night-Ghost out chasing after Sasquatch Lady and Mr. Morton, and Titan and Maria a few miles high on that runaway missile, this left just Aquarius, Skymaster and The Wizard in the basement to deal with Mrs. Flembaugh's rampaging Falcons.

The Wizard had removed one of the mind-control transmitter's side panels and had climbed inside to deactivate the explosive heart of the thing. Thankfully, he had the technical diagrams of it, which made his job a bit easier (if dismantling a bomb can ever be called "easy"). *[Warning: **DO NOT** attempt to defuse a bomb unless you are a fully trained and fully qualified superhero-scientist whose brain can instantly figure out any mechanical or electrical system at a glance! ...Or unless you're a member of the police department's official bomb squad, I suppose.]*

So with their scientist partner busily clanking away inside the machine, Aquarius and Skymaster were left as the only heroes in the room with the pack of crazed football players — and Titan had taken only five of them away on the missile-ride. This left the flier and the fish-boy facing fifteen foes!

Pinned to the floor by three of them, Skymaster screamed, "Aquarius! You have to get me out of here! I have to get up there and save Maria— I mean, save *everyone* on that missile!"

Busy with his own pack of brutes, Aquarius shouted back, "Do you have some sort of plan to save all of them?"

Skymaster's hopeless response was "No. All I know is that they're in the air, and that makes it my job!"

Aquarius cast his gaze all around, searching for some quick inspiration; some brilliant move that would free his flying partner from the fight, so he could get up there in the sky and do his job. Knowing that the electro-burst death-ray cannon had fallen to the bottom of the missile's launch-pit, the green-clad amphibian zigzagged through the room, headed for that immense hole in the floor. He dodged a Falcon's flying tackle, then did a perfect baseball slide across the floor and over the edge of the missile-launch-pit. As he plummeted toward the bottom of the pit, he caught hold of the rope that still hung over it and slid down. Well, actually he only slid *partway* down the rope. It had been weakened by the missile's fiery take-off, and it snapped under his weight.

He dropped the last ten feet to the cement floor of the pit, hitting the bottom with a thud. After painful moan of "Didn't hurt!", he found the electro-burst death-ray cannon. (Actually, he had *landed* on it, which was no picnic.) Discovering a ladder on the side of the pit, he scrambled back up to the boiler room, carrying with him the massive weapon he had jumped down there to retrieve.

With his electrical-cannon in hand, the amphibian rushed to Skymaster's rescue. "OK, Tweety-bird, don't worry about a thing! I got me a far-out weapon here! I just gotta plug it in and... Oh, crud!"

Yes, he had suddenly realized that the cannon had not survived being at the bottom of the pit during the burning blast of the missile's launch. Its rubber power-cord had completely melted away to a blackened stump.

But this is where Aquarius' insane sense of humor came into play!

He produced a series of loud "zip-zap" laser noises with his mouth, getting the attention of every zombie in the room. They turned to look at him, and he aimed his useless cannon at them. In his best "sea-dog voice," he snarled, "Alright, ye scurvy dogs! You're done-for now! I got the principal's ultra-zap-o-matic... gun.. thingy... *And I'm gonna roast the lot of ya!*"

With another outburst of those phony "zip-zap" sound effects, he actually made the football players flinch. He had them believing for a fraction of a second that they were getting zapped.

And that fraction of a second was all that Skymaster needed to break free and zoom into the air!

A quick cry of "Thanks, Aquarius!" and The Fearless Force's flier raced out through the open ceiling.

"Sure; no problem," groaned Aquarius, as he realized that he was now the last visible superhero in the room, facing fifteen zombie athletes, and armed with nothing but a useless electrical-cannon.

He dropped the worthless weapon and shouted to his scientist-friend who was somewhere inside the transmitter, "Wiz! I need some gas!"

The Wizard's none-too-pretty answer was "Eat a bowl of beans!"

"Thank you, Mr. Science!" the amphibian shrieked, while running for his life. "Gimme a knockout-gas-bomb, ya big comedian!"

"I already told you: the room's too small. You'll knock yourself out along with all those zombies!"

"No, I won't!" Aquarius howled. "I got a brilliant plan!"

A grenade came flying out from the transmitter, and Aquarius caught it. He instantly pulled the trigger-wire and flung the little canister at the feet of the Falcons. Those zombie footballers suddenly found themselves surrounded by a flurry of pink smoke. In just a few short seconds, they went weak at the knees and dropped to the floor.

As for Aquarius? He wasn't affected by the gas. As he had said, he had a brilliant plan.

In the corner of this basement, there was a janitor's utility sink — a big, ugly basin that looked like a place to clean mops, tools, paint brushes and whatnot. Attached to the faucet was a short hose. The water-breathing hero, just stuck this hose in his mouth, turned on the water and breathed it into his amphibious lungs. With that endless supply of water to breathe, there was no need for him to breathe the air, which was now clouded with knockout-gas.

He just stood there, casually sucking-in the water and grinning in victory as those zombie football players dropped into sleep all around him. (The Wizard didn't have to worry about any of his knock-out gas affecting him. With the touch of a button on the side of his helmet, a clear plastic face-shield slid down over his eyes, and the sides of the helmet closed-up to meet in the middle and cover his mouth. This entire system of shielding sealed itself tightly, and a set of air-filters on the front cleaned-up the air that he breathed.)

With the ceiling opened-up from where the missile had launched, the gas quickly floated up and out of the place. Leaving the football players in a sleepy heap and Aquarius laughing in triumph — a gurgling laugh through a mouthful of water. When it seemed safe to do so, he spat out his "breathing water," and popped open the side of the transmitter, where he found his scientist friend working at a superhuman pace.

"How's it going in there, Wiz?"

Keeping his eyes on his work, The Wizard replied, "If I can disconnect the primary memory drive, I should be able to find the coaxial lead and follow it to a main override mechanism. Then I can tap into the circuit that—"

"Don't map it out for me, egg-head! Just do your job!"

"You don't want to talk to me? I thought we should have *some* kind of conversation, considering we only have fifty-six seconds to live."

"A minute!" The amphibian paced anxiously around the room. "Say, 'a minute!' I hate it when you get exact!"

A few machine parts sailed out and clanged on the floor.

"Found it!" shouted the voice from inside the huge contraption.

"Found what?"

"The coaxial lead that goes directly to the main—"

"Forget I asked!" screamed the panicked water-breather. "Shut your cake-hole and save our skins!"

The Wizard worked his science quickly. Switching the yellow wire with the green one, changing around the orange and the blue ones, he then reached outside the machine, and tapped three switches on the command console. The giant device let out a click, a buzz, a whir, and a great gasp of steam. It was now completely dead, except for a single monitor screen, which read...

Transmitter Deactivated
Self-destruct Sequence Terminated: 00:08

The Wizard stepped out of the machine with a proud grin. "See? All under control. And we still had a whole eight seconds to go, you worrisome water-lily."

With the mind-control transmitter shut down, the Falcons sleeping on the floor all twitched with a sudden shock, then instantly woke up. They looked around, confused and silent. The last thing any of them could remember was showing up for football practice that afternoon. And now they were in a basement somewhere with a blue superhero and a green superhero standing in front of them. Needless to say, none of this made any sense.

After a long pause, Aquarius smiled his silly smile. "Boy,

did we ever work-up a sweat! You jocks got any Gatorade?"

Meanwhile, a few thousand feet above the town...

The rocket was still circling madly, and the fight still raged on. Titan was drawing back his fist for a good, fierce punch on one of his foes when he noticed it was Eddie Thigpen under the helmet.

"Oh, this is gonna be a pleasure!" the orange-clad hero laughed.

But, before he could swing his fist, Eddie woke from his trance. He blinked several times and shouted, "Huh? What's goin' on?"

The other four zombies blinked and woke up as well. (This was, of course, the moment that The Wizard had finally shut off the mind-control transmitter.) In one quick, baffling moment, the former zombies realized that they were turning random spirals on a runaway missile. Their screams of fear almost drowned out the sound of the rocket engine.

"*Now* they snap out of it!" Titan grumbled, "Just when I noticed it was Eddie and I was gonna get mean!" He turned back to Maria, saying, "Remind me in my next fight that I wanna get mean *right away.*"

She didn't respond, for right at that instant the situation got serious.

Maria was the first to notice that the rocket's engine was sounding peculiar. With a note of dread in her voice she said, "I think we're running out of gas!"

Sure enough, the engine began to sputter as the fuel tank spent its last few drops. The missile was rapidly losing altitude.

Titan snapped into action. He helped the five bewildered peewee players into the empty compartment where the satellite had been before lift-off. Then he bent a steel panel over the opening to seal them all safely inside.

He told Maria, "Their football padding should protect them during the crash."

" 'Crash'?" asked Maria with a sick feeling.

"Well, a *controlled* crash," Titan replied. "I think I can steer this thing by bending the tail-fins into whatever direction I need to turn it. I'm gonna try and skid it to a stop in the meadow behind our neighborhood."

"So the football players should be safe if you can do that." Her voice was full of growing concern as the world below got closer. "But what about *me?*"

Titan grinned. "Your ride home just showed up!"

He pointed off into the distance, where Maria could only just barely see a dark spot in the dark sky. In a split second it became clear that the tiny spot was Skymaster racing to the rescue.

The airborne hero was moving at top speed toward the missile as the missile sped towards him. This meant that he'd be passing by the missile at *twice* his top speed, which would make it tough for him to snatch Maria off the side of the thing. She stretched out a hand to him as he made his flyby; he likewise stretched out his hand...

But the rocket's engine gave a little sputter, forcing it to veer sideways a few feet. Skymaster's and Maria's hands missed each other by mere inches.

Skymaster changed course as quickly as he could, but the missile was falling fast out of reach. With his fists thrust out before him and his every muscle tensed in concentration, he pushed his flying power to its absolute limit and chased after the descending rocket.

Maria looked at the ground racing up at her and the flying hero trying desperately to catch up behind her. "We're going too fast for him!"

Climbing to the back of the rocket, Titan grasped one of the tail-fins and twisted it sideways as if it was made of the cheapest tin. This caused the rocket to slow down and turn to the left.

He bent another tail-fin backward, causing the rocket to pitch upward.

"Here's the plan!" he told Maria. "I can run really fast — super-muscular legs, you know. So, you hold onto me, and I'll jump off the back of this thing just before it hits the ground. If I can hit the ground running at the same speed as the rocket, I think we'll be safe."

"Sounds logical," she replied uneasily.

By bending those fins into this shape and that shape, Titan aimed the rocket's flight-path towards the open meadow by the woods. The engine finally ran completely out of fuel, stopped sputtering, and shut itself off. There was now no sound but the whistling of the wind as they rushed downwards.

But the closer they came to the ground, the faster they realized they were going. Before Titan knew what was happening, he had overshot the meadow and the woods altogether. The runaway missile Titan was responsible for steering was headed for the quiet homes of his own neighborhood.

He jumped and stomped on the rear end of that missile, trying to force its nose upward; to give it a tiny skyward nudge. Those small triangular fins on the rocket caught the wind and its flight-path was redirected just as Titan had hoped, rising slightly and zooming over the chimneys of the unsuspecting houses below. He gave the tail-fin another bend, reshaping it to steer the thing off towards the soccer field at the school.

"Here it comes!" he warned Maria, as the field raced up at them. He wrapped one of his iron-muscled arms around her waist and told her, "Hold on!"

But just as Maria hid her eyes on his shoulder and braced for the coming impact, Titan changed his mind and screamed, *"Let go!"*

Before she knew what was happening, Titan had ripped her loose from him, and flung her straight up into the air.

Shrieking in horrified confusion, she sailed through the empty night, tumbling end over end. Then — *bam!* — she found herself in Skymaster's embrace.

To have caught her so suddenly, Skymaster was thrown into a spin by her weight. After a confusing (and generally harrowing!) tumble through the night, he righted his course. When he was flying smoothly again, he whispered, "You're safe, Miss Fuente!"

"...Huh?"

In a flash, it all became clear to Maria what had occurred: Titan had noticed that Skymaster had gotten close enough that she could be thrown to him. (Unfortunately, there hadn't been time to explain this change of plans to Miss Fuente!)

She hugged tightly to Skymaster and looked below to see the missile with Titan on the back going in for its "controlled" crash-landing.

The speeding rocket smacked sideways into Palisades Elementary School's soccer field. Its metal frame groaned, creaked, and screamed as it skidded on the earth. Titan dropped off the back, and rolled violently across the terrain, turning at least fifty bone-jarring somersaults. Meanwhile, the missile crashed into the side of the school, punching a hole in the building right above the basement boiler room.

When the wreck was over, Skymaster and Maria floated down from above, while The Wizard and Aquarius came out of the basement through the hole that the missile had bashed in the wall. Next came all the football players that had been down in the basement with them. They stepped through the clouds of dust and smoke and looked at the missile that had slammed through the side of the school. (Needless to say, this scene only made those confused athletes all the more confused.)

The Wizard and Aquarius stared at that crashed rocket for a moment. Then they casually said to each other at the same instant, "Well, *there's* something you don't see everyday."

Titan shambled across the soccer field drooping at the shoulders and just on the edge of total exhaustion. Maria realized that this was the first time she had ever seen him worn out. None of his superhuman bones were broken, but that powerhouse adventurer *finally* looked like he had taken a beating.

Without a word, the strongman ripped away the metal

panel that he had put in place to protect the five Falcons inside the rocket. The football players inside stumbled out, looking just as befuddled as the befuddled football players who stood there watching them stumble out. All as one, the Falcons (the so-called "toughest team in the league") fainted into a collective heap.

Recognizing one of the kids who had been inside that missile, Aquarius shouted at Titan in exasperation, "You saved *Eddie Thigpen?* Are you out of your —?"

He stopped at the sound of approaching voices — people coming out of the gymnasium to see what had caused all the bangs and booms.

The Wizard gave out a quick command for his fellow superheroes to *"Scatter!"* (He was, after all, in charge, seeing as how Night-Ghost was off chasing Morton and Sasquatch Lady.) But before they could follow this order, he stopped them and gave them a big thumbs-up. "Well done tonight, guys!" He bowed to Maria (in that stage-actor fashion, the way Night-Ghost would have). *"And* Miss Fuente!"

Maria responded to the scientist's gentlemanly bow with an oh-so-proper ballerina's curtsey.

The Wizard reminded her, "Remember: you still have to call me a jerk twice!"

She dismissed it with a smile and a wave of her hand.

Then the heroes performed their "scatter" — The Wizard, Titan and Aquarius bounding off into the nearby woods; Skymaster and Maria vanishing behind the school building.

Just as those colorful costumes were swallowed by the shadows and surrounding darkness, the adults arrived on the scene, running clumsily through the grass in their silly grown-up shoes.

Seeing the devastation, they quickly summed up what had occurred.

After the group's gasps of surprise, a man in the crowd said, "Yep. Morton was right." He pointed to the twisted metal of the missile wreckage and the hole it had knocked in the wall of the building. "Look: the water-heater blasted itself right out of the basement!"

Seeing the unconscious football players sprawled on the ground, a panicky lady shrieked, "They're hurt! Someone call an ambulance!"

That lady's piercing cry woke the Falcons from their faint. One by one they looked around and blinked their eyes.

Another man in the crowd saw his son amongst that team and rushed to him. "Are you OK, Jimbo?"

Of course, poor Jimbo's memory of his time spent as a mind-slave was a foggy mess. He could only offer a confused, babbling answer: "...Yeah... I think so... There were superheroes here... a guy with a blue helmet... green swim-fins... really strong guy... flying guy..."

Rather embarrassed that his son would concoct such a wild tale, the father rapidly told the crowd, "He's just shaken up by the excitement!" As he led the baffled Jimbo to the car, he explained to him, "What happened was that your team was practicing in the playfield, and the school's water-heater exploded. *That's* what blew the hole in the wall."

The weary peewee quarterback could only shrug and mumble, "Whatever you say." He was too drained from an all-out war against a team of super-powered crime-fighters and a rollicking ride on a runaway missile...

...even though he wouldn't remember much of it in the morning.

Chapter 38

Dan or Skymaster

Running madly through the deserted, moonlit playground, Maria towed Skymaster by the hand. She stopped at the monkey-bars, then checked this way and that to make absolutely certain they were alone.

All out of breath, she said, "Night-Ghost's going to get me!"

" 'Get' you?"

"He's going to wipe out my memory! And then, he says, you guys will make extra-sure you never cross paths with me again! And before he gets me, I just wanted to tell you—"

"Is this because you know his secret identity?"

"I know *all sorts of stuff* I'm not supposed to know! Yeah, that's what happens when Maria Fuente: Girl Detective is on the case!"

He drooped in misery. "I wish you knew *my* secret identity!"

Instead of admitting that she did, she asked, "And why is that?"

"Forget it." His voice went quieter and quieter. "It's nothing — just that the guy I really am would like it an awful lot if you knew he was a superhero, that's all."

"So, tell me who you are." She crossed her heart, and pledged with all the honesty she could put into her voice, "I *promise* I won't tell anyone. And Night-Ghost's just going to make me forget it, anyway. So... who are you?"

"I wish I could tell you who I am." His heart was crushed under the weight of this wish. "But that's just a terrible idea."

"Because of your superhero's oath of secrecy?" she asked.

"No. Because... Well, the guy that I really am is this stupid nobody. There's nothing under this helmet but a klutz! I almost killed you today, dropping you from a couple of miles up! Sheesh! What an idiot! I'd better get out of here before I do something even stupider!"

He threw his cape back, climbed up a little higher into the monkey-bars, and got ready to leap into the night sky. She knew that in a moment he'd be gone and she'd never see him again. (Well, she wouldn't see *Skymaster*, anyway. Of course, she'd still see Dan in class every day, but she'd never know that he was a superhero. After Night-

Ghost wiped out her memory, she'd only see Dan as she had before: a shy little boy too scared to speak.)

"You're not an idiot!" she said quickly. "You're a superhero!"

He stayed put, but kept himself turned away from her. "Superheroes can be as stupid as anyone else, you know. Remember when you asked if my super-suit was what gave me my super-powers? Well, it *does*. Sort of. Not the power to fly. It gives me a power that's way better than that."

"What could possibly be better than the power to fly?"

"The power to talk to you. If I didn't have this mask on, I wouldn't have the guts to say any of this to you."

A crafty little smirk jumped to life on her lips. "And that's because you're Dan."

Still facing away, he couldn't see her smirk; but he could hear it in her voice. He instantly denied everything: "Dan? Dan who? I don't know any Dan."

In that little instant of realization she saw him as the most magical creature alive. He was more amazing to her now than when she had first seen him fly; more amazing than when he had waltzed her through the clouds.

She saw before her a boy who was full of fears — fears of everything from heartless bullies to pretty girls — but who led the perilous life of a superhero regardless of those fears. The terrified boy who was afraid to say a word to her in class could have swept her up and flown her around the classroom at any time during the day, but instead he just kept quietly at his desk. Even now, when she had admitted that she knew the identities of all his teammates, he stood firm on his oath to keep his own a secret.

She told him, "I knew it was you when you wouldn't inject Sasquatch Lady's serum into my arm."

Of course, he didn't remember anything that had gone on during his time as a zombie. "I wouldn't?"

"Nope. I said, 'Please don't do it,' and you stopped. And you quit listening to Sasquatch Lady just because... just because I asked you to." (Yes, Maria neglected to tell him that she had promised the zombie Skymaster that she would give him a kiss if he refused all of Sasquatch Lady's commands. Much to her own surprise, she was feeling a little shy about it now. And, since he didn't remember any of what had gone on, she decided that maybe she just wouldn't tell that part of the story.)

"You can take the mask off now," she told him.

He shook his head in silence.

"Your superhero's oath doesn't count anymore," she said. "I *figured out* who you are!"

"Yeah, just some totally un-cool little twerp."

She reached up, took his hand and gently brought him down off the bars to stand and face her on the ground.

"You're *not* un-cool! Do you know how cool a guy has to be to keep the fact that he's cool a secret? Oh, the heck with 'cool'! Who needs it! People acting cool is what's *wrong* with the world! Who's cool, anyway? Eddie Thigpen, that's who! He beats people up, steals things, and says, 'I didn't do it!' But you! You *save the world* and say, 'I didn't do it!' " A brilliant thought popped into her head: "I finally know the difference between a *regular* hero and a *super* hero!"

"What?"

"If you save people you're a hero," she explained. "But it takes something extra to save people and never tell anyone. If you can keep all your good deeds a secret; if you can disappear when it's time for everyone to thank you... well, that's when your heroics become super."

"Very well put," said a third voice.

Both Maria and Skymaster spun around to see who had spoken. There stood the purple-cloaked leader of The Fearless Force.

"I'm here to fix everything like I said I would," Night-Ghost told them in his overly-dramatized way.

"Oh, go ahead and get it over with!" Maria felt utterly defeated, like when it's time to wake up from a glorious dream. She knew that once their secret identities were erased from her memory, then her time with The Fearless

Force would be over. Those five heroes would make sure they ducked out of sight whenever she came too close to their adventures. She'd never again get to live through perils like the ones this night had provided. She'd spend the rest of her life being just another person who sees a wrecked missile and thinks it's a broken water-heater.

"But first," said the hypnotist-hero, "take your mask off, Skymaster. Tell her she's right. She guessed your real identity."

Skymaster's heart pounded in anticipation. "Can I really?"

"Go ahead," said Maria. "He'll just wipe it out of my memory a minute from now."

Skymaster's trembling hands slowly unbuckled his helmet and slid his mask down.

Night-Ghost smiled a sly smile, then turned around and walked away.

Skymaster was baffled that the escape-artist was just leaving like that. "Hey, boss? Aren't you gonna hypnotize her?"

Night-Ghost stopped and thought for a moment...

...then answered, "Nope."

"But what about the promise we had to make when we became superheroes?"

The purple-cloaked hero replied, "I just heard her

promise that she wouldn't tell anyone. That's as good a promise as any."

"Wiz, Aquarius and Titan are gonna be awfully cranked-off when they find out!"

Night-Ghost smiled cunningly. "And that's why we're not going to tell them. You want to keep a secret? Keep *this* one."

Skymaster was speechless, standing there with his mask hanging loose around his neck.

As the escape-artist/acrobat/captain of The Fearless Force walked off and vanished into the shadows, Maria asked, "Is he serious?"

"Always!" Dan replied firmly.

With the purple-cloaked hero gone, Maria and Dan stood in silence. Their faces sprang to life with matching smiles as they suddenly became best friends — or, rather, suddenly realized that they had been best friends for a while now.

Maria asked her new friend, "Do I get a lift home?"

"OK, but no dancing!"

They hugged each other as closely as possible — no fear or embarrassment this time. Certainly, their hearts jumped a bit, but not with fear or embarrassment. This was the wonderfully uneasy joy of very best friendship... or perhaps that other, grander thing: the "L-word." Who can say? It's a subject ten-year-olds refuse to discuss.

With a little push of Skymaster's willpower, their feet were raised up off the earth.

The bold adventurer and her flying friend floated up and up into the starry, deep-blue September atmosphere. The world high above their neighborhood was silent — silent for everything but their hearts, which were *both* thundering like drums.

And up in that wide-open stretch of empty wind between heaven and earth, Skymaster thought, "If there was ever a time to kiss a girl, this has got to be it!" But he just couldn't risk it. "No. I'll probably drop her again!"

Then he thought, "Maybe I can just say something really smooth — something like, 'If I had never been able to fly... I sure could tonight!' Yeah! That's perfect!" Sadly, he chickened-out on this too, and the words never made the journey from his brain to his mouth.

So, he would have to settle for a silent flight through the night sky with the girl of his dreams as all the victory his heart would enjoy. And judging by the contented sigh from Maria as she rested her head on his shoulder and gazed around at the stars, it was a grand victory indeed.

Not only was she hoping there would be many more adventures to come, but she hoped that they would all end with this same peaceful float through the sky.

And as their dual silhouette levitated higher and higher into the jeweled velvet of night, a purple-cloaked figure was stuck way down on the ground, watching from the shadows. He thought, "Maria's right. The thing that's wrong with the world is people acting cool... like when a stubborn idiot of a superhero says, 'I don't have time for romance!' "

Epilogue

The Boiler Burst

A fast-moving figure flitted through the headlights of Officer Rocco's patrol car. The policeman's eyes caught a fleeting glimpse of a fluttering patch of white-flecked purple. He recognized it immediately: the flapping cape of that kid who called himself Night-Ghost.

Turning his spotlight on the so-called superhero, the officer called out through his car's loudspeaker, "Freeze, Ghost-Knight!"

With a sigh of defeat and a droop of his head, Night-Ghost surrendered himself to the officer of the law. Just like the night before, Officer Rocco brought the masked hero over to his squad-car, shut him in the back seat, and got in the front.

After a brief report into his radio microphone and a scribble on his clipboard, he asked the make-believe adventurer, "Are you out pestering the neighborhood girls again?"

"Not at all." Night-Ghost explained his evening as if it were all quite ordinary: "I was just heading home after my fellow superheroes and I stopped my teacher from ruling the world with a mind-control machine. She set the self-destruct on the machine and almost blew up the town. Thankfully, I know a super-scientist who was able to defuse the bomb, and—"

The officer wasn't the least bit convinced. "I just got a call on my radio that said the water-heater at the school exploded. Tell the truth, kid. Did you blow up the water-heater at your school while you were playing superhero?"

"No," answered Night-Ghost. "The hole in the side of the building is from a missile that crashed into it."

Officer Rocco tried to sound shocked, but he faked it poorly. "Oh, really? And where did this missile come from?"

Night-Ghost answered calmly and without delay: "My crazy teacher bought it from the government. They sell old rockets to anyone — even to supervillains, I'm sad to say."

The policeman was doubtful. "And did Uncle Sam sell your teacher the mind-control machine, too?"

"No. Supervillains usually know mad scientists who will supply them with those bizarre sorts of weapons. That's where my principal got his electro-burst death-ray cannon, his gravity-wave-disrupter, his heat-ray-pistols, his—"

Officer Rocco wondered, "How do they afford all this space-age gear?"

"They steal lunch money from kids."

"A missile, a mind-control machine, and a gravity-wave-death-ray — *that* stuff I'll believe," the policeman joked. "But now you're saying your teacher steals lunch money? You're making that part up."

"She doesn't steal it herself. The playground bully does it for her."

"So your playground bully raises funds for an operation to rule the world?" The policeman was finally laughing out loud. "It's so weird it's brilliant!" He turned around to tell the kid in the purple costume, "You could grow up to be one heck of a writer, kid!"

But as he spun in his seat, his jaw fell open in astonishment. In a repeat of the previous night's occurrence, the back seat was empty and the door was wide open. Night-Ghost was gone.

"No way! I made *sure* it was shut this time!"

He jumped out of the front seat and examined that back

door to see if there was anything wrong with the latch.

"How the heck does he keep doing that?" he yelled. "This door has *got* to be defective!"

In order to test the latch, he got in the back seat and shut the door on himself. In an instant, he found that the latch was working fine... and he was now stuck in the back seat of his own car.

He realized he was going to have to use the walkie-talkie on his belt to call for help, but had no idea what excuse he'd give for getting locked inside his own patrol car. This story was certain to be told and retold all over the police station. He'd be taking a cruel ribbing for this blunder, and he knew it. He could feel the bruises on his pride already.

A deep breath, a roll of his eyes to heaven, and he finally called for assistance on his walkie-talkie.

"Unit seven requesting back-up; 300 block of Century Boulevard. *Not* an emergency. Just don't ask!"

In the silence of waiting for help (and mockery) to arrive, he muttered, "*Is* there such a thing as a ten-year-old escape-artist who chases monsters and fights crime? ...No way! ...Maybe?"

The End

Special thanks to . . .

Bunny for continuing to be the responsible one; Selena for continually helping in the hunt for the proper green; David E. Peterson for his endless generosity and for keeping the computers functioning; Julia Reece for editorial brilliance; Paula Howard for more editorial brilliance; Jay Irwin for even more editorial brilliance; Geoffrey Mckenzie for the gift of time (which, believe me, people, is more precious than gold!); Rod Fichter for alerting Geoffery; Lorie Vanderwalker (who probably did more to promote Sebastian Reckless than I did!); Betsy Gellert (Thanks for the donut suggestion! ...I hope that doesn't sound too weird.), Mae Scott & Gregory H. (does "H" stand for something? I mean, do you have a last name?); Kristi Smith and her brilliant little charges; all the teachers and administrators at Lake Youngs Elementary, Pine Tree Elementary, Seabury School, Washington-Hoyt, Our Lady of Guadalupe, St. Vincent's in Federal Way, Meeker Middle School, Meridian Elementary, any school I might have left out; Kenny Sinner for expert advice (Sorry about the punch in the face!); Barb Wood and Mitch Wood for securing all those totally confusing computer programs for me! (I'm slowly learning how to use them!); Greg Gamble for brotherhood; Christy, Nathan, Laura, and Princess Danielle; Ase, Jordan & Christina for reading the thing; Erin & Chuck for more belief and energy (they never seem to run out of either!); Dan and Lana; Aunt Ruth for teaching me to draw; Aubrey Reece for being fan number one; Kevin Reece just because; Alex Cole for the word "fluffy"; Shirley Deranleau, Sherri Stevens, Scott Daggatt and Alan White (even though the end result didn't quite happen this time).

And, mostly, every teacher or principal who understands that it's a book that makes an author an author, not a multimillion-dollar contract with a massive corporate machine!

And finally, all the superheroes that I knew: John Jones, Pat Crawford, Fred Bahr, John Mahoney, David W. Peterson, Dan Hughes, Clay Howard, and all the rest who came and went on various adventures, utilizing their powers to keep evil at bay.

If you didn't see your name listed, it's not because I don't love you, but it wouldn't hurt to take me out for some fish 'n' chips and pretend to enjoy my jokes!

About the author/illustrator:

Rushton Howard was born in 1963, and was known throughout his school years as "the guy who draws the cool pictures." He slacked-off from his drawing to become an actor, which led to writing plays, which led to writing books, which then needed illustrations. So there you are: he's "back to the old drawing board." Though he continually swears that he'll never again work on the stage, he continues to write, direct, and act in plays, also occasionally producing publicity art for local theatre companies. With Greg Gamble, he co-wrote *The Last Touchy-Feely Drama on the American Stage (and Other Plays)*, a collection of one-act satires that have seen production all across the U.S. and Canada (and even a couple of times in New Zealand!). He currently lives in Tacoma, Washington with his wife, Bunny.